Goodness &
Mercy

Patti Hill

Goodness & Mercy

ISBN: 978-0-615-77611-8

Cover photographs and cover design by Tania Settje of
www.CatchingKeepsakes.com.

Visit Patti Hill's web site at www.pattihillauthor.com.
www.Facebook.com/PattiHillAuthor

Unless otherwise noted, Scripture quotations are
taken from the King James Version.

Other Novels by Patti Hill

The Garden Gates Series

Like a Watered Garden

Always Green

In Every Flower

The Queen of Sleepy Eye

Seeing Things

For Kathi

Is solace anywhere more comforting

than that in the arms of a sister?

–Alice Walker

Surely goodness and mercy shall follow me

all the days of my life:

and I will dwell in the house of the LORD forever.

Psalm 23:6

Mercy

October 10, 1943

Mama had high hopes when she named me Mercy. She expected me to be kind even when people didn't deserve kindness. And for the most part, I hadn't disappointed her or her memory.

But Mama could not have known there was anyone like Mrs. Nadel in this world. Mrs. Nadel served the orphans sour milk and looked the other way when Verlan Custer Sawall threw the ball at the girls' heads at playtime. Worst of all, she thought nothing of separating me from my brother, Goody. Forever.

Of all the boys at the orphanage, a farmer and his wife chose my brother to be their son, even though they already had five daughters. They promised to come for him the minute they emptied part of the attic for his room.

Since Mrs. Nadel told me about Goody's new family, I've never fought harder to be what Mama had hoped for. Maybe Mrs. Nadel would see me trying with all my might to be kind and let Goody stay with me. I did everything she asked me to do. If she wanted silence, and she almost always did, I swallowed my words and dreamed of being somewhere else, like in my very own bed. Dreaming of home busied my heart too much to blurt that Betty cried all night long or that Cook had forgotten to pick the weevils out of the oatmeal again. Things worked out much better when I kept my mouth shut.

But Goody would rather swing a skunk by its tail than please

1

Mrs. Nadel, not that he worked at being contrary. Goody only knew how to be Goody, and that was plenty contrary for Mrs. Nadel, so staying on Mrs. Nadel's good side was all up to me.

That wasn't as hard as it sounded. For some crazy reason, Mrs. Nadel liked me. She dragged me to ladies' Sunday school classes all over Sauk County. Goody was not invited. He walked to the First Baptist Church with the other children from the orphanage, where the teachers served him cherry punch and sugar cookies. And because I wasn't present at Sunday school, I missed putting stars on the chart for memorizing Scripture verses and bringing my Bible. I kept hoping Mrs. Nadel would find another little girl to like, but that never happened.

That Sunday was no different. We visited a Sunday school class in Portage, Wisconsin. When class was over, Mrs. Nadel drove back to the orphanage with all the windows rolled up tight and the heater blowing hot air, even though the morning had warmed up real nice.

By the time she parked the car in front of the orphanage, the car was blistering hot, and I couldn't wait to get out. Plus, the car smelled like Dr. Drake's cough syrup. Goody said Dr. Drake's tasted like witches' brew, and while he had no way of knowing anything about witches or their brew, he was one-hundred percent correct about Dr. Drake's cough syrup, that is, if it tasted as bad as it smelled, which was awful. That smell was the very thing I thought of whenever I saw Mrs. Nadel. But, of course, I never said anything about that.

After she turned off the car and put the keys in her purse, I figured I was free, at last, to escape and find Goody in the dining hall. We always ate our lunch real fast on Sundays, no matter what Cook put on our trays. Our big sister was on her way, and we sure didn't want to miss a minute of Lucy's visit.

Mrs. Nadel laid her hand on my arm. "Before we go in for lunch, Mercy, we have something to talk about."

I wasn't in much of a mood to talk. I'd done what she'd asked. I sat in a cold church basement with a bunch of old ladies who asked me lots and lots of questions about heaven—some that I could answer, some that I couldn't. No matter what I told them, they didn't believe one word I said. They were much more interested in forking big bites of cake into their mouths than hearing about

Mama's garden. The cake was the yellow kind with dark chocolate icing, my very favorite. And they never even offered me a piece. I don't know why they didn't. I knew not to talk with chocolate on my teeth. Some of those ladies had not learned this from their mamas.

Mrs. Nadel leaned closer. I pressed my back against the door. Even though she'd eaten a handful of those pretty mints they put by the coffee percolator, she still smelled like Dr. Drake's. "I would like to talk about Lucy's visit today."

I sucked in a breath. "She is coming, isn't she?"

"I don't see why not. She's here every Sunday."

I worked at slowing my breathing while Mrs. Nadel used the mirror to put on lipstick. Finally, she turned back to me. "I need your help with Lucy. If she thinks you're happy about Goody's new family, she will be too. Lucy can be a bit headstrong, but you know that, don't you? We want this to be a smooth transition for Goody. Lucy has a way of riling things up. Let's be happy for Goody's sake."

After all I'd done to make life easier for Mrs. Nadel, she hadn't noticed at all. All that kindness had gone wasted with nothing to show for it. Could it be that she didn't know what kindness looked like? Could it be that I hadn't tried hard enough? I didn't know the answers to those questions, but I knew she hadn't changed her mind about sending Goody away. My stomach twisted and my chest burned. I opened the car door to spill my breakfast on the gravel.

In no time, Mrs. Nadel ran around the car and pulled me out. She held my arm real tight. "This kind of behavior isn't going to help your brother. You have to be the big sister, Mercy."

She wasn't making any kind of sense. Sure, I was born first, but Goody and me celebrated our birthdays on the same day. Isn't that what twins do? And how could Goody be better off with five sisters he didn't know? Those girls wouldn't think to put cinnamon in his oatmeal or that he needed help buttoning his shirt. And they sure wouldn't know how much he hated being called a cry baby.

"Are you going to be sick again?" she asked.

I covered my mouth with both hands. Splashing Mrs. Nadel's shoes wouldn't help anything.

"You'd better go, then."

I turned and ran as fast as I could, through the play yard and over the grassy field toward the woods. The bushes scratched my legs as I ran deeper into the trees. I wanted to put as much ground as I dared between the orphanage and me. I leaned over a fallen log and more of my breakfast came up. It burned like crazy.

I wiped my mouth on my sleeve and worked up a good spit like Goody had taught me. One spit wasn't enough to clean my mouth of the sour taste, so I worked and worked until more spit bubbled on my tongue. A couple more spits did the job.

I found a place where the sun lit a patch of ground. I sat there, hugging my knees to my chest with my skirt pulled to my feet. I planned on staying in the woods until Lucy came. I would need that long to figure out how to tell Lucy about Goody. And to start missing him bad.

Lucy took being our big sister very seriously. She wouldn't like that Goody wasn't going to be our brother anymore. That news was better coming from me than Mrs. Nadel, especially now that she was breaking her promise to Lucy. And I wasn't about to pretend Goody's new family made me happy. That would be an out and out lie.

Five new sisters? Goody would hate that more than just about anything, seeing how he wasn't very keen with the two sisters he already had.

I thought on it real hard, but the right words to tell Lucy wouldn't come, so I thought about birthdays without Goody. I also thought of long winters buckling my own boots. It was Goody who climbed up on the counter for the boxes of cereal. He held my hand when we walked on ice, unless someone was watching, and then he would push me right down. He always told Mama he was sorry later. As Mama would say, that was the bitter and sweet of it.

Since we'd been real small, it was my job to worry about Goody. How was I supposed to worry about him if he lived with another family? I could see him at the orphanage just fine, so I had plenty of reasons to worry. First, he believed he was the Lone Ranger. This got him in all sorts of trouble. Second, he was smaller than the other boys. Third, he didn't eat very much. Fourth, the boys ganged up on him. Fifth, he didn't do his homework. Sixth, he hardly ever smiled. Seventh, he didn't know his multiplication tables. Eighth, he wet his bed when he was scared.

As sure as the sun rose in the sky, Goody would always need someone to worry for him. Would his new papa worry for Goody?

His new mama? More than likely, they would get plenty mad at him instead. That was how people usually reacted to Goody.

The wind rattled the leaves and stirred my thoughts. How small could a family get and still be a family? Our family was getting smaller all the time. First, Papa got killed at the ammunition factory, and then Mama fell in the river. Now, Goody was being adopted by another family. That left me and Lucy.

Are two sisters a family?

I worried about Lucy, too. It wasn't her fault Goody got himself a new family, but she would think it was. She wouldn't cry. Lucy was sixteen, way past the days of crying when she didn't get what she wanted. After all, she wore a bra and lipstick. No, Lucy didn't cry. She cleaned out the ice box or scrubbed the walls. The day Papa died, she stripped the wax off the kitchen floor and laid down two fresh coats.

People back in Prairie du Sac were always saying how sorry they were that I'd lost my parents. Losing them was a sadness that truly blistered my heart. Now, I was losing Goody. I wear an undershirt, not a bra or lipstick. I'm only eight and I cry plenty. So I squeezed myself into a ball and cried, mostly for myself, which, for some reason made me feel even worse.

My tears dried up, but it was too cold to sleep, so I leaned against a tree, hoping the bark still held some of summer's warmth, but it didn't. Leaves lay on the ground like hands that had touched wet paint. Some red. Some gold. Some gold with red that bled from their veins. A few were still green. Most were splotched with brown. Soon, when all the leaves lay on the forest floor, the whole world would be leftover colors—gray, brown, white. Lots of white.

I rubbed hard at the goose bumps on my arms.

The woods sighed, and a shower of leaves spun to the ground. One tapped the top of my head and fell to the ground at my feet. This was a leaf to keep—a maple hand, perfectly gold, not one spot of brown, a million times brighter than the star on top of the Christmas tree.

It was then I heard the song of coming, the stirring of the air, the clatter of leaves. I put my hand over my heart to feel it beating faster. I sat up straight, looked around. I was alone, even though I didn't feel alone.

I lifted my face to the sky. The clouds parted, so I closed my eyes against the sun's brightness. My eyelids glowed the color of mercurochrome. I wasn't cold anymore. I was back home under the covers in my bedroom. The sheets smelled of sunshine, and the radio played in the kitchen. Dust fairies danced where the sun squeezed into the room. There was a burn mark on the freckled linoleum where Goody once lit a firecracker. That was home, all right.

Back when we all lived together in the apartment above Mrs. Devendorf's garage, the weight of the blankets and quilts held me in bed, unless, of course, Lucy started frying bacon in the kitchen. Then I got out of bed quick and ran to stand over the grate until the heat made a bell of my nightgown.

The orphanage was never warm, not even in the summer.

And just like that I knew how to tell Lucy about Goody. Lucy liked things straight. There was nothing to do but tell her out loud about Goody's new family. When Goody squinted down on his target to show Lucy he was still the best ranger in the world, that would be my chance. I would tell Lucy the news. But telling her wouldn't be any kind of easy. My tummy sloshed something awful just thinking about telling her.

I sat very, very still. Papa had taught me how to do this. I'd inherited his stomach, he'd said. I breathed nice and slow how Papa had showed me and looked around for something peaceful to watch. I'd seen plenty of trees. Geese honked overhead. I chanced a look. They flew in a wavy V that tumbled my tummy even more, and I lost what I hoped was the very last of my breakfast.

Sometimes, throwing up was the easiest thing to do.

Lucy

I met the gaze of passengers with a scowl as they shuffled by, a surefire way to enjoy a bus ride without company. It also helped to sit on the aisle, so anyone daring to take a seat by an unhappy teenager would have to squeeze between me and the seat. Not many people owned that kind of fortitude. Most took one look at me and kept moving toward the back of the bus.

I wasn't heartless. I just wanted to be alone. Unless a soldier climbed onto the bus.

They alone received my brightest smiles, even doe-eyed requests for help when I was perfectly capable of hefting a grocery sack to the overhead rack myself. In my way of thinking, no one facing the threat of war should travel alone. Unfortunately, not many soldiers traveled between Prairie du Sac and Baraboo, Wisconsin, but when they did, I wished the trip had been much, much longer.

As for the other travelers, it wasn't that I didn't like people. I liked people fine. I made my living being nice to customers all day long at the Badger Café, and that suited me. But a girl grew tired of explaining why she traveled to Baraboo and back each and every Sunday.

A woman huffed with the effort of climbing aboard the bus with a makeup case and a lumpy cloth bag. She greeted each passenger as she sidestepped down the aisle, snagging her broad bottom on each seat as she pressed by. Passengers leaned away from the aisle to avoid getting a face full of her heinie. Our eyes met. Her face was as cheerful as a sunflower, although I'd never seen a sunflower dab sweat from its brow. I couldn't help myself, I smiled.

"Scoot yourself on over," she said and lowered herself into the seat beside me. Her hip pressed me against the side of the bus. "Morning," she said, nearly laying her head in my lap to stuff her bag under the seat. She used the makeup case to elevate her feet. They swelled like rising dough out of her shoes. "We certainly have a beautiful day for a journey. Where you going, honey?"

"Baraboo," I said, hoping I hadn't invited a conversation about arthritis or hemorrhoids.

She brightened as if I'd said Paris, France. "Our county seat! Visiting family, are you? I was in Prairie du Sac to visit my third grandchild. I wish they lived closer, but I can't complain, not in these perilous times.

"Are you from Prairie du Sac? Maybe you know my son and his wife. He's gone and enlisted in the army, but he's selling insurance for the R. Gakin Agency until his orders come through." She pushed her glasses up to rub hard at her eyes. "Maybe your parents have done business with him. He's very good at what he does." She bent with a grunt to pull the bag out from under the seat. "I bought this yarn at the mercantile to make my newest granddaughter an afghan. Feel the yarn, honey. I've never felt anything softer. I dipped deep into my egg money to buy this here yarn. Did you say you was visiting family in Prairie du Sac?"

She'd finally run out of breath and expected an answer. We hadn't even pulled away from the bus station. "I live here," I said without elaboration.

My family was not a topic for small talk. Talking about my parents only dug a deeper hole of ache in my chest. And the twins? I missed them horribly, which had turned out to be a big surprise, what with Goody constantly shooting his popgun in my ear and Mercy forever championing a cause. I must have frowned over these thoughts because the woman egged me on with a tilt of the head. I relented under the spell of her chattiness.

"My twin brother and sister are in the orphanage there. They're eight, almost nine."

"Why in the world—? You aren't saying—?" She covered her mouth with a gloved hand and then touched my arm. The warmth of her breath lingered on her cottony fingers. "Honey, what happened? Are you all alone in this crazy world?"

I was the last peanut in the tin. "I have the twins."

"No grandparents? No aunts or uncles you can live with? However do you manage?"

"The people at church—"

"What would we do without the brethren?"

"And our landlady. The twins love her like an aunt. She helped the doctor birth them." But Mrs. Devendorf had left Prairie du Sac to nurse her ailing father soon after Mother's accident. I only saw Mr. Devendorf when the rent was due.

This lady didn't need to know we had a real aunt, my mother's sister, or that we had never heard her name spoken in our house, not ever.

"We're doing fine," I told the woman. "I have a good job waitressing at the Badger Café."

"I've eaten there." She looked at me over her glasses. "I thought you looked familiar. They serve the most wonderful meatloaf. I don't suppose you know the recipe."

"Mr. Stiefler makes the meatloaf before I arrive."

"Is that so? My goodness, I'm always on the lookout for a new recipe."

She looked so disappointed I felt obliged to offer her something. "He buys the ground beef and pork from South Central Butcher. That's all I know."

"My husband won't touch my meatloaf, says he prefers dog food. Even if you could talk your Mr. Stiefler out of the recipe, there's no promise Marvin would try it." She rolled the bag of yarn closed, sighed, smoothed the front of her dress. "But you were telling me about your family. How are those little angels managing in an orphanage?" She shuddered when she said orphanage.

"The twins have lots of friends, and the cook there feeds them well. Goody's getting a belly on him. The director, Mrs. Nadel, has taken a special interest in the twins. She makes sure Goody practices his spelling words. He's doing better than ever in school. And she reads Bible stories to Mercy every night. In just over a year, when I'm eighteen, they'll come home with me. By then, I'll have a fat savings account. We won't have any trouble making ends meet."

That was the story I told folks when they asked about the twins. In truth, I'd doctored yet another wound on Goody the week before and heard about the fight from Mercy. I also punched a new hole in Goody's belt with a hammer and nail I'd borrowed from the custodian. Goody complained that the food tasted like old socks, but again, there was no pickier eater in the whole wide world than Goody. And one of the orphans had ripped the last pages from Mercy's library book. She feared she would be banned from the Baraboo library forever, a fate worse than death. As it was, I carried Mercy's doll back and forth each week to prevent its decapitation. I also carried Goody's popgun. The miscreants at the orphanage destroyed everything they touched. The Baraboo orphanage wasn't Boys' Town, and Mrs. Nadel sure wasn't Father Flanagan.

I hated lying to the woman—the part about the twins coming home when I turned eighteen was true—but I'd discovered early in my days of traveling to and from the orphanage that people got awfully upset by the stories I told, so I made up the best story I could. There was no sense troubling good people with our problems.

The woman frowned, so I added, "This is only temporary. We'll be fine. You shouldn't worry."

She patted my hand. "You're a brave girl, a very brave girl."

I shifted to lean against the window. Even though the sun warmed my shoulders, I shivered. Sixty-six more trips. With the return trip, that made 132 times past the Lower River State Park turnoff, a silo with a tree growing out of the top, and about a million cows. As the bus strained against a rise, I closed my eyes and feigned sleep.

The woman nudged my shoulder. "Honey, you're likely to miss your stop if you fall asleep. How many hours are you working? I wish my youngest daughter would take an interest in something besides boys, but I have no one to blame but myself.

"Do you have a beau? May Ann's my baby, and I'm afraid I've spoiled her rotten. She spends every possible moment at the cinema. That girl will get whiplash, the way she looks at the boys in uniform. Oh dear, that's Baraboo coming up." She opened her purse and handed me a folded bill. "Maybe this will make things a bit easier for you, honey."

"Thank you," I said around the knot in my throat.

When the bus pulled out of sight, I unfolded the dollar. My stomach growled at the thought of the eggs and bread I would buy at the Water Street Market.

The sight of the orphanage gates made my legs leaden. I never knew what I would find inside. I patted my pocket. There were bandages, just in case, and an apple for the twins to share, plus a box of Kix for Goody in my bag.

Lucy

Once inside the gates of the orphanage, I expected to see Goody and Mercy. They usually waited for me on the steps to the main door. They weren't there or on the playground or helping in the kitchen. That was odd. Goody always raced to claim his popgun and Mercy, well, she folded herself into me. This day, I had to look for them. Very, very odd. I finally found Mercy gathering leaves in the woods that bordered the playground. Goody, back at the orphanage wall, flailed at a group of boys grabbing for his Lone Ranger badge. Once again I would try to talk him into letting me take the badge home for safe keeping. I doubted he would go along with such a plan.

While Goody ate the Kix, I turned my attention to Mercy. She held out a fistful of maple leaves, more a torch than a bouquet. "It's your turn to be the bride," she said. "Remember to smile as you go down the aisle." Her smile was half-hearted, probably a stomachache. In a rush to catch the bus I'd left the peppermint on the kitchen table.

"Is your tummy hurting?" I asked.

"I'm fine." Mercy hummed the wedding march, my cue to walk slowly, smiling like a simpleton with the bouquet to my heart. Just as I approached the altar of leaves, a cardinal's whistle drew my eye to the molting branches of a tree near the orphanage door. How I envied the bird's oblivion to the purpose of the building.

Although someone had attempted to build an orphanage that

looked like a real home—two arched windows flanked an imposing door—the building resembled a train station. And the red roof tried too hard to be cheery. I hated thinking of Goody and Mercy waking up on opposite ends of the building.

Mercy clutched my waist. "I'm tired of playing wedding."

She was a championship hugger, that was for sure, but she didn't usually squeeze the breath right out of me. Something was up. I tugged her arms free to study her face for a telltale sign of trouble. There was nothing unusual about the crease between her eyebrows or how she bit her lip, or was there?

"How about elephant girl?" I suggested. "Would you like that better?" I knelt in the grass, but Mercy didn't shimmy onto my shoulders. "Come on, you'll be high above your adoring fans." I straightened against the ache in my back and waved at an imaginary crowd with the bouquet of leaves before offering them to Mercy.

Her chin dropped to her chest. Mercy tended toward the melodramatic.

I shook the leaves under her nose. "These are your feathers, collected in the jungles of India. Don't feel obligated, but I tiptoed through a pit of cobras to find the most colorful feathers on the continent." This, I was sure, would coax a smile from Mercy. She knew I hated snakes more than anything.

Instead, she slumped to the ground to rip grass by the fistfuls. "There's something I've got to tell you, and you're not going to like it."

I sat next to her on the lawn, not sure at all that I wanted to hear what she had to say.

"Goody spent the night somewhere," she said.

"Spent the night somewhere?" The children did not go on overnight outings. "What do you mean he spent the night somewhere?"

Mercy lay on her back, her hands folded over her heart as if she lay in a coffin. I stretched out beside her, grabbing her hand, holding it tightly.

Mercy said, "I couldn't find Goody."

"When?"

"A few days ago. I'm not sure."

"Go on."

"I told Mrs. Nadel. She said I should play with the girls for a change and that Goody needed to play with the boys. I was about

13

to tell her how the girls made fun of me, and the boys liked to throw rocks at Goody, but Cook came to say the grocer had added wrong on the bill again. Mrs. Nadel followed Cook back to the kitchen, so I kept looking for Goody. I looked in the playroom again, but he wasn't there, so I went outside, thinking maybe he was practicing his tracking skills."

My fingernails dug into my palm. "Go on. It's okay. I can't fix the problem until I know what's happening."

Mercy was too kind to smirk, but her gaze held a question: When have you ever fixed anything? And she was right.

"There was a man," she said.

"The custodian?"

"No, not Mr. Duffy. Another man. With Goody. Out front. He made Goody get in his truck."

"Are you sure about this?"

"Positive."

"Where did he go?"

"I don't know. I didn't see Goody until the next day, and he wasn't talking."

Goody had filled his tummy with Kix and started target practice with his popgun. I rose up on an elbow to watch him press the cork into the popgun's barrel and take aim.

"Mercy?"

"Yes?"

"You have to tell me everything."

She crawled into my lap and pulled my face to hers. "He came back yesterday," she whispered.

"Who? The man?"

"With a lady."

"And?"

She sucked in a shuddering breath. "Goody wet the bed last night. Mrs. Nadel won't let him drink anything."

Mercy bit down on her lip, which meant she wouldn't say another word, a maddening trait for a girl who spoke reliably unless something or someone had pushed her to the brink. If she believed Mrs. Nadel had treated Goody unfairly, she could remain mute for days. I didn't have time to unwind a mystery about Goody, so that meant talking to Goody, and getting Goody to talk was like convincing a fox to cough up a chicken.

Goody lay prone on the ground, sighting the popgun on a can, his ranger hat pushed off his forehead. He possessed the intensity of a warrior, no matter that the target stood less than a yard from his nose. He pressed the trigger and sent the can tumbling into the grass. To hear his story, I would have to pin him to the ground. Goody would only spill his guts to buy freedom.

I eased Mercy off my lap. "Goody, come here," I said, fighting against a prickly dread.

He picked up the can and eyed me with the suspicion of a stray dog.

I stretched my legs out, crossed my ankles, trying my hardest to look casual and nonthreatening. "You haven't given me one hug since I've been here." I opened my arms, hoping to entice him within striking distance.

Goody shifted his weight from one foot to the other. "I'm busy."

I stood to rummage through my purse. "You need a target that will challenge you, cowboy."

"I ain't no cowboy; I'm a Texas Ranger," he said, lifting his chin. Behind his ranger mask, his eyes narrowed.

I held up a tube of Mother's lipstick, the small bit of her I could still hold. "I bet you can't hit this."

He cocked his head, studying the shiny cylinder. "That ain't nothing."

"Prove it."

He walked toward me warily to grab for the lipstick. I withdrew it. "A target for a hug. That's the deal, Ranger Richter." Goody took a step back. I feigned a Texas drawl, "I reckon you're a-scared of missing this here target, ain't ya, pardner?"

He leaned in and patted my shoulder. I lunged at him. He twisted as I grabbed his waist and rolled over him. He kicked me with the heel of his boot, but I held on. "What's going on, Goody? Who's coming to see—?"

He kicked again, harder. I gasped. I managed to catch one of his wrists and pin his legs with mine. He wriggled under me. It was all I could do to hold on. A cool breeze up my skirt meant I was dangerously close to showing my underwear to the world. I caught his other wrist and whispered in his ear. "We have to stick together, Goody. That's what Papa said. No secrets. We're a family."

Mercy cried, "Don't fight. Please, don't fight."

She distracted me enough that Goody worked a leg loose. His boot cracked against my shin. I released him to rub the rising lump. "It would be so very helpful, Goody, if you could, this once, talk to me."

He backed away. "Sometimes a man has to do the hard thing."

"Who told you that? Did the man in the truck say that?"

His eyes flitted to Mercy. "I can't tell you nothing or I won't see Mercy, not ever. Don't ask me anymore questions. You can't! You can't!"

"I promise, no any more questions."

He fell into my arms. Within moments, my chest was wet from his tears.

I unbuttoned my coat in the pressing heat of Mrs. Nadel's office.

She added folders to a pile on her desk and sat down. "Sit, Lucy. I haven't much time."

I kneaded the strap of my purse and perched on the edge of the chair, staring at her, willing her to grow a heart as I watched.

She said, "Things have changed around here in the last three months. They're sending me more and more children, and I have nowhere to put them. I'm running out of space and money to do my job. And I'm expecting the numbers to rise. They always do in the winter." She finally met my gaze. "Influenza. You understand."

I bit down on my words. "But you promised."

"So you keep telling me. And I'm telling you this is a wonderful opportunity for Goody. He's the kind of boy who will do well with a father's direction."

"Goody only wets the bed when he's upset."

She thrummed her fingers. "I'm trying to be patient, Lucy. You've been through a lot. You're still a young girl yourself. This is not your decision to make. I decide what's best for the children, and being with a family is just what Goody needs."

"Then why is he wetting the bed?"

She took off her glasses to rub the bridge of her nose. "His bed-wetting has nothing to do with his daytime experiences. We learn about these sorts of things in our college studies." She belched into her hands, releasing a heavy sweetness across the desk. "Children at this age, especially boys, revert back to wetting the bed. No one knows why. It happens. We try not to get too upset about these sorts of regressions around here."

"But you won't let him drink."

Her eyebrows rose. "Mercy told you that, didn't she? That girl has an active imagination. Of course, you know that better than I do. She says the most outlandish things."

"She never lies."

Mrs. Nadel looked at her watch, straightened a thick stack of folders with a sharp rap on the desk. "Goody will thrive on a farm. He's an active youngster. Hard work will teach him responsibility and self-control, something he's sorely lacking." She stood to adjust her hat in front of the mirror.

I pleaded with her reflection. "Goody's different. He's changed since last week. Something's not right. He wants to be with his family, with us. Didn't your college teach you that?"

She rested her hand on the doorknob. "The family taking Goody is wonderful. They're known in this community for raising well-behaved, clean children. Their little girls sing like angels. But fate has not been kind. The mother has delivered two stillborn sons. The husband needs someone to help him on the farm. If you will stop being a silly girl for one minute, you'll understand that Goody will inherit that farm someday. This is the best possible outcome for a difficult situation."

I blocked the door with my foot. "The best possible outcome is for Goody to be with his family. I'm his family. Mercy is his family. Those people are strangers. That's why he's upset. Please, Mrs. Nadel, you have to help us."

"I won't talk to you about this anymore, Lucy. It's time for you to go."

I'd left the twins on the playground over an hour. "I'll leave after I've said goodbye."

Mrs. Nadel looked at her watch. "The children are eating their supper. I won't have you disturbing them." She worked at loosening something from her teeth with her tongue. "The family is coming for Goody next Sunday. I can't guarantee he will still be here for your regular visit. I will ask them to come in the afternoon. That's the best I can do."

"I'll come as early as I can on Sunday. You can't let him leave before I get here. I have to meet these people."

Mrs. Nadel turned back to me, studied me hard in the day's dimming light. "I've come across older siblings like you before,

Lucy. You tend to be reckless. If you have any ideas about taking matters into your own hands, know this: I will make sure you're prosecuted to the full extent of the law. There's no place you can hide from me. The law is on my side. Do we understand each other?"

I honestly didn't know what she was talking about. How could I take matters into my own hands? My only hope was to make her believe I intended to win a cooperation award from the Sauk County Child Wellness Society. "You don't have to worry about me. I have no intention of taking matters into my own hands. You've been so good to the twins." I nearly gagged on those words, but I needed her to believe I meant them. I didn't. "I'm just asking you to keep your promise. I'll be eighteen before you know it. Please, don't separate us. Please."

She turned for the door. "Be here early next Sunday. I don't expect Goody's new family until church lets out. They're very devout."

Ada

Lucy, you scoundrel!

I thought I'd satisfied you with stories of endless piano scales and the making of sauerkraut in Mutter's *kitchen. I should've known better. Your curiosity is inexhaustible. If you surrender this obsession with the past, we could travel to exotic locales instead. My walker folds as flat as a pancake, and I'm very amenable under the influence of French pastries. As it is, I'll be writing day and night.*

Yes, I'm stalling. Won't you allow an old woman her peculiarities? Consider my age, darling girl. My biggest worry is a steady supply of prune juice. And now this.

To be honest, telling this part of the story is more painful than you know. The days of the war were much too uncertain for my taste. Gil's letters came with agonizing infrequency. When they did come, I couldn't help but wonder if I was reading the letter of a dead man.

On top of all this worry, add the crushing weight of running the ranch. Without Gil to guide me, I feared everything would fall apart. As you know, I take my responsibilities very seriously, perhaps too seriously.

I do promise to handle your heart like a mewing kitten, my dear. I've hurt you enough. You see, don't you, that I've made every effort for your happiness since we came to our understanding? I so hope you do. While I will be tender, I will also be truthful. I won't have you accusing me of coloring or hiding the facts. When doing so is necessary, I'll show myself in the harshest light. This is the least I can do.

Let's start at the letter, where you stated quite plainly your dilemma. I found this most heartbreaking, for you were trying so hard to be brave for a girl of sixteen. I admired you immediately. Had I received your letter on an ordinary day, far from the turmoil of war and the agony of absence, I pray I would have answered you differently.

As it was, your first letter came to me only days after I'd received a letter from Gil. He was still in Africa, but his time of waiting had come to an end. He couldn't tell me directly about the European invasion, but we had concocted a code. He wrote: "Be sure Geronimo gets new shoes before the end of July." This meant: "I will parachute behind enemy lines before the end of July."

My knees ached from all my praying against Hitler's army. Surely, if I'd figured out Gil was to jump into Italy, Hitler knew as well. In fact, I wanted to burn the Palisade Tribune down for all its speculation in the months leading up to the invasion, as if that would have changed anything.

Oh bother, I was a mess. My Gil, who saw the war as a grand adventure, was heading into harm's way, and you wanted to bring the twins to live with me. Your request was quite impossible. You see, I believed my future to be absolutely grim. I never would have admitted so then, but I was scared to death. I didn't deserve Gil's love, and I hadn't inspired God to spare him on my account. As for Mother Heller, she wanted more than I could give. She had long dreamed of a daughter-in-law to gossip with over coffee, someone to titter over a bolt of fabric or a new recipe. That wasn't my way. If Gil didn't make it home, I saw no reason for her to keep me around. So you see, my life was quite unsettled when I received your letter. And, of course, there was my promise to your mother.

None of this is very convincing, is it?

Honestly, I had no intention of reading your letter at all, although I studied your script on the envelope in every private moment. Such contradictions of emotions nearly drove me insane. You may not have thought of this, but I was terribly upset at Magda and Thomas. I felt betrayed in the worst sort of way. This didn't help my frame of mind. I carried the letter to the incinerator more than once, but I couldn't complete the dirty deed. Instead, I kept it tucked into my brassiere, close but out of sight, until I could not resist the draw of your words one moment longer. I fully expected your words to flatten me. I was sure you hated me and wrote to tell me so.

I waited for Mother Heller to leave the house. She attended those weekly committee meetings for the migrant labor camp. She had barely turned out of the lane when I opened the letter with the tip of a butcher knife and sat on the bench under the apricot tree to read it.

I steeled myself for the accusations I'd expected, certainly not prepared for news that my sister had died, the furthest thing from my mind. The words pinned me to the bench like a mounted butterfly. Hours passed. Mother Heller returned and parked the car, shielding her eyes from the setting sun as she walked toward the house. Did she shake her head? I think she did. Anyway, she paused briefly before entering the house through the kitchen.

Every few minutes, she pulled back the curtains for a look at her crazy daughter-in-law. The day evaporated. Yellow light flared each time Mother Heller sneaked a peek at me around the blackout shade.

I didn't dare cry. There would be questions aplenty about sitting like a lawn ornament in the dark and why I hadn't come in for supper. How could I explain that I grieved a sister no one knew about? I hadn't spoken one word about Magda since I'd left Wisconsin to Mother Heller or anyone.

I sat under the tree until the house went completely dark. Mother Heller never came to me. She wanted to, I know that, but I wasn't someone who welcomed that sort of intimacy. Back then, I was delighted she didn't come to me. Now, I wish she had. I wish I'd told her everything.

You understand, don't you, Lucy, why I didn't?

I couldn't possibly keep the letter, so I hid it in the barn, in the hayloft above Bessie. I left it there for a long time. I'm sorry, I don't remember how long. But the loft wasn't a solution, just a way to keep a piece of you near, although I didn't understand that at the time. I made a plan to destroy the letter.

I sneaked out after Mother Heller had gone to bed, retrieved the letter from its hiding place, and headed for the pond on the east edge of the orchard. At the pond, I folded the letter into ever smaller squares and pressed the lump of paper to my heart. How tempting it was to read one more time your youthful script of fat loops and energetic flairs. But what good would come of such an extravagance? I'd held on too long, risked too much. I wasn't one to break promises, and I'd already compromised everything I'd worked for. No, the letter had to go. I'm so very sorry, my dear. I was a stupid, stupid woman.

I dropped the letter into a flour sack. The stones in the bottom of the bag clattered as I cinched it closed. The bag broke the water with a plunk. I imagined the bleeding of ink into the water, how the words first smeared and then lifted off the page, gone forever.

I wrote to you the very next day, not even trying to explain my reasons or sparing you the brevity of my rejection. Lucy, while I've tried to explain why I couldn't allow you and the twins to come to me, the real reason, the reason I couldn't minimize, even in light of Magda's death, was the promise I'd made to your mother.

Well, dearest, that's the story. I hope you don't regret asking. Now, I'm tired. I've asked Laurie, the CNA on duty, to bring me a hot prune juice with a pat of butter stirred in. This is my new "cocktail" for evenings. Works like a charm! Good night, my dear.

Love,
Ada

Lucy

Pete Devendorf made my life perfect misery.

On the very day Papa, Mother, and I had moved into the apartment over his parents' garage, Pete chased me around the yard with a garter snake until I ran down the street crying. I was four years old. A lot of garter snakes lived in Wisconsin, and I'd met most of them in the twelve years we lived on Maple Street, all thanks to Peter Benedict Devendorf.

Pete could be charming, in his own way. And for whatever reasons seemed to please him at the time, he turned that charm on me. And like the silly school girl I was, I surrendered my heart to Pete. There were times when I thought he knew, and he seemed to like the idea. He would offer me the last cookie on the plate or compliment my hair, but never in front of his friends. With them around, I was nothing but a bug. And then I would snatch my heart right back but never for long.

No matter. I had bigger problems to solve, like seeing the twins before the farmer came for Goody. For that reason, I forced all of the longing and loathing I'd felt for Pete behind me. I needed Pete to do the one thing he was least inclined to do—help me. No amount of wishing or praying would get the bus to Baraboo early enough to see the twins before Goody's new family arrived that next Sunday. Only a car could get me there in time, and Pete owned a car.

I'd hurried home from the diner to wash the grease out of my hair that Monday. I agonized over what to wear. I wanted to seem older, and if at all possible, pretty. Anything to persuade Pete. In the end, I wore the last dress Mother had made for a customer's daughter. The girl had never come to claim it. With ruffles everywhere, the dress was too fancy for school or church, so it hung in the closet like a museum piece. For convincing Pete to sell me his car, the dress was perfect if a tad light for the chill of a fall evening. I covered the dress with Papa's heavy jacket while I waited for Pete. I drank in the scent of Papa that lingered in the wool and swiped at my nose with a hanky. I counted back on my fingers the number of months since Papa had died.

Eight.

Forever.

All this waiting and primping could have been eliminated if Mr. and Mrs. Devendorf hadn't left for Appleton that morning. Mrs. Devendorf would have driven me to Baraboo herself, at any time of the day or night, to see the twins. Her love for us was that kind of crazy. But I didn't want to go knocking on the door and give Pete the idea that I was desperate for his help, even though I was. No, I wanted him to believe my appearance was pure happenstance, that maybe I was heading for a dance or movie.

The longer I sat on the bottom step, waiting for Pete to come out of his house, the more I feared I'd missed him or that he had decided this one Monday night to listen to the radio with his sister Joanne. Pete had never done such a thing. Now that he'd dropped out of school to join the Marines, Monday night meant drinking with his friends or a movie at the Midway.

Just as I rose to climb the stairs to the apartment, Pete hopped jauntily down his porch steps and stretched into an optimistic stride, completely missing my presence in the shadows.

I hung Papa's jacket on the newel post and followed Pete. Goose bumps rose on my arms.

"Hey, Pudge," he said when he saw me and socked my arm. "Where have you been?"

"For the love of—" I bit the inside of my cheeks. Pete waved over his shoulder as he walked down the driveway and turned south away from town. As much as I wanted to abandon my idea and watch him disappear into the night, I ran to catch up. "I hear you're leaving for basic on Friday."

"That's right, Pudge. No more childish games. I'm a Marine. I'll be shooting live ammo at Camp Lejuene by the end of next week. First and foremost, a Marine is a rifleman."

Oh brother! I smoothed my dress and blurted, "Are you selling the Tin Lizzie before you leave?"

"To you? I don't think so. You don't even drive, Pudge," he said with a smugness that made me want to slug him. I thought better of it.

"I was hoping you could teach me," I said with practiced sweetness, practically coughing up a hairball in the process.

"Not tonight." He laughed. "Besides, Pudge, I'll need a car when I get back. You aren't wishing the worst for me, are you?"

"Heck, no. I need a car is all. I have money."

He stopped, looked me up and down. "What's going on?"

Waxing or waning, I couldn't tell you, but there wasn't much of a moon that night. Still, in a flash of concern that made Pete's face go all earnest on me, a fist of longing gripped my heart. A crush? On Pete? I turned away from his gaze. This was no time for silliness. Not now. Probably never. Not with Pete. I wasn't anything like the girls he preferred. "The twins. Things have changed," I said as evenly as I could manage.

"They're not sick, are they?"

This was the Pete, the one who showed up much too infrequently—the one who was present, aware, caring—that kept my heart off balance. My face warmed. "No. They're fine. It's just that—"

He shrugged and continued walking, assuming I would follow him like a puppy, which I did. This was the Pete I knew and knew well. I trotted to catch up.

His cologne stung my eyes. And why was he walking so fast? I skipped every few steps, yet only managed to stay within a pace. "I used to wish my folks had brought the wrong baby home from the hospital," he said over his shoulder. "Now that Ernie's in the army…" He turned suddenly and I ran into him. He lifted my chin. "Hey, Pudge, you aren't crying, are you? I haven't seen you cry since—"

Was he schizophrenic? "I'm perfectly fine, you toad."

He pressed his hands deep into his pockets. "Then why are you chasing me down the street? Make it snappy. I'm expected somewhere."

Pale flesh rimmed his ears, and there was a razor nick on his neck. When did Pete start shaving?

Pete wasn't heading for the theater or the lodge. He was practically sprinting in the direction of Mildred Faschingbauer's house. Hadn't they broken up?

With a jerk of his chin, he beckoned me to follow. "You can walk along, just to the end of Broadway."

Mildred Faschingbauer? Really? She'd flunked Home Ec., for goodness' sake.

I brushed the grit off my heart and fell in step with Pete. I wished I'd worn my work shoes instead of my Sunday shoes. The patent leather pinched my toes something awful. "A family is adopting Goody."

He stopped and I nearly ran into him again. "What about your agreement?"

"That doesn't mean anything to Mrs. Nadel, not anymore."

"Come on." He pulled me by the hand toward the river. "Tell me about the family."

"I don't know much. Goody visited a farm, spent the night. They have five daughters. Mrs. Nadel says they need a boy to help out."

"I was afraid of this." He pressed me to sit on a log. Pete loosened his tie, ran his hands through his hair. "Oh boy, this isn't good. Let me think for a minute." He rolled his shoulders, cracked his neck, and spat on the ground.

"How is this helping?"

"Is there any chance in the world this Mrs. Nadel will change her mind?"

I remembered Mrs. Nadel walking out of her office, her heels clicking sharply on the linoleum, her warning. I shook my head.

Pete sat beside me. "I'm going to ask you some questions. I don't want to hear the answers, but I want you to think about the answers real hard. You're the twins' only hope. It shouldn't be that way." He paused, looking off toward the river and then back to me. "I wish to God I could stay and help you. You know I can't, don't you? I'm not leaving you high and dry. I would help if I could."

"I know that, Pete." And I did know, even though the knowing surprised me.

"You have to be very careful. You can't tell anyone what you're going to do or where you're going, if you're going anywhere, that is. If anyone asks me, I'll say we never talked about your plans. Do you understand?"

Pete studied me. What was he hoping to see? This seemed like an awful lot of intrigue for a visit to the orphanage. "Why should anyone care that I'm visiting the twins? I think all this soldier stuff has gone to your big, fat head."

I made to rise, but Pete stopped me with a hand on my shoulder. "Then you're perfectly satisfied with never seeing Goody again? You're okay that he'll be some farmer's slave? I thought better of you, Pudge."

"What are you suggesting?"

"I'm not suggesting anything. I'm just asking questions, giving you stuff to think about."

"Go on."

"Are you willing to leave Prairie du Sac? Can you get away without raising suspicion?"

"Are you crazy?" He meant for me to take the twins from the orphanage. Where would we go? Wouldn't I be a kidnapper? Mrs. Nadel thought so. This was the rash behavior she'd warned me against, I was sure of it. Taking the twins from the orphanage was definitely taking things into my own hands. But letting Goody go off with another family—could I? Honestly, I should have thought of this myself.

"How will you keep two talkative eight-year-olds from spilling the beans to everyone you meet along the way?" he asked.

I imagined the twins sitting in the backseat of the Tin Lizzie with gags in their mouths.

"Avoid the main highways. That's where the state patrol will look for you."

The state patrol? They hung kidnappers, didn't they? And then I remembered the promise I'd made to Papa. *Ich werde sie nicht verlieren.* I wouldn't lose them. But I had lost Mother.

Pete waved a hand in front of my face. "Hey, Pudge, are you listening? This is serious. You have to go someplace you've never mentioned to anyone. You'll need a job. An apartment. Food."

Did he think I was an idiot?

"Go to a city. That's where the defense jobs are. You'll have to lie about your age. Can you do that? Who will watch the twins? You can't trust just anyone. Forget the large city. Find a small town. Rent a room from a widow. Make sure she isn't too nosy. Heck, Lucy, I have no idea how you're going to do this."

27

He'd never called me Lucy before.

Pete pulled a cord in the middle of the garage and a single bulb reflected off the Tin Lizzie. He rubbed at a spot on the hood with his sleeve. "The key's in the ignition."

"How much?" I said, opening my purse.

"Put it away, Pudge. This is a loan. Letting you drive the lizzie around will keep the carburetor clean."

We looked at each other across the hood for a long moment. He looked older, kinder. It suited him.

"Just promise me you'll be good to the old gal," he finally said, patting the fender. "She'll need lots of oil, so make the gas-hop check every time you fill up." He handed me a ration book from under the seat. "There are a few extra stamps in there. Hopefully, you won't run across an overzealous gas-hop. You deserve the gas as much as anyone. This is all about keeping your family together, right?"

"Won't your parents…?"

"Can you see Mom driving the lizzie?"

Mrs. Devendorf liked her homemade donuts too much. She wouldn't fit behind the steering wheel. "I should pay you something. Your family has given us so much. It doesn't seem right—"

"If you try hard enough, you can talk me out of this, Pudge, so you better shut your clap. Wish me luck." And he was gone.

I leaned against the garage wall, listening to Pete's footsteps crunch the gravel until all that remained between us were the crickets' songs. I breathed in dust and oil, clutching the keys over my heart like amulets.

Before the war, Pete had packed the lizzie with his friends. The girls squealed with surprise when the car backfired. And plenty of times, I was pressed into washing and polishing the thing to ransom my laundry he'd stolen from the clothesline. The car had come to represent all I'd disdained about Pete. But in the soft light of the garage, the lizzie shone like a jewel. What was I to think about Pete now? I didn't like being muddleheaded, so I shook off thoughts of him to sit behind the wheel, petting it like a cat and tapping the pedals with my feet. One of them surely made the car move.

The garage door opened. "Pete?"

He stood by the driver's window, breathless. "Who's going to teach you how to drive?"

"It can't be that hard."

He opened the door. "Scoot over."

"What about Mildred?"

"She's a good gal."

"You can't tell her anything, not about teaching me to drive, or the car, or—"

"I'll think of something. Don't worry. I know how to handle Mildred."

We drove the farm roads where we were less likely to see anyone. I hardly knew where I was for all the orders Pete barked. "Not so fast! Take it easy on the brakes! Clutch! Shift! Clutch! Ease on the gas. Stop!"

My calf cramped from pushing the clutch in so many times, but Pete insisted I practice until I shifted without grinding the gears. By the time the sun brightened the far hills, Pete approved of my driving—until I tried to back up.

"That happens to me too. The old girl is showing her age." We switched places. He backed the car into the garage. When the time came for my Sunday visit, I would be nervous enough, and backing the car out of the garage was one less thing to worry about. "If you pay attention, you won't have to back up much."

I'd known her long enough to say with authority, "Mildred's going to be mad."

Pete snugged his tie to his Adam's apple. "She's crazy about me. I'll tell her the boys took me out for a beer, and they wouldn't let me go until I shot out the light on the co-op."

"Pete…" I started, but he put a finger to my lips.

"Don't thank me." He reached into the backseat. "I've got a notebook here somewhere. And a pencil." He wrote out his military address, a crazy mix of numbers and letters that made no sense at all. "Let me know where you end up, Lucy. I don't want to lose you."

Lucy

I pressed Goody's head down.

"Stay down," I said through my teeth. In the rearview mirror, I watched the farmer and his wife amble up the orphanage steps, him in a suit that no longer buttoned over his belly, the wife in a cotton dress so thin the sun outlined her plump legs. Mrs. Nadel greeted them with opened arms.

Goody said, "How come we have to hide to take a ride in Pete's old car?"

"There's a hole in the floor," Mercy said.

Pushing the clutch to the floor, I pumped the accelerator and waggled the gear shift. I took on a conspiratorial tone. "Because we're breaking out of this joint, see? And we ain't taking any prisoners. In fact, we ain't stopping until we reach the Colorady border, see?"

The engine rattled to life, and Mrs. Nadel and the couple turned toward the sound. My stomach clenched. I'd managed to get the twins into the car before the farm couple had arrived, having told Mrs. Nadel that I couldn't bring myself to meet them after all. I wasn't about to give the twins up now. The farmer said something to his wife, but they turned back toward the orphanage and entered.

"My Lone Ranger badge, it's under the mattress," Goody said from the floor of the backseat. His voice trembled.

Goody treasured his Lone Ranger badge above everything and

anything. He'd proven that in the past. And once he figured out I had no intentions of letting him retrieve it, he would invent new ways to torture me. He might even jump out of the car to run back into the orphanage for it. I couldn't let him do that. As it was, I'd forgotten to park where I didn't have to back up, and now I struggled to find reverse. A conversational diversion could work with Goody. "I heard Mitch talking with his parents at the diner. He was begging for the *new* Lone Ranger badge."

"There ain't no new badge. I got the official badge. Mitch don't know what he's talking about."

The gears ground metal against metal. "He seemed awful sure of himself. He saw a kid wearing a new badge in Milwaukee."

"He's crazy!"

"Goody, it's not nice to call someone crazy," Mercy said.

"But he is crazy. You can't have more than one official badge. That don't make no kind of sense."

I waggled the gearshift again and prayed. *Oh please, oh please, oh please.* Still, the gearshift resisted.

"I can't be the Lone Ranger without my badge," Goody said, his voice rising to the octave of panic.

Finally, the car lurched out of the parking space.

"Sissy," Goody pleaded, "what if we see some bad guys. They won't know I'm the Lone Ranger."

"Didn't I tell you? Aunt Ada has a white horse named Silver." I watched the rearview mirror and prayed that my lie would put miles between us and the orphanage.

"Honest to goodness?" Goody's head popped up.

"Get down!"

And surprise of surprises, he sat on the floorboard again. "A white horse?"

"Yes, and he wears a silver saddle."

I crossed my fingers against the lie and pressed the gearshift into first. Mrs. Nadel appeared on the front steps of the orphanage. She guarded her eyes against the sun to watch me drive away. I played at wiping away tears and gave her a half-hearted wave. I took my first breath when we turned onto Highway 33 toward Reedsburg, the first of many twists and turns I'd mapped for our journey to Colorado.

"I can see the road through the hole," Mercy said. "It's going by pretty fast."

I checked the rearview mirror for state troopers, something I planned on doing all the way to Colorado or anyplace else we ended up, probably until the day I died. "You can sit on the seat now."

Goody crawled over the seat to the front.

"I told you to stay in the back."

"So we ain't going back to the orphanage?"

"We'll get you a new Lone Ranger badge, Goody. There's no sense getting upset over a piece of tin."

"How far to Colorado? Is it close to Texas?" Goody sat on the edge of the seat, bouncing as he gripped imaginary reins. I should have made him get into the backseat, but this was the happiest I'd seen him in a long time.

"It's a pretty big hole, Sissy."

I shouted over the engine to Mercy, afraid to look away from the pitted road. "Sit on the other side. I'll put something over the hole when we stop for gas."

"Are we almost there?" Goody said.

Mercy hugged my neck until the pressure against my windpipe got to be too much. I patted her arm, and she loosened her grip to lay her head on my shoulder. Her breath warmed my neck. "I guess Jesus liked my prayer because he changed Mrs. Nadel's mind, just like I asked."

This bit of news didn't help. I was already struggling over what to tell the twins about what I'd just done. If I told them I'd kidnapped them from the orphanage, Mercy would want to go back. She had a highly developed conscience for an eight-year-old. For Goody, being kidnapped would mean adventure. He got downright unbearable when riled up. That wouldn't do either. Mercy's words decided the question. I was more than willing to give Jesus credit for the twins' exodus.

"I memorized a new mercy verse," she said.

Ever since Mercy had realized her name showed up in many, many Scripture verses, she set to memorizing all of them. As I was in the middle of kidnapping my brother and sister from the orphanage, a Scripture verse was the last thing I wanted to hear. "Sure. Go ahead." I tightened my grip on the steering wheel.

"'Have mercy on us, O LORD, have mercy upon us: for we are exceedingly filled with contempt.' Psalm 123, verse three. What's contempt, Sissy? Mrs. Nadel didn't know."

At the mention of Mrs. Nadel, my blood ran cold. I must have shivered.

"Are you cold?" she asked.

"I'm excited is all," I lied yet again. "Contempt means hating something or someone."

"We aren't supposed to hate."

"You're right, Mercy. But sometimes it's very hard not to hate someone who hurts you or the people you love."

She squeezed my neck again, more gently. "I contempt Mrs. Nadel, just a little, I guess."

If I'd had any doubts about taking the twins from the orphanage, they dissipated with Mercy's whispered words. I felt Goody's eyes on me, but I didn't dare look away from the road. My arms ached with the effort of steering the car around pot holes.

"I contempted everything about that place," he said.

"It's good we're together." I reached to touch him. He seized my hand.

"Is Aunt Ada nice?" This from Mercy. We were traveling at one hundred questions per hour. What did I expect from two eight-year-olds?

Goody released my hand to whinny at horses grazing in a pasture.

"It's hard to tell about a person from a letter," I said, although in the weeks since I'd received Ada's reply, I'd spent many nights wetting my pillow over her terse answer. And she never even mentioned Mother. "We should wait until we meet her face to face."

"It would be better for Goody if she were really, really nice."

Goody pointed his finger like a pistol at a sign announcing Highway 23 and shot off a full round.

I prayed Aunt Ada owned a tender spot for boys who aspired to be the Lone Ranger and for a bucketful of mercy to come my way. No one was so exceedingly filled with contempt as me.

"I am not carrying you, Goody."

"The Lone Ranger can't go into a town without his mount."

I marched rather than walked to ease the rub of my shoes against growing blisters on both heels. "Even the Lone Ranger gave Silver a day off, Goody."

Behind me, he yelled to my back, "I ride into town or I don't take another step."

"Fine."

October was usually a friendly month—warm, refreshing, free of mosquitoes. But if this was October's way of befriending travelers, I was rethinking my loyalties. We'd been walking through a light snow for nearly an hour, hoping for the village of Mt. Hope, Iowa to come into view. I was in no mood to be placating Goody's delusion about being the Lone Ranger, especially when he insisted that I play the part of Silver.

Goody's boots pounded the road behind me. "I'm not much of a ranger without my badge."

"Come on, Goody. The town can't be that far." Mercy said, walking like a soldier beside me.

Rather than focus on my raw heels, I negotiated with Goody. "Well, kemosabe, would you consider walking if Mercy and I walked behind you?"

"What good would that do?" He sat down again.

Negotiations ceased. "Okay. Fine. Enjoy the view." I shifted the bag to take Mercy's hand. I took on the exuberance of a May robin. "Mt. Hope sounds like a lovely place. I'm sure the good residents of such a pleasant hamlet will be glad to see us. It's customary in these parts to offer a cup of hot chocolate to sojourners."

Mercy stopped, pulled her hand from mine, and looked to Goody. "I'm not thirsty."

This sort of behavior maddened me. Everything was black or white with Mercy, and leaving her brother on a road to be squished by a truck definitely merged to black in her eyes. Of course, she was right.

I stooped and Goody nearly vaulted onto my back. He used my braids for reins. "When I pull on the right rein—"

"I turn right."

"And when I pull the—"

"If you pull hard, I'm leaving you in the ditch. Do you hear me?"

He stroked my shoulder. "Easy, boy. Easy now."

When the lizzie had dropped something hard onto the road and rolled to a stop, we'd waited for a car to drive by, hoping for a lift to the next town. But folks had long since grown drowsy from their Sunday lunches and settled in for a long nap. The sagging clouds meant more snow was on its way. At first, the twins had complained about leaving behind their belongings. I'd assured them we would return after we found help. Now, Mercy asked me to carry her doll, and Goody wanted me to trot.

When we crested a hill, the town's grain elevator rose like a welcoming hand. My heart felt glad for it. The gladness didn't last long. The village of Mt. Hope was nothing but that grain elevator, a post office, a church, a tavern, and a market, all of them closed on a Sunday afternoon. I lowered Goody to the ground to look up and down the four roads that fed the village. Only the roof of a barn peeked over a far hill.

I banged on the doors of the businesses, hoping someone had come in on a quiet Sunday to do bookkeeping as Mr. Stiefler of the Badger Café had often done. I stood before the tavern for a long time before I rapped quickly on the door and walked back to where I'd left the twins on the market's steps. The store's alcove provided the only protection from the wind. The snow fell heavier, and I pulled the twins close, considering which window I would break to find shelter and food.

"I'm hungry, Sissy." The quaver in Mercy's voice told me she was much hungrier than she would say.

"Me too," Goody said. "I could eat a buffalo. All I've got is these lemon drops I took from Mrs. Nadel's desk."

I patted my pockets and pulled out the contents, a few saltines and an apple. "Lemon drops for dessert, then." Foolish me, I'd considered the bag of groceries in the car too heavy to bring along. "You'll have to share."

Goody cupped his hands to peer into the market and pounded on the door.

"No one's in there, bud," I said, taking him by the shoulders. Below his cheekbones, his face was drawn and his chin was more defined than I remembered. I polished the apple on my coat.

I handed the apple to Mercy first. "I won't hear any arguments from you. You have to eat half before you give the apple to Goody. Understand?"

"She always goes first." Tears slid over Goody's freckled cheeks.

"I'm not hungry anymore," Mercy said.

"That doesn't matter," I told her. "You have to eat."

She handed the apple to Goody. "He shared his half of the

sandwich. He doesn't like mayonnaise, remember?"

She didn't say this as an accusation, but she should have. Goody despised mayonnaise. I'd forgotten that about him in the few months they'd been in the orphanage. What else had I forgotten? A breeze lifted the flap of my coat, and the cold needled my thighs. We needed shelter. I remembered the barn in the distance. "We better get moving."

I woke up rubbing my arms against the cold. The moon reached through the barn's walls with silvery fingers, outlining a tractor, a wagon, a cultivator. When I sighed, my breath was a vaporous pouf. I pulled Mercy closer and tugged her cap down to touch her scarf I'd wrapped around her mouth and nose. At least her face would be warm hidden behind Mrs. Devendorf's knitting. I reached for Goody, such a wild sleeper. If I didn't keep him close, he would end up trampled by the milking cows. The rascal had scooted out of arm's reach. Reluctantly, I left Mercy behind to search on hands and knees, feeling through the straw for his boot or an arm.

A cow complained from the corner. "Goody?" I whispered, fighting to keep panic from my voice, more for my sake than Goody's. He deserved any discomfort his wandering caused.

Large animals shifted. I crawled faster.

"Goody?" I said through chattering teeth. I called out again, louder. "Goody!'

The barn door clattered open. "I'm here!"

Behind him stood a man large enough to block the moon's light. I scrambled to my feet and pushed Goody behind me. "Mister, I'm sorry. We didn't take anything. We just needed a place to sleep."

"The little mister here explained how your car broke down."

"I have some money. I could pay you—"

"You ain't horse thieves or cattle rustlers, are you?"

Goody stood in front of the imposing man. "I'm the Lone Ranger. If you've got problems with thieves and rustlers, I'm your man."

The man laughed and the knot in my stomach relaxed some. He asked me, "You're traveling alone? You don't got your folks nearby?"

Goody tapped the man's elbow, and the man looked down. "Our folks are dead."

"Well now, that's a big piece of heartache right there." His voice came from a deep well. "Let's get you all inside before the misses makes me sleep out here with you."

From the way Ernst and Lillian Langstrom welcomed us into their home, I wondered if they received midnight visitors to their farm on a regular basis. Lillian turned from the stove where a large pot steamed. "Children, sit here at the table."

Ernst lowered Mercy into my arms.

"Ernst, get the blankets around those children like I told you." Lillian took the blankets from Ernst and tucked them around our shoulders. She paused to lift Mercy's cap. "Still sleeping. Now, there's a tired child. Take her on upstairs, Ernst. Put her in the big bed. And add another quilt."

I watched Ernst carry Mercy down a hall toward the stairs.

Lillian patted my arm. "Don't you worry about your sister. She's in good hands." She pulled cups from a cupboard and adjusted the flame under a pan of milk. "Me and Ernst raised us eight children in this house. Come a Sunday, all the children and their spouses bring the grandchildren here for fried chicken. Had one of my daughters-in-law living here up until a couple weeks ago, seeing as our son is fighting Hitler over in Africa. She's gone home to be with her own parents. Can't say as I blame her, but I sure miss that Timmy of hers. He kept my mind from worrying so much about his daddy. I never dreamed in a hundred years one of my babies would end up in Africa." Lillian ladled hot milk into cups and set them in front of me and Goody. She paused, ladle poised, and frowned. "I can't remember why I told you all that." She settled in the chair across from us.

Ernst shuffled into the kitchen. Goody chose that exact moment to forget his manners. "Maybe you was going to offer us some of your fried chicken."

Lillian lowered her glasses to look at Goody. She popped out of her chair. "Bless my soul, that is exactly what I was going to do." The ice box opened like the window of heaven. Out came pickled beets and the chicken Goody asked for, plus mashed potatoes that Lillian patted into circles and fried in bacon grease. She sliced thick slabs of bologna and spread lush swaths of butter on slices of homemade bread. I nearly swooned. "And I got some chocolate cake left. With all them grandchildren swarming around the kitchen, leftovers are a bit of a miracle."

After we ate, Goody and I joined Mercy in a quilt-laden bed under a sloping ceiling. With a full tummy, Goody fell asleep during a quick telling of "The Three Little Bears." Since both of them missed our goodnight prayers, I decided to pray on their behalf, thanking God for the kindness of the Langstroms, especially for the good food and warm bed, things I couldn't provide for the twins.

My arms and legs felt stuffed with sand, but my brain was free to tiptoe through a garden of worries. What if Mrs. Nadel had called out every policeman and state trooper in Sauk County? What if the police found Pete's car in the ditch and followed the road to the Langstroms' farm? And what was I going to tell Pete about his car? I had no answers, and so I did what I always did when sleep wouldn't come—I remembered a better day.

I chose a summer day back when we were a family of three, just me, Mother, and Papa. Mother had made us matching swimsuits covered with sailboats to wear to the lake. The sun warmed my bare shoulders as Papa grunted and groaned, wrestling the rowboat from the top of the car and into the lake. At Mother's insistence, our family trips to the lake were for swimming, not fishing. Papa groused about that. We expected this of him because he loved fishing more than anything other than me and Mother.

Once the rowboat lay belly up on the shore, Papa raced me to the end of the dock, and we plunged into the cold water. When I complained about the chill, he told me to swim harder. I pulled at the water as if plowing a watery field. I swam a wide path around Papa and back toward the dock. After lunch and the torturous hour of waiting to enter the water again for fear of certain death by drowning, the three of us rowed to the middle of the lake. Mother treaded water with languid sweeps of her hands. Her hair remained perfectly dry.

I dove from the back of the rowboat with a rope tied to my swimsuit. With every stroke, I reached, stretching and splaying my fingers to stir the stewy bottom. If I stayed under the surface too long, Papa tugged me back to the surface at Mother's command. That day, I brought up a turtle for my prize. I'd kept Snappy in a glass bowl until he'd bitten me.

The remembering faded into a dream. Instead of water weeds, I grabbed a fistful of hair. The hair tangled around my arm, and I planted my feet on the lake's bottom to pull away, but the hair wrapped around my legs, too. My lungs screamed for a breath. I clawed at my arms and legs to free myself. Above me, the sun outlined the rowboat. My mother leaned over the side and reached for me. I pushed off the bottom.

I woke with a gasp, panting and sucking in icy air until the twins complained in their sleep. I dared not close my eyes against the darkness again.

We stayed with the Langstroms for three days. Lillian insisted it took that long to work the chill out of bones, but I worried every day that tarrying meant my next bed would be in a jail cell for taking the twins.

Ernst offered to bring the car to the farm where he could take a good look at it, which settled my worry some. He found the lizzie right where we had left it and declared it dead in the water on account of the transmission being scattered across the road. He promised to keep the lizzie's carcass in the barn until Pete could retrieve it after the war.

Ernst used his kerchief to wipe grease from his hands. "That's the least I can do for one of our boys." No doubt, Pete would return to a car that ran better than he'd left.

Lillian and I hung her wash on a bitingly brisk day. I could tell she was aching to ask why we were roaming around the countryside. As we shook a sheet out to hang, I told her we were headed to our aunt's house in Colorado, dismissing Pete's admonishment to keep our destination a secret. He could not have meant for me to lie to someone like Lillian.

She snapped a clothespin in place. "Now that your car's kaput, how will you get to Colorado?"

I'd given this question some thought. "How far are we from the nearest train station?"

"You got money for the fare?"

I'd sold everything worth anything from our apartment. The good people of Prairie du Sac opened their pocketbooks and pressed extra coins into my palm. Since I hadn't had to purchase

Pete's car, I'd earned more than enough to get us to Colorado. I lifted my skirt to show Lillian how I'd pinned dollar bills to my slip like fish scales.

"You're an awfully clever girl, Lucy. Cedar Rapids is where you need to go," she said. "That's where the westbound trains come through, more than usual these days with all the boys headed for the Pacific, but you still might face a long wait." She turned to give me a sympathetic look. "The boys travel first."

The next morning, I came to the kitchen to find Mercy already nestled in Lillian's lap. She'd fallen back to sleep against Lillian's cushiony bosom, looking more peaceful than I'd ever seen her. The woman blotted her eyes on her sleeve. A smile creased the corners of Lillian's eyes when she saw me. She nodded toward the coffee pot. I poured a cup and sat across from her.

"Your sister has a gift."

I'd hoped to put much more distance between us and Baraboo before Mercy said anything to draw more attention than we needed.

Not everyone will understand," she said.

I stared into my cup. "She says things. I'm awfully sorry."

Lillian touched my arm. Our eyes met. "You don't have anything to apologize for. She speaks with a tender authority. It's like talking to an angel, although I must say I've never talked to an angel before, but it must be like this. She had no way of knowing, no way at all." Lillian's tears flowed again.

"You've been so good to us," I said. "I hate to see you cry."

"She..." Lillian kissed the top of Mercy's head. "She lives up to her name, is all. If I'd a known that was how it worked, I would have named all my boys Peaceful and all the girls Quiet. Your mama was very wise."

Lillian begged off accompanying us to the train depot, claiming she had a basketful of mending that simply had to be tended. I was greatly relieved. One more second under Lillian's care, and I was sure to ask if we could stay with her and Ernst forever. But staying this close to Baraboo was impossible. I felt foolish for becoming complacent and for planning so poorly. The twins would find themselves in the orphanage again, if we didn't keep moving. I meant to keep my heart in check from then on, not allow myself to get caught up in imagining a life that could never be.

On the train platform, Ernst took each of our hands in turn, a bass swallowing minnows, and squeezed. I squeezed back, willing his strength to become mine. He smothered Goody's shoulder with his hand. "You're the man in charge of these fine women. Get them to Colorado safe and sound, now. Don't go taking your eye off of them for one minute."

"Fine women? They ain't nothing but dumb girls," Goody said.

"You'll feel differently about them someday. I guarantee it, young man."

"All aboard!"

A gust of wind pressed my skirt to my legs. We huddled closer. Nearby, a mother wiped her tears and rested a hand on her soldier son's cheek. His buddies called from the train and he bolted, only to return for one more hug. "I gotta go, Ma," he said. The mother and I exchanged glances for the briefest moment, but in her eyes I saw the universe tear apart. I pulled the twins even closer, not nearly as eager to leave as I had been.

Ernst raised my chin. "Lillian and I agree on this: God is with you in a mighty way. He will get you through."

"Last call! All aboard!"

I nodded, wanting to believe him but remembering Aunt Ada's stern words: *Under no circumstances are you to come here. You would do better to go back to school and encourage the adoption of your brother and sister. Do not contact me again.* But I also remembered a young Ada in the photograph with Mother, smiling like she had opened the most wonderful birthday present ever. Surely, Aunt Ada would smile like that again when she saw Goody and Mercy, carbon copies of her lost sister.

Ernst shepherded us toward the train. "You better move along, now. It won't do for you to miss the train while we're standing right here. Lillian wouldn't let me hear the end of it, that's for sure. Get on there, and may the Good Lord bless you." Ernst walked the platform as we inched down the crowded train aisle. His face scrunched with worry, gesturing a question with his hands that I couldn't answer. Mercy held the hem of my coat and I pushed Goody ahead. Besides the soldiers, there were young mothers with babies and suited men reading newspapers. There weren't two empty seats together, let alone three.

I'd once taken the train with Mother to Chicago to see *The Nutcracker*. That was the Christmas before the twins had been born. Those passengers had spoken in hushed tones and laughed into their hands. This train was an anthill. Soldiers stood in the aisle and sat on the floor. Whispers that warmed my ear called me "babe" and "sweet cheeks," and someone tugged at my coat sleeve. I pulled away without looking to see who it was. I'd had boys tell me I was pretty before, and I didn't like it. These boys sounded like they hadn't eaten in weeks, and they intended to make me their next meal.

I looked out to the platform. Ernst still waved his hanky, his face folded with concern. If he were to beckon me off the train, no doubt I would live in Mt. Hope, Iowa to the end of my days. A conductor pressed past me and ordered me to follow. He asked a woman sitting alone to sit next to a man reading behind a newspaper. She scowled at me as she wedged herself into the seat. We sat in a seat meant for two, but I was glad for the twin's closeness. They were all that was familiar to me. The train lurched.

"Where are you going?" the conductor said.

Goody crowed at the top of his lungs, "Colorado, here we come!"

The conductor braced himself on the seats. "You need anything, you come to me. I'll be on until we get to North Platte, and I'll make sure Simon knows you're here. You got somebody meeting you in Colorado?"

"Yes, sir," Mercy said, "our Aunt Ada invited us to live with her because our Papa and Mama died."

He held his cap to his heart, revealing a shiny pate. "Well then, I better take extra good care of you. I wouldn't want Aunt Ada mad at me."

Mercy giggled and my heart melted. The conductor was more right than he knew to avoid Aunt Ada's ire. In just over a thousand miles, I would come face to face with her.

Could I compose a speech pretty enough to change her mind about taking us in?

I was betting everything that I could.

Lucy

I left the ladies' lounge wearing Mother's felt hat and her Midnight Serenade lipstick.

"You look stupid." Goody spoke loud enough to turn heads.

I squeezed between the twins and gave him the evil eye.

"You look like the clowns at the circus," he said, managing to keep his voice low, which meant he knew what he was talking about, but what was I to do? If someone saw twins traveling with a teen-aged girl, they might remember reading about kidnapped children, not that I'd seen a headline like that. I'd only imagined such things in every unclaimed moment since we'd driven away from the orphanage.

Goody's face squeezed into a question that crowded his freckles. Mercy searched me with knowing eyes. My heart snagged on a deep longing. Mercy was a mirror likeness of our mother, her hair glistening shades of bittersweet chocolate and eyes as warm as cocoa powder balls. Goody's coloring was softer by a tone, only milk chocolate, but still very much our mother. And so, here we were, a clown of a girl, a nymph as alluring as chocolate, and the Lone Ranger. No one would dare cast a suspicious eye our way.

The train lumbered along, the wheels clicking rhythmically with every juncture of the rails. We played *Old Maid* and *Go Fish* until the outside world disappeared into blackness. Inside, soldiers took off their tunics and rolled up their sleeves, celebrating winning hands of poker with whoops and shouts that startled Mercy out of sleep. When the lights inside the car dimmed, the poker games folded and the glow of cigarettes rose and fell like fireflies.

Someone strummed a guitar and sang of an unfaithful lover. I played with the rim of Mother's hat as I let my head fall against the headrest but willed my eyes to stay opened. Goody leaned over my lap to watch the soldiers and, no doubt, to hear their ribald stories. This would never do. I didn't want Goody talking like an old salt by the time we reached Colorado. Aunt Ada would send us packing for sure.

"Come on," I said, waking Mercy and pulling Goody along the aisle toward the ladies' lounge.

Goody dug in the heels of his cowboy boots and refused to budge when he saw the door. "I can't go in there."

"Sure, you can. This is our assigned sleeping area."

"Who ever heard of sleeping in the ladies' bathroom?"

Mercy put an arm around his shoulders. "You always feel better after a good night's sleep." Goody didn't argue because this bit of truth and wisdom came from Mercy, not me. That's how it was with the twins. They spoke to each other with an odd familiarity and no resentment. Still, Goody didn't follow me until I yanked his arm. Mercy followed. She always did.

The ladies' lounge was two rooms, one mirrored along two walls with a vanity counter. The other room was the lavatory. I made a bed of paper towels under the vanity. With a little coaxing, Goody agreed the vanity resembled a tent the Lone Ranger and Tonto might sleep under on a rainy night. He put his back to the wall and fell asleep almost immediately, a trait he'd inherited from Papa. Mercy and I nestled like spoons in a drawer. I stiffened each time the door opened, sure that someone had complained to the conductor, and we would be forced to give up our bed. A woman nudged me with her shoe. "Aren't you the smart girl to be sleeping in here? Did your mother teach you that? You can't be too careful riding the rails. Don't let the bedbugs bite now, you hear?"

After that, I let sleep pull me into its cocoon.

The next morning, I stepped over sleeping soldiers as I looked frantically for Mercy. I found her sitting with the woman who had nudged me. Mercy's cheek bulged on one side. A heart-shaped box of chocolates with empty wrappers rested in her lap. Beside her, the woman took a long drag off a cigarette. Through the window, the burdened clouds had turned to metal gray. Snow would fall again before the day ripened. The woman wished me a good morning.

I tugged Mercy's arm. "You need to come with me. I've been looking all over for you."

Mercy offered the box of candy. "Goody was snoring."

The woman smiled and winked. "How about that? Men start snoring when they're nothing but lads. I guess they can't help themselves."

I'd never spoken with a woman like her. It wasn't what she said as much as the directness of her gaze. She was no farmer's wife. "You shouldn't be bothering the nice lady with your wild stories."

"She's no bother to me." The woman's voice was honey poured out in a heavy stream. "I don't sleep much, especially not on trains, and I've been on this train for what seems like forever. Pull up a duffle bag and visit with us. They don't serve breakfast for another hour."

At the mention of breakfast, my stomach growled. I extended my hand to Mercy. "We can't leave Goody alone, sweetie."

Mercy leaned back in her seat.

"This isn't a good time, Mercy. Come on, brother might wake while we're gone, and he'll never forgive us for leaving him in the ladies' lounge."

Mercy wrapped her fingers around the woman's hand and leaned to whisper to me. "I haven't told her what she needs to know yet."

"About what?" I whispered back. But I knew. It was one thing to whisper comforting words to someone like Lillian Langstrom. Speaking the messages from heaven to a woman like this was quite another. In fact, what would a child like Mercy have to say to a worldly woman? "Nice to meet you, ma'am," I said and pulled Mercy out of the seat, lifting her over a sleeping soldier and many duffle bags and carrying her all the way back to the ladies' lounge. I set her down.

Before I opened the door, Mercy pulled her hand away, something she had never done. "Sissy, you came too soon."

I knelt down. "I know you want to help, but we have to be careful. We're not home anymore. All kinds of people live in the world, sweetie. We have to be cautious."

"But she—"

"Why don't you pray for her?"

Mercy looked longingly down the aisle. "It's not the same. I should go back."

"Family comes first. That's the way it has to be. There will be plenty of time to visit with ladies on trains when you're older, I promise." What I did not say to Mercy was how dangerous her messages could be. To do so would mean telling her that I'd kidnapped the two of them, that drawing attention to us might mean going back to the orphanage. This was my burden to carry and my sin to bear.

Mercy met my gaze. "Okay then, let's pray."

I said my prayers at every meal, bowed my head with people watching, and I recited the Now-I-Lay-Me prayer every night, otherwise I couldn't fall to sleep. Mercy's prayers were very different. We bowed our heads, and she prayed for the lady named Margie.

"Jesus, Margie doesn't know how much you love her. I don't know why, but her mama forgot to tell her. I wanted to tell her, but Lucy won't let me. Please bring someone to tell her, and that someone better not have a big sister. Amen."

Before the sun set that night, the train crawled with agonizing slowness the steep slopes of mountains. The engine nearly met the caboose as we wound our way ever upward, along rushing rivers that glistened like ebony ribbons against snow. On one side, the train barely cleared a wall of solid rock. On the other side, Goody and Mercy pressed their noses to the window, mouths agape, to marvel at the plunge to the icy waters below. Keeping Goody alive in this terrain would take every bit of wit I could muster. Perhaps I would fashion a leash from his belt.

Once the sun set, the twins peppered me with questions I didn't know how to answer: How do you stay in bed in a mountain house? Does food roll off your plate? Will we live in a log cabin? Can I shoot a bear? The questions continued as I laid a fresh bed of paper towels for our second night on the train. Will I roll to the bottom of the mountain? Do balloons pop on the mountaintops? When will we see a purple mountain? Where do the mountain goats live? The torrent of questions slowed to a trickle, and soon Goody's snoring sounded like that bear he'd wanted to shoot.

"We'll be closer to the sun, won't we?" Mercy asked.

"I suppose so," I offered, not believing anything I said.

"Will it be hot?"

"I'm awfully tired, Mercy. Let's get some sleep. We'll be in Palisade by supper tomorrow."

"Tell me about the picture of Aunt Ada and Mama."

"I've told you a thousand times."

"Tell me again."

"And then you'll go to sleep?"

"I think so."

"Well, Aunt Ada is wearing a cotton dress with a satin ribbon tied into a big bow. She is hugging Mother around the waist."

"The sun makes her hair seem white."

"Who's telling this story?"

"Go ahead."

"And Aunt Ada is laughing so hard, her head is tilted back. She's probably laughing at something Mother said."

"Is Mama happy in the picture? Is she laughing?"

"She looks like she wants her little sister to stop talking and go to sleep."

"That's not how it goes."

"It's how it goes tonight."

Lucy

Not one window glowed from within Aunt Ada's house. No shuffling of hooves came from the barn. No dog rushed to bark a welcome. I'd seen friendlier farms in the Sears and Roebuck catalog. Even so, the moon tinted a lacy crust of snow a silvery blue, beguiling the farm into an unnatural slumber. I surely expected our arrival to upend that peace.

My footprints crunched as I walked through shadows reaching like bony fingers across the lane. My resolve faltered at the door. What had I thought? No one knocked on a door at this hour unless flames threatened the house. But I sure didn't want to sleep in another barn, and the twins were depending on me.

Goody called out from the mailbox where I'd left him with Mercy, "Hurry up, Lucy. It's cold out here."

"Shh. Stay where you are."

I counted on Mercy to chat with God on our behalf, for that was how she prayed. It was a conversation, one-sided, no exalted salutations, no greasing of the skids with a promise of good behavior, just talk between a child and a beloved parent, the kind of parent who celebrated a childlike faith and held no expectations for perfection. Where had she met this God?

"Hear Mercy's prayer, Lord."

I knocked. Waited. Knocked again. "Hello?" I said. "Is anyone home?"

A woman, whom I assumed to be Aunt Ada, stepped onto the

porch and closed the door behind her. She clutched her robe to her neck to study me, and when she spoke, her voice lobbed words as hard as stones. "You had no business coming here. You got my letter. I told you as much. You're to take the next train right back the way you came." She turned toward the door.

I could no longer feel my feet. "The twins are at the mailbox. Please, let us stay just for one night. We'll leave first thing in the morning, I promise."

"You brought the twins?" She stepped closer. Aqueous eyes caught the moon's light. Her hair fell in waves past her shoulders, but she no longer resembled the little girl in the photograph. From the creases between her eyebrows, the grownup Ada had forgotten how to laugh at jokes. "Please go," she pleaded. "You can walk back the way you came. There's a motel, the Elberta Motel. You can see it from the depot. The Mountaineer goes to Denver every morning. I'm sure you can make whatever connections you need from there."

At midnight? With two small children? "We slept in the ladies' lounge. On the floor. The soldiers, they said things, terrible things young children have no business hearing."

"Lucy." Her sigh was a cloud of frost. "You have no idea the trouble you're bringing to me. I'm asking you to go. Go now. Please."

Warmth seeped from the house. "I'll go, but take in the twins. They're eight years old. What kind of trouble—?"

The door clicked open, sending a dull rectangle of light across the porch and down the steps.

"Go," Aunt Ada hissed.

"Who's there, Ada?" The woman, as slight at a hummingbird, stepped beside Aunt Ada. "I don't think we've met, dear. Ada, bring the girl in. No one will freeze to death at Honey Sweet Ranch, not while I'm alive." This last part sounded like a scold.

"The girl was just leaving, Mother Heller."

And because Goody had never obeyed me for more than a minute, usually less, the twins stepped into the light, marching in place to warm their feet.

"Oh, my." Mother Heller ushered the twins up the porch steps and into the house. When I hesitated, she said, "Come on. This is no night to be counting the stars."

"They can't stay," Aunt Ada said, her voice squeezed by panic.

"Why not?" asked Mother Heller.

"They're taking the next train to Denver. Salt Lake."

Mercy snuggled into the folds of Mother Heller's robe. "It's quite a challenge to travel both east and west. Tonight, the children will sleep in a warm bed to prepare for this odd journey you're sending them on. Ada, what's gotten into you?"

Mother Heller told us to call her Lotti. She was Ada's mother-in-law, but Ada never said as much. She didn't have to. Aunt Ada was winter to Lotti's summer, which had nothing to do with their coloring and everything to do with their temperaments. Aunt Ada's eyes were a roiling storm. Lotti squinted as if facing into the sun, even at this hour. No, these women were not related by blood.

Lotti sent Aunt Ada to collect quilts, but Aunt Ada lingered, biting a cuticle until Lotti shooed her toward the stairs. Lotti moved from the icebox to the stove and back to the icebox. The hem of her quilted robe trailed her movements on the floor. She was a bee, refusing to land until she provided for the hive. Aunt Ada returned with the quilts. She snapped each one open to drape over our shoulders. They smelled of cedar and promises.

A knock came to the kitchen door. A man mussed from sleep stepped into the kitchen's light. "I heard voices." He looked us over with eyes much too small for his head. "Is there anyone else? Should I take them to the hotel?"

Lotti offered him a cup of coffee, but he waved it away, never taking his eyes from us. Here was the watchdog for Honey Sweet Ranch, but he wasn't barking a greeting.

"Heaven's no. The Elberta is a flea trap."

"Okay then, if you think everything's all right, I'll be heading back to the bunkhouse."

Lotti wrapped a piece of cake in a towel and pressed it into his hands. "Thank you for watching over us, Corky. See you in the morning." He looked us over again, lingering with a questioning eye on me, before he left.

I realized I'd been holding my breath, only to notice Aunt Ada stood over us like a gargoyle. It was probably my imagination, but she studied me with more intensity than she did the twins. I tested this by looking up from the cup of hot chocolate periodically, each time hoping to catch her in the act. Aunt Ada averted her eyes each time. What was she looking for? Horns? A forked tail? Once Lotti had warmed us from within with hot cocoa and scrambled eggs, she joined us at the table. Aunt Ada crossed her arms and leaned against the sink. Still, I felt her gaze settle on me.

"Now, children, how did you come to be out in the cold this close to midnight?" Lotti asked.

You can tell a lot about a woman by her kitchen. Lotti's was clean and tidy, not fancy or cluttered. The walls glowed sunshine yellow, a color reserved for optimists. Her stove housed two ovens. She was generous, a good thing in light of how scrawny Goody had become. A large coffee pot gleamed on the counter, gurgling away. Such a welcoming place. No one remained a stranger at Honey Sweet Ranch. Most telling of all, a pink elephant cookie jar winked at us from atop the ice box. Lotti knew how to have fun.

I dared not look at Aunt Ada as I answered Lotti's question. "I'm very sorry. The train was late. There was an avalanche."

"An avalanche? And here it isn't November yet. Was it Soldier Summit in Utah? We're in for a tough winter, if that's the case."

Goody's hot cocoa sloshed on the table when he slammed his cup down. "Heck, no! There was a long tunnel—"

"Moffat Tunnel," I offered.

"The snow was real deep." Goody was nearly breathless. "It was clear past the windows."

Lotti leaned in. "Just where did you come from, young man?"

"Well, we started out in—"

"We came from the east," I said, careful to keep our origin vague.

But once Goody started talking, he was hard to stop. "You should have seen the soldiers on the train, but they didn't have any guns. I don't know how they expect to kill Japs without guns."

Lotti frowned and asked, "And now you're headed home?"

Mercy found my hand under the table and squeezed hard.

Aunt Ada straightened. "Let's get your hands washed. I'll take you upstairs. You must be exhausted."

"What's this about? Ada, do you know these children?"

Aunt Ada looked from Goody to Mercy and rested her gaze on me. "These are my sister's children."

"That's quite curious." Lotti's eyebrows rose over her glasses. "And so, these would be your nieces and nephew, is that right?"

Aunt Ada looked at the floor. "Yes, that is correct."

"And where are your parents?" Lotti asked me, but Mercy spoke before I could gather the words.

"Our parents are with Jesus in heaven, so Mama doesn't have to cry anymore."

Lotti studied Aunt Ada for a long moment. "No, she doesn't, does she? Isn't that lovely?" Lotti reached across the table for Mercy's hands. "I'm very glad you came and brought Lucy and Goody with you." Light glinted off Lotti's dark irises and the creases around her eyes deepened. "Any family of yours, Ada, is my family, too. Now, children, I can see that you need your rest. Don't bother unpacking tonight. There will be plenty of time for that tomorrow. Get your pajamas on, and your Aunt Ada will be in to say prayers with you."

Aunt Ada tightened the ties of her robe. "Come along," she said, lifting the suitcase. "You'll have to share a bed."

Once in bed, Mercy inched closer, and Goody stretched along the foot. I drew up my knees to avoid his kicks that would surely come. If we stayed in Colorado another night, I would take the clippers to his toenails. As for tonight, I wanted him as near as possible.

Goody rose on his elbow. "Maybe I should sleep on the floor, just in case."

"That won't be necessary. You haven't had a problem since you left the orphanage." And I prayed again, this time for Goody's bladder to do its job. A soggy mattress wouldn't improve Aunt Ada's disposition one bit.

The windows rattled and a great swooshing sound pressed the house until it creaked in complaint. Had it been up to Ada we could have been out in the wind and cold. Perhaps, we would be trudging in the mountains the next night. I had to prepare for the worst. The next day, I would find a button for my coat and darn Goody's wool socks. That was about as prepared as I could make the twins, which would be sadly inadequate.

The twins breathed in unison, something they had done since birth. I pulled the quilts over my nose, matching my breathing to theirs until the knot in my stomach loosened. Although the room was as black as ink, I listened wide-eyed, waiting for the angry whispers Lotti and Aunt Ada were sure to exchange. Instead, the toilet flushed. A door clicked shut. Bed springs groused. The ache between my shoulders I'd nurtured since Baraboo melted away.

Piano music rose from downstairs. I didn't recognize the song. My chorus teacher would have called it classical music, not a toe-tapper, that was for sure. The notes tiptoed on an icy pond. I pictured Aunt Ada at the piano, blue in the moonlight, her icy breath filling the parlor.

My heart hardened.

I felt perfectly obliged to hate Aunt Ada. My mother, despite all her oddities in the last years, would never have dreamed of sending children into the night. The more I tried to picture Aunt Ada and Mother sharing confidences as sisters, the more impossible it seemed that they were related at all. The picture and the inscription were wrong. Grandma and Grandpa Stauffer found Aunt Ada on their doorstep, left there because she cried around the clock, and the young mother couldn't take another minute of her howls. No wonder Mother had never spoken of her. Milk curdled as Aunt Ada passed. Rainbows faded in her presence. Daisies wilted under her gaze. And to add to her offenses? She played music that froze the spine.

Yes, I definitely hated her. I would no longer call her Aunt Ada. And for Lotti's sake, I wouldn't call her the name that repeated in my head either. Ada was no aunt to me and certainly not to the twins. They would have frozen to death if Lotti hadn't intervened. I ached to rise and dress, do whatever it took to put distance between me and the woman who stirred the night with her music.

But where would we go?

Lillian and Ernst would welcome us back with opened arms and plenty of donuts. But having climbed through the Rocky Mountains, I appreciated the barrier the mountains put between us and the orphanage and whatever punishment I deserved for taking the twins. And to the west? Nothing but the unknown lay there. Besides, only a few dollars remained pinned to my slip.

The music stopped.

Ada climbed the stairs heavily. Mercy was a light sleeper, so I touched her shoulder and held my breath. It wouldn't do for Mercy to wake up crying. Ada's steps stopped outside the door. I imagined her long, rough fingers on the doorknob. A shoe scuffed against the floor and her steps receded.

The harsh words she'd spoken at the front door deserved a reply. I slipped out of bed and stepped into the hallway to knock on Ada's bedroom door.

"What is it?" she said from the other side.

"I need to talk to you."

"It's late. I'm nearly in bed."

"I have to talk to you. Tonight."

The door cracked open. "What is it?"

"We won't stay where we're not wanted."

She opened the door wider, leaned out. "What are you talking about?"

"We'll leave. Tomorrow. First light."

"No. You're here. There's no sense—"

"But you said—"

"Yes, I know what I said, but Mother Heller wants you to stay."

"And you?"

"Yes. Stay. That will be fine. Good night." And she closed the door.

Ada

Dear, dear Lucy,

    I would accuse you of having a heart of ice had I not been the object of your endless kindnesses over the years. The things you're asking of me, however, rattle my bones. Let's do get this part past us, shall we? I'd hoped you'd forgotten all about the night you arrived with the twins. This is what I remember:

    You caught me studying you in Mother Heller's kitchen. From the scowl on your face, it was clear that you hated me. And yet, I couldn't keep my eyes off of you. I've never been subtle. I've proven this to be true over and over. I'll tell you this, I came as close to madness that night as anyone ever has without crossing over into the darkness with all my flip-flopping from joy to terror.

    That you hated me hurt the most, but I was helpless to do anything to change your mind, not then, not with Mother Heller looking on. How I resented her ease with you. Of course, with all these years separating me from the emotions of that night, I'm extremely grateful for Mother Heller. Her love was a magnet and a shelter for the three of you.

    After you went to bed, I sat at the piano, fingering the opening bars of a Bach fugue without pressing the keys. So you see, I didn't mean to wake you. Unfortunately, only fingering the keys didn't provide the clarity I needed. And so, I played, yet I sounded like my clumsiest student playing a Sousa march.

    Just knowing you were in the house made hammers of my fingers. Your name hung from every note. And here I must tell you the truth as I promised: I considered your name wholly unsuitable. I feared you would never grow up with a name like Lucy, that you were destined to be a waitress until your dying day. Surely, no one would take you seriously.

You should have started your life with the name Julia. Had I told you that? Magda and I had written a hundred names on a piece of paper before choosing your name. Thomas had gone fishing. He contributed exactly nothing to your naming. I suppose we should all be happy he kept his distance, or you might have ended up with a name like Walleye Marie or Muskie Anne.

Evidently, Magda had a change of heart about your name. As it was meant to happen, by your achievements and steadfastness, you elevated the name Lucy to new heights. It is now the dearest name to my ears.

While I'm telling the truth so recklessly, I must add I was also dismayed to see you had grown into such a pretty young woman. Beauty is a curse, my darling. It is better to be homely. A girl left to rely on her wits learns to conquer the world. And there was that willfulness in your eyes. You needed a strong hand. Is this all sounding familiar?

Eventually, the C-sharp fugue combed the knots out of my thinking. I determined to let you and the twins stay as long as you accepted my guidance. This, of course, seems ridiculous to me now. What guidance did I have to offer?

You also asked about my first impressions of Goody (I'll never learn to call him G.T.) and Mercy. As you've already suspected, I groaned inwardly about their names, too. I'd always believed my sister too religious for anyone's good and much too trusting and obedient, blindly so. And now her children carried ridiculous names. If you had asked me then—and I'm glad you didn't—I would have told you Magda was a fool, much too idealistic. And to her I would have said, "Life is not a cloistered order, Magda. Your children are no more saints than you are."

I consider it one of God's great graces that I never got the chance to say such a thing to Magda. With age comes many undesirable changes, but time does clarify some things and tends to assign true value to people and relationships. I hold Magda in the highest regard, as I have for many, many years. Not a day goes by that I don't ache at her absence.

As for Goody, I saw he would be a handful. A storm brewed in his eyes, even as tired as he was. He possessed the same weak mouth as Thomas, along with the dimple in his chin. This was a disappointment, but only until I got to know the little rascal better. He was his father's child, no doubt about it.

Magda and Thomas. Now, there's a mystery I've yet to solve. What did Magda ever see in Thomas? A child? A lost puppy? Surely not a man, although man enough, it can be argued, to father twins. I don't say these things to hurt you. I know you loved him, but you asked for honesty.

Mercy was a lamb, a baby, but she didn't blink, not once. At first, I saw her as impertinent, but I came to view her as sharply astute. The quiet ones turn out to be the strongest. That Mercy had a spine of iron, didn't she?

Oh, dear, I've strayed off the point quite nicely. Back to that night. Once I'd decided to let you stay, the minor scales became crystalline, and my thoughts stopped chasing each other, enough so that I closed the piano and went to bed. I'm sorry, but I don't remember that we spoke at my bedroom door. I'm quite useless to help you with that conversation.

I'm off to bed for the second time tonight.

Love,
Ada

Lucy

The morning after our arrival, I woke long before sunrise and waited for the light, as soft as chimney smoke, to bleed around the blackout shades. I intended to meet Palisade, Colorado face-to-face, so I dressed in the clothes I'd lain on the chair and tiptoed down the stairs and out the front door.

Broad, flat-topped buttes filled the horizon in all directions, but they weren't so different from the Baraboo hills at home, just taller and flatter. It seemed to me the sun should have been up, but it had stalled behind a mountain to the east, which stood buttresslike over the valley. I'd never actually seen a buttress, but this was exactly how I'd imagined one.

I turned the corner of the house and stopped dead in my tracks. Down a long row of russet-tipped trees, not a mile away, a drapery of gray and tan stone rose like a leaning wall to meet the blushing sky. A mantle of stone capped its top. As far as I could see, nothing grew on the sloping sides.

I stepped back. An unreasonable fear of the mountain collapsing like a giant wave made my heart race. And still, I stood there, inching back but caught by the grand scale of the mountain. I finally stood my ground, only to lose track of time, watching the shadows deepen the folds of the slope as the sun rose.

Lotti startled me out of my stupor with a touch on my shoulder. "Mt. Garfield doesn't make the best first impression. He's a bit stark and imposing. You will find the mountain a comfort over time. In fact, I find that I miss its grandeur whenever I leave the valley."

I doubted I would ever miss such a menace. "It's so bare."

"Isn't it though? I was only thirteen years old when my parents brought my brothers and sisters and me here. I took one look at the dry, lifeless ground and climbed back in the wagon. The engineers hadn't built the irrigation canals yet. How my father ever believed peaches would grow here I've never figured out. He was a true man of vision or a touch crazy. Or both."

Lotti slipped her arm around my waist and pulled me closer with the strength of someone who had wrestled life out of rock. "That's a long story. One better suited for a warm summer morning. I came out to say breakfast is ready. The twins are up and dressed."

I turned toward the west and the south. "There are mountains all around. How did we ever get in?" I really wanted to know how to get out.

"Getting in is the easy part." She winked and guided me to the kitchen door. "Nothing gladdens the heart quite like a good breakfast."

"Lotti, are you sure it's okay for us to be here?" I said, following her. "I don't want to start trouble between you and Ada."

"You've missed your chance to start trouble between us. You'll have to settle for eating a good breakfast."

Goody spooned oatmeal onto his toast and plowed the mess into his mouth. I whispered his name through my teeth, hoping to remind him of his manners. He looked up from his breakfast, but he dug at his oatmeal like a dog after its bone.

Ada entered the kitchen and poured herself a cup of coffee. She was almost to the door when Lotti said, "Ada, look at that boy eat. These children need some protein to build their muscles. Fry up some eggs, will you?"

Ada turned back to the room slowly.

I stood. "I can fry eggs."

"I promised Melba Wood a dozen eggs," Ada said. "She's making custard pie for the potluck."

"Thelma's custard would make better mortar." Lotti shooed me back into the chair. "You're our guest. Sit down."

Lotti pulled Mercy onto her lap. She looked to me. "How long since your parents went to heaven, Dearie?"

Instead of answering, I watched Ada at the stove for any sign she cared one lick how her sister had died. She broke an egg into the pan and poked at the yolk.

Mercy leaned into her hand. "Papa got killed at the factory last winter. Mama fell into the river. It was terrible swollen from the rains."

Lotti looked to me, a question creasing her brow.

"That was May," I said. "Mother wanted to see the river. She hadn't been out of bed…She'd been sick for quite some time."

Ada moaned, her hand poised motionless over the bowl of eggs.

Lotti squeezed Mercy. "That was six months ago." It was more of a question than a statement.

Goody spoke around the toast in his mouth. "Seems more like a hundred years to me."

I kicked him under the table. I didn't want Goody talking about the orphanage. All we needed was for Ada to find out I'd shanghaied the twins out from under Mrs. Nadel, and we would be on the next train back to Wisconsin.

"What?" he said, spitting oatmeal onto the table. "I didn't say nothing about the—"

I kicked him harder.

"Ouch!"

Lotti reached for my hand. If not for the softness of her eyes, I would have pulled away. I deeply regretted coming to Honey Sweet Ranch. I should have known Goody would spill the beans about the orphanage before one day passed. "I'm sorry for being so nosy," she said. "You're under no obligation to answer my questions. Tell me anything you like about yourselves. It's been ages since we've had children in the house." She glanced at Ada's back. Ada stiffened like a flag pole.

I didn't want Lotti to think we were hiding anything, so I told her all about life in Prairie du Sac, minus the part about the twins living in the orphanage. "Our landlords are real nice, more like family than neighbors. They lowered the rent when Papa died and then again when Mother fell in the river. I worked as a waitress at the Badger Café. I made good tips from the regulars, and the owner had raised me a nickel before we left."

"You were right to come, Lucy," Lotti said. "Taking care of your brother and sister is too much responsibility for a young girl."

I sat up straighter. "I've managed just fine."

"Yes, you've done a very good job. You're strong, but God put us in families for a reason. This life is tough enough. There may come a time, Lucy, when He'll ask you to walk alone, but not now. You're here with us."

Ada scooped eggs onto plates and set them before us.

"Are you traveling alone?" Mercy asked Lotti.

Lotti studied the contents of her coffee cup, frowning. I was about to clarify Mercy's question when Lotti answered her. "My Bernhard's been gone three years now. My son, Gil, is off fighting the Germans, or, at least, he will be fighting the Germans very soon. God has given me Ada, and now I have you. So no, I am most definitely not traveling alone."

Lotti stood, removed her apron. "Children, I have a sick friend to call on this morning and a migrant labor board meeting this afternoon. I won't see you until supper. I'm terribly sorry. I would love to show you around and get to know you better. Save your best stories for after dessert. I'll open a jar of peaches."

"*The Lone Ranger* is on the radio tonight." Goody scraped the last bit of oatmeal from his bowl, and his head snapped up. "They do have *The Lone Ranger* in Colorado, don't they?"

The answer came too slowly for Goody. Tears threatened to spill from his eyes.

Lotti's voice was a warm quilt. "Of course we do and *The Shadow* on Sundays. It was Gil's job to warm up the Sparton, so that task goes to you, Goody. After tonight's program, perhaps we can get Ada to play us a rousing rendition of the *William Tell Overture*."

Ada glared at Lotti. "You know I go to bed early."

There had been times on a Saturday when Mother felt well enough for me to go to a movie. Since I had to wait for the twins to fall asleep, I always arrived late. I got pretty good at recreating the part of the movie I'd missed. The actors gave clues in their dialogue, like who talked to whom or who didn't.

So far, being in Lotti's house with Ada was a lot like walking into a clever movie much too late. Clearly, the two women tangled. Unspoken rules had been settled upon for getting along, but the women still tested the limits of those rules. I had no clue as to why, besides the fact that Ada was a shrew. They exchanged a look like two boys deciding whether to fight for their place on the playground. I hoped Lotti bloodied Ada's nose.

Instead, Lotti ruffled Goody's hair. "It's no matter. I have a recording of the overture. We'll dust off the Victrola, that's what we'll do."

And she was gone.

Ada wiped her hands on a towel. "Well, you've managed to worm your way into Lotti's soft side, but I won't have you taking advantage of her. You will do your fair share of the work around here. And you won't stay a moment longer than you must."

"You can be sure of that," I said. I didn't see any reason to play at politeness for Ada's sake. She felt no such obligation toward us.

Ada pushed Lotti's cup aside and took her place at the table with a Big Chief tablet and a pencil. "The key to a well-run home is organization and cooperation."

"What the heck is that?" Goody said around a piece of toast.

"The first rule is: Don't speak with your mouth full. Chew and swallow before you speak."

"What if you've got something to say?" Goody asked.

"Didn't your mother teach you these things?"

"She was sick," I said through clenched teeth.

Ada let out a sharp breath. "Well then—"

"She was sad sick," Mercy added.

"Still, a mother must do what a mother must do. Now—"

I couldn't let a challenge to our mother go unmet. "How many children do you have, Ada?"

She narrowed her gaze. "You are a child still, although you think you are more. There are things you don't understand. It's best not to speak unless you're asked to speak."

Goody's head snapped in my direction. Mercy closed her eyes. No one prayed more than Mercy.

"You don't know Lucy very good," Goody said to Ada.

"Very *well*," Ada corrected him.

More than anything I wanted to leave the house, leave *Ada*, immediately. Instead, I took in the kitchen. The icebox bulged with food, and a full loaf of bread sat on the counter. And warm air rose through a floor grate. This house, even with Ada present, was the twins' best chance, at least for now. I bit my tongue.

"No, you don't know Lucy very good," he said. "She told the

pastor's wife to go away and not come back."

"This is so?" she asked me.

Pastor Bennett's wife had suggested my mother didn't fall into the river by accident. "I had my reasons."

"We all have our reasons, Lucy, but only a fool acts on them."

Ada opened the tablet and wrote our names across the top. She listed chores under each.

"I've run a household," I told her. "I'm not afraid to work."

"There's always plenty of work on a peach ranch. You won't be disappointed."

She put Mercy in charge of the hen house. "Report to Corky when you've finished here. He'll show you where the egg basket is kept and how to water and feed the hens. Stay clear of the rooster, and always remember to hook the coop door. Corky is famous for forgetting that little detail. There are plenty of wild things in the desert that would love a chicken supper."

Mercy's eyes widened.

Goody slunk low in his seat when Ada gave him the job of collecting coal for the furnace. She shook her finger at him. "You'll take the bucket to the Palisade Mine every day—rain, snow, or shine, and on the way you'll scavenge pieces of coal along the railroad tracks. We welcome any opportunity to reduce expenses during these times."

"Who takes care of Silver?" he asked.

I yanked Goody out of his chair. "Time to get started. We don't want Lotti sorry she invited us to stay. Mercy, put our dishes in the sink before you head to the henhouse. Goody, get that coal bucket filled, now." I plunged my hands into the soapy water to wash the dishes.

The sharp tap of Ada's heels withdrew from the kitchen. I expelled a long breath.

Goody crossed his arms to pout. "That chore list is too long. When will I ride Silver?"

"I won't have Ada calling us freeloaders. You'll get your work done, and that's the end of it." I turned him toward the stairs and swatted his bottom. To soften the blow that was sure to come, I added, "Don't get your hopes up about that horse. This is a peach ranch, not a movie set."

Goody waved me off, and I wondered if he already knew I'd lied to him about Silver and so many other things.

Since Ada assigned breakfast, lunch, and supper dishes to me, I tested the water and added more hot water from the tea kettle and started scrubbing at the scorched oatmeal. I felt Mercy's stare on my back. I dared not face her. "If you're going to stand there, you might as well help dry these dishes."

Mercy joined me at the sink. It wasn't like her to be silent, not that she was chatty exactly. No, not that. She filled any pause of a conversation with a hymn or a song about Paul Bunyan or the railroad. That morning, she dried dish after dish without saying a word.

"What?" I said, finally.

"You should be nice to Aunt Ada."

"Perhaps she should be nice to me."

"She wants to be nice. You should let her."

"Oh, no you don't. I'm not some stranger on a train. I'm your sister, your older sister. Don't be telling me what to do, not about Ada." I took the towel from her. "Go feed the chickens."

Her face fell, so I pulled her to my belly. "I'll be more careful about what I say. And I'll think about letting her be nice." We touched foreheads. "Will you pray for me? You know how sassy I can be."

She nodded and I covered her face with kisses just as Mother had done for me. "And don't worry about those wild things. Ada exaggerates." At least, I hoped she did.

Lucy

"Will Mercy like it?" Lotti asked, holding up a calico dress with a white collar. "I found a lovely blue sweater, too. We'll have to wait on shoes. Thompson promises to ring the moment the new shipment arrives. Oh, blast this stupid war. These children need shoes."

I wiggled my toes against the rug through holes in my soles.

Ada opened pleading palms. "We have plenty of flour sacks to make clothes for the little ones. Why did you do this?"

Lotti collapsed the dress into her lap with a rustle of tissue. "Are you questioning how I spend my own money, Ada?"

"It's a long time to harvest."

"You can take my clothes back," I said. "I won't be going to school."

Both women frowned, but Lotti spoke first. "Nonsense. What's done is done. You can't go to school in rags."

I tugged my skirt to cover my knees. "I quit last spring. There's no sense going back now. I'm used to working. I'll get a job and pay you back whatever you spent on Goody and Mercy's clothes."

Ada made tight balls of her hands. "You stupid, stupid girl. There is no question; you will go to school."

Lotti leaned back in her chair and rolled her eyes.

Ada paced in front of me. "What kind of future do you expect without a diploma? Where did you get such a crazy idea?" She raised a hand to stop my answer, and it was a good thing she did because I was about to say regrettable things. "Have you been working all this time?"

"Yes."

"And taking care of the twins?"

"Yes."

"Are you a good student?"

I'd been the first girl invited to join the math club, and I'd published a story in *The Wisconsin Student Review*. "I liked school, all right."

Ada continued her pacing. "For you to stay in this house, you must go to school. Otherwise, you can get back on the train and go—" She rolled her shoulders. "You will earn nothing less than a B. The high school is tough here. The community expects its children to contribute to the world. You'll have to work harder than your usual. You will take Latin—"

"I've taken two years of Latin."

She studied me. A light flashed in her eyes, and then it was gone. "Algebra, then."

"I'd planned on trigonometry."

She perched on the edge of a parlor chair. Her cheeks flushed. "And science? Have you taken chemistry?"

"They didn't offer it at my old high school."

"They do here. And you will play an instrument in the band."

I met her gaze. "I'll sing in the choir."

Lotti clasped her hands together. "How I loved choir. Singing was always my choice as a girl. When you know how to sing, you carry music in your pocket." She folded Mercy's new dress. "As a member of choir, Lucy won't have to lug around an instrument. Choir is a splendid choice."

Ada's frown deepened. "She won't learn music theory quite so well in choir."

"But, Ada, the girl will be happy."

Later, when I opened the closet to hang up our new school clothes, I found two dresses already hanging there, grandmotherly dresses of gray and navy worsted with lace collars. Ada entered the room and reached past me to take them. "I saw that you'd outgrown your dress. You won't need these now that Lotti has seen to your needs."

I remembered my promise to Mercy to let Ada be nice. "The fabric is good." This was the only nice thing I could say about the dresses. "I might find an occasion to wear one." If someone died, perhaps.

Ada withdrew her hand, averting her gaze. "That's fine, then. Yes. Okay. Keep them."

That night in bed, the twins and I sat cross-legged under the quilts. "There's nothing but a stupid old mule and an even stupider cow in that barn," Goody said.

I shushed him. "Keep your voice down."

"They don't even have a dog," he continued, louder. "How can you have a ranch without a dog?"

I grabbed into the darkness, catching Goody's arm, a good piece of luck. "Do you want Ada coming in here?"

"Heck no," he whispered, and I giggled much louder than I should have.

"The chickens are nice," Mercy said. "Reaching under the hens is like putting on a friend's mittens. And the hens talked to me."

Goody said, "What's a chicken got to say about anything?"

Mercy knew better than to challenge Goody. Instead, she said, "I've seen people ride mules."

"It's getting hot in here," he said, digging his way out of the quilts. "I ain't riding no mule." He climbed out of bed.

"Where do you think you're going?"

"That bed is too soft for a Ranger. I'll lay out my bedroll on the floor."

"What bedroll? Goody, get back in bed. You'll freeze on the floor."

Even in the darkness, I sensed Goody's drop-jawed incredulity. The snow had melted, and although the mornings remained cool, we'd started slipping out of sweaters by noon. The weather of Colorado certainly was fickle. We changed our clothes three times a day.

I made a bed of quilts for Goody and plumped his pillow. "Thank you, ma'am," he said and crawled between the covers. We said our prayers, and soon Goody was snoring, and Mercy kicked me in her sleep.

Tomorrow, we would be going to new schools. The thought of meeting kids my age appealed more than I would have dreamed. I'd never lived anywhere but Prairie du Sac. I revisited my decision to wear the belted jumper Lotti had bought me. Perhaps the skirt was too long or the color too bright. I didn't want to attract attention. The girls in Prairie du Sac wore their mothers' remade dresses. The younger ones wore dresses made out of flour sacks with brown cotton stockings. I never considered wearing the blue dress I'd worn to beguile Pete. It stayed in the suitcase. I wasn't sure why. Who would know that it wasn't really mine? Maybe for Easter, if we stayed that long. I pulled the quilts over my head when I thought of rows of students shifting to make room for me to sit among them alphabetically.

Perhaps the other girls wore skirts that had been let down many times like my own. Back in Prairie du Sac, I'd resented Ruth Madsen something awful for all her new clothes, the matching sweaters and the brilliant white socks. I wasn't anxious to draw that kind of ire from the girls of Palisade. On the other hand, I loved that no one had ever worn the jumper. It smelled of sewing machine oil and cardboard, which smelled a million times better than someone else's sweat and soap and cooking grease. Yes, I would wear the jumper.

Mercy draped her arm over my waist. "Lucy?"

"What are you doing awake, Pumpkin?"

"I don't like going to new schools, Sissy."

"We'll put something extra in your lunchbox. There's no better way to make friends."

"It's the teacher I'm worried about."

"Third grade teachers have to be nice. That's the rule. If teachers aren't nice, they make them teach high school."

"Are you nervous?"

"A little." I was very nervous. School had been in session for more than a month, and teachers loved assigning makeup work. I'd seen it many times with the kids moving to Prairie du Sac, all of them with fathers working at the ammunition depot like Papa. Teachers enjoyed occupying every waking hour of their students' lives. Things would only go worse for me if they found out I hadn't been in school since last spring. Ada would happily inform them about that. My heart fluttered. Yes, I was very nervous about returning to school.

Mercy squeezed my hand and soon her breaths warmed my back. The house creaked and popped as the day's warmth left its timbers. Just as the silliness of a dream tugged me to sleep, I resisted. I decided to wear my old dress, the one Mother had remade from a dress she bought at a rummage sale. She had fitted the bodice and added tucks at the shoulders. The first day I wore it, I worried someone would recognize the fabric from a grandmother's dress, but no one did. Besides, the new jumper would only make my old shoes look shabbier, if that were possible.

I hadn't let myself think about Mrs. Nadel or her warning since coming to Honey Sweet Ranch. Part of me believed if I didn't think about her, she would evaporate and go away. But being twitterpated about school weakened my resolve.

In the dark, I imagined Mrs. Nadel discovering Goody and Mercy absent from the dining hall at the orphanage, followed by a frantic search of the grounds for the twins. The farmer walked behind, waving his arms and calling Mrs. Nadel incompetent, which only made her angrier for letting me drive away. Before long, the county sheriff arrived at the orphanage with lights flashing. Mrs. Nadel was inconsolable. "The twins are in great danger," she told the sheriff and pointed down the highway we had taken.

"This isn't helping."

"Sissy?"

I had to swallow hard before answering Goody. "I'm okay. Just a bad dream. Go back to sleep."

Lucy

To my way of thinking, being poked with a stick would have been preferable to standing in the lobby of Palisade High School with Ada clenching my elbow. Students poured through the door, shifting their books from one arm to the other, shouting out to friends, and looking me over like someone's 4-H steer.

The woman on the other side of the counter raised an eyebrow. "How is it, young lady, that you have come to be in this world without a birth certificate?"

I acted at smoothing my skirt when I was actually wiping my palms dry.

Ada jumped in. Ada always jumped in. "Myrtle, this is craziness. Who else would these children be? I saw this girl being born."

Ada had been with Mother at my birth? Why hadn't she told me? I wanted to ask her, but this wasn't the time, not with Myrtle staring at us.

Myrtle Hanson had the face of a bulldog—small, round eyes, pillowy jowls, a resolute chin—but she sat with hands folded, possessing a serenity that defied saints. Ada couldn't shake her. I liked Myrtle immediately. "Let the girl talk," she said.

"I don't know. I found the twins' birth certificates in my mother's Bible. Mine wasn't there. I didn't think to look anywhere else." This was true.

"Well then, how about your school records?" Mrs. Hanson asked. "Do you have those?"

70

What else had I forgotten? "No."

"No problem." She uncapped her fountain pen. "I'll drop a line to your old school. Where are you from again?"

I'd known the secretary at Prairie du Sac High School my whole life. She'd been my Sunday school teacher since cradle roll. No one loved gossip more than Mrs. Eucklund. Once she started talking, everyone in Prairie du Sac would know the twins and I had made our way to Colorado. Within a day, there would be no one else to tell. Even the Sauk County sheriff would know, and that spelled trouble.

"I do have them," I said.

"Wonderful. Just bring them with you to school tomorrow."

"Not here. I don't have the records here in Palisade."

"Is there someone who can mail them from Wisconsin?"

"I might have lost them."

Myrtle tilted her head. "Either you have the records or you lost them. Which is it?"

"Lucy, this isn't the time for double talk." Ada increased the pressure on my elbow. "Myrtle is a busy woman."

Think! "I lost our school records. I'm very sorry. I was carrying a satchel. Our school records were tucked inside, along with photographs of our parents and the twins' baby pictures, all things dear to us. All of our baby books were in there, too."

"Oh, dear. Go on."

Hadn't she heard enough? "We got off the train for supper. I don't know where we were exactly. It was dark."

"Yes?"

Someone else on the train had left a satchel behind when we stopped for lunch in Nebraska. I decided that borrowing a piece of a stranger's life was innocent enough. "We'd barely started eating when the whistle blew. In the rush to finish and get the twins back on the train, I left the satchel in the depot. We'll never see it again. The twins cried for an hour." There, that should satisfy the bulldog.

"I could write the depot, see if anyone turned your satchel in to lost and found. That is, if you can remember the name of the town."

I'd only managed to confuse the bulldog's trail, not dissuade her. More was needed. "You won't need to do that. The twins made such a ruckus the conductor asked after them. He promised to check all the depots on his return run. I gave him Aunt Ada's address. If the satchel turns up, he'll send it to us." I was getting pretty good at this lying business.

"All right. I guess there isn't much more we can do about that. If you don't hear from that conductor, we'll have to piece your records together, but I can't give you better than a C in any of your classes."

There had been a day when the threat of a C unhinged me. Today, a C was better than alerting all of Sauk County where we'd ended up and a possible jail cell. "Thank you. That will be fine."

On the walk home from school, Goody kicked at a pebble. "The teacher didn't let me wear my mask, and she made me write a stupid essay while the other kids went out for recess. She said writing an essay was the best way to see what kind of thinker I was. I could have told her I didn't think much about writing essays, but she didn't ask."

"What did you write about?" I asked him, a little worried what secrets he might have revealed.

"About how the Lone Ranger met up with Tonto. Now, that's important to know."

And Mercy? "Did your teacher ask you to write an essay?" I held my breath.

"I wrote about driving across Wisconsin in a holey car, and they all laughed. It wasn't a mean laugh. They raised their hands when I finished reading. They wanted a ride in a holey car, too. I told them the car broke down in Iowa."

"Anything else?"

"I told them about the soldiers on the train, how they played cards most of the night and how they told stories you didn't want Goody to repeat, so we slept in the ladies' lounge."

Goody kicked hard at a bigger rock. "The boys wouldn't shut up about it."

"Don't say *shut up*, Goody," Mercy said. "We aren't supposed to say bad words."

I couldn't keep track of all the things I shouldn't say, the lies I'd told, or what might give us away. How could I expect Goody and Mercy to say the right things? Before we turned down the lane to Honey Sweet Ranch, I knelt before the twins to ask if they'd told anyone about the orphanage.

Mercy crossed her heart. "No, Sissy, not a word."

"Goody?"

"Nope. I never want to think about that place again."

"You trust me, don't you? We're going to forget the orphanage ever existed. Okay?"

Goody studied his boots and nodded tightly. That had to be good enough for me.

Palisade was smaller than Prairie du Sac, but instead of corn fields growing up to our back fence, there were peach trees in arrow-straight rows behind the stores and along the railroad tracks and within spitting distance of the kitchen door. You could walk just about anywhere worth going in Palisade, including school, in ten minutes. I liked that.

Mercy and I sang "Old MacDonald's Farm" as we walked. Goody squeezed my hand. I promised myself to treasure the pieces of a day like this when the three of us were just kids, a brother and his sisters, doing what brothers and sisters do.

After supper, I settled on the bed to read *The Scarlet Letter*. I was behind the rest of the class by nearly a hundred pages, which made me a bit nervous. From the bottom of the stairs, Ada called me to the dining room. That woman! Did she wait for me to be busy with something—anything—to exert her considerable will over me? I pretended not to hear until she climbed the stairs heavily and knocked on the door. It was a small victory, more than petty, but I relished the conquest.

In the dining room, Lotti sat at her place bent over an oddly shaped piece of paper I recognized as a sheet of V-mail. She stuck her tongue out in concentration as her pen scratched across the paper.

Ada pulled my chair out. She'd left a blank V-mail and a pen at my place. I'd wondered how long it would take Ada to demand I join her and Lotti in their letter writing. "Lotti and I write Gil every night. He loves to hear what's happening at home. He says our letters soothe his loneliness." She patted the back of the chair and I sat down. "You're old enough to do your part to encourage our boys. There is precious little else we can do from so great a distance. A boy from church is fighting in Europe. You will write him."

Most of the girls in Prairie du Sac had written to soldiers. The girls came into the diner comparing stories the soldiers told, the endearments they'd shared, promises made. As I poured coffee and iced tea, I listened as they read flirtatious lines to each other. I wouldn't have minded corresponding with a handsome soldier, but I was too busy managing a home, working six days a week, plus visiting the orphanage on Sundays. Now that I had the time, I found I liked the idea of writing a soldier very much, but Ada's bossiness irked me. "I'm not writing a stranger."

"It isn't as hard as you might think," Lotti said. "I write several boys besides Gil. The Red Cross provides the names. I write about the weather and the people I know. They seem to like funny stories best. And, of course, I write about the orchard. Many of the boys come from farms or ranches, even orchards. They like to hear about the pruning and spraying and harvesting. One of the boys asked if he could visit when he returns. He didn't believe a peach grown in Colorado could taste as sweet as one from Georgia. I hope with all of my heart he will come. His name is David, a strong warrior name, if ever there was one. He doesn't mind that I'm an old lady. Any distraction will do, I suppose."

I remembered my promise to write Pete. "There is a soldier I promised to write. Our families have known each other for years." I was getting good at leaving out details, too.

"That's perfect," Lotti said. "If you're more comfortable writing someone you know, we'll find someone else to write Lilla's grandson."

The truth was I'd forgotten all about my promise to write Pete until that moment, not that I found the idea objectionable. I was surprised by how much I liked the idea of writing him, especially him. However much Pete had tormented me through the years, I knew my secret was safe with him. He would be my one contact with the past.

Besides, I was sure Pete made a handsome enough soldier. His coloring reminded me of the fields tilled in spring—his eyes nearly black like the damp soil and his hair, lighter and warmer, parted in a straight furrow. I preferred blue eyes and blond hair, but no one like that preferred me. I was too tall, and I'd heard often enough that my nose was too snoutlike. Pete would have to do. I didn't mind sharing him with Mildred, much.

Oh, and I liked dimples. Pete had two as deep as thimbles.

I stared at the paper for a long time, not knowing where to start. It didn't help that Ada stood over me. "You're making this harder than it needs to be," she said and sat down. "Tell him about the first day at your new high school. Everyone can relate to an experience like that."

"I'm not sure I need to write on V-mail. He should still be in basic, in North Carolina, I think."

Ada slapped a brand new tablet on the table. "Then you won't have to write so small."

I'd known Pete forever. I should have had tons to say to him, but my mind went completely blank. I took Ada's advice and wrote: *The kids are nice. The teachers are nice. We arrived in Palisade in the snow, but now it's warm. Signed, Lucy.* He would see from the return address where Goody, Mercy, and I had landed. What else was there to tell? I sure wasn't going to tell him what happened to his car. *The Scarlet Letter* waited. I scooted my chair back. "Done."

"Let me read that." Ada scanned the page. "When he receives this he will go AWOL and be shot for treason. Try again. And this time, write as if you're talking to him about the most wonderful day of your life. He needs to know you're doing well, that what he's fighting for is important to you." She tore my first attempt to pieces and tossed them into the trash. "Don't move until you've written a letter worthy of your friend's sacrifice."

Something about the challenge of making a perfectly awful day sound wonderful for Pete awakened my creativity. I closed my eyes to recall the smallest details—the startling crispness of the air and the severity of the blue sky that hung like a watery bridge over the valley. By the time I finished, Lotti and Ada had already moved to the parlor to listen to the radio. Mercy read on the floor, and Goody practically touched the radio with his nose. Ada knitted socks for the soldiers. I asked her, "Do you want to read my letter?"

"No," she said, her brow creased in concentration at the news report about fighting in Italy. The announcer spoke in somber tones about the German's Tiger tanks against our grenades and bazookas. When he finished talking, Ada leaned back and closed her eyes.

Lotti looked up at the chirping cuckoo clock and then back to me. "Your friend will be glad for that letter, Lucy. Leave it on the desk. I'll put a stamp on it and drop it at the post office tomorrow."

Back on the bed, I splayed *The Scarlet Letter* across my stomach and tried to imagine Pete reading the letter on his bunk. He propped one foot on his knee and cradled his head in his hand. He'd laugh over me spilling milk down the front of my dress on the very first day at school; and he'd cock a wistful grin when he read about the twins walking hand in hand to their new classrooms, Goody to the second grade and Mercy to the third.

After listening to the war reports on the radio with Ada and Lotti, I hated the idea of Pete facing any kind of tank. How much better for him and his family—and me—if he flunked out of basic training and returned to Prairie du Sac, where he would be safe. His father would give him a job at the mercantile, and Mildred would happily marry him. I pictured the two of them walking down Broadway with a baby carriage.

On the other hand, maybe it was better for Pete to see this war through. After all, sometimes a man had to do the hard thing.

Lucy

The late-October sun glinted off the trees and barn and each blade of grass, gently warming my face like a touch. The day had started cool, crisp, cunning. We'd worn sweaters buttoned to our chins to church. Back at the ranch, we'd all headed for our rooms to change into summertime clothes. And now, as evening squatted, we congregated on the porch, sweaters close at hand to enjoy the fading day.

I pretended to read *The Scarlet Letter*. The day was too mild for such a haunting book. Ada, the queen of industry, cast yet another sock onto her needles, and Lotti rocked with her eyes closed, not asleep because she wasn't snoring, nor awake because she wasn't describing the sunset we all saw plainly for ourselves. Corky whittled a stick to a lethal point. Goody had been gone quite a while, collecting treasures of questionable value with his new friends. I should have gone looking for him, but the gentility of the sun had lulled me into complacency. Mercy spun lazily in the tree swing Corky had hung while we were at church. She was praying. I could see her lips moving.

Ada dropped her knitting into her lap and sniffed the air. Her face twisted like she'd taken a swig of sour milk. "What's that?"

Lotti opened one eye. "Probably coyotes. They'll drag their kills into the orchard."

Coyotes? I set the book aside. "How long has Goody been gone?" I rose to scan the lane to the road. And there he was, ambling as if the bolts in his joints had loosened. A dog trotted behind him. At least, the creature's gait was doglike and the size was about right for such a creature or a small pony.

"Hey, look what I found!" Goody called.

Assuming the creature was a dog, it was a sad specimen to be sure. Only one ear cocked toward Goody, and its coat lay flat in places, curled in others, and sores oozed on his hind quarters. A stiff knot of hair rose from his haunch where a tail should have been. The closer the duo came, the more my eyes watered from the stench.

Ada lifted her hand like a traffic cop. "Stop where you are. I won't have that beast on the ranch." She covered her nose with her knitting. "Take him back where you found him." When Goody didn't move, she stomped her foot. "Now!"

I had to agree with Ada. "You need to do as you're told and do it now, young man."

Goody pouted and turned his soulful eyes to Ada. "There ain't no one to take care of him. All he eats is rotting fish and garbage. You would smell bad, too."

Corky nipped his thumb with his knife and uttered a curse.

"He needs me," Goody said.

If I owned a nickel for every time Goody had begged for a dog, there would be steak on the table every night. And what stood before us wasn't even much of a dog to beg for. It needed to see a veterinarian, and where was the money for that? Still, I liked how Goody moved like a bag of bones with the animal. I should have said something, intervened on Goody's behalf, but I was concentrating too hard on keeping my lunch down.

Ada hugged her belly. "If he isn't out of here in—"

"We always had a dog running around the place when Bernhard was alive," Lotti said. "Old Tipperton followed him everywhere. That old dog wandered off the day we buried Bernhard and never returned." Lotti stood to get a better look at the creature sitting beside Goody. She fanned at the stink, but the enormity of the task got the better of her, and she moved to stand behind her rocker. "A ranch needs a dog, don't you think so, Goody?"

"Yes, ma'am." I'd never heard Goody call anyone ma'am.

"You have to get that dog clean, meaning Ada can't smell him. She's the one you'll have to please. If you can do that, the he can stay."

Goody turned his pleading eyes on Ada. Wasn't that Lotti a conniver, passing the decision to Ada?

Ada appealed to Lotti. "The vet bill alone—"

"I suppose you have a name for your new friend?" Lotti asked Goody.

Goody studied the dog who whined at the attention. "Tonto. His name is Tonto."

Corky clicked his knife closed and stood. "For the love of—"

"There's no reason to be profane, Mr. Miller," Lotti said.

"No, I reckon there isn't, unless you're downwind from that dog." Even as he said this, he met Goody's gaze and cocked his head toward the barn. Goody and Tonto followed double time. "Let's go, young man. Getting that dog clean will be a two-man job."

When the trio was out of sight, we exhaled together. Lotti laughed first, and then she snorted and laughed at her snort. I couldn't help but join her, which caused her to snort again. Our laughter worked to hook Ada. Lotti wiped at her tears with the hem of her apron. "That boy's going to be washing that dog half the night."

Ada worked her needles. "There's school in the morning and chores to do before that."

"A boy needs a dog," Lotti said. "Tonto may not look like a gift from heaven. In fact, I can't think of a time when a gift from heaven looked like much of anything. Remember, the Lord Jesus was uncomely."

"The Lord Jesus smelled a good deal better than that dog," Ada said, jabbing her needles into the ball of yarn.

"He smelled of sweat and sawdust, I know that much," Ada countered. "And he prepared fish for his followers that morning on the beach. You can't cook fish without the smell of it clinging to you."

"Smelling of sweat and sawdust would be a huge improvement for that dog."

Lotti made sandwiches for Goody and Corky to eat in the barn. Tonto was still a long way off from being presented to Ada. Mercy took her bath while I folded back the covers and laid out our school clothes. I caught the swinging light of a lantern making its way toward the barn. Through the lace curtains, I watched Ada set down the first-aid kit to open the heavy barn door.

I brushed Mercy's hair in front of the window to tell her the story of "Goldilocks and the Three Bears," only this time, Baby Bear ate Goldilocks because that was the level of tension I felt in my gut. In all that time, Ada stayed in the barn.

"We should pray that Goody gets Tonto clean," Mercy said.

And so I prayed Tonto would smell better. Mercy prayed Ada would fall in love with the dog. That pretty much summed up the difference between my faith and hers. Mercy settled under the quilts and fell into a child's sleep. I stared at the ceiling, waiting for Goody, feeling guilty for leaving him to deal with Ada alone but not guilty enough to smell Tonto again. I turned to my side and drew up my knees.

A pleading howl from the barn woke me just as Goody returned to our room. I helped him out of his clothes and into his pajamas. Outside, Tonto yipped and barked.

"He wants to sleep with me," Goody whispered.

"Ada would never—"

"He can sleep on the floor with me, just like the Lone Ranger and his Tonto."

"Goody—"

The howling stopped. Goody ran toward the window, but I caught him by the waist. There was no telling what Ada had done to stop the ruckus. "Let me look first." By the time I peeled the shade back, toenails tapped in the hall. Goody opened the door, and Tonto rushed in to cover him with licks. Mercy pushed past me to greet the dog. "He smells like soap!"

Ada stood at the door. "This is for tonight only, so we can all get some sleep. He can't stay unless he learns his manners."

Goody draped an arm over the dog and Tonto rolled into him. That settled it. I would do anything to keep that dog for Goody. I followed Ada into the hall. "The dog is clean. He obviously loves Goody. Ada, please, let him stay."

Ada caught a loose strand of hair in a bobby pin. "I won't make a decision now. Not tonight. Go to bed."

Just as I was dozing off, the music of the piano startled me awake.

Ada's playing evoked the marching of soldiers, doom, and foreboding. I imagined a soldier running a trained finger along a saber before plunging it into its scabbard. The interlude, a tickling of notes, brought both the beauty of a flowered field and the threat of something unseen. And then she remounted the melody, both conspiratorial and menacing. Up the scale she went. Pounding. Pounding. A trill. Silence.

While Goody may have finally won his Tonto, I wondered how many nights of sleep I would lose for crossing Ada. I covered my head with my pillow, knowing this wasn't the last time Ada would exact her unique brand of revenge.

Mercy

I used to think of postmen as a kind of Santa Claus, bringing letters and catalogs as if they were gifts, but it turns out they do a lot more than that, and most of what they do is boring, some of it scary, like when a dog growls at them. And sometimes the dogs bite. Most postmen carry treats for the bad dogs, hoping the dogs will learn to like them. If it were up to me, the good dogs would get the treat. It's funny how you can think you know all about something, like what a postman does, and know just about nothing at all.

I'd believed Veronica Allen was the happiest girl in the class. She was definitely the prettiest. Her mother set her hair in rag curls every night and tied her hair with ribbons to match her sweaters, and she wore different shoes to church, to school, and on rainy days. All the girls wanted to be her friend. They followed her around the playground, inviting her to play tag or hopscotch or jump rope. Sometimes, Veronica played with the other girls, but most of the time she told them to go away. And then she sat under a tree all by herself.

I copied the first question from the social studies book and chewed on the end of my pencil, while I considered what I'd learned about the job of a postman. A flash of Veronica's pink sweater caught my eye. She was headed for Mrs. Z's desk again. It was the third time this week.

Today, Veronica held her hand over her stomach and screwed up her face. When my stomach hurt, my face turned white but felt green and my eyes watered like crazy. Veronica's cheeks were as rosy as ever. I added the date under my name on my paper, but I kept one eye on Veronica and Mrs. Z. Surely, Mrs. Z would tell Veronica to march back to her seat and do her work. Veronica cupped her hand to whisper into Mrs. Z's ear.

Mrs. Z frowned and asked Veronica questions I strained to hear as I turned the page of my book, trying hard to look interested in postmen and dogs and sorting the mail. Finally, Mrs. Z asked for volunteers to walk Veronica to the nurse's office. I didn't raise my hand. Mrs. Z always picked one of the girls who begged with their eyes and bit their lips to keep from calling out. I went back to answering the questions from the book, a little disappointed in Mrs. Z, to tell you the truth.

Mrs. Z said, "Mercy, will you walk Veronica to the nurse?"

The class sucked in a breath.

I stood too quickly and knocked my book to the floor. The class thought that was pretty funny, but I kept my eyes on Veronica. Although she tried to keep up her act of being sick, she was having a hard time because she was so surprised Mrs. Z had picked me.

Mrs. Z handed over a paddle with *nurse* burned into the wood. "Come back as soon as you can, girls. It's almost time for recess. Veronica, I hope you're feeling well enough to play outside," Mrs. Z said this with a wink. She knew Veronica was faking. Adults sure confused me.

"Hold Veronica's hand, Mercy."

Veronica seemed unsure about which hand to give me, the one she held over her stomach or the one that held her pencil. She handed her pencil to Mrs. Z and off we went.

Veronica's hand dropped from her stomach and she stopped moaning the minute the door hissed closed behind us. The tapping of her shoes filled the hallway. I stopped outside the fifth-grade classroom. They were reciting the Gettysburg Address so loud that every word came through the door. "Your stomach doesn't hurt a bit, does it?"

"Are you going to tell?"

The whole class, including Mrs. Z, already knew she'd faked her way out of class. "Who is there to tell?

"My mother?"

"I don't know your mother."

"Mrs. Z, then?"

"She doesn't care. She's the one who lets you go."

"You're an odd girl," Veronica said this with a sneer. She wanted to hurt my feelings, but I'd heard lots of people say I was odd. It hardly mattered anymore.

"You're the saddest girl I've ever seen, and I'm real sorry about that," I said.

She yanked her hand away and stepped back. "You're crazy. What do I have to be sad about?"

"I sure don't know, but you're sad, all right."

She looked at her shoes. I had to lean forward to hear what she said. "The classroom is awfully quiet today."

The classroom was quiet, mostly because Jimmy Otis was home with the mumps. The quiet had a way of making you think about things you'd rather not. "When it's quiet like that, I can't help but remember how much I miss my mama and papa," I said. "I try to concentrate, but the next thing I know, I'm thinking about cuddling with Mama in her bed or sharing a tomato in the garden with Papa. Quiet makes everything louder."

Her shoulders shook, so I hugged her. That's what Lucy did for me when I cried. I expected Veronica to push me away, but she didn't, so I rubbed her back, and soon I was crying, too.

When I cried over missing Mama and Papa, I couldn't help remembering how happy they looked in heaven. It was real nice to see them smiling and laughing. I only wished they could be happy right here with me. I stopped crying long before Veronica did.

With all her sniffling and gulping for air, Veronica didn't say anything for a long time, but when she did talk, she said, "I miss George."

Who was George? Was he more important than missing a chance to grab a jump rope for recess? "We better get you to the nurse."

"All right." Veronica wiped her eyes and walked about as slow as a person could walk. "My brother pulled my doll's head off."

Why did boys have to do that? They couldn't seem to help themselves. The boys at the orphanage pulled my Ruthie's head off every chance they got. "Is that why you're sad?"

"No." Veronica stopped again. At this rate, we would never get to the nurse's office, and all of the jump ropes would be gone.

"You don't have to tell me if you don't want to," I said, tugging on her arm.

Veronica blinked and two perfect tears rolled down her cheeks. "George liked to see me cry. That's what Pop said. Pop told me not to cry, and George would stop pulling Dot's head off. But he didn't. I tried to be brave. I tried not to cry. But I wasn't very good at it. I cried every time, and George just laughed and laughed."

"That's a boy for you."

"And he threatened to pull her arms out, too."

That made me glad Goody was my brother and not George.

Veronica searched my eyes. "I wished him dead. I screamed it real loud. He was so shocked at what I said that he gave Dot back."

"Good for you," I said.

Veronica looked at her feet. "No, I wasn't good. In fact, I'm about the worst person in the whole world."

Up and down the hall, chairs scraped against the floor inside classrooms. Students called out for jump ropes and balls. "We have to get going," I said.

"I know a place."

"What for?"

"So we can talk."

"Shouldn't we——?"

"Mrs. Z never gets mad."

Veronica led me by the hand past the custodian's room, out the door, to the alley behind the school. "We have to cross the road before the bell rings." Once we crossed the road, we slid down a grassy slope on our backsides to the bottom of a ditch. "You can hear the bell from here. We'll go back after recess."

I wasn't too sure about leaving the school, even if we could hear the bell, but Veronica lay back in the brittle grass like she'd done this a million times before. Her eyes reflected the blue, blue sky.

"Are you any good at secrets?" she asked.

"I have an older sister." Lucy asked me to keep secrets all the time. Some of them didn't make any kind of sense, like not telling anyone about the orphanage. What kind of trouble could that bring?

"It all happened last summer. I got scarlet fever and passed it on to George. We were sick a long time. The whole summer went by. About the time school started, I got better, but George didn't. They said the fever damaged his heart."

I had a bad feeling this wasn't going to be a happy story. "Did he get better?"

Veronica shook her head and her eyes got all watery again. "It's because I wished him dead. I killed George as surely as if I shot him with a gun."

"That's not how it works."

Veronica sat bolt straight. "How do you know?"

I closed my eyes. The sun was a fiery ball beyond my eyelids, the color of the trumpet flowers in my mama's heaven garden. Lying there, I heard the bees and the rush of the river on the other side of her garden wall. I sat up to look Veronica right in the eye. "I don't understand everything, but you didn't kill your brother. I'm real sure about that. Heck, he doesn't mind one little bit about living in heaven, especially if he likes to fish."

"He likes to fish, all right."

I'd told Veronica just what she needed to know, but she shuddered and started crying harder than ever. That was the funny thing about learning the truth. It hurt almost as much believing a lie. Veronica put her head to my shoulder, and I held her tight, hoping I could squeeze the hurt right out of her. My hand warmed where it touched her back.

The recess bell rang. I released her, but Veronica didn't move. It made me nervous not to return to class, but it didn't seem right to leave her alone in the ditch, either. We sat there long after the shouts from the playground faded. Just as Veronica's sobs slowed, I heard footsteps in the gravel and then a voice. It was the principal, Mr. Frieling, standing right over us.

"You girls are in big trouble."

Lucy

Goody pushed through the front door hard enough to slam it against the wall. Tonto followed him, his toenails as sharp as tacks on the floor. The dog's tail, having been liberated by his bath, now stood at attention above his scabby haunches.

I intercepted boy and dog at the door to the kitchen. "Ada wouldn't like Tonto being in the house. You better get that dog out of here this very minute."

"I can't help him following me everywhere I go." Goody pushed past me to pile his books on the kitchen table. He pulled the elephant cookie jar closer and lifted the lid. "Did you go to the library like you said?"

"Of course I did."

He pressed a whole cookie into his mouth. "Did you check me out a book on mules?"

"People don't write books about mules, so I found a book on the care and feeding of horses."

"What good will that do?"

"Mules are half horse." I'd learned this from the librarian. I made Goody wash his hands before handing him the book. "Read half the book. I don't care. It's the best the library could do."

Goody dropped to the floor where he'd stood and opened to the middle of the book. He happened on a page with a white horse rearing to paw the sky. "Silver!" He clapped the book shut. With a pocketful of cookies, he ran for the barn and the recalcitrant mule now named Silver.

"You're welcome!" I called after him.

I poured milk for me and Mercy, filled a plate with cookies and took a seat at the kitchen table. The screen door squeaked behind me, and I braced for whatever Ada commanded. Instead, Mercy wriggled onto my lap and leaned her head against my shoulder. "I missed you today, Sissy."

I breathed in the heat of her scalp and plucked bits of grass from her hair. With Goody guarded by Tonto and actually reading a book, and Mercy so at ease, I was tempted to let my heart settle in this place, but doing so was impossible. Sometime soon, something would surely happen. Someone would ask one of the twins a question, and they would answer without thinking. Mercy would tell how she came to live in an orphanage, or Goody would spill the beans about the farmer and his wife. At night, long after Ada had serenaded us with haunting melodies, and Goody was snoring in unison with Tonto, and Mercy's arm had turned leaden over my chest, I imagined a car driving up the lane. Mrs. Nadel sat in the passenger seat, and a state trooper drove. They allowed no protests from me. The state trooper clamped handcuffs on all three of us and drove us back to Wisconsin.

I kissed the top of Mercy's head. "Honey, we have to get a start with supper before Ada comes home."

"Something happened at school today."

Mercy nearly pushed me over from trying to stand so close. Lotti and Goody stood alongside us on the porch. I was about to send Mercy to feed the chickens when the woman pulled up her daughter's blouse to show a red handprint on the child's back. "Does this look like something I imagined?"

Lotti dismissed the evidence with a flip of her wrist. "Thelma, Mercy isn't the kind of girl to hit someone. I don't know what Veronica told you."

Veronica looked over her shoulder at her mother. "I told you, Mama. Mercy never hit me."

Thelma smoothed her daughter's blouse. "Yes, I suppose you did." She looked to Lotti. "She's been crying since she got home. What was I supposed to think about that? Veronica never gets in trouble. She's very upset by the attention and having to sit in Mr.

Frieling's office. I tried to calm her down. She was so dirty. I thought a bath might soothe her. When I took her blouse off—"

"Mama!"

Thelma put a finger to Veronica's lips. "When I took her blouse off, I found the shape of a handprint. As it turns out, getting into trouble and this mark were caused by the same girl." She tilted her head toward Mercy, who buried her face in my back.

"All right then. Bring Veronica inside where we can get a good look at that mark," Lotti said, but she looked at me with a question on her face. I shook my head and followed with Mercy in tow.

Ada joined us in the parlor. "What's this about?" she asked.

"Mercy socked Veronica in the back," Goody blurted.

"She did no such thing," I said.

Veronica tugged on her mother's hand. "I want to go home. I won't cry anymore, I promise."

"We'll go when I'm satisfied the one responsible for this mark is punished."

Veronica, pale with red-rimmed eyes, bent under a lamp and let her mother lift her blouse again.

We all leaned in. Lotti said, "Why, that's a rash, Thelma. Look at the blisters."

Goody shouldered his way in between the women. "Holy cow, Mercy. You walloped her good."

I grabbed Goody by the collar and pulled him toward the stairs. "Go upstairs, now."

"I didn't do nothing. For once Mercy's in trouble and I want to see her get her due."

"Only a fool delights in the suffering of others," Ada said. I wished I'd thought to say so.

"You heard Ada. Leave this to the grownups." I patted his rump. He shot a poisonous look over his shoulder. I'd only seen Goody move slower when there were Brussels sprouts on the dinner table.

Lotti held a magnifying glass over Veronica's back. "This is peculiar. I've never seen anything like it."

Thelma yanked Mercy's hand over the mark. It matched perfectly.

I asked, "Mercy, do you have any idea how this happened?"

From the day she was born, Mercy had been as transparent as water. One look at her face, and I knew she hadn't hit the child,

Patti Hill

but I had to ask the question. "Did you hit her?"

"No."

"Did you touch her?"

"Yes, I did touch her."

"Were you trying to hurt her?"

Veronica shook loose of her mother's grip and pulled her blouse into place. "Mercy walked me to the nurse because my tummy hurt. When we got down the hall a ways, I started to cry."

"Oh, Veronica," her mother cooed, "did it hurt that bad?"

"Let her tell her story, Thelma," Lotti said.

"Mercy patted my back, like you do, Mother, when I've been crying hard. That's all. It doesn't hurt. It never did."

Ada crossed her arms over her chest. "You put too much starch in her blouse, Thelma. Veronica has always been a sensitive child. You and I both know that mark wasn't caused by a slap. It's Dr. Opp you need to be seeing."

"No!" Veronica cried and pressed her face into her mother's belly.

Thelma's face puckered with pain and the tears came. Ada heaved a sigh.

Thelma said, "She won't go, not since...It's been terribly difficult."

Lotti cradled the back of Veronica's head with one hand and touched Thelma's cheek with the other. "Your family has suffered greatly with your loss. Sorrow has a way of working itself out, even when we don't know how to express it. If there's anything we can do, you mustn't hesitate. In fact, I have an apple crisp cooling on the table. Mercy, why don't you wrap the crisp in a tea towel and bring it for Mrs. Allen?"

Once Mercy stepped out of the room, Thelma said apologetically, "You can imagine how I felt when I saw that handprint on her back. I hope you won't think the worst of me."

Goody called from the second floor landing. "Is Mercy going to get a spanking or not?"

If only spanking Mercy would shift the attention she attracted somewhere else. No, I wouldn't spank her, but I would warn her—again—to not care so much, to keep her hands to herself, to please be like every other eight-year-old girl in the world—unremarkable and annoying. I would certainly settle for that.

90

Pete

November 3, 1943
Camp Lejeune, NC

Lucy,

    Sure glad the lizzie got you to your aunt's house okay. You can stop worrying now. You're a long way from Wisconsin, and from what I hear, resources are pulled pretty tight these days. I doubt anyone is looking for you. To be on the safe side, don't draw any attention to yourself. Maybe you should lock Goody in the barn. That might help.

    Mom has no idea where you are and I promise to keep it that way. She's still taking care of Grandpap in Appleton. She isn't answering my questions about him, so he must be pretty sick.

    Boot camp wasn't anything like Camp Wild Rose. Remember counselor Backstedder? My drill sergeant looked just like her. He ran us hard. Nothing could have prepared me, not for this.

    I guess all those days of cleaning kennels for old Doc Bingham paid off. I've been assigned to the 3rd War Dog Platoon. We met our dogs today. Cuff is the biggest malamute I've ever seen. When he jumped up on my belly, he looked me straight in the eye. Turns out, I should have run for my life. In civilian life, Cuff guarded a bar in Chicago but he got too difficult for the owner to handle. Since he got here, he's gone for a couple throats. I wondered why no one else wanted him. Now that we're paired, no one wants me for a partner either. Cuff's not the kind of dog you'd care to meet in the dark. But when a dog chooses you, I guess you'd better go with it.

The guys think your letters are swell, especially when you write about Goody and Tonto. I've never seen a dog chase a train before. That's one ambitious mutt. He would make a fine Marine. Anyway, keep the letters coming.

Send a picture. I know thirty Marines who want to marry you.

Your friend,
Pete

Lucy

Christmas was awful.

All that filled the day—the tree, the soggy dressing, gifts opened after church on Christmas day—seemed off. Everything, especially the people, were rearranged or absent. All was familiar but strange. Instead of Mother and Papa, Lotti and Ada handed out gifts. There was a sense of the familiar about it, traditions that gave the day a beat but the absence of Papa's laugh and Mother's favorite dishes from the table had stolen the day's melody. Christmas couldn't end too soon for me.

Lotti, Ada, and Corky watched us open our Christmas gifts with the same anticipation and anxiety Mother and Papa had expressed only one year earlier. To stave off any disappointment on their part, I *oohed* and *ahhed* over a rose-scented bath set from Lotti and a pair of knitted socks from Ada. They were made of the same yarn she used for the soldiers. If I ever mounted an invasion on the Artic, the socks would keep me plenty warm. Corky presented whittled gifts for the three of us, the likeness of Tonto for Goody and a fat hen for Mercy. He probably felt obligated to make something for me, so he'd whittled a sleeping kitten. I wasn't sure what to think about the gift. I wasn't a kid anymore. All this fussing embarrassed me. Eventually, I would pass the carving on to Mercy. She loved cats.

Later, I caught Goody admiring himself in his new Lone Ranger hat. "You look mighty fine, Ranger."

He whispered, "I miss my frog."

"What frog?"

"The one in the bucket. Papa's bait pail. Out by the shed."

As so often happened with Goody since Papa passed, we were talking about a frog and not talking about a frog. "There's a pond here," I offered.

"I saw."

"Come spring—"

"I don't care much for frogs anymore."

"You know, I miss that old frog, too."

Once the dishes had been dried and put away, I found Mercy rearranging the furniture in the dollhouse Lotti—a very generous Santa Claus—had given her. I marched the blue father figurine into the kitchen where Mercy's pink mother figurine set the table. I spoke in my best father voice, "Hey there, Pumpkin, I'm starving."

Mercy's eyes flew open in surprise. "You sound just like Papa."

I reached for her hand. "I'm so sorry."

"I'm tired," she said and climbed the stairs to our bedroom.

Watching Mercy go, I vowed our next Christmas would be different. I would cook a goose and fry up some walleye, chop down the tree with Goody and make paper garland with Mercy. And none of this opening gifts on Christmas day. That wasn't right. And although I would never cut the snowflakes as lacy as Mother had, I would use her sewing scissors to snip away until they came close, and then I would paint them with paste and sprinkle on glitter.

I couldn't quite picture Christmas happening anywhere but our apartment in Prairie du Sac. That was a problem.

Ada

March 28, 1994

Dear Lucy,

I was terribly afraid of this. You've asked a question I can't answer. I'm ashamed to admit that I don't remember one bit of our first Christmas together. I'm so very sorry, my dear. I've talked to the nurse about this. Honestly, I was a bit worried about slipping into some sort of oblivion. She kindly assured me that the memory is still in my brain but inaccessible. I don't see how having memories locked into my brain is any different than losing them altogether. They're lost to me either way. Please, Lucy, you must promise not to add any meaning to my lapse. I'm sure of one thing, since I'm sadly consistent, that I was most probably quite horrible on our first Christmas. Your ability to forgive astounds me. Thank you, again.

To prove the capricious nature of my memories, I can tell you, as you asked, about a Christmas with your mother. You'll understand why I remember this particular Christmas once you've read my story. If Magda already told you this story and remembered it differently, do this old gal a favor and keep that bit of news to yourself. I still enjoy a pinch of delusion in my day.

Christmas 1919. The Christmas I remember most was the year Magda was eighteen and I was eleven. This would have been our last Christmas together under our parents' roof, for Magda had become engaged to Thomas, then a young German immigrant who apprenticed the building trade with Mathias Klug. He barely spoke English, and I think that was what Vater liked most about him.

Thomas spent the day with us as he came to this country without his family, and Mutter *couldn't bear for anyone to be alone on Christmas. Thomas couldn't keep his eyes off Magda. Our brothers considered his adoration an affliction and teased him unmercifully.*

Sleep never comes easy on Christmas. That night, in particular, the boys whispered in the attic above us long after Vater had tried to silence them with a rap of the broom on the ceiling. Magda and I whispered under the eider down, too, mostly about Thomas and their coming wedding. I never wanted the night to end, but even Christmas is only 24 hours long. Magda rubbed my back until I fell asleep.

Magda didn't sleep. We teased her that love made her an insomniac, but Vater believed God had charged her with saving our lives that night. She ran down the hall, banging on doors, yelling for us to wake up. The barn was on fire. Already sooty and breathless, Fritz, the youngest of the boys, met us at the back door, saying he had gotten the cows out. Vater wanted to know about the hogs. Fritz couldn't answer. He only hung his head.

The flames from the barn drew neighbors. They came with the pounding of hooves and the rattle of wagons. The younger men took turns at the pump as bucket after bucket sloshed its way toward the flames. The women gathered in the kitchen. We kept the coffee pots full and helped Mutter cut ham for sandwiches. Even through the glass, we felt the heat on our faces and heard the hiss of snow shoveled onto the cinders.

The next morning, when the charred posts of the barn stood like ribs from the smoking remains, and the sunrise brightened the horizon to the faintest gold, the men praised God in their many languages. Their piety struck me as odd since they looked like goblins with their hair blown back by the heat and held in place by dried sweat. And their eyes glowed white in their soot-covered faces.

Fritz confessed to smoking in the barn, and an empty bottle of gin was found in the ashes. Although Mutter cried and clung and cooed, Vater's mind would not be changed. Before breakfast was served, Vater hitched the horses to the wagon and drove Fritz to the train station. I don't know what happened there, but Vater never spoke Fritz's name again in my hearing. This was only the beginning of Vater's disappointments. If Mutter received a post card or letter from Fritz, I never saw it. Fritz ceased to exist, and he was the brother I loved best.

Mutter stopped baking Christmas cookies, including my favorite, lebkuchen, for the neighbors, and the goose got smaller and smaller each year. Magda and Thomas moved to Wisconsin, where he tried his hand at being a butcher, a tailor, and a truck driver, but those are only the occupations I heard about from the letters Magda wrote to Mutter.

I stayed in my parents' house five more Christmases, none of them as remarkable or as painful as that one. Oh, dear, I didn't mean to make my Christmas memories of Magda sound so glum. We loved Christmas at our house. We helped Mutter prepare, starting in the summer with the fruit we preserved for the baked goods. Magda sewed our new dresses all through fall, and we fussed over gifts for everyone in the family. Perhaps I should have kept that bit about Fritz to myself, but now I'm too tired to start over. Feel free to do what you will with that portion of the letter.

When you come, let's plan on attending the opera in the city. I'll get tickets. Their productions are quite spectacular. Bring your pearls!

Love,
Ada

Lucy

Ada rapped on the bedroom door, the sound so sharp I wondered if her fist was made of wood. "The men are here," she yelled. "Put that book away. Do you hear me, Lucy?"

"I hear you fine."

She opened the door. "I'm counting on you to cook the best lunch these men ever tasted. Are you up to it?"

In the months since coming to the ranch, I'd done everything she had asked of me and more. There was no way in the world I would feel beholden to her for taking us in. When the time came to leave Palisade, I would walk out the front door without a backward glance, unless Lotti stood there. And then, well, I teared up just thinking about watching Lotti staunch her tears with one of her hankies.

I pressed the bookmark into the crease of the book and closed it slowly. "The potatoes and carrots are peeled. The roast will be in the oven the minute I take the cake out."

"Fine. Let's go, then." She turned sharply away.

I mouthed to her back, *Fine.*

Lotti ushered me to the porch before I had a chance to put on a sweater, and it was still January. She could be an impetuous thing. I hoped to be just like her when I was old. She greeted the men coming to prune the peach trees, about a dozen of them in plaid jackets with knitted caps pulled over their ears. They jumped from the back of a truck. Their greetings fogged the air.

"You have to see this," Lotti said. "We don't do much that's acrobatic around here. This is your one chance to see the men perform. I can tell you they're glad that last bit of snow has melted, but I've seen them prune in drifts of a foot or two."

"Ada wants the roast in early," I said, shivering.

Lotti opened her sweater and pulled me close. "She's feeling pressure to do Gil's job. He would be with these men, going from ranch to ranch to do the pruning. That's how things work around here. We help each other. A season will come when one of these men won't be able to do his part, and Gil will happily go to that man's ranch to prune. Ada has been on this ranch fifteen years. She's seen how we manage without keeping track of who owes what to whom." Lotti squeezed me. "Watch now. This is our big show for the winter."

The men climbed a ladder to sit on the shed roof like birds on a wire. Corky and a couple boys I recognized from school brought each man a pair of wooden stilts, which they strapped onto their feet and secured just above their knees.

The screen door slammed closed behind me. Ada pulled on gloves as she walked past us and down the steps. "The cake is going to burn," she said over her shoulder.

Lotti rolled her eyes. "Stay put. I'll get the cake. You enjoy the show." She left me her sweater.

The men laughed and nudged one another as they stood and stomped to test their footing. Now they were storks, walking as if wading through watery weeds, using their bent arms like wings to steady their gaits. The slant of the morning sun stretched their shadows beneath the trees, and their pruning shears snipped at branches hungrily. Piles of russet twigs gathered on the ground. My nose ran from the cold, so I returned to the warm kitchen. All through the morning, as I mashed potatoes and frosted the cake, the men's shouts rang out with friendly jibes. These men knew each other and liked each other.

At lunch, the men sat shoulder to shoulder around the dining room table. The two boys, Hank and Carl, sat at the kitchen table. I balanced the rolls in one hand and refreshed their coffee with the other.

Hank said to me, "I overheard you explain the law of cosines to Andy in trig the other day."

I glanced at him, noting his cocky smile. This Hank thought

more of himself than he ought with his wavy hair and clear green eyes. Sure, he played football for the Bulldogs, but where would that get him in this life?

I shifted my weight to one hip. "So?"

"Your explanation made sense. I wasn't getting it at all. Maybe you should be teaching the class."

My face warmed. "If you didn't understand, you should have asked Mr. Wagner."

"That old goat. I'd much rather ask you."

Did he wink?

"Coffee?" I said through my teeth.

"Yeah. Black."

"Funny, I took you for a cream and sugar boy." I could give as well as I got. Working at the Badger Café had taught me that. I returned to the dining room where the men raised their cups to be filled.

After cleaning the kitchen, I joined Ada, Lotti, and Corky under the trees to rake the debris. Although the sun shone bright, the cold pricked the inside of my nose. I breathed into the tent I made of my gloves. Ada worked her rake furiously down the row. I swiped my nose on my sleeve and matched her movements stroke for stroke, and then I pulled my rake faster, grabbing at the twigs. I inched past her, and still, I worked faster. The ditch where the twigs were to be burned lay not twenty feet off.

Without missing a stroke of her rake, she called to me, "You're missing twigs. Slow down."

Her sniping only spurred me on. My shoulders burned with the effort, but I beat her to the end of the row, only to face another and another and another long row of twigs to rake. Had the orchard been this big the day before? Staying ahead of Ada would kill me.

All through the afternoon and evening meal, I'd managed to keep my sore muscles to myself. But when I slid below the hot water of the tub, I moaned. A rap of knuckles startled me. Ada spoke through the door. "Next year, you will put the roast in an hour earlier. The meat was tough."

I cocked my arm to throw the soap at the door, but I held it to my heart instead. There might not be a next year, not if Mrs. Nadel found us. Rather than making me fearful, the thought saddened me. Living at Honey Sweet Ranch—the hard work, seeing the twins growing back into their skin, all thanks to Lotti's cooking, even the constant tiptoeing around Ada, and yes, testing of Ada— made me feel more at home than I had in a long, long time.

From the top of the stairs, the dim light of the parlor spilled onto the hall floor. Even here, so far from either coast, we lived under strict blackout guidelines. I slumped on the top stair. When did Ada sleep? It was nearly eleven.

I chewed on a wet braid, weighing the benefit of retrieving my English book from the kitchen table against the torture of composing something pleasant to say to Ada. She never missed a chance to harp at my failings. Simply walking into her presence put me under the microscope. Had she forgotten that the world burned with hate? In the grand scheme of things, an undercooked roast seemed trite, hardly worth mentioning.

Dispirited by the prospect of her bite, I rose to return to bed. Reading could wait until tomorrow. Or could it? There would be church until noon, and Lotti had invited the Stone family for lunch afterward. There wouldn't be time to read the assigned chapters of *The Red Badge of Courage* unless I started that night. I promised myself not to leave my school books on the kitchen table ever again.

To quiet my steps, I eased my weight onto the edge of each tread, and still the wood creaked loudly. But Ada didn't call out. I stretched to see her, leaning into the feeble light of an abalone-shell lamp, something she and Gil had brought back from their honeymoon in California. The sight of Ada dabbing at tears as she read held me in place.

When Lotti received a letter from Gil, she read every word out loud while the rest of us ate supper. We all enjoyed his letters, although Lotti wished he would write more often. His stories about life "somewhere in Africa" made Lotti blush, like the time he took a bath in a camel trough, but she kept reading, trying not to show her delight but always failing. Goody begged Lotti to read the letter about the exploding canteens again and again. Even in wartime, boys we'd thought to be men delighted in playing with CO_2 cartridges from their life vests. In the end, Gil claimed their experiments concocted something similar to the sodas we drank at the Peach Bowl Café. Goody loved listening to the story so much he nearly missed *The Lone Ranger* one night. Now, Gil was in Naples. His latest letter told of smashing glasses on restaurant tables and riling its owner. Goody was doubly impressed with his uncle. Ada raked furrows into her potatoes with a fork as Lotti read.

But tonight, from the way Ada cradled this particular letter in her hands, I knew why she didn't share the letters Gil sent her. It was intimate, meant only for her. Would I ever receive a letter that robbed me of sleep and made my cheeks bloom with color? As much as I anticipated Pete's letters, they only confused me. He was no longer the boy I'd known in Wisconsin. Was Gil a changed man, too?

Ada wiped her eyes, and my heart thumped a warning beat. I'd meant to ease back into the kitchen's shadows to wait her out, but watching Ada with the letter was like watching a chick hatch; she was an unexpectedly fragile occupant.

Ada moved her lips as she read and ran a finger along the edge, just like Mother had run her finger along Papa's arm when they'd forgotten I was in the room. I stifled a gasp. Such tenderness from Ada. How could this be? I stepped into the kitchen and grabbed the book.

When I came out, Ada was stuffing the letter into the pocket of her apron. "How long have you been standing there?"

"I was getting my book." I held *The Red Badge of Courage* up as evidence.

"You move like a cat. Show your manners. Let people know you're about. And don't ever forget that you're a guest in this house."

"Okay."

"Yes ma'am, Lucy. Yes *ma'am*."

I didn't know how I managed to repeat her words, biting my tongue as I did, but I spat them out, and she waved me off. That was fine with me. How could I forget my position in this house? She reminded me daily in the way she watched my every move. She was impossible to please, and although I loathed admitting it, I did try to please her. She narrowed her eyes. Her scrutiny was hot rock under my bare feet. I trotted toward the stairs.

"Walk like a lady, Lucy."

If I walked quietly, I was a cat, presumably sneaky. If my steps were heard, I was a buffoon. I stepped into the pale light. Ada frowned, which only emboldened me. "In the middle of the night? In the privacy of my own—?" *Don't forget you are a guest in this house.* "When no one is watching? What is the point of walking like a lady?"

"Being a lady is self-respect. You don't stop respecting yourself when no one is watching. Take the stairs one at a time, if not to demonstrate your dignity, at least to allow other people in the house to sleep peacefully. I'm sure you can manage that kindness."

I turned toward the stairs. Paused. Turned back to Ada. "You were crying. Is Gil all right?"

She didn't answer right away, and I couldn't read her expression in the stingy light. I waited. She blinked and swallowed. Still, she said nothing. I was about to walk—like a lady, of course—toward the stairs when she said, "I told Gil I wanted nothing of coy letters, so he tells me more than he tells Lotti. There are times when I wish I hadn't insisted on such honesty."

I stepped closer. "What is he telling you?"

She sighed and crossed her arms over her chest. "They're preparing for something big. I can't imagine things getting worse. Although his letters to me are frequently censored, sometimes the censors let things go through I wish they hadn't. I've heard about bazooka rockets bouncing off German tanks like tennis balls and the importance of recovering the dead. His company is shrinking. I read the newspapers, try to piece it all together. It's driving me crazy."

Pete's letters had gotten more detailed, too, but he tempered his stories. I was sure of it.

"What about the boy you're writing?" she asked. "What's his name?"

"Pete's on Guadalcanal, I think. He writes about his dog, telling me just enough to worry me to death, and he never answers my questions, not really. He sounds different—older, bossy, more serious. He has complete confidence in Cuff—that's his dog—he tells me not to worry, but …"

"That's a man for you. They think they're invincible. You must pray for Pete. I don't know how God will decide which man will survive this hell and why another won't, but it can't hurt to ask for mercy on Pete's behalf. There's precious little we can do." Ada blew her nose. The force of it must have reminded her to whom she was talking, and yet she spoke with unsettling kindness. "There's church tomorrow. Don't read too late."

Tonto smelled of wet fur and dead leaves when I bent to pull Goody's blankets over his shoulders. I slid under the covers beside Mercy. Talking to Ada had sucked my last ounce of initiative. I couldn't face *The Red Badge of Courage,* not with Harry echoing Pete's quest for glory. It soured my stomach. Men—boys, rather—were incredibly shallow. I left the book on the side table. Raking had left my arms leaden, so I fell asleep without the usual cataloging of worries, but my weariness didn't leave me too tired to dream.

The dream was never the same, although it contained similar elements, like my mind kept rehearsing the same scene, changing the location or the characters until finally, I hoped, I got it right, at least in my dream world. Tonight, the current of a swollen river pressed me against a fallen log.

The shore lay only an arm's length away, but I couldn't wrestle free from the water's icy grip. With one hand, I clung to a stump. With the other, I pulled at the grass that wrapped around my arms and neck and face. The moment I freed myself of one strand, another took its place. The tendrils squeezed and pulled me downward. I looked into the water to see Mercy's face just under the surface. I screamed, but, of course, no sound came out. Her eyes stared at me without seeing, and her skin was the color of the moon. I wrapped my legs around her and with one hand I grasped the fabric of her dress. Although I knew it was too late to save her, I strained to lift her face out of the water. The river tugged at her. I tightened my grip but the pull of the water freed my legs, and Mercy slid away.

I sat bolt upright, stifling my cries with the crook of my arm. The cold chased me back under the covers. I stared into the blackness, waiting for my heart to slow and for my breaths to ease. I scrambled for a memory to replace the dream. I knew I wouldn't sleep unless I did.

As if on cue, Ada's piano music began, a waltz by the count of it but not a waltz to set you dancing, unless you danced by yourself. The song flared for a few bars, but then turned melancholy again, so much so that I turned in my mind to the day the twins were born.

I'd run deep into the cornfield on the other side of the fence until the saturated air had softened my mother's birth cries. There I sat, breathing the tangy sweetness of the corn's new growth. The tassels hung as still as death. Even so, Mother's labor wails punched the air to both pull and repel me. I lay back in the cushioned earth to imagine myself as the fastest girl in the world. Spectators fingered coins in their palms. They paid a nickel to see me outrun a cheetah. Cheering schoolmates filled the grandstand, a measure of popularity I'd never enjoyed in real life.

Mother's next cry startled me upright. I pressed the heels of my hands to my eyes as I imagined riding an Arabian stallion to outrace a band of desert thieves, and then I was a pirate girl leaning into the wind over the bow of my ship, the Fair Winds. But none of the stories withstood my mother's agony.

And I was confused.

The pastel-covered birthing books my mother had collected from friends said nothing about torturous pain. Was Mother doing something wrong? With the next scream, I covered my ears. Dr. Warner drove to the house throughout the day to check on her. This was worrisome. Dr. Warner only showed up when things went bad, like the time Mr. Kelly lost his arm in a baler or Mrs. Quinn's lungs filled with fluid and she died.

Would the baby kill Mother?

I lay back down, crushing dirt clods between my fingers as I contemplated a life without Mother. In my imaginings songs silenced. Games ceased. Secrets held no mystery. Fevered cries went unanswered. A chair sat empty at the Christmas program. I faced the beginning of each day without the silky comfort of her lap. This was unthinkable.

I rubbed at my eyes, straining to conjure the early days of Mother's pregnancy when hope ran high. Word of the long-awaited Richter child-to-be had hummed through our tiny town. Men slapped Papa's shoulder and shook his hand like a pump, saying God had shown His favor to him just like Abraham. Women gathered around my mother, whispering about the miracle of a child coming so many years after my birth. Offers of prayers and crocheted blankets had bubbled from the tight circle.

In the cornfield, I worried over having misplaced my hope or vexing my mother with pessimism. I wanted to believe the buoyancy of my parents' friends, but my nature inclined me to prepare for the worst. I stood and sang "My Country, 'Tis of Thee," the most solemn song I knew, as a prayer.

Our landlord and neighbor, Mrs. Devendorf, called to me from the landing of our apartment. "Lucy! Your sister is here! She wants to meet you!"

I started to run toward the river to tell Papa, but the thought of a sister proved too delicious. I ran up the stairs two at a time. At Mrs. Devendorf's insistence, I scrubbed my hands as I counted to one hundred.

My fingertips stung from the nail brush when I finally sat on the sofa with a pillow on my lap. I looked toward the closed doors of my mother's room, my chest raw with longing. I held out my arms for a bundle too small to be of good use to anyone. I'd seen bigger cats. I was disappointed. I'd imagined a sister to share tinseled Christmases and walks through carpets of crisp leaves.

"Support her head, now." Mrs. Devendorf placed my sister in my arms. "This little darling never even cried, not the whole time I cleaned her up. Mark my words, this one will be a thinker. That's how it is with babies. You can tell by how they're born what kind of people they'll be—this one will see all the details of life whether you want her to or not."

The baby squinted against the brightness of the room and fell asleep. Her breaths came as puffs and I breathed in the scent of her—the metallic tingle of spring's first rain. Light passed through her nose like through a marble. The heat of her warmed my belly, and my heart nearly burst. I ached all over. I wanted to cry and laugh.

I touched her silken hair but pulled my hand away fast. Her scalp pulsed under my fingers. Maybe she wasn't done forming yet. She was soft in the middle, like a cake taken from the oven too soon. And her face, her skin blotched red and folded into tucks like it was too big for her head. Such homeliness was sure to exile her to the far corner of the playground. I vowed death to the bully who dared to hurl insults at her.

Mother shrieked again. Mrs. Devendorf snatched my new sister just as I stood to rush to Mother's aid. Mrs. Devendorf stood like a wall before me, her blouse translucent with sweat and her hair coiled into ringlets around her face. "Whoa there, young miss." She followed my gaze to Mother's door. "Your mama's rest is over, child. For all of her waiting and praying, she's been rewarded with a special blessing. You've another brother or sister on the way."

Maybe the next one would be prettier, I thought, but thinking this shamed me. "Is Mother all right?"

Mrs. Devendorf ran a finger along the baby girl's face. "Don't you worry, child. The doctor has everything under control. Another baby means more to love, my darling. Go now. Find your father. Tell him the good news." Mrs. Devendorf smiled as she spoke, but the corners of her mouth strained from the effort. My heart fluttered under my cotton dress.

"Don't dawdle. Your father asked me to send you with the news. The next one may be a boy."

I ran under the reaching arms of oaks toward the Wisconsin River. Papa's rowboat bobbed on the current; his pole bent like a harp. I stood among the bushes, watching him run the stringer through the fish's gills before I edged to the end of the dock, kicked off my shoes, and splashed the cool water.

I should have called out to him, but the moment seemed too frail to disturb. The light glinted off the water to make a silhouette of my father right in the middle of the day. More truthfully, I waited because I was unwilling to dispel the magic. Besides, I couldn't hear Mother's cries from the dock.

Papa ruled the rills and eddies. Almost daily, fishermen rowed within shouting distance of where he fished to ask what kind of bait to use and where the big ones were biting. When he told Mother about becoming a fishing guide, they argued until Mother threw a vase at him. From then on he walked like a condemned man. His hair fell down over his forehead. He started smoking cigars, which made Mother furious.

What my mother siphoned from Papa, the river replenished. He laughed at my schoolyard riddles and told me stories from his boyhood home of Elleangen, stories filled with mischievous older brothers who took great delight in tormenting him.

The river caressed him and sheltered him, just as the cornfield sheltered me. He fished whenever Mother pulled one of my baby teeth or a splinter. With twins squalling for their bottles, I feared we'd never see Papa again.

I waved at him and shouted the news. "*Es ist ein Mädchen, Papa!* It's a girl!"

"*Ist gibt nichts mehr?*" he yelled.

She wasn't pretty at all, but that seemed a cruel announcement for a baby's first hour of life. "There's another one coming out!"

He sagged to the seat. The tip of his pole bobbed raucously. Papa didn't notice. The sight of him carrying the weight of his expanded family was too much for me. I ran home where Mrs. Devendorf greeted me with a baby boy. He was red-faced and screaming. His balled fists punched the air. When I stood on tippy-toes to get a better look, a sour smell wafted from him, and he wasn't yet ten minutes old.

A boy. An angry, yelling, stinky boy. Had I not prayed hard enough?

Mrs. Devendorf finally ushered me into Mother's room. She lay back on her pillows like wet tissue paper. Even her freckles had faded from the effort of birthing the twins. She raised her fingers when I entered, beckoning me closer, although I wasn't at all sure I should. But I couldn't resist Mother for long. Her hand against my cheek was cool and damp. Before I had a chance to ask her why, the doctor placed my sister in Mother's one arm and the wretch of a brother in the other. Her eyes closed and her head sank into a mountain of pillows.

"What will you name them, Mrs. Richter?" the doctor asked with a pen poised.

"Goodness and Mercy," she said.

"Goodness, huh? And which of these creatures will be burdened with such a moniker?"

She folded the answer in a sigh. "The boy."

"And Mercy is the girl?"

She nodded and her head lolled to the side.

Mrs. Devendorf picked up Goodness, bouncing him to raise a bubble. He burped but he cried on. "And so, Goodness and Mercy will follow you all the days of your life, will they, Magda?" she said.

Had a person not known my mother well, they would have missed the slight brightening of her eyes. "Yes, Goodness and Mercy."

If the river revived Papa, the birth of the twins depleted my mother. Gone were the songs while coating and frying chicken. Blanket tents disappeared from the clothesline. Monday remained wash day; she cooked three meals a day, changed diapers and fed the twins, cleaned the house, and bought the groceries. But she scuffed rather than walked. I helped all I could, but the garden lay fallow each spring. Impromptu coffee klatches with friends ceased. A powdering of dust coated the cookie plate. My father fished every day after work. If Goody wasn't wailing, Mother's pencil scratched at a frenetic pace in a notebook she'd bought at the drugstore. Life turned flat and quiet, except for Goody's crying and Mother's pencil.

By the time the twins started school, Mother stayed in bed most days, writing in her notebooks and listening to the radio. Goody, Mercy, and I went to Mrs. Devendorf's kitchen after school for cookies and milk. Pete and Joanne, her own children, scowled as the twins and I were offered first choice of the cookies. We stayed at the kitchen table until we all finished our homework. Afterward, we played in the front yard to avoid waking mother with our games. When father brought home his evening catch, I fried the fish in butter with extra pepper.

It went just as Mrs. Devendorf had predicted. Nothing escaped Mercy's attention. She knew when Herb Wright asked Martha to go to the Fall Fling instead of me, and I hadn't said a word, not about wanting him to ask me or that he hadn't. And she understood Mother best, warned us to be quiet or suggested a bouquet of dandelions to cheer her. Goody, well, he clattered, tumbled, and bellowed through life. Papa nicknamed him Jaybird since he carried home anything that glittered, crawled, or wriggled.

Lucy

"Can I carry your books?"

Hank, the boy from trigonometry class, the one who helped with the pruning at the ranch, walked beside me. His swagger, so typical of the football players, rankled me. Was all this posturing absolutely necessary? Would he preen next?

I clenched my books to my chest. "They're not heavy. Besides, I carry them home every day." I hadn't meant to sound harpy.

We walked in silence to the railroad tracks. Finally, he said, "Your sister looks like a weakling, but she sure got the best of Veronica. I heard she blistered her back good, not that Veronica didn't deserve it. My sister says she's stuck on herself."

That did it. No more small towns for me. You couldn't sneeze without everyone in town calling out, "God bless you!" I was breaking one of Ada's biggest rules by being alone with a boy, not that anyone else had asked to walk with me, and now he turned out to be a dope. "You can't believe everything you hear. My sister didn't hurt anyone."

"What about the handprint? How do you explain that?"

I couldn't. "Mercy didn't hurt her!" I walked faster.

Hank caught my arm. "Whoa, wait a minute." His pleading voice warmed me. "I'm sorry, Lucy. I'm terrible with girls. I turn soft in the head. You're right; I never should have listened to Jerry. He'll say anything." Hank reached for my books, and I let him take them, even hoped his hand might brush against mine, but it didn't.

He smiled shy like, and I couldn't help myself. I smiled right back, although now I was mad at myself for wanting and not wanting Hank to walk with me. What kind of craziness was that?

Once we hit our stride, all awkwardness dissipated. I learned that his family ran a peach orchard about a third the size of Lotti's, but his dad was president of the First National Bank. "My grandfather started the bank." Without even trying, I pictured a string of pearls at my throat as I hosted the wives of lawyers and doctors who kept their accounts at the bank. Even in my imaginings, I spilled coffee on the starched tablecloth. I woke up from this daydream in time to hear Hank ask about my parents.

"You're an orphan then?"

"We're fine." I wanted to tell Hank that Ada hated me, although probably less than when we'd first arrived and the safe feeling I got from living in Palisade could be the very thing that undid me. It was a good thing I didn't. I knew better. With all the connections that crisscrossed between people in small towns, the chance of that kind of news looping back to Honey Sweet Ranch ran high. Besides, the way Hank talked about the town, you would have thought the twins and I had landed in the foyer of heaven. I wasn't surprised. Hank had been born in Palisade, so he felt obliged to defend the place. Still, I couldn't help asking, "Do you plan on living in Palisade for the rest of your life?"

"Heck no, I'm joining up the minute I turn seventeen."

It was plain un-American to hope he would do anything else, but a groan I never intended leaked out. Too late, my hand covered my mouth.

He grinned like he'd found a gold nugget in the flour. "That's good, real good. You'll be sorry to see me go. Good thing we have plenty of time to get to know each other. My birthday isn't for another six months. Ma wants me to wait until graduation, but that's over a year away. The war will be over by then."

Did Hank listen to the radio? Read the newspaper? Watch the newsreels? How could he know when the war would end? There was no sense trying to talk sense into him. He was a boy, after all. Instead, I asked, "You'll come back here? Do you ever think about living in a place like California?"

"My dad's looking to buy another orchard, maybe put in some cherries and pears to stretch out the harvest season."

"And you'd work it?"

Hank's shoulders drooped. "I don't let myself think too far ahead, not with the war."

I hated that the war made us consider our mortality and not our futures, especially someone as nice as Hank. When we reached G 7/10 Road—yep, seven-tenths of a mile from G Road and three-tenths of a mile from H Road—I told Hank I could make it home with no problem. I reached for my books. "There's no need to go so far out of your way."

"I'm enjoying myself, Lucy."

"Oh."

"I've been thinking about walking you home for a while."

That made me smile so big my teeth dried and stuck to my lips. Plenty of kids had been friendly to me, but none had welcomed me into their circles. "Where do you live?" I asked.

"At the end of Iowa Avenue, but our orchard is down in the Vinelands. You should come there sometime. There's a place to swim in the river. It's a little cold now, but we all meet there in the summer."

The thought of swimming in a river brought bile to the back of my throat. "I can't swim."

"I'll teach you."

I'd enjoyed our conversation to this point. Now I found his confidence incredibly annoying. Who did he think he was? "I'm not interested."

"I didn't figure you for one of those girls who doesn't like to get her hair wet."

"I'm not."

On down the road, dust billowed, and I prepared to be nettled by a spray of pebbles from the passing truck's tires, but the truck locked its wheels and skidded to a stop. Ada leaned out the window, waving at the dust. If her anger had been any more righteous, she would have wielded a sword of fire. "Get in the truck, Lucy."

Mother had raised me to always offer a polite greeting. So, to give Ada a chance to redeem herself with Hank, I said, "This is Hank, Ada."

"I know who he is. I changed his diapers in the nursery. Now, get in the truck. You know the rules."

Just then, I learned how ready Hank was to face the battle-hardened Germans or Japanese. He stepped toward the truck and extended his hand to Ada. She let him stand there with his hand out. "It smells like snow, Mrs. Heller. My father has high hopes for the year, though he worries where the labor will come from at harvest." Hank stuffed his hand deep into his pocket.

"Tell Ralph he has good reason to worry, but that won't get him the pickers he needs. It's time he came to a Control Board meeting. Your father has a habit of letting other people do his work for him. If he thinks pickers will magically appear from the Midwest, he's delusional. They're having their own labor problems out there. I don't doubt Ralph will be feeding peaches to his hogs with that attitude. You can tell him that."

Hank inched back from the truck. I took my books from him and skedaddled to the passenger side. He raised a hand to me and said, "I'll see you in home—"

Ada gunned the engine before Hank finished. And here I thought Ada and I had reached an agreement of sorts. I nearly spat my words. "You can't say everything that comes to your mind, Ada." And then I said what I really meant. "I don't need you watching over me like an old farm dog. We weren't doing anything wrong."

Her glance cut like a cleaver. "It's surprising how stupid a girl can be in this day and age. You have no idea what a boy has on his mind every hour of every day. You will not walk home with boys, especially not boys like Hank Wagner."

"There's nothing wrong with Hank. He's a gentle—"

"No boys, Lucy. None. Good girls don't walk with boys without an escort. I won't discuss this anymore. If you break the rule, I'll find a way to make your life miserable."

It wasn't beyond me to accept Ada's challenge, but I doubted my life could be more miserable than it already was. I'd lost both of my parents, and I daily feared arrest for taking the twins from the orphanage. But for Goody and Mercy's sake, I kept my mouth shut.

"You better make up your mind. It doesn't seem right to be writing one boy and walking home with another," she said.

"Pete's a friend, nothing more."

"You practically run to the mailbox."

"I don't have anything but chores and homework to keep me busy. Pete's letters are a diversion."

"Does Pete feel the same way?"

I had no intention of telling Ada about Mildred or explaining how I fought loving Pete every day. I let her believe whatever she wanted. She would anyway.

By the time I sat down to write Pete that night, the end of the pencil was nearly chewed off from wondering if I should tell him Hank walked me home. And then I had to wonder why I wouldn't tell him. In the end, I told Pete the whole story, including the part about Ada riding in like the cavalry to save me from absolutely nothing.

Goody moaned in his sleep. Since I wasn't asleep anyway, I rose onto my elbows to listen. Tonto whimpered. Fearing Lotti's cabbage rolls had soured Goody's stomach, I felt my way through the dark. Cold air cascaded to the floor from the window. I vowed this would be his last night on the floor. Goody could resume sleeping like the Lone Ranger in the spring.

When I knelt over Goody, Tonto stole a kiss, so I scratched the dog behind the ears. "Your job is to keep him warm, fella." The scolding earned me another kiss.

"Goody. Honey." I shook his shoulder. "Is it your tummy? Does it hurt?"

Goody sniffed. "I'm fine."

His voice rasped as if he'd been crying. I laid another quilt over him. "Did you have a bad dream?"

He rolled toward the wall. "No," he said, as if I'd asked him to wear a dress to school.

I lay next to him, nestled in like Mother used to do when I woke in the middle of the night, only I had slept in a soft bed. The cold seeped through my flannel nightgown. "I'll keep you company for a while. I can't sleep either." I draped an arm over Goody's shoulders before I thought better of it. To my utter surprise, he didn't shrug me off.

His breaths shuttered under my arm. "I miss Mama and Papa."

I drew him closer. "Me too."

"I miss playing Cowboys and Indians with Mama when she hung up the sheets."

She did that? When? I hung up the sheets.

"I miss—" I tiptoed through my memories of Mother, hoping to match my recollections of Mother with Goody's. I knew the mother of gentle surprises and leisured walks, the mother of my childhood. But Goody would only know his mother—a sullen woman, an explosive woman. A woman tangled in the sheets, lashing out at the slightest provocation. Or so I'd thought.

Mother played Cowboys and Indians?

Grief had a way of smudging our memories, most of all for little boys it seemed. I squeezed down hard on the tears that stung my eyes. "What I miss," I said, "are the times Mother made donuts on Saturday mornings. The powdered sugar felt cool to my tongue, just like snow."

"I remember that," he said, his voice brighter. "And Mercy spilled her milk on Mama and Papa's bed."

I'd forgotten all about the spilled milk. The scene came back to me with unsettling clarity. Mother had grabbed Mercy by the arm, her fingertips digging into Mercy's flesh. I pried at Mother's fingers, begging her to let go, promising to change the linens, terrified by the dispassion of her face. When I finally worked her fingers free, beads of blood rose from the crescent marks in Mercy's flesh. Mother eased back onto her pillows and drew up her legs.

"I'll be back to clean the bed," I said.

I'd kept Mercy home from school until the bruises faded on her arm.

"Mama—" Goody started.

"Mother liked a tidy bed," I said. "And if I remember correctly, I was the one to clean up that mess. Nothing new about that."

"That's because you're the big sister." Goody turned toward me. "I dreamed I was fishing with Papa."

My voice pinched. "Did you catch a fish?"

"Huh?"

"Were you at the river or the lake?"

"The lake, I think."

The lake pried my memories open—the cool green water and the fried chicken under a checkered towel. Laughter. The sting of sunburn on my shoulders. Buzzards circling overhead. What did Goody remember? Mother staring into the lake at the edge of the dock? Papa handing out bologna sandwiches? Silent rides home? I hoped he remembered swimming through my legs.

Goody snorted. His breathing had slowed to soft tea-kettle whistles. He was asleep.

"Good night, Goody."
Mother played Cowboys and Indians. How about that?

Lucy

The next morning, I peeked around the shade, a habit since I could remember. Was it snowing? Raining? Sleeting? Above the fortress-like escarpment, the sky blushed at the coming day. Straight up, the sky had not yet found its full color. My breath clouded the window.

Since it was Saturday, I tucked the mussed covers around Mercy and paused to watch Goody sleep. His tears from the night before had left powdery trails to his hairline. I wet my finger to wash the trails away but thought better of it. Goody at rest was Goody out of trouble. The scent of sweet vanilla wafted up from the kitchen where Lotti waited.

I eased the bedroom door open a crack. Below me, the front door clicked shut. Ada had left to teach piano in Orchard City. I should have said a prayer for those hapless students, but I enjoyed my freedom from her too much to let myself be concerned with their welfare.

When I got downstairs, the coffee pot percolated gleefully. "Are you hungry?" Lotti asked. "I've cobbled together a coffee cake. I doubt it will be sweet enough, but I added some of Clara's honey, just in case."

I sat with my back to the oven, Ada's usual place. I was that greedy for the warmth the oven offered. I hadn't raised the cup to my lips before Lotti started asking questions. This wasn't unusual. Lotti philosophized, questioned, and sermonized. She spoke plainly from a wellspring of love that completely disarmed me. When I thought of leaving Palisade, it was Saturday mornings with Lotti that tugged at me to stay.

She fingered the handle of her cup. "How are things going for you? Do you like school? Have you made friends? Being new can be terribly difficult. Small towns are friendly, but they're not always welcoming. I'm still not sure Ada feels like she belongs here and she's lived here fifteen years."

I set my cup back on its saucer.

Lotti continued, "Are the twins adjusting? They've had so many changes in their short lives. Goody knows how to keep himself busy, that's for sure. When we're listening to the radio, I swear he's off somewhere else. What an imagination that child has. He reminds me of Gil in that sense.

"When Gil comes home, he and Ada won't live here long. Ada doesn't think I know, but she's saving every penny to buy a place of their own. This is Ada's doing. I'm sure of it. Bernhard and I lived with his parents our whole married life until my mother-in-law, Henny, passed. We were such good friends. Things are different now. Children want to make their own way in the world. Gil and Ada won't be any different. When the war is over, I suppose I'll sell this place and move into a little house with a small yard. It wouldn't do to be without a garden." She set her coffee cup on the tray with a rattle. "Good heavens! I'm prattling on. You have to stop me, Lucy." She held her hands to her heart. "I've come to enjoy our Saturday mornings together. I collect questions and thoughts all week. You mustn't let me take advantage of your patience."

I smiled at her, and she started again, only now her hands rested idly in her lap and her eyebrows creased together. "I had a very interesting conversation with Mercy the other day."

I crossed my arms over my stomach. "Really? She's the one with the imagination."

"She seemed deadly earnest."

I'd worried Mercy would give a "message" to Ada or Lotti. "Did she upset you? I'll talk to her."

"Oh no, not at all. I want her to feel like she can tell me anything." Lotti sipped her coffee. "She's been to heaven, has she? She spoke in great detail about your mother's needlework. About the garden where Magda works. And there's a river. But you know all about this, don't you?"

I'd heard enough about Mercy's trip to heaven to realize a little girl wanted to believe her parents were happy and safe out of her seeing. But I stopped Mercy from telling me anything more, although she pressed me often to do so. Her stories only reminded me that I never should have let Mother stand that close to the river. "I don't know why she tells such stories."

"She believes what she saw."

"Yes, she's convinced herself." Had she?

"We all have our oddities, don't we? Ada certainly does. She's not a bad girl, not Ada. I'm only an observer, but it seems she's afraid an awful lot of the time. I wish I knew what scares her so. Of course, there's Gil being away, but long before he left and there was talk of war, Ada shied from her own shadow.

"More than anything, I had hoped by now the two of you would have come to terms. I'm more than a little disappointed in her. You're her niece, for heaven's sake. True, she's had her share of sorrow, but I didn't expect her to become your mother. We all benefit from the tenderness of family."

I was more than happy to shift our conversation from Mercy. Besides, I knew exactly why Ada and I hadn't come to terms. "I disappoint her."

"We all disappoint Ada, so you mustn't think there's anything especially wrong with you. You deserve better than you're getting from her."

Did I want more? "She's great with Goody and Mercy. I'm grateful for that."

"Unless you're putting itching powder in her bed at night, I don't understand her behavior."

"I can be hard headed." Papa had said so first.

"That you can, but Ada invented hard headed." Lotti poured more coffee into my cup. "I have a proposal for you. You can think about it as long as you like, and a refusal won't change my affection for you."

I stirred honey into my coffee. Lotti laid her hand over mine. "Darling girl, may I be your aunt, and if not your aunt, then a friend? You can depend on me to step in front of a train if needed."

Her mouse eyes glistened as she searched my face for an answer. I grasped her hand. I didn't trust my voice. And in that moment, my desire to stay outpaced my fear of being found out.

She said, "When you're strong, it isn't easy to ask for what you need. I hope your Pete is a trustworthy fellow to whom you can expose your heart. I'll not ask you to bare your soul to me. I'm just here. To talk. To listen. Although I'm much better at talking." She smiled at that. "And I'm here to enter the fray as needed. I'm fearless, you know." She kissed the back of my hand. "I think I know your answer. No more is to be said. It will be our secret. To the end." She looked up at the clock and jumped out of her chair. "Good heavens!" She opened the yawning mouth of the oven, reaching for the cake with a folded towel to protect her fingers. "I've been spared. Ready for a piece of cake?"

After such a generous offer, any thoughtful person would have dropped to their knees to thank God above for providing a ministering angel like Lotti, especially one who could bake and love so richly. Oh, I was thankful all right, but I was angry, too, at Mrs. Nadel. She had wheedled her way into a moment in Lotti's kitchen that had bordered on holiness. It could be argued that Mrs. Nadel had, in her odd way, driven us to a new home and family but spitefully, it seemed to me, she lurked behind every sweet promise and unguarded moment in hopes of snatching it all away. She would surely drive me to madness if I didn't find a way to put distance between us, either measured in miles or—what? This was my conundrum.

Mercy shuffled into the room and climbed into my lap, smelling of dried saliva and the last traces of lavender soap.

"Did you have sweet dreams?" I said, combing her hair back with my fingers and pushing thoughts of Mrs. Nadel to the back of my brain.

"I didn't have any dreams."

"You will dream of honeyed pillows after you taste what Lotti has baked."

"I'm hungry."

"Go get Goody."

Lotti sliced the coffee cake at the table. "God is pleased with you, Lucy. You must believe that. Not many could have accomplished what you've done so early in life. By holding your family together, you are mirroring His nature." She placed a fat slice of steaming cake on a plate and pushed it toward me. "He meant for us to be in families."

Pete

April 2, 1944
Someplace hot in the South Pacific

Dear Lucy,

I want to apologize for giving you such a hard time back home. It took me traveling halfway around the world to realize you're an amazing woman. Thanks for putting the past behind us and writing this poor sap.

Tell Goody I enjoyed the drawing of Tonto. Don't tell him I said so, but that's one ugly mutt.

Cuff and me got some sleep last night, so I should be able to muster enough energy to finish this letter before I drop off. You asked for details about what I'm doing. I can't really tell you much. Just know that Cuff and I are busy cleaning up a heck of a mess over here, and Cuff deserves more credit than me. He's one tough Marine. He out sniffs anything on four legs. And the ears on that dog! I'm so lucky he picked me. He's saved my life more than once. If he alerts, I pay attention. I would be a fool not to.

You're beginning to sound like a rancher (a very pretty one). I like how you talk about the peach orchard coming to life. I never paid attention when I was back home, but I will from now on. There aren't any peach trees around here, but they have trees that look like broken umbrellas and the houses don't have any walls. That sure wouldn't work back home, would it?

I was like you. I wanted to see the world. I thought I was missing something being holed up in a nothing town like Prairie du Sac, but I'm here to tell you, home is a place to long for with your whole heart. It would be paradise

121

to swat at mosquitoes on my own porch, sipping Ma's lemonade or something stronger. Sometimes I can see the beauty of what this place used to be, but it doesn't last long, not with the way it smells and the sounds I won't describe.

I got three of your letters today. I'm sorry I can't write as often as you. They keep us pretty busy and when I get a chance to sleep, I take it. Promise me you won't count the days to the end of school. All they say about high school is true. These are the best days of your life. You haven't mentioned that joker Hank in some time. Did he move to Mongolia? You can't blame a fella for hoping.

About Ma—she's still in Appleton. Her letters are full of doctor visits and runs to the druggist. She seems real tired but she doesn't complain.

Because of you, I'm the envy at mail call. Keep 'em coming!

Love,
Pete

Lucy

Love, Pete?

I dug for the bundle of letters I kept hidden under my panties in the top drawer of the dresser, the one place Goody would never look, and took them to the bench under the apricot tree. Within seconds, my nose was running like a spigot from the cold.

I started with the most recent letter, skipping all the talk about Cuff to read Pete's sign off.

Your Friend, Pete

I worked back through the letters and opened another.

Your Friend, Pete

And another.

Your Friend, Pete.

This was new. What was he doing?

Love, Pete?

He must have been under tremendous pressure. Perhaps lack of sleep had dull his thinking. I'd seen the newsreels, heard the radio reports. The Pacific was a nightmare.

Love, Pete?

This was a slipup. He probably wrote Mildred every day, signing his letters the same way. He simply forgot who he was writing. It was a mistake. A boo-boo. A tired boy's bungle. Pete was popular back home, mostly for his good looks, and he had a way about him. Girls loved him. I'd tried hard not to be one of his fawning crowd, but, to be completely truthful, I had allowed myself to relish

123

his attention on occasion much more that I should have or wanted. And here I was doing the same thing.

This was about the car, wasn't it? He thought I had his car. In his eyes, that was reason enough to be nice to me. And I did like him being nice to me. If he didn't ask about the car, and he hadn't, I saw no need to write of its demise until absolutely necessary.

I gathered the letters and considered tossing them in the incinerator, but I couldn't. I would miss reading them too much. Yes, that, but even more, I hoped, beyond reason, he'd signed the letter as his heart had wanted, maybe not his head, not yet.

And he thought I was pretty, very pretty.

I tied the ribbon back around the bundle of letters, and as I did, my heart trembled over his words: *Love, Pete.*

Mercy

Aunt Ada stomped through the orchard, calling my name. I'd gone and lost track of time, all because I'd found a real nice branch to sit on to read my library book, a story about a girl who found a silver thimble and then all kinds of wonderful things happened. I hadn't found a silver thimble, although I had been looking, but I sure liked sitting in the peach trees now that they were all pink and ruffly with blossoms. It was like sitting inside cotton candy. I tried to tell Aunt Ada about the story. She was much more interested in getting the grocery shopping done.

Me and Aunt Ada did the grocery shopping every Saturday afternoon, when she finished with her piano lessons, which meant we had to hurry before the store closed. And even when we hurried, working through the store took forever with everyone in Palisade catching up with their neighbors, blocking the aisles as they talked, never even noticing we wanted by. I didn't mind so much. Sometimes I saw my teacher, Mrs. Z, in her overalls or ran into Veronica and her mother. According to Aunt Ada, it only took two chatty people to clog the whole works. Lots of chatty people lived in Palisade.

Aunt Ada groaned real loud when we rounded a corner, and there stood Mrs. Reed. She was the fattest woman in town. Her lacy slip peeked through the gaps between her buttons. I tried not to look, but it was a wonder to see a pink slip. I don't think Aunt Ada liked her, but I sure did. She didn't go on and on about the weather, and that was something in a town of ranchers, no matter where you lived.

Mrs. Reed greeted Aunt Ada with a smile full of teeth. I'd never noticed before, but her hands seemed too small for her arms. "The orchards look good, Ada, mighty good. The trees are bustin' with blossoms. With all that's going on with the war, it's a blessing to look forward to a good harvest."

Here came the labor shortage speech again. Ada loved telling people they were foolish. "Sure it looks good, but if we don't get the pickers, the peaches will rot on the ground."

Mrs. Reed's fingers fluttered over her mouth. "Donald says the pickers always come. They go where the money is. This year won't be any different, will it?" She didn't seem too sure about Donald's opinion.

"We're living in a different world. Nothing is the same. We can't do things like we've always done and expect to get our peaches picked. I don't know what it's going to take to make some people believe that."

Aunt Ada shuffled through the ration stamps in her purse. She wanted Mrs. Reed to get on with her shopping, so we could get on with ours. Instead, Mrs. Reed waggled a finger at Aunt Ada. "If you ask me, I think we should get those German prisoners in here to do the picking. They're just sitting around, practically eating food off our tables. We might as well get some work out of them."

Aunt Ada narrowed her eyes at Mrs. Reed for the longest time. Finally, she said, "You're fortunate not to have anyone fighting in the war. Otherwise, you would never consider such an idea. Goodbye, Nadine."

We left the store without our groceries.

The ranch was always busy. That was a fact. Aunt Ada and Lotti pulled lists of chores out of their pockets just as one of us reached for a book or dared to sigh. And now, with the coming of the blossoms, the whole town of Palisade seemed to be primping for a party. Folks painted their pickets, weeds got hoed deep into the soil, and storekeepers raised banners of welcome for Blossom Sunday visitors, a day of true celebration for peach growers. The last possible night for a killing frost had passed. Ranchers smiled all the time now, even when they spat their tobacco and patted one another on their backs, like they had had anything to do with the weather.

A man from the newspaper thought so highly of the Blossom Sunday potluck, he came to the house to ask Lotti a lot of questions. She plucked a fat chicken thigh out of the frying pan with tongs. "The people we invite to harvest our peaches deserve the dignity of a clean place to sleep and bathroom facilities with flushing toilets."

The reporter wrote down what she said.

"We've been calling dysentery the peach-fuzz flu for years. The plain truth is our water is contaminated by the rush of people in the valley. The sooner we get the laborers suitable living conditions, the sooner we can say goodbye to drinking water contaminated by human waste."

The man looked up. His mouth dropped open.

Lotti wiped the grease from her hands. "As I remember it, Tom, you got sick last year. I made some chicken soup, gave it to Susan at church." Lotti wrapped a piece of chicken in waxed paper and handed it to Tom. "I sure hope the newspaper takes better notice of our fundraisers, Tom. I'd hate for you or your children to get sick again."

"When's that camp going to be completed?" he asked, trading his dull pencil for a sharp one.

"If the turnout for the Blossom Sunday potluck is good and folks like you show up for workdays, I suspect we'll open in time for this year's harvest."

Tom gave a quick nod. "You get the information to the newspaper office for whatever you're doing, and I'll get the word out in the next edition. Don't forget the Wednesday deadline."

Lotti assured him she would be Johnny-on-the-spot with all the details as she walked him to the door. I didn't remember them playing a game, but Lotti sure looked like she'd won the grand prize.

People drove all the way from Orchard City to gawk at the blooming peach trees. The way their mouths opened wide, I'm sure more than a few of them swallowed a bee. I couldn't blame them. The trees didn't know anything about the war or the sadness around them. They bobbed in the breeze like it was just another fine day in the world. Who wouldn't feel happy looking at an ocean of pink?

It seemed like everyone in town showed up with casseroles and cakes and breads to go along with Lotti's fried chicken. And anyone who didn't bring food, hung crepe paper streamers—pink!—and set up row after row of tables and chairs. It all happened the way Lotti had hoped. Many of the people who came to Palisade to see the trees, stayed for the Blossom Sunday potluck. It nearly killed me and Goody, but, at Aunt Ada's insistence, we left all the preparations to take a bath.

Once we smelled like Ivory, Aunt Ada rushed us out the door. Aunt Ada always liked to be first, but what she told us was this: "It's rude to show up late when people are expecting you." She didn't like us arguing with her either, so we followed close on her heels. We left Tonto locked in the barn. Goody said he could hear him howling from the park, but I sure couldn't.

We sat close to the dessert table where Aunt Ada set her Peach-a-Bye Dream Cake at the very beginning of the line. Plenty of folks admired how smooth the icing was, and that was a good thing, because we'd been eating oatmeal without sugar for a month just so Aunt Ada's frosting would be sweet enough.

Women marched across the lawn toward the serving tables with their pans and crocks and platters covered with kitchen towels like they were the wise men taking presents to baby Jesus. The ladies peeled the towels off their dishes, and you could see the relief on their faces, especially the ones who'd brought a molded salad.

Goody ran off to play with some boys, and Lucy helped a lady using a muffin tin for a cash register sell tickets. Once Ada had filled her plate, she insisted we all sit together as a family. This was odd and wonderful to hear from Aunt Ada. Odd because she was our mother's very own sister but a stranger to us until we'd traveled all those miles from Prairie du Sac. And wonderful because being part of a family felt extra good to me. But then, just thinking about being part of a family that didn't include Mama and Papa made my heart ache, and I wondered if I was having a heart attack.

I saved Lucy a seat next to me, which was one of the chairs from the Sunday school classroom, the ones that pinched your bottom if you didn't sit down kind of careful. Aunt Ada drummed her fingers, waiting for Lucy to join us. Already, Lucy's deviled eggs were stained green from the Jell-O salad. When Lucy did come to our table, she wasn't careful and she got herself squeezed good by that chair. "For the love of—"

Ada's shoulders snapped back. "Watch your mouth, Lucy. 'Thou shalt not take the name of the Lord thy God in vain.' Once you break one commandment, sin is a downhill slide to hell."

Lucy looked around the table and bit down on her lip. I said a prayer for her and crossed my fingers for extra measure. I could tell she was about ready to burst. She only bursted when someone embarrassed her, and Lucy would definitely be embarrassed if someone thought she was on a downhill slide to hell. Lucy's hands rested on the edge of the table. She was making a huge effort not to sass Aunt Ada, and Aunt Ada didn't even notice. She was too busy taking the skin off her chicken.

Lucy shifted in her seat. I could tell she wanted to rub the sore spot on her bottom, but we both knew better than that. Lucy scowled at Aunt Ada, and I was worried she might go ahead and burst, but she took a big bite of chicken leg instead, all the while looking straight at Aunt Ada. Lucy's lips were shiny with grease, but the pained look lifted from her face. Lotti's chicken was that good.

I was so proud of Lucy that I quoted a verse for Aunt Ada. "'He retaineth not his anger for ever, because he delighteth in mercy.' Micah, chapter seven, verse eighteen."

Aunt Ada frowned. "That's a peculiar verse to be quoting just now." She folded the chicken skin into her napkin.

Lucy answered before I swallowed my bite of potato salad. "It's her latest mercy verse. That's all. It doesn't mean anything." Lucy raised her eyebrows at me, a warning.

"It means something," I said to Aunt Ada. I didn't dare look at Lucy, but I felt the heat of her glare. "It means God doesn't hold a grudge."

Aunt Ada's eyes got all squinty. "You're an interesting girl, Miss

Mercy."

That's what she said, but a blush rose up her neck to color her face.

"Go find your brother," she said. "The food will be gone by the time he finds his way back."

Aunt Ada wasn't one bit worried Goody would starve to death. When she was thinking hard on something, her eyes danced around like they didn't know where to land. They were dancing like crazy right then. But I was happy to leave the table. My skin got tight when Aunt Ada and Lucy got cross with each other, which always surprised me. I'd never seen two people more alike.

Aunt Ada and Lucy had the same color of hair, and they were about the same size, but Ada had blue eyes and Lucy's eyes were dark, dark brown. When they were angry, they both sucked their lips in and they got all squinty eyed. And even though you would have thought they were the two bravest people on earth, they sure weren't. Don't ask me how I knew, I just did. They should have been the best of friends.

I wove through men balancing heaped plates and women herding children. I was heading toward some trees where, more than likely, Goody tracked make-believe cattle rustlers. I was about to scoot past a group of men patting each other on their backs when I noticed a woman sitting at the last table.

She was more of a statue than a real live woman. She was the exact same color as stone with her gray velvet hat and gray dress. The family sitting at the other end of the table had turned their backs just enough to let her know they didn't want to talk to her but not enough to let the world know how rude they were being. This reminded me too much of the orphanage, so I sat across from her.

She kept her eyes on her plate. "I never serve ham without trimming off the fat," she said.

"I wouldn't know anything about that."

The lady stopped cutting and looked at me with eyes the color of an angry storm. "And I never sit down with anyone without asking their permission. It isn't polite."

If she was trying to shoo me away, I was ready to skedaddle, but I was too curious about why she was cutting the ham into such tiny pieces. I could see that she still had all of her teeth, so it wasn't that she couldn't chew. "May I sit with you until my brother comes back?"

"Looks to me like you're already sitting. It's still a free country, unless you want to drink a cup of coffee after supper, that is. I don't see what fighting Hitler has to do with coffee beans."

I didn't know anything about Hitler or coffee, so I told her my name and she sniffed loudly. "In my day, children didn't speak unless they were asked a question."

This lady was going to need lots of chances to be nice. "How did the children ask for a story?"

"My mother read a chapter from the Bible every evening at seven o'clock, sharp. If any of us were late, we got a whupping. I don't suppose a little girl like you gets whupped nearly enough."

If only she knew. Papa had taken me to the Devendorf's tool shed plenty of times. I had a knack for following my nose, only I didn't know I was following my nose until it was too late. A fine spring day drew me outside, and then a bird might sing, or the light might make a puddle sparkle. The next thing I knew, I was much farther away from home than I intended. And that scared Mama into a good mad.

Papa would pull his belt through the loops and scowl as he lectured me on the importance of always telling Mama where I was going. His voice was like a boat scraping a rocky shore, and I forgot myself sometimes and started to cry. Then he'd wink and kiss my head. "Are you ready?" he whispered.

I nodded and dropped my chin. Otherwise, I might giggle and give us away. Papa slapped his hand with his belt. That was my signal to howl and carry on like a wild banshee. I didn't know what a banshee was, but Papa seemed awfully pleased with my performance. We couldn't go into the house until my eyes were good and red, and I grew a rash under my eyebrows, so I worked up a good cry, too. I thought about Bambi's mother, and the tears just gushed out of me. I guessed those spankings worked because I got better about telling Mama where I was going. I'd hated making Papa redden his hand for me.

"My papa took me to the shed when I wandered off without telling Mama," I told the lady.

"And that's supposed to make your rudeness acceptable? Glory be, but we're raising a generation of insubordinates." She looked through her glasses perched on the end of her nose. A web of hairs filled each of her nostrils. "Well, if you must know, my name is Miss Melba Zimmerman Wood. My family came to this valley when it was nothing but creosote bushes and rattlesnakes. It took some imagination and a good deal of hard work to make this place inhabitable for humans, but I don't suppose you're the kind of little girl who appreciates that sort of effort." She propped her knife on her plate and laced her fingers. "I'll have you know this place killed my mother. She worked with a pick ax to break up the soil and hauled rocks to clear a garden plot. If it hadn't been for her, we would have starved the first year.

"My father was the head engineer on the irrigation system. Oh, others had tried. They were nothing but mud slingers. No, my father used what he had learned at Harvard University in Cambridge, Massachusetts. Once word spread about what he'd accomplished here, how he'd brought life to a dead place, he worked on irrigation projects all over the west. My mother refused to leave the garden she'd worked hard to start, so we stayed here, and Father returned when he could. His work eventually took him around the world. He was a very important man." She poked a tiny piece of ham with the tine of her fork.

A family with a crying baby and a little boy sat next to Miss Wood. The mother dug through her basket for something to quiet the baby. The boy took one look at Miss Wood and tugged on his mother's sleeve. He whispered in her ear. The mother met Miss Wood's gaze and traded places with the boy.

Miss Wood chewed the ham without so much as a nod to the mother or the boy. The family unpacked their basket of dishes and cups and service, and before the mother would allow the boy to fill his plate, she wiped his hands with a damp cloth. I liked the way she did that, not rough as if scrubbing to the bone but tender. That's how Mama used to wipe my hands, pulling the washcloth down the length of each finger, and then she kissed the backs of my hands. Watching the boy and his mother made my chest ache all over again.

And still Miss Wood chewed. Her lips pursed out and the hairs on her upper lip rose and fell. Finally, she worked her tongue over her teeth. "What does your father contribute to the world? Is he off fighting in this godforsaken war?"

"Papa is living in heaven. He catches fish for the banquet."

"That's a good bit of storytelling someone has filled your head with."

I remembered Lucy's rules just in time and kept my mouth closed about heaven. And then it happened, my heart knew the truth about Miss Wood. I didn't want to talk to her one more minute, but what was to be done? She wasn't mean because she wanted to be mean. She was mean because someone had hurt her. "Who hurt you, Miss Wood?"

"You impertinent child. No one can hurt me. I live in the nicest home in this town. I sit on the school board. I am the treasurer of my mission circle."

Those were all nice things. "Maybe you wished your father liked to stay home with you."

"As I said, he was a very important man. He made crops grow where no one believed he could. He had better things to do than go to my recitals."

I tried to picture Miss Wood singing in front of an audience. The ladies who sang in church smiled and their eyes sparkled. Miss Wood's eyes were as deep and cold as a cave. "You don't sing anymore, do you?"

"Who are you?" She scanned the crowd. "Are you here with your family?"

Lucy had a rule about talking to strangers, but poor Miss Wood needed a friend. "Who's Henry?" I asked.

"Henry? I don't know any Henry."

Yes, she did. "Are you sure?"

Miss Wood slapped the table so hard the silverware jangled. The family with the small boy turned to watch us. Miss Wood leaned toward me. When she spoke, she splattered me with spit. "Who have you been talking to? Where are your parents? This has to stop!"

I said the first thing that came to mind. "'I will be glad and rejoice in thy mercy: for thou hast considered my troubles; thou hast known my soul in adversities.' Psalms, chapter thirty-one, verse seven."

"Enough!" Miss Wood reached across the table to grab my arm. She was a lot stronger than she looked, and she pulled me right out of the chair. "Who do you belong to?" She tugged me past tables of people, some holding forkfuls of food in front of their open mouths, all with a question creasing their brows. Not one of them moved to help me. She lowered her face to mine. "You're not one of those retarded children from the home, are you? Did they bring you on a bus?"

"You're hurting my arm."

"Point out your people, and I'll let go, not a moment sooner."

I looked over the crowd to find Lucy or Aunt Ada or Lotti. And there she was, Lotti, the easiest to find with her pointed hat, the one that made her look like Santa's happiest elf. Lucy was there, too. I pointed the way. "I'm here with Lotti and Aunt Ada and Lucy. I haven't found Goody yet."

Miss Wood squeezed my arm tighter. "You're the child who burned little Veronica. It's no small wonder you live with Lotti." She pulled me through the tables, telling people to mind their own business when they asked why I was crying. I lost track of how far we'd walked, but soon the adults were yelling at each other, and Lucy scooped me into her arms and kissed the place where Miss Wood's nails had made dents in my skin.

Lotti inched closer to Miss Wood. When she tilted her head back to get a good look at Miss Wood, her hat tumbled off her head. "What's the meaning of this, Melba?"

"I should ask the same of you, bringing this hateful child to a celebration for people of the community. She shouldn't be allowed to roam about to assault people."

Onlookers turned in their chairs to watch. I buried my face in Lucy's neck. I couldn't bear to see people all red-faced, snarling like dogs. Lucy's heart beat against my chest.

"The girl doesn't weigh forty pounds, Melba. What did she do to you?"

"That girl has a mouth on her—"

I couldn't stand the suspense. I looked in time to see Aunt Ada step between Lotti and Miss Wood. I was relieved because Aunt Ada was bigger and stronger than Lotti. Aunt Ada spoke in a low voice.

"You've let your imagination get the best of you, Melba. Why don't you return to your meal? You don't want your food to get cold."

"What are you going to do with that child? She deserves nothing less than a lashing."

Aunt Ada didn't blink. "Go back to your plate, Melba." Miss Wood didn't move for a long time. A man sauntered up with his emptied plate, and I could tell he was looking for more of Lotti's chicken. He took one look at Aunt Ada and Miss Wood and backed away. Miss Wood *humphed* and turned sharply. Aunt Ada looked like someone had punched her in the stomach.

Seeing her like that only made me cry harder. My tears soaked Lucy's blouse. I tried to think of other things, nicer things. I remembered the warmth of Mrs. Devendorf's kitchen. I saw Goody holding a baby bird in his hand as if it were made of glass. That was wonder enough, but I also caught Mama smiling at him. I thought of Papa holding us, Goody in one arm and me in the other, telling us stories from the homeland, a place called Germany. Lucy was there, too, sitting in a chair all by herself, and I'd wished Papa had a bigger lap.

Lucy rubbed my back. "I'm so sorry, *mein Sonnenschein.*"

Lucy

Lotti wrung her hands and Ada fingered the lace of the tablecloth. "You know we love Mercy, don't you, Lucy?" Ada said.

"Of course, she does." Lotti frowned at Ada before turning back to me. "What you need to know, dear, is that you have done an amazing job with the twins. They're smart. Caring. Thoughtful. Each in their own way, of course. That Goody is a sprite." Her focus faded for a bit, but she returned her gaze to me. "If there is something we need to know, something that would help you carry the burden of raising your brother and sister, we're here to help."

I looked from Lotti to Ada. Mrs. Nadel had said much the same thing: *I'm here to help you, Lucy. You trust me, don't you? We must do what's best for the twins.*

Lotti's frown deepened when I didn't answer. Ada didn't need to know everything about Mercy. She already carried so much. Gil told her everything about the war. The ranch fell on her shoulders, too. And now she felt the weight of her sister's children. Most importantly, this question begged to be answered: Would Ada see Mercy's peculiarities as a reason to send us packing? We couldn't leave yet. I hadn't earned enough to get us to California.

Lotti continued, "Is there…is there anything we should know about Mercy? She's a darling girl. In some ways, a bit of an angel and as sweet as butter. In other ways, well, she seems to carry the world's sins on her shoulders—that's not to say she's naughty herself, but she's aware of what goes on in people's hearts. Wouldn't you agree?

"I've never seen Melba that upset. I dare say she would have cried, if she'd stood there another minute. I attended her mother's funeral. Her eyes remained stone dry all through the service, the graveside, and the early supper the girls put together. So you can see why this whole episode is strange." She leaned forward, her fingers laced together. "Has anything like this ever happened to Mercy before?"

I didn't dare look into Lotti's eyes as I remembered the first time. Instead, I looked past her, out the window to where Mercy was reading to Goody under the apricot tree.

At church, Mercy had slipped off Papa's lap to trot up to where Mrs. Sprecht, my fifth-grade teacher, sat and patted her right on the knee. The woman startled. I sank in my seat. Papa nudged me to retrieve Mercy. She was almost four at the time. His arm held Goody in place like a paperweight. Mother had stayed home. Just as I rose from the pew, Pastor Sanderfoot started reading the Bible passage. I sank back in my seat. Only his voice and the ticking of the clock filled the stillness. Pastor Sanderfoot stopped reading when Mercy said, "Poor, poor mama. Poor, poor mama."

Mrs. Sprecht bent toward Mercy. "I'm not your mama, little darling."

Mercy put her doughy hand to the woman's cheek. "Don't cry, lady." And then she sang, "Jesus loves me, this I know." Tears streamed down Mrs. Sprecht's face. At the end of Mercy's song, the woman pulled her into her lap and rocked her, murmuring, "Thank you, little angel. Thank you." The congregation, with noses usually pointed toward the pulpit like true north, goosenecked to see what was happening in our corner of the sanctuary.

The magic broke when Goody said, "I gotta pee, Papa."

We didn't learn the wonder of what had happened between Mercy and Mrs. Sprecht until the gossip in the fellowship hall reached us. Mrs. Sprecht's son had been arrested for stealing a car the night before.

How in the world did Mercy know that? Or did she?

The people of Prairie du Sac embraced Mercy. In fact, they made her a bit of a celebrity, passing her from one set of arms to the next, hoping to hear a tender message for a buried pain. They were content to own her. They had no need to hold her up to scrutiny. I couldn't be sure Palisade would be so protective. She wasn't one of them. She'd gotten into trouble at school and caused a ruckus at their potluck.

No doubt about it, I needed to talk to Mercy again, remind her how important it was for us to fit in, at least until the end of harvest, only five more months. Then, with the money I earned packing peaches, we would move to a big city where we would be far less conspicuous.

Aunt Ada leaned forward. "You are very protective of the children, as you should be, but we need an answer to Mother Heller's question. Has anything like this ever happened before?"

"Never."

Lotti's eyebrows rose. When she spoke again, there was a hint of incredulity in her voice. "Really? Never? You're saying that Mercy has never displayed a special talent, a gift for knowing what is hidden?"

"Mercy is liked by everyone," I said with a sharp nod of my head. I was so angry with myself. Had I believed Mercy would become a different child once we'd left Wisconsin?

Lotti laid her hand over mine. "Don't let your heart grow cold for the people of Palisade. We're all under the stress of the war, and with the men gone, there's more for everyone to do. We're more suspicious. Those who were once our friends and neighbors have become our enemies. It's all so very confusing."

Ada pushed sharply away from the table. "This is craziness. There's too much to do to be talking about fairy tales."

Lucy

Fingerling leaves and tongues of pink and yellow hinted at the peaches to come. The trees were caught between what was and what ought to be, just like the whole wide world those days.

Pete didn't tell me everything, but I caught the tension in his letters. I'd known him long enough to see he was trying to sweeten the telling of his story. I lifted my face to the breeze, hoping to feel with the earth's breath an assurance that Pete was fine. I wanted Cuff to be fine, too. According to Pete, he owed his life to that dog. He sure wrote plenty of flowery prose about Cuff. And here I was, sitting under an apricot tree, thousands of miles between us just as anxious for a dog's safety as Pete's.

But his writing about Cuff was much better than endless ramblings about Mildred. In fact, Pete never once mentioned Mildred or their plans for the future, and I didn't ask. Pete was my connection to the past and my dream for the future. I saw us on the porch of a bungalow near Main Street in Palisade, not Prairie du Sac. That surprised me some. I felt him walking beside me to school and back, and I imagined him reading the paper at the table while I washed the dishes. I laid my head in his lap right there under the apricot tree. And since Cuff had become so important to Pete, the dog slid into my daydreams, too.

I was nothing better than a dope. Surely Pete wrote lots of girls, including Mildred, but he made me feel like I was the only one.

Was that enough?

For now, yes.

I needed his letters. His words, although deeply personal, were written to someone else, the someone I hoped to be and needed to be—a woman more than a girl, strong and resilient.

Besides, I couldn't complain too much about Mildred and all the other girls because there was Hank right here in Palisade. I liked him fine. He walked me as far as the railroad tracks a couple days a week. He dared not walk me farther for fear of another encounter with Ada. Hank, too, would be gone soon, and I would miss him like sunshine. He asked to hold my hand once and I said no, not yet. I was thinking of Pete but still wanting to be loved right there and then. It was all, as Lotti had said, so very confusing.

With the days getting longer and warmer, I spent more and more time under the apricot tree to do my school work. Between the radio forever blaring war news and Goody asking to tie me to a chair so he and Tonto could rescue me, I needed its sanctuary. I sat in the umbrella shade of the apricot tree. The apricots were still hard as rocks, useful only if I needed to lob at the neighbor's rooster who considered the bench his personal roost. If the reading got too boring, which it almost always did, I pulled out a blank V-mail from my notebook to write a letter to Pete.

This was our place, only he didn't know it yet.

"Yup, it's going to be a hot one." Charlie the postman leaned on the pummel of his saddle, fanning himself with a pile of letters as he talked. One was a windowed envelope that could be a V-mail from Pete or Gil.

"I'm sure you and Lucky want to get your route done before it gets any hotter." I stroked the horse's neck, collecting horse sweat and hair on my hand. "He sure is spent."

Charlie pushed his hat off his forehead. "I'm powerful thirsty."

He wanted some of Lotti's iced tea, but that would only delay the reading of Pete's letter. I looked Lucky over from nose to tail. "I've never seen a more haggard animal than Lucky. Is he sick?"

Charlie dismounted, took hold of Lucky's bridle at the bit, and looked at him head on. "Why, he don't look any worse than he usually does."

This wasn't the response I was looking for. "Charlie, can I have my letters?"

"You mean this here V-mail addressed to one Miss Lucy

Richter?"

I grabbed for the letters, but Charlie held them over his head. "You're a scoundrel! Give me the letter!"

Charlie smiled broadly. "But there ain't one letter in this pile for you."

"But you said…"

Missing teeth made a cavern of his mouth. "Miss Lucy, there are *two* letters from Pete in this pile."

I snatched the letters from Charlie and ran toward the apricot tree. Behind me, I heard Charlie laughing as he mounted Lucky and plodded toward the river. Goody said he'd once found Charlie sleeping under the cottonwoods with his mail pouch as a pillow. All those folks on the other side of the river probably didn't get their mail until near sundown. Lucky for me, Honey Sweet Ranch was on this side.

May 4, 1944
The Hot and Lonely Pacific

Dear Lucy,

Don't spend a minute worrying about me. By the time you get this, I'll be as good as new. Cuff and I got a little too close to a mortar round is all. He took the worst of it. His whole side was filled with shrapnel and his hindquarters wouldn't move. I was plenty scared he would be put down. To make matters worse, Cuff bit the corpsman when he tried to treat my wounds. That guy will be telling his grandchildren he got wounded by a dog in the war. How about that? My wounds didn't amount to much. They got me cleaned up in the field hospital, but it was Cuff I was worried sick over. We hung back for a week. I put APC tablets in his dog food every day, and after a week, he was as good as new. You can't get rid of us that easy.

I have to go. The unit is packing up to move out. Things are getting crazy over here. Don't forget to pray for me. I want to come home to you with all my pieces.

Love,
Pete

I stuffed the letters in my pocket and ran up the stairs. I fell to my knees beside the bed. "Father. God. Jesus. Keep Pete safe. And thank you he didn't die. Please, bring him home. This war makes a mess of everything. It just has to stop. Do something quick, God. Amen. Wait! I shouldn't be feeling this way about Pete. I'm all confused. I don't know what you can do about it, but I would appreciate your help. Amen."

The second letter was all about Ted Williams and Pee Wee Reese visiting the war dog platoon for an exhibition game. I dropped the letter to my lap. He was 10,000 miles away, and still Pete drove me nuts. One minute, he was wounded, and I pictured him writhing in pain. The next minute, he was playing shortstop in a baseball game. How was I supposed to pray about that? Did he need a healing or a homerun?

My emotions tumbled like wrestling puppies. I read the rest of the letter. Pete gushed about Ted Williams being a Marine pilot. Well, if Mr. Williams was such a great pilot, what was he doing playing baseball? There were plenty of Japanese lobbing mortar shells at Pete who needed bombing themselves. I read on. There it was, the constant in every letter, Cuff saved the day. Mr. Williams hit a homerun and just as he was rounding third base, Cuff dropped the ball at Pete's feet. I would never be more exciting or perfect than Cuff, that was for sure.

I wadded the letter I'd already started writing and pulled out a fresh piece of paper. The day would come for Pete to say goodbye to Cuff, but would he ever say goodbye to Mildred? I had to know.

Ada

April 6, 1994

Dear Lucy,

I have no idea what happened to Gil's letters. I meant to keep them until the day I died. I'm still here, but the letters are lost forever. This makes me sadder than I thought possible. After all, they're only paper with words. Still, they were Gil's words. You don't suppose I left them in the attic? Maybe you could take a look?

Before I answer your question, I want to tell you how distracting you were. I was used to grinding through each day as if the balance of the universe depended on me getting my work done. You changed all that. I watched you constantly. You were such an enticing mystery. It took every ounce of self-control I could manage not to torpedo myself into your life.

When Charlie delivered letters from Pete, I watched you reading under the apricot tree and writing feverishly in return. Plainly, he had become more than a friend to you. I didn't know a thing about him. He could have been a gangster, for all I knew. But he was in the middle of a horrific mess. The chances of him returning were slim. I wanted to wrap your heart in cotton wool to protect you from that possibility. Of course, I knew better. The ecstasy of love is the pleasure and the pain it brings. To be human, to love, means embracing it all.

Later in the summer, when the time came to Tanglefoot the trees, watching you evoked very different emotions. If you had moved much slower, the turkey vultures would have taken you for dead and alighted to pick your bones. I yelled at you from the porch to pick up the pace. But my admonishments only encouraged you to slow your progress. What an obstinate child! No wonder you were as brown as a chestnut. I busied myself with paying the bills. I even closed the shade and worked under lamplight, vowing not to yell at you again. If you insisted on sitting in the hot sun all afternoon, that was your business. Of course, I broke my vow almost immediately. You were all that stood between the peach bore and the peaches.

I peeked around the shade, and there you sat under a tree with the brush dripping Tanglefoot on the ground, staring off into nothingness. I left the house, stood at the edge of the orchard, and came as close as I'd ever come to taking the name of the Lord in vain. Instead, I yelled for you to get moving.

Isn't this the truth of love? Love obliges to seek the best, even when doing so drives us to the abyss of madness.

Still, in spite of the heat, you didn't give up or complain. I remember checking the thermometer. The mercury quivered near one hundred that day. In that way, I saw myself in you. Both of us stubborn to the bone. I knew this would be your strength or your undoing. It became your strength for the most part. I admire you so.

Only the bravest bloomers showed their colors in that heat—Rose of Sharon, the trumpet vine, and the coreopsis. What would we do without their brilliance to cheer us? Simply put, some plants and some people thrive in the heat. You were one of them and so was I.

But this isn't what you asked about. You asked about my early days in Palisade. Quite simply, I was a silly, frightened, stupid girl when I arrived. Finding a job at the Peach Bowl Café was my best piece of luck. I learned to serve cream before a customer asked, and I remembered who liked catsup on their scrambled eggs, all in hopes of earning higher tips, which I did. I also learned to deposit my wages at the bank before returning to the Kline homestead after work. I slept under their rafters in exchange for some cooking and cleaning. If I didn't deposit those coins, they disappeared. I suspected the middle child. He tried to ingratiate himself to me, but he never won my favor.

Like you, I got my start in peach ranching by painting Tanglefoot in the orchards. I didn't understand the damage peach borers could do to the trees. Still, I followed the rancher's instructions. I wonder if the trouble my back gives me wasn't born in the orchards that summer. My doctor blames osteo-something. That sounds like something for old people.

After packing peaches later that summer, my savings account swelled to the point of amazement, at least in this girl's mind. I considered going back to Wisconsin, but I'd made a promise to Magda, an unreasonable promise to be sure but one I kept.

Many people traveled toward California in those days, waxing about golden opportunities and everlasting summers, but such promises made me suspicious.

They still do. No place on earth can be heaven, especially not California in those days, filled as the state was with the sad-faced, broken-down people I saw passing through Palisade.

And there was Gil, a little older and devilishly handsome. From the first time he came into the café, he scared me to death, having known his kind before, or, at least, thinking I'd known his kind. He persisted, quite unreasonably, despite my rebuffs. He wore me down and more than won my heart, pulling me toward an unfamiliar openness. I fell in love with him despite myself.

When you came to the ranch, you had not a clue to be cautious with your heart, to guard what only you could give to a man. Am I being too coy? You understand my meaning, don't you? In any case, you needed someone to watch over you. Do you remember how I insulted Hank when I found him carrying your books? I knew too well what could come of an innocent flirtation. I would not have that happening to you.

I read back through this letter to discover I hadn't finished the story about the first time you painted Tanglefoot on the trees. Since Tanglefooting is part of our heritage, I'll tell you the end of the story now.

As I remember, you finally tired of staring at the escarpment, but I understood your fascination with the naked slopes and gullies. You had never seen anything like it. You came from a place of rhythmic hills. In Palisade, the mountains are brazen, unpredictable, a menace in their boldness, a true staccato. By that summer, the nearness of the walls had come to comfort me. They were a shelter and a constant source of amazement. I prayed you would find shelter there as well.

You definitely had me agitated, but in so many ways I admired you. Mercy had finished the school year without causing another public display of hysteria, although she remained a focus for the pricklier members of our community. There will always be those who thrive on drama. You understood Mercy's odd ways, which was more than I could say for myself. Besides the guidance you offered her, you earned straight A's, something even Vater's strong hand never extracted from me. Thomas, I must admit now, was a good influence on you. His gentleness allowed you to grow unfettered. I know you miss him, and I'm sorry for your pain. That his passing brought you to me is a kind of redemption. I desperately hope you share this sentiment with me.

You will look for Gil's letters, won't you?

Love,
Ada

Lucy

Ada shouldered Bessie's rump, and the cow sidestepped. "You can't pussyfoot around. She expects you to take charge. First, you'll need to clean her up. You don't want hair and dirt ending up in the milk." She spoke to Bessie, "Looks like you enjoyed some time in the mud this afternoon, old girl."

Bessie eyed me with pure contempt. "Ada, I'm not good with large animals."

"What do you mean? Bessie is a sweetheart. I've never known a gentler cow. She won't give you a problem. In fact, I've found her to be a good listener."

"I might hurt her." I didn't care if I hurt the cow. I was fighting for my time. I already carried my load on the ranch, and I had my school work besides. I also wanted to finish a letter to Pete. "How can I milk the cow and pack peaches?"

"They don't start packing until three. You may not be able to help with every milking, but when I'm preoccupied with the pickers or arranging shipping, having another milker will be helpful."

"What about Corky?" I asked, sounding as desperate as I felt.

"Bessie is not fond of men."

"How do you know?"

"She gets agitated."

"Does she bite? Kick?"

"You're worrying about something that won't happen. At the very worst, she will flick you with her tail." Ada plucked debris from the brush. "Back to your lesson. Before you place the pail, you must clean her coat." She offered the brush. "You try."

Once I took the brush from Ada, I would be the sole milker on the ranch. She had a way of adding chores to my list. This one meant predawn trips to the barn only to return every afternoon. What little social life I enjoyed would completely disappear. Who was Ada trying to kid? I was born in Wisconsin. I knew a few things, like a farm—or a ranch—could come to own you. "Goody brushes Silver. He does a good job. Maybe he—"

Ada fanned the bristles with her thumb. "I balked at first. Milking was below me. I had students to teach. Meetings to attend. Committee members to call. I was not a milk maid." She scratched Bessie's ear. "I've come to treasure the quiet of the barn. Bessie's sweet compliance and generosity are quite refreshing. I thought, perhaps, you would find solace here." She turned as if she was done with me. "I was mistaken," she added quietly.

Lotti entered the barn. "Ada, what are you doing? You don't expect Lucy to do the milking. She has plenty to do."

"It's good for her to learn. We haven't experienced a harvest without Gil. We don't know what sorts of things will come up. We aren't even sure what kind of workers we'll get."

Lotti rubbed her palms together. "That's what I came out here to tell you."

"Have you heard back from the McKnights? The Krammers? Are they coming?"

Ada handed over the brush, not to tend Bessie but to give her full attention to Lotti.

"No, they're not coming. And the Simpsons have decided to stay home. The trip is too much with their boys gone. There's no one to look after things at home."

Ada snatched the brush back from me to rake Bessie's side with long, deep strokes. "We should have recruited from Mexico. They're hungry for work. The committee, they wouldn't listen to me. We can't panic. Others will come. People need the work."

"I never intended to panic," Lotti said. "I've put in an order for a dozen German prisoners. They'll be here next week."

Ada stopped brushing Bessie. "You did this without asking me?"

"Ada, your contributions on the ranch are invaluable." She put her hand up to Ada. "I won't argue that point or my right to make decisions without conferring with you on every point of managing it, at least for now." She stepped closer to Ada, lowered her voice. "We can't wait until the last minute to fill our picker slots. As for the Germans, they were offered on a first come, first served basis. The opportunity presented itself, and I was thankful to be in place to secure the workers. The peaches won't wait—I've heard you say often enough, and you're very right—and neither will I."

Ada balled her fists. "You know, of course, if things had worked out differently for those German soldiers, they would be shooting at Gil right now. I will not have them on the ranch, Mother Heller. The pickers we have are good, hard-working people. They've never let us down. They'll be good examples to any new workers we find."

"*If* we find any new workers, Ada. The only returning picker we can truly count on is Kansas Johnny. I'm happy to have him, but he's getting older and slower. We need healthy, strong workers. Soldiers are certainly that."

"This is craziness. What will Gil say?"

"He'll say, 'Aren't you clever ladies, using our enemies to bring good? Now, that's redemption.'"

Tears collected in Ada's eyes. "And what if Gil doesn't get the chance to tell us how clever we are? How will you feel about that?"

Lotti drew Ada into her arms. "I will weep a canyon of tears. We both will. But what are we to do? I've prayed and fretted and prayed some more about bringing the Germans to the ranch. Dear girl, these are unfathomable circumstances for simple people like me. The war still rages, and yet our enemies will serve us. It's truly an extraordinary opportunity."

Ada returned Lotti's embrace.

I looked away, embarrassed by their shared tenderness, but too curious to keep my gaze away for long.

Lotti rubbed Ada's back. "In all of my years, I've turned to God in times of plenty and trouble. He's never failed me. And so, I've decided to rely on Him yet again. We will heap coals on the heads of our enemies with the kindness we show. If any other justice is to be administered, we will commend the German soldiers to God."

Bessie lowed and nudged Ada. She backed away from Lotti, wiping her eyes. "I'll milk Bessie tonight."

Lotti beckoned me to follow her out of the barn. She looped her arm through mine. Once we reached the house, she said, "Yet another miracle in a stable, I do believe."

Pete

August 16, 1944
Some crazy place in the Pacific

Dearest Lucy,

Something has happened that will change me forever. It's only fair that I should tell you about it. We were pressing to take an airstrip. Nobody had slept for 60 hours or more. This makes you a little crazy. The decision was to sleep or live, so we kept moving toward our goal. Cuff alerted me to Nips hiding in the trees several times. Otherwise, you would not be reading this letter.

Once we reached the airstrip, we found the Nips were dug in pretty good, so it took us a long time to scare them out and win it back. This was the worst time we'd had so far. When the place was finally secured, I dug a foxhole to get some shuteye. When I woke up, it was just me and Cuff. I'd slept straight through a mortar barrage, and from the looks of it, the Nips had followed up with a close-in grenade attack. I never heard a thing, Lucy. Every single one of my buddies is dead.

There were some truly great guys in my platoon. I'm not one of them by far. I thought that God had gotten His signals crossed, so I pulled out my pocket Bible to see what He must have been thinking. I opened to a verse that I'd never read before. This guy Paul talks about how hard it is to stay in this world when dying and being with Christ would be so much better. In the end, he decides to stay alive for the sake of his friends, to help them grow in their faith.

I read the passage a hundred times. It was like I wrote the words. I don't want to be here, and there have been times when I've envied those who died.

They're out of this mess, and I'm still in it. But this verse made me think that maybe God didn't make a mistake. Maybe there is something out there for me to do. More than anything, I hope He wants me to be with you.

I've given a lot of thought to that night by the river when we talked about the twins. I hope I didn't push you toward something we will both regret. Keep your wits about you. Don't run off scared. You have a good situation in Palisade.

I should have said something about Mildred a long time ago. She sent me a Dear John letter while I was still in basic. She met an army pilot at the USO in Milwaukee. The way I see it, I'm awfully glad she did. She helped me see how much I cared for you. Now that we got that out in the open, can we talk about the future? I don't want to rush you. You're still young and I'm getting older by the minute. I'll need plenty of hot water bottles and mentholated rub when I get home. Do you mind?

It may be some time before I can write again. Don't ask why. Everything in the Marines is hush-hush. Thank your aunt—she's not so bad—and Lotti for the letters and prayers. You're praying for me too, aren't you? Tell Goody to cheer for the Brewers for me and give Mercy a squeeze from good old Pete.

Love Always,
Pete

Ada

Lucy!

We've lost two residents this week. This is to be expected, but it's always a surprise, nevertheless. A man—have you met Lawrence?—who sits at my table likes to say there will always be death and taxes. We're like an Abbott and Costello routine because I say, "Yes, but death doesn't get worse every year." No matter how many times we repeat this joke, everyone at the table laughs, and not that bashful sort of laugh either. We turn our faces toward death and guffaw.

And yet, when the time comes and one of us passes, we mope about like schoolgirls without dates. We actually envy those who move on. Does that sound macabre? You're not to worry about me. I tremble in my slippers on the topic of death like anyone. It's the unknown or nearly unknown, the bit about crossing over, that puts my faith to the test. Will I walk through a door? Will curtains open? Will shedding this body be painful? I'm quite accustomed to pain these days, so more pain won't matter so much. What about that bright light at the end of the tunnel? I'll know soon enough, I suppose.

Honestly, I'm a tad morose today. A story about Goody will surely brighten my outlook. I'm very grateful for the new assignment you gave me.

Let's see, I was in the barn, finishing up the afternoon milking when Mother Heller came with a letter from Gil. Goody shadowed her like one of the barn kittens looking for a saucer of milk. That surely was not his way. Mother Heller struggled to keep a straight face as she held the letter under my nose, pointing at Gil's words, as if I wouldn't read them greedily.

151

I soon understood their conspiratorial looks. Gil wrote about fond memories of driving the hoopie. From his eighth year on, Gil drove the thing up and down the rows of trees and to the packing shed. It was a rite of passage, he said. My duty, in Gil's estimation, was to teach Goody how to drive the hoopie for the harvest. My first inclination was to snatch the letter from Mother Heller's hand and eat it. Then I pictured Gil on a hillock in Britain, snickering to himself. He didn't think I could do it.

I made the mistake of looking at Goody. Such earnestness in his expression! Talk about being painted into a corner. When I told Goody I would teach him, he threw his arms around my neck. His exuberance unsettled Bessie, and she kicked over the milk pail.

I delayed the first lesson as long as I could with excuses of meetings and errands. In those few days I bought, Goody sensed I was observing him. He stood straighter, swallowed his food before speaking, and begged at dawn's earliest light for extra chores.

Corky took it upon himself to fit blocks on the hoopie's pedals and donated his pillow to boost Goody closer to the steering wheel. I came within an inch of canceling the driving lesson once I saw how small Goody looked behind the wheel, but when he caught my eye, you would have thought I'd crowned him king of the world.

On that first day, my plan was to simply teach Goody how to ease the clutch out and move a few feet before braking. I figured we would drive up and down a couple rows of trees and call the day's lesson complete. I never dreamed we would drive off the property on our very first day. At first, I stuck to my plan. We worked at learning how to clutch and shift. Up and down the rows of trees we went. Everyone in the household had found something else to do, but I don't doubt you all peeked around the shades to watch. Most surprising of all, I really liked teaching Goody. He didn't whimper when I yelled at him for grinding the gears. Instead, he set his jaw and asked for another chance until he drove that beast better than I or Gil.

Something changed between Goody and me that day. He approached me more openly. I expected better things of him, and he never disappointed. I should have taken him driving much sooner. Gil, even from so far away, understood Goody's need for ever greater responsibility.

We did experience one small mishap that day. The string of events remains foggy, but I do remember Tonto jumping off the hoopie to chase a cat. At any rate, we drove through Melba Wood's freshly hung laundry. She never came to claim her bloomers.

I hope this story made you smile as it has me.

Oh, I almost forgot, again. Have you heard from Mercy? I didn't like the *tone of her last newsletter. Is it possible she isn't well? Would she tell us? That child! See if you can find something out before we talk on Sunday. I can't imagine the demands the orphanage puts on her.*

All my love,
Ada

Lucy

The pages of Pastor Pennington's Bible crackled as he flipped to the day's passage. Although the windows were wide open to Main Street, Palisade's habitual breeze had forgotten to show up. Women fanned themselves. Men sat like statues in their suits, the same suits they had worn all winter. A bead of sweat slid past my ear, over my jaw, and down my throat to my collar. It was almost 11:35 by the sanctuary clock.

A careful look at the congregants revealed a tension about the eyes, a drumming of fingers, a squirm here and there. Even if Pastor Pennington announced the date, time, and address of Jesus' Second Coming, I doubted anyone would have noticed, except Mercy, of course. She wasn't one to miss anything about the Second Coming.

A train whistle blew in the distance.

Goody's knees bounced wildly. He turned toward the doors at the back. I grabbed his hand, which was sweaty and gritty, only to release it. My job every Sunday was to keep Goody in his seat without distracting the congregation. It wasn't easy. When Mercy turned toward the dancing voices of women outside the windows, I nearly conceded defeat.

The whistle blew again, closer.

Pastor Pennington stopped mid-sentence, looked toward the door. His own son writhed in his wife's arms in the front pew. Pastor cleared his throat as if to refocus his own attention. "This is a crucial passage in understanding the true calling of the committed

Christian."

Was he trying to convince us or himself?

Goody tugged on my skirt. His grasp left a deep crease I would have to iron before next Sunday. "They're coming, and I'm going to miss everything," he said too loudly.

Mrs. Dorset, the woman who clerked in the mercantile, turned to look down her hooked nose at me. Why was that? I sat quietly. I wished Ada would step in, but she didn't. I elbowed Goody, hoping he would stop talking. For once, he understood.

He slouched in the pew and kicked the seat in front of him. I stilled his feet with a touch on his knee. He scowled at me, but I held my gaze on the pastor as if every word was a sip of chocolate malt. If Goody believed his behavior addled me, and most certainly he did, he would fidget, burp, and scratch in inappropriate places until I sent him outside. That would surely result in a lecture from Ada about proper church decorum when all I wanted was to write Pete a letter under the apricot tree.

Pastor Pennington didn't seem to notice Goody's quest for freedom. "Let us read from the Holy Scriptures. 'Behold, a sower went forth to sow; and when he sowed, some seeds fell by the way side, and the fowls came and devoured them up.'

"Interesting passage, isn't it? We are a generation who has known hardship. When but a young boy, my family left our home near Chicago. We took only what we could carry after my father lost his job. At thirteen, I hated just about everyone, especially the factory bosses who had fired my father after years of faithful service. And there were the bill collectors who hounded and belittled him, not to mention the banker who foreclosed on our home. My father, a once-strong tower of a man shriveled before my very eyes.

"After a day of unsuccessful job hunting, when yet another day ended with him indebted to my aunt and uncle for room and board, he found me in their garden drawing unflattering pictures of his tormentors. I can hear him still. 'Ah, Kenny, don't let your heart grow bitter.' And he poked me with a hard finger." The pastor rubbed a spot on his chest. "I still have the bruise to prove it."

A self-conscious laugh swelled through the congregation.

"My father said, 'Your heart is God's garden. He plants seeds of love for Himself and others, but the ground must receive the seed.

It must be soft. Kenny, don't miss the love of God for anything, no matter how hard life gets for you or those you love.'" These last words were spoken with a tightness that forced Pastor Pennington to swallow down his emotion before he continued. "This is the best advice I ever received, an echo of the Lord's words written here. And I share them with you."

The train blew its whistle, very close, at the depot. The Germans had arrived in Palisade.

Pastor Pennington looked toward the doors. His brows twisted into questions: Should I continue? Will the congregation listen?

As much as I wanted to see the Germans as prisoners on our very streets, I also wanted Pastor Pennington to continue. Would he have an answer for the bitterness I harbored?

He hurried on. "We have a unique opportunity to practice this love in our town. Many of you have sons in the armed services. They have been taken from you by the bloodlust of evil men. The future is as uncertain for our boys as it is for us. Will you receive this Word, this seed? Will you trust the Sower of your heart's garden, or will you, by ruminating on injustice, allow your heart to resist His Word and love?"

Church bells pealed and through the windows, voices of men joined together to sing. Robust. Commanding. Triumphant. Not the songs of a Sunday hymn. They sang in German. Goody looked at me as if in great pain. I raised my chin to him ever so slightly, and he slipped out of the pew and sprinted for the doors.

The pastor said, "It seems our visitors have arrived. It wouldn't do for the church not to welcome them. Let's take a short break, say ten minutes until they march by, and then we'll continue with the service."

Congregants shifted in their seats, glanced toward the yawning doors and the pounding of boot leather on the pavement. Pastor Pennington strode down the center aisle, his robe billowing. "Let's go," he said, gesturing his congregants out of the pews. "History is being made in our town."

Lotti was among the first to lean out of a window for a better view. As short as she was, this was the best place for her. Ada loitered behind the row of spectators who jostled for an aspect from a window. I pulled Mercy outside. "Stay with me. And keep an eye open for Goody."

The streets were lined with women in Sunday dresses and broad hats. Men carried their jackets over their arms and loosened their ties as they shouldered their way into the crowd. Wives and children followed close behind, shielding their eyes from the intense sun. Many had skipped church services for a chance at the best seats along the route from the train depot to the Civilian Conservation Corps camp, where the POWs would be housed. Residents and migrant workers who had come to pick peaches, packed the sidewalks and spilled into the street. Goody had disappeared, probably with his posse of friends.

The singing intensified and the excited whispers stopped. Onlookers inched back. The power of the voices and the confidence of their words didn't belong to defeated soldiers. I stopped walking and Mercy bumped into me.

"What are they singing?" she said.

"It's in German."

"But you—"

I put a finger to her lips. Like grass in the breeze, the people bent toward the sound of the singing men. Watchful. Blinking. Sweating. "Not now, Mercy. Not now."

A family accepted an invitation by Mr. Tomlin, a merchant, to watch from the rooftop of his store. They scrambled to rise and follow him. We stepped into the spot they'd left at the curb. "Stay with me," I said, holding Mercy's hand.

Necks strained. Hands shielded eyes from glare. The heat was forgotten. A few babies cried out. Boots pounded the pavement like war drums.

The Germans advanced.

A hum moved through the crowd. *They're here. They're here. They're here.*

Flanked by armed American soldiers, the prisoners came singing and marching in their imposing, straight-legged gait, arms stiffly swinging by their sides. Their chins jutted. Their voices resounded like a waterfall. Their burnished skin made their eyes glow unnaturally. They were tall, giant tall. They sure didn't look like prisoners. These men sang as if they anticipated a great victory. I tightened my hold on Mercy.

But they weren't the snarling, drooling monsters I'd expected, either. Some were only boys, and the men looked like anyone you would care to meet in Prairie du Sac or Palisade. Their features were familiar and intelligent. And except for the PW stenciled on their navy uniforms and their German songs, they looked like Americans. The sensation was like licking your finger expecting salt and tasting sugar.

Wir sind das deutsche Afrikakorps!

As they sang, their eyes flitted to take in their new surroundings. I willed myself to be too small for them to notice, but one of the German prisoners met my gaze and held it for the brief moment he marched by. His eyes were the blue of the sky, equally startling and defiant. I expected a sneer, but he smiled. Small. Just for me. A spark warmed my face.

Between the rows of marching men, I caught a glimpse of Goody on the opposite side of the street. He had run the several blocks to the ranch and back to bring Tonto with him, who barked and snarled at the Germans while Goody took aim with his play six-shooter. Behind his Lone Ranger mask, he squinted in determination.

This was all fodder for my next letter to Pete. Even with all the drama of POWs marching in front of me, just thinking about Pete squeezed my stomach. I needed to take control, get things in perspective, stop being a silly girl.

The last of the prisoners marched by, followed by two jeeps filled with our American soldiers. The crowd cheered wildly. When the jeeps passed, Goody ran across the street to join us. "Did you see that? Did you see how tall they are? And they're our prisoners!"

"We should get back to the church." Tonto jumped up on my skirt, leaving two perfect paw prints. "Goody, you're to take Tonto home and come right back."

He countered, "I heard what Pastor said. My heart sure ain't hard."

The boy constantly surprised me. Mercy squeezed my hand. "Okay then, take Tonto home and change your clothes." Goody and Tonto bolted toward the ranch right through a huddle of onlookers. "And don't go leaving your good clothes on the floor." I doubted he heard that.

Back inside the church, Pastor Pennington stood in the pulpit, shuffling his notes. Lotti leaned across me to speak to Ada. She said, "The Germans are certainly strong enough to pick peaches, don't you think?"

Lucy

Kansas Johnny wore his bedroll like a sash and walked toward the house with a long, loping gate. I welcomed him at the kitchen door.

"Is Miz Heller 'bout?" he asked.

Even though I was two steps higher than Kansas Johnny, we stood eye to eye. "If you mean Lotti, she's gone to town. She said to make you welcome. I'm not to let you talk me out of feeding you. If you mean Ada, I'm afraid you missed her, too, but you still have to eat my cooking."

"Thank you kindly, miss, but I don't need nothin'. I reckon I'll throw my roll in the usual spot."

I'd expected a younger man, seeing how he had walked all the way from Kansas City, Missouri, to help with the harvest, but then if he had been a younger man, he would have been trudging around the Pacific like Pete or through Europe like Gil. That Johnny could walk at all was amazing. Perhaps it would have been better for old men to go to the war. With their arthritic knees and weakened hearts, the whole matter would have been settled in days, if they managed to start a war at all. Leave the daddies at home to fix bicycles and the husbands to clean the eaves and the brothers to torment their sisters. The world was much too lonely without men around, and by men I meant Pete.

I should have taken Johnny at his word, sent him on his way,

159

and finished cleaning the kitchen, but Johnny was the most interesting man I'd ever seen, like a mutt with legs too long for a short body. Nothing seemed to fit about his face either. His eyes were small and slanted downward like he'd seen all the sorrow in the world. He was certainly old enough for that to be true. Valleys combed his face. His scruff of white whiskers couldn't soften the sharp angles of his chin. I expected his bones to rattle like pencils in a box when he moved, for jutting bones topped each shoulder. I dried my hands and pushed open the screen door.

"I have roast for a sandwich. It's already cut up. It wouldn't be any bother, and if I can tell Ada you've eaten a sandwich, things will go much better for me. Won't you come in, Mr. Johnny?"

"There ain't no mister in my name, missy." He dipped his head to enter the kitchen. "Beef, you say? I reckon a bite of cow will kindle my fire a mite. Took me two weeks to pass them mountains. I ran clear out of vittles some days back. Found me one of them whistle pigs along the road. Hope it don't come to that again."

I reached to relieve him of his satchel. He withdrew a step and put a hand to his bag. "I'll keep my bag," he said.

I motioned him to take a seat and introduced myself to let him know how I fit into the new order of things at Honey Sweet Ranch.

"This is the best ranch in the valley," he said. "I've worked at more than I can count on two hands and a foot. That's how I reckoned this is the best one. The trees knowed they're loved, and they grow the biggest peaches, and the workers are cared for real good, so we pick faster. Yep, you landed yourself in the best possible place. And I like the music the younger Miz Heller plays at night. Nothing dampens loneliness quite like a pretty song."

Johnny didn't turn out to be much of a talker once food was placed in front of him. He downed that sandwich in three bites, so I made another and served him half a pie. It was gone in a wink. He backhanded his mouth on his sleeve and stood to leave.

"I've always fared better on the outside of a house." He gestured toward the door. "I'll be going."

I watched Johnny sauntered toward a patch of grass under the cottonwood where he finally unslung his bedroll and rolled it out. He lay out on the bedding with his arm over his eyes, and if I'd been closer I would have heard his snores. He fell asleep that quick. If Kansas Johnny proved typical of the people who traveled to Palisade to harvest the peaches, the days ahead suddenly seemed wondrous. Who knew what could happen next?

"Did you hear that?"

We stood in the middle of the orchard in our nightclothes, pulled out of our beds by Ada. Just when I thought I was beginning to understand that woman, she did something completely unexpected. Lotti giggled and opened her robe for Mercy to step inside.

"Was it an Injun?" Goody said, adjusting his mask.

Lotti drew him closer too. "Heavens, no. Now, listen again. Carefully."

Through the trees, yellow spots of the migrants' campfires dotted the night, but for the whisper of the breeze in the treetops, the world was silent.

Ada squeezed my elbow. "There's another. Did you hear?"

"Is this like a snipe hunt?" Goody said with no small amount of disgust in his voice.

"Hush. Listen. Something miraculous is taking place. I wouldn't want you to miss it."

"I'm sleepy," said Mercy.

Ada turned, arms outstretched. "The calendar tells us the day is near. The pickers drive into town, set up their tents. Johnny walks up the lane. And then, the peaches can't hold on for all the sweetness inside." On every other day, Ada's voice was a punch to the arm. With the moon muting her skin to the color of cooled wax and the sweetness of the peaches filling the night, her words were like papery embers dancing on a fire's heat. "Listen."

And there it was, a thud as soft as an angel's footstep.

"Shouldn't we be picking them up?" I said.

"Oh, dolly, the fall bruises the flesh," Lotti said. "That peach is useless for market. Only perfect fruit makes it into the stores. Gleaners will come to can the peaches for their pantries. Tomorrow, the picking begins. Tonight, we find one of the fallen peaches and share it. It's a family tradition started by my father. Now, who will find the first peach?"

Tonto barked.

Ada snapped on her flashlight. "I won't be sharing my peach with a dog. Turn on your flashlights. Goody, come with me."

Goody ran through the trees behind a tremulous beam of light bouncing from ground to branches to sky. At that rate he would stomp more peaches than he found.

"Come on, Mercy," Ada coaxed. "I know the trees that ripen first."

Ada thought she knew everything. "I'm feeling lucky," I said. "I'm heading this way." I turned in the opposite direction.

Lotti called after us, "I'm going in to start the coffee. Daylight will be here before we know it."

As it turned out, I wasn't lucky at all. I heard a triumphant whoop from Ada. Mercy giggled. I caught a flash of Ada's white nightgown as she ran with Mercy through the trees. I snatched a peach from a tree and dropped it to the ground. "I found one!"

The predawn visit to the orchard had done little to quench the anticipation of the day. The sun had just winked over the mesa by the time Lotti and Ada returned outside to set three-legged ladders against the barn and heap canvas picking bags into a pile on the ground. Corky drove the hoopie loaded with bushel baskets. He distributed the baskets along each row, all within easy steps of the trees. I watched the activity from the kitchen window, where it was my job to keep Goody and Mercy out of the way.

Goody jumped up from the breakfast table, sending his spoon rattling across the floor. Despite convincing myself the Germans would come, do their job, and leave with nary a hiccup, I started at the noise.

"I'm ready," he said.

"Eat your toast," I retorted with added heat in my tone, just in case he missed my seriousness. "We're not to go out until the pickers have arrived and are hard at work."

Goody slouched and groaned.

"'Blessed be God, which hath not turned away my prayer, nor his mercy from me.'" Mercy looked from Goody to me. "Should we pray?"

Lotti entered the kitchen with Ada close behind. "Are you ready?" Ada said. "The peaches won't wait."

We all turned at the sound of a truck growling up the lane and moved to look out the window. My stomach tightened into a knot. The brakes squealed to a stop, and an American soldier jumped out, rifle held casually to his side, his stomach squeezed by his belt. One by one, the Germans stepped out of the truck. They looked even taller in the yard.

They carried themselves like soldiers, not field hands—heads held high, chests out, shoulders squared. Despite their posture, they tried to seem relaxed, like they labored in peach orchards thousands of miles from home every day—all as they studied the road, the house, the orchard, and the imposing mountain. They were dressed in crisp, navy shirts and pants stenciled with PW in letters that nearly covered their backs. Someone set on revenge must have chosen the dark color to sponge the heat of the Colorado sun. And long sleeves? That was what they got for setting the world on fire.

"Come on, come on. We don't have all day," yelled an American soldier from the truck's cab.

"They're here!" Goody bolted for the door.

I caught him by the belt. "You're sticking with me, young man."

Behind me, Mercy said, neither accusingly nor plaintively, just in that matter-of-fact way she had about certain things, "We didn't pray."

I kissed her forehead. "You pray for us."

She caught my hand. "You don't have to be afraid."

"I ain't afraid," Goody said, straining against my grip. "I have to go."

Mercy squeezed my hand. "Mercy is a river flowing from heaven. It's for everyone, absolutely everyone."

"This isn't a good time, Mercy. I have things to do and a renegade to contain."

Goody glowered over his shoulder. "I ain't no Injun. Let go of me."

I put my nose to his. "I will gladly let go of you when the time is right. But hear this: If you give me an ounce of trouble or worry today, I will lock you in the root cellar until next spring. Got it?"

A soldier with a clipboard strode toward the porch where Mercy played with her doll and I restrained Goody. I steadied my breathing, swallowing down the sour taste of fear. Ada greeted the soldier at the bottom of the steps. "You're late." She walked past him toward the Germans and stopped.

The soldier blinked before he regained himself to say, "Sergeant Salvatore at your service, ma'am. Here's your workers, delivered as promised by the United States Army. Me and Corporal Tibbs are here to keep an eye on them guys. We'll make sure they earn their wages and don't give you no trouble."

Ada turned sharply to face the sergeant. "There are only ten men here. We ordered twelve."

He shrugged. "Some of the prisoners complained about being sick this morning." He leaned in to Ada. "They're allergic to work, is what I think."

"I'm not interested in your theories. I have ten days, twelve if I'm lucky, to harvest my crop. If you can't get the workers I need, tell me now."

"The doctor is looking the men over, something about the Geneva Con-ven-a-tion or something like that. There are rules about these things. The best I can do is promise healthy Germans to pick your peaches by tomorrow."

"What I am learning, Sergeant, is that the army is good about making promises they can't keep."

Ada and the sergeant continued talking, but the Germans held my interest. They lit cigarettes and blew smoke over their heads, laughing into their hands like this was the first day of school and they were nervous about making a good first impression. They didn't fool me. At any moment, they would sprout horns and grow pointed tails.

"Hey, have you guys killed—!"

I clamped my hand over Goody's mouth, but I was too late. The Germans, all ten of them, turned to look at us. The one with startling eyes, the one who had smiled at me as he'd marched by, stepped forward. What were the chances? He smiled and nodded his head ever so slightly, like we shared a secret. A chill gripped my bones.

Lotti saw him, too. She swept us toward the front door with broad gestures. "Get in the house, the three of you. Now."

"I just wanted to ask a question," Goody complained.

"If you have questions, you can read a book," she said. "The library is full of books. I won't have you around those men, Goody."

"You said they're just like us, that they're fathers and sons and stuff," Goody countered.

"Well, they're a lot taller than I thought they'd be."

"I can't stay in the house all day. I have to drive the hoopie. Gil said so. Remember?"

Lotti sighed heavily. She knew all too well what it meant to break a promise to a boy, having raised one ambitious son in Gil. "You will drive the hoopie, but you must promise to be careful. Those men have been through very difficult circumstances. I want you to keep your distance. Don't go volunteering any information about yourself or us. And for goodness' sake, don't tell them there isn't a man of the house."

Goody looked wounded. "I'm the man of the house, ain't I?"

Lotti cocked her head. "I guess you are. I'm a little rattled. I trust you implicitly to take care of us."

"You won't be sorry. I'll do a good job." And out the door he bolted.

Lotti turned to me. "You know your job, right?"

I'd stuffed a list as long as my arm into my apron pocket. I would be doing everything that wasn't related to plucking peaches off a tree. Laundry. Preparing meals. Changing the beds. All of this was my ticket to packing peaches with the other girls of Palisade. I would report to the shed at three in the afternoon and stay until the last peach was wrapped and packed, sometime before dawn. At five cents a box, the socks Aunt Ada had knitted me for Christmas would bulge nicely by the end of a week, and then, if the worst happened, meaning Mrs. Nadel found us like she'd promised, we would have options. After nearly a year on the ranch, even with Ada's contrary ways—she was so much bluster—I prayed we could stay here forever.

That first day, the Germans did a fair job of picking the peaches but not great. Some picked faster than others. It was the others who vexed Ada. She yelled orders at them: "Faster, faster! No! These are not ready yet! Are you a simpleton? Use the gauge, for goodness' sake!"

The prisoners didn't speak English, but that didn't stop Ada from yelling. I should have helped, but to do so meant admitting I could have helped sooner. It was better to let Ada work her problems out with the Germans in her own good time. She would love taking credit for that.

She drove me to the packing shed without saying a word. No doubt, her silence meant she was planning another day of browbeating for the German pickers. I hoped Ada succeeded, even if she was hard to live with for a while. We all wanted and needed a good harvest.

My hand pulled up on the truck's handle the second it rolled to a stop. "Not so fast," Ada said. "You've never worked anyplace like the packing shed. Most of your coworkers will be girls you know from school. They're good girls, here to help their parents by earning money for school. There are a few girls, however, who drift into town to make a lot of money in a few days. They aren't the kind of girls you're used to. They smoke and go drinking when they should go home to bed. You'll hear language unfitting for a respectable girl. And they like to tell their stories. You'll know who they are. They strut about, puffing on their cigarettes. You're not to have anything to do with them. Pick a nice girl to work next to, one of the girls from church is preferable. Do we understand each other?"

I nodded. I understood very well that Ada did not want me to have any fun.

The girls came to the packing shed in pairs and larger groups, talking and tying their hair into kerchiefs. They didn't look like they were reporting to work. Theirs was the slinging gait of girls going to a sleepover. They wore slacks and long sleeves, and for once, I was glad I'd listened to Ada. It was three o'clock, and the heat was only ripening. It seemed like craziness to cover my arms, but after thirty minutes of packing peaches, I understood.

The peaches came and came. I picked the fruit out of bins to wrap in tissue and pack into a wooden crate. First, my shoulders burned. Before long, my fingers stung from paper cuts. Not long after that, peach fuzz filled the air, and I began to itch. No one had warned me, so I touched my face, my nose, my neck. And soon, I itched down to the bone. Five cents a box seemed like a lot of money when the girls in class had talked about packing over two thousand boxes during the harvest. Now, I saw why they packed so fast—to be done with the itching!

Despite the ache, the paper cuts, and the incessant itching, I enjoyed the energy of the packing shed. The motors that drove the grader and belts laid a foundational hum to the place. The girls talked constantly as they wrapped the peaches, and the radio blared Glen Miller tunes and the Andrews Sisters and Frank Sinatra. When one of Frank's songs came on, we all cried out his name and sang along. Girls shouted barbs and challenges across the shed, and the pace quickened. We sang patriotic songs, and when we did, the wrapping and packing intensified again. I didn't hear any swear words or bawdy stories.

That Ada, she thought she knew everything. This proved she didn't.

I saw, at last, a break in the flood of peaches. I rolled my shoulders and reached for my purse. Just then, another truck pulled up to the loading dock. In unison, we moaned its arrival. I stepped back into my station, making sure I had plenty of tissues and boxes, and waited for the peaches to cascade into the defuzzer, lope along on the sizer, and start to fill the bin. The girls who had done this for years, packed a box in less than a minute. I was slow, and the supervisor told me to pick up speed more than once.

Finally, the peaches thinned and the motors went quiet. My arms were rubber and my feet burned inside my shoes. I'd never worked harder in my life, but I was too tired to complain. The girls ambled off as they had come, only now they called out plans to meet at a diner or one of their houses.

"Do you need a ride home?" It was the girl who worked the station behind me. I recognized her from home economics. She'd scorched her applesauce.

"I don't live that far," I said.

"Come on, we've got Coke in a cooler. There's always room for one more." She was a moon-faced girl, friendly and open, and I wanted to say yes to her more than anything.

A horn honked. I shielded my eyes against the headlights. It was Ada, waving at me.

"Maybe tomorrow night," the girl said.

"Maybe." But somehow I doubted very much Ada would let me arrange my own ride home.

Ada said, "You're done with the packing shed."

I turned stunned eyes on her. What had I done wrong this time? "You're needed at the ranch," she amended. "Lotti has a hare-brained idea to get the Germans working faster."

Wasn't that exactly like Ada? I was doing something I enjoyed, making money doing it, and she thought she could snatch me away. I blurted before I had a care to be cautious, "I'm *not* quitting the shed. I need the money. I promised I wouldn't stay at the ranch any longer than necessary. To get out of your hair, I have to work through the season. You'll have to think of another way to motivate your Germans."

That shut her up for a good minute.

"Of course," she finally said. "That's a fine idea. You continue on with the packing shed. You and the twins can make your way in this world far from the toils of the ranch. Perhaps you'll end up in Hollywood." Her sarcasm smacked. "Meanwhile, the peaches will rot on the ground. There won't be money to pay the taxes or the grocery bill or the druggist for Lotti's pills. When you're sunning yourself on the beach, think of Lotti and me, won't you? We'll be living in one of the migrant worker cabins down by the river, at least until someone kicks us out."

This was a new side of Ada. Either she was angry or terribly frightened. Until I knew which, I refused to exchange barbs with her. "Perhaps if you asked the Germans nicely they'd work harder for you. Mother always said honey sweetens better than vinegar."

Ada shot me a sideways glance. "Magda knew how to work on a farm. She milked the family cow from the time she was six-years-old, every day, two times a day. She never missed. From planting to harvest, she helped mother prepare lunch for the field hands. She never shirked her responsibility. And she never complained to Mutter about my poor work habits. It's a wonder she didn't. I gave her plenty of reason to resent me."

What was more intriguing—the notion that Ada was lazy or that we shared common memories of my mother? Like an irresistible current, Ada's reminiscing pulled me through my own memories of Mother, back past her days of brooding behind the bedroom door, back beyond the fits of rage at my slightest mistake, back through the sweltering days of her swollen tummy to the mother who woke me with whistles from the kitchen.

To urge more about Mother from Ada, I gave voice to my memories. "Mother canned both sweet and pie cherries. Her garden was the envy of the neighborhood. She planted tomatoes, kale, potatoes, turnips, peas, and beans...and snapdragons. We played with them like puppets."

Ada's face glowed green from the dashboard lights, but she remained silent.

I prattled on, "Papa repaired a discarded washing machine. She crushed her middle finger in its wringer. The doctor had to cut the finger off to the knuckle. She baked my birthday cake the very next day."

"She never complained."

We drove past the post office and the depot. I wasn't about to leave off my memories with something as silly as a birthday cake. "The thrum of her sewing machine made my bedroom wall vibrate. She sewed beautiful dresses with pleats and ruffles and tucks, complete with covered buttons. The merchants' wives kept her busy copying dresses from the magazines."

Ada wiped at her eyes and let the truck roll to a stop. She looked straight out the windshield, way past the place where the headlights illuminated a jumble of cars belonging to the migrants, some tethering tents of heaving tarps. A hopeful goat pulled against his fetter to see what we might offer. The engine shimmied and died, and the crickets' chirrups rushed the cab. "Magda sewed all of my recital dresses. Did she ever tell you that?"

No.

"I was terrible to her. The dresses had to be perfect. I don't know how she put up with me. She never wore dresses so fine. Vater insisted I was the best-dressed girl at the recital. He wouldn't have anyone saying farmers didn't have the sense to dress properly. I traveled to my recitals with Aunt Gerta. She paid for my lessons.

She'd married a banker and thought her husband's prestige bought her license to meddle in other people's lives. I never thought to complain on Magda's behalf."

Ada pumped the accelerator and twisted the key. "That was a long time ago." The engine moaned but didn't start. "I loved those dresses." Ada leaned her forehead against the steering wheel. Her shoulders shook. "Your...your mother, she loved me more than I deserved."

Ada's tears surprised and embarrassed me. I never dreamed she cared about Mother. I held my hand over Ada's shaking shoulder, then withdrew it. "What is Lotti's plan?"

Ada wiped her face on her sleeve. "Mother Heller hasn't been to bed. She's home baking a German pastry from her grandmother's recipe box. I think she may have nodded off at the kitchen table because the first attempt burned." She shook her head dismissively. "Mother Heller believes if we treat the Germans with respect, as guests and not prisoners, they will respond in kind and work harder for us. It's their disposition, she says."

"Kindness begets kindness. That's another of Mother's sayings."

Ada looked at me sideways. "The Germans are not fat merchants' wives, trying to look citified. They are hardened killers. Their comrades in arms have shot their rifles at Gil. And they will again. He won't stay in England much longer. He can't. He'll face the Germans again, sooner rather than later, soldiers just like our pickers."

I recalled newsreel pictures of soldiers being carried off the battlefield. "What part do I play in Lotti's plan?"

"You've heard Gil's letters. He's constantly writing about food—when it's plentiful and when he's forced to scavenge in the field. He's lost nearly thirty pounds. He certainly didn't have thirty pounds to lose when he left here. At any rate, he's completely preoccupied with his stomach."

Obviously, hunger had never eaten a hole in Ada's stomach.

Ada continued, "I can't teach you much, but it is true men are very serious about their stomachs. In that way, and that way only, the Germans may be similar to our boys. Some of the pickers have been fighting for five years. They're hungry for home cooking, all right. Mother Heller intends to give it to them. She can talk you through each day's meal, but her place is in the orchard with me. The pickers need supervision, and as I learned today, the guards need supervision as well. It's up to Mother Heller and me to keep a count of the boxes taken to the shed. We're much too busy to prepare a large meal."

Even though my shoulders burned with fatigue, what tired me more was Ada's low estimation of my abilities. "I don't see the problem. I can cook for the pickers and pack peaches. You promised I could work."

"Cooking for a crew of men is a full-time job, Lucy. You can't be sleeping all morning and expect to prepare a hearty meal. Mother Heller has it in her mind to rival the wedding feast of the Lamb."

At the Honey Sweet Ranch sign, she pulled hard on the steering wheel to drive down the lane. I didn't have much time to plead my cause. "Ada, *please*. I'll sleep after I clean up the kitchen. We don't start packing until three. That gives me a few hours."

Ada pushed the truck door open and stepped into the night. I joined her. She stood with her face to the moon, ready to take on the universe for her cause and expecting to win. She turned toward me. "This is how peach growing works. We have ten days—and ten days only—to earn one paycheck each year. Since Mother Heller chose to use the Germans as pickers, we must now motivate them the best we can or lose the harvest. We desperately need their strength. If I could do it all, I would."

"I've gotten by on less sleep," I countered through my teeth. This wasn't true, but I'd seen how quickly the nickel per box turned into dollars as I'd packed. I paced, forcing out panic with sharp breaths. How quickly a well-devised plan could be shattered. I half expected to hear Mrs. Nadel's laugh. What if someone did arrive on the next train from Wisconsin and started asking after the twins and me? Without money in my sock to flee, I would end up in a jail for sure, and the twins would be lost to me forever. I couldn't bear to disappoint Papa, not like that. "I'll cook for the Germans and pack peaches. I do both or I do nothing at all," I told Ada.

With her back to the moon's light I couldn't read her face. Finally, she sighed. "You're like your mother in ways you will never understand. If you slack at either job, you will quit the packing shed. I have eyes and ears everywhere in this town."

She was so smug, thinking she knew who I was like and what I could do. But a more terrible thought occurred to me. Maybe she did know me in ways I couldn't know myself, so I jabbed at her with the silliest playground insult. "The Germans scare you, don't they, Ada?"

She cocked her head. "No, they don't scare me. They're too smart to hurt us."

I *was* afraid of the Germans, no matter what Mercy had said, but Ada didn't know that. I wasn't about to admit such a thing. Instead, I took on an officious tone to say, "There are only two guards, and they are too busy riding the hoopie with Goody to be of any use."

"Since the time of Homer, soldiers only want to go home. Their quest for glory is a sway-backed horse. It tires quickly. Soldiers want their mamas and wives and children and, luckily for us, a home-cooked meal. There is no kindness like the familiarity of home or the illusion of home." When she said this, her voice was wistful and sad.

She stopped when we reached the porch steps. "You are old enough to understand that all families have their secrets. Each generation protects the next from their foolishness. What is sheltered away must stay sheltered away. For people like you who are strong-willed and clever, it's tempting to resuscitate the past. It's better for everyone if you leave the past where it lies. Understand?"

I didn't have a clue of what she was talking about. Was Ada

capable of foolishness? It hardly seemed possible. And was she capable of a foolishness that could harm future generations? That seemed a far stretch. I, however, knew all about secrets and how they could threaten the future of innocents. In that way, I understood her perfectly.

"I'll do as you've asked."

I leaned against the bedroom door and listened to Ada's footsteps as she walked past our room. Goody snorted in his sleep when I stepped over him. A breeze lifted the curtains and chilled the room, so I stooped to cover his brown arms with the sheet he'd kicked away. A train whistle blew low and pining. Tonto's bony tail pounded the floor. "Not tonight," I whispered and patted the dog's head. Mercy sprawled across the bed like a bug on the windshield. I nudged her onto her side. When had she gotten so heavy?

Morning would come soon enough, and I would be peeling potatoes and plucking chickens. Lotti had written out a menu and left it on the kitchen table. Biscuits? My biscuits would never be considered an incentive for anything but a trip to the dentist. The Germans preferred dark bread, the kind Mother baked for Papa with rye and wheat flour. On the other hand, my biscuits might be written up in history books as the very thing that broke the teeth of the German army.

Of all the nights when a piano tune might have helped me straighten my thoughts or lulled me to sleep, Ada snored louder than Lotti or Goody. More than anything, I wanted to read Pete's letter again. The way he scrawled my name was enough to warm my face. That night, just the thought Pete's hopes for our future warmed me in new places.

Mercy

Goody kicked at Silver's ribs, as if that would make that dumb ol' mule walk any faster. With all of the honking of horns, his ears twitched every which way. I expected him to send the both of us flying into the dirt any minute. Goody yelled at people to move out of the way, and he wasn't saying it nice, either. He was good and mad because the sergeant was driving the hoopie and he wasn't. "The sooner we get back, the sooner you'll be driving the hoopie," I said, hoping to get his mind off being mad and on the job of delivering the soap. But Goody didn't get distracted, and today was no different.

I thought the migrant camp would be quiet with all the workers in the orchards, but children ran between the cabins, squealing and yelling for someone to pass the ball. Silver's muscles twitched under my legs. Oh, my goodness. If one more squealer came around the corner, there was no hope for me and Goody.

Mothers worked over large kettles and milked goats. A few leaned on the shady side of the cabins to smoke their cigarettes. Even though they didn't look like the ladies at church, they whispered behind their hands and laughed just like the church ladies. They straighten when they saw me looking. I guess nobody liked to get caught gossiping.

Some kids took notice of me and Goody. They tugged at our feet, asking for a ride on Silver.

"This ain't no typical mule," Goody told the growing crowd of children. "This mule was found on the plains by the Lone Ranger himself."

"Ain't so," a boy said. He said this like he'd punched teeth out of boys who had tried to tease him.

I don't think Goody noticed, or if he had, he didn't let the boy scare him. He talked right to the boy. "You can see the scar on his shoulder here. That's where a buffalo gored him. Silver nearly bled to death before the Lone Ranger nursed him back to health, and Silver was plumb wild, lived with a herd of mules with no one to call master. From that day forward, Silver didn't let no one ride him but the Lone Ranger."

"You're lying!" another boy said.

A boy with a patch over one eye added, "The Lone Ranger don't ride no mule. He rides a white stallion."

I held onto Goody's belt because he didn't like being called a liar about anything, the Lone Ranger least of all. "We have to deliver the soap to the center," I whispered in his ear.

Goody clicked at the mule, and Silver bolted to a trot. The children ran with us for a little way, but it was too hot to keep that up for long. "What do they know?" Goody said over his shoulder.

The mule shuddered to a walk, and my teeth clanked together. I slid off. "Go on home. I'll deliver this ol' soap." I hefted the bag so he saw that I could manage it.

"Honest to goodness?"

"You go," I repeated. "I'll be just fine."

Goody slapped the mule's haunch and tugged hard at the reins. "Turn around, you miserable bag of hair and bones," Goody yelled. "It's time I got back to driving."

It was hot, hot, hot at the camp. The only trees were nothing but sticks with a few leaves. The dust from the road stuck to my legs. I was some kind of miserable. Instead of thinking about how thirsty I was, I tried to see the migrant camp like I'd never seen it before, which wasn't true because Lotti brought us to the camp plenty of times. Each time we came, there were more cabins. This had made Lotti grin like Christmas. Rows and rows of the tiny cabins lined the camp. The migrants kept chickens that pecked at the ground, all the while making that worried sound chickens make. It was a sad sound, and I wished I could tell them everything would be okay.

I swiped sweat from my forehead, but I wasn't careful enough, and the salt stung my eyes. Why I ever told Goody I would do this alone, I did not know. And I didn't know why Lotti's volunteers put the camp's community center so far from the road. The soap bag was getting heavier by the minute. I nibbled on the dried flakes of skin on my lips, all the while thinking of a chocolate soda from the drug store.

Trumpet vine covered a fence, just like the flowers of heaven. They glowed the brightest orange and reddest red. I slid my finger into a flower, feeling its velvety throat and the tickle of its innards. Seeing those flowers made heaven seem close, even though nothing else around me was anything like heaven. Not one bit.

Up a ways, a woman sat bent over in a rocking chair. She wore a calico bonnet and her black skirt covered her feet. She should have been sitting in the shade. There was a lumpy old bag, the kind you might expect a hobo to carry, and an empty glass on the ground beside her that needed filling with water. That was all.

"Would you like some water?" I asked her, hoping she would say yes, so I could get a drink for myself at the same time. "I'm headed for the community center. It wouldn't be any trouble."

She raised her head and leaned forward, twisting to the side, and wincing. Her eyes were milky marbles. I felt awful for making her work so hard to see me, but she nodded. I was right. She needed a drink.

That lady didn't talk much, and I surely understood. The heat sucked the talkative right out of me. I took her glass. "I'll be right back." I didn't want her to think I was stealing her glass, so I bent closer to her ear. "I'll be right back," I said again, louder. From the people at church, I'd learned old people had trouble hearing the first time.

She tried to stand up by leaning on skinny arms that shook under her weight as she pushed against the chair. Standing up was not a good idea for that lady, so I touched her shoulder. Her bones were hard and pointy under her dress. "You don't have to get up. I'll get the water for you. It's awful hot. I'll be right back."

I held my breath as she lowered herself down, wondering how I would pick her up if she tumbled into the dust. It took about a minute, but she finally sat down. The woman's hands were stained with coffee-colored spots and deep-purple bruises. They looked like scoops the way her fingers stacked on one another and her wrists turned inward. I'd never seen anything like it.

"Do your hands hurt?"

"Some." She pulled at the fabric of her cotton dress with her fingertips, bunching the skirt in her hands to lift the hem. Her feet were lumps of bone and flesh, half in and half out of her dirty slippers. "My feet hurt some, too."

"Can you walk?"

"It's all I can do to get to my bed at night. I stay here until my children return from the orchards."

I knew for a fact that the pickers worked late into the day. The thought of the lady sitting in the hot sun for all those hours without nothing to do or anyone to talk to sounded like the worst kind of punishment ever dreamed of.

"I'll be right back," I said, running for the community center. When I got back, I held the glass to her lips for a long drink.

"Thank you, kindly," she said.

"Can I touch your hands?" I could see she was surprised by my question but no more surprised than I was. There was nothing soft about her hands. They were hard and strange looking, but I couldn't help thinking that the warmth of my hands might be a comfort to her.

"Not many folks want to come near me."

I held my hands over hers. "Tell me if I hurt you." Tears slid over the hills and valleys of her cheeks. I pulled back. I'd gone and hurt her already. "I'm so sorry."

"No. No. You go on, now. I'm just fine."

Under my hands, her skin slid over her bones. I feared I might tear her thin skin with my touch. My palms were hot with sweat. I hoped she didn't mind. She sighed, and it was a sigh of comfort, so I let the weight of my hands settle on her. My palms grew warmer and warmer, and her fingers wiggled under mine. Sure I was hurting her, I pulled away.

"No, child. Please. The warmth takes the pain away."

"It does?" My heart raced. "My aunt will wonder where I am."

"Just a little longer, child. Just a little while longer, if you please."

It was the pleading in her voice that made my eyes burn with tears. Finally, she pulled her hands from under mine. She wiggled her fingers, opening and closing them, stretching them out like she was saying she was ten years old, but no one would ever believe that. Somehow her hands looked a whole lot better.

"Are you an angel?" she asked.

"No." I pulled away, but as quick as lightning, she clamped her bony fingers around mine. I pulled but couldn't free myself. "Please, let me go."

"Are you an angel?" she asked again, only this time I saw she was serious.

"No, ma'am. I'm just a girl." I remembered what Lucy had told me and buttoned my lip.

She loosened her grip. "I didn't mean to scare you." She watched her hands open and close, first with her palms down and then with her palms up. Her fingers were rod straight and not one bit lumpy. And the knot of bone at her wrist was back where it belonged.

She looked to her feet again, and with great effort, lifted them one by one out of her slippers.

"Oh," I said, and right away I felt bad about opening my big mouth. It wasn't her fault she had ugly feet. But she didn't frown at me or anything.

I sneaked another peek at her feet. They were a wonder. The big toe hid under her little ones, the ones that go to the market for roast beef and wee, wee, wee all the way home. Her toenails were yellow and thick as quarters. Strangest of all, it looked like a new toe was trying to grow where her big toe should have been.

"Would it be any trouble for you to touch my feet?" she asked, and the shake in her voice made my chest ache.

I looked at her feet again. Cracks as deep as buckets collected dirt around the edges.

"I can barely stand to look at them myself," she said. Then she looked at me. "I sure would like to help my daughter-in-law with the young ones."

I was all kinds of confused right then. This had never happened before. I wanted to run back to the ranch. Lucy would know what to do.

The lady dropped her skirt over her feet. "I understand. I completely understand, child."

"It's not your feet," I blurted. "I blistered a girl's back, although I didn't mean to, and I got into plenty of trouble. And I made a lady real mad when I said the wrong thing. If I touch your feet and something happens—I'm not one bit sure anything will happen— but if it does, I might get in deep trouble."

"His mercy doesn't run dry. It won't hurt to ask, will it?" she said.

That stopped me short. "Have you been to heaven?" I asked, remembering the river that ran on the other side of Mama's garden wall.

"Why no, I ain't gone over, if that's what you mean."

"But you know about mercy?"

"I learned that from the Good Book. Everybody knows that."

Everybody did not know that, but I didn't see any sense in arguing with the lady, so I knelt in the hot dirt and laid my hands as softly as I could on her feet. I waited for the heat to come into my hands again. I waited to feel her bones straightening under my touch, like they did with her hands. I waited for her to wiggle her toes. Nothing happened. I wrapped my fingers around her feet and held my breath against the stink. Inside, I was praying harder than I'd ever prayed before.

Maybe I should have prayed out loud like the preacher on the radio. Then again, I didn't want to scare the lady. I just wanted Jesus to heal her. Instead, I quoted the first mercy verse that popped into my head. "For I desired mercy, and not sacrifice; and the knowledge of God more than burnt offerings." I didn't say the reference. I couldn't remember it. My hands warmed against the woman's skin, but it was hard to tell if my hands were warm because of the heat or because God was doing something wonderful for her feet, too.

"I don't feel anything," she said.

It was the heat.

"Maybe God is done with me today." Her voice spilled from her like water.

"Do my hands feel hot to you?"

She sighed a little groan. "No, nothing. Not like before. Come on off the ground, child. I won't be greedy with the Lord's goodness. He has done a wondrous thing by giving my hands back. It's more than an old woman could dream about, and here it has happened to me."

The sweat from my hands had muddied her feet. I couldn't leave her like that. I ran to the community center for more water. I told the woman there that I needed a bucket big enough for feet. It took some convincing, but they handed over a roasting pan and a bar of the soap I'd brought with me from Lotti. I lost half the water with it sloshing out on the road. Some children followed me back to the lady's cabin and stood a ways back.

The woman was right where I'd left her, but she was knitting so fast her needles clicked. She looked up. "I thought I'd forgotten how. It come back to me like I done it yesterday. The Lord is good. The Lord is very, very good."

I set the pan in front of her feet. There was barely enough water left to cover her toes. The children murmured mean words about her feet as if the lady couldn't hear. "Don't you have something better to do?" I said over my shoulder to them. "This isn't a picture show."

The children shuffled, looked at their feet.

The lady said to them, "You know where the candy is. One to a customer."

While the children rummaged for candy inside her cabin, I washed the lady's feet. "I'm sorry the water is cold."

"Don't worry, child. I thank you for all your kindness…and the kindness of the Lord."

"I have just the thing." I rubbed that soap between my hands until the suds were as thick as cream, just the way Lucy did for me. When I was done, her feet smelled like lavender. "I don't have a towel."

"Use this." The lady pulled her stitches off the knitting needles and handed me a square of knitting smaller than a washcloth.

I dried her feet and helped her back into her slippers.

"What's your name, child?"

"Mercy."

"If that don't beat all. I've never heard a child called by that name. It fits you perfect, don't it? Before we leave Palisade, I'll knit you a scarf and some mittens. It won't always be this hot. Winter will come, and you'll be in want of some wool to keep you warm."

I didn't feel right accepting a gift from the lady. "You don't have to do that."

"No, I don't reckon I do, but I'm going to do it. I got me a sweater I don't wear no more. The yarn still holds plenty of warmth. I hope you like blue."

She covered her heart with her hands and closed her eyes. Her bottom lip trembled. "You know what? The Lord told me something wondrous was going to happen. He told my soul, not my ears, because I thought to ask my son to bring that old sweater even though it's terrible hot here. Claude looked at me like I'd asked him to bring my snowshoes to Colorado. He's a good boy. He didn't say nothing. He found a place for that sweater in this old bag." She covered her mouth with her hands, and her eyes opened wide. "Claude gone and put that sweater in my old knitting bag. I never give that bag a bit of notice since I hadn't used those needles in so long. The Lord whispered to his soul too, don't you see? And now I intend to make you a gift." She clapped her hands. She was smiling now. "I can help my daughter-in-law put up the peaches. Knitting? Canning? Why, there's lots of things I can do with these old hands. Oh, the Lord has made me glad this day."

Until I figured out what had just happened, I made up my mind to keep this whole business to myself.

Lucy

Corky set the sawhorses down and adjusted his hat. "Whenever you ladies are ready, I'll be in the barn."

Ada slapped her gloves against her thigh, a sure sign she wanted nothing to do with arranging a lunch table for the Germans.

Lotti dried her hands on her apron for the umpteenth time. "We want our guests to be comfortable. The shade is deepest under the cottonwoods at noon, but the barn blocks the breeze." Lotti turned toward the apricot tree. "It's always cooler here. Or we could set the table on the porch. What do you think, Ada?"

Ada tugged on her gloves. "Do what you want." She walked into the orchard with long, confident strides. How much of that was bravado?

Inside, Lotti and I gathered dinnerware, culling out chipped plates. Lotti wondered if we shouldn't use the china, the set her mother had packed in flour for the trip from Chicago. Finally, she put the china back in the hutch. "Men don't notice things like that. Everyday dishes are good enough." With a fistful of forks in one hand and knives in the other, Lotti seemed to study the cobwebs in the corner before turning her gaze on me. "People want kindness more than breath or water. And we shall give these men kindness, as much as their stomachs will hold. If I'm wrong, and these fellas don't work their fingers to the bone, Ada will never forgive me this extravagance."

I failed to stifle a yawn. I'd barely slept two hours before Ada woke me.

Lotti filled a shoebox with the forks and knives. "I heard the screen slam about one in the morning."

I added the spoons to the box. "I'm sorry. I didn't mean to wake you."

"I wasn't asleep. I never sleep well during harvest. I'm too excited. And this year, with Gil gone, well, it's just us girls...and a dozen German soldiers, Corky and Kansas Johnny, and the sergeant and the corporal. That's all. Nothing special." She counted out eighteen napkins. "Ada told you, didn't she, that the children will be eating in the house, away from the Germans?"

Yes, she'd told me, and this one time I had to agree with her. "It's a good idea."

Lotti sighed, seemingly pleased to change the subject. "How was the packing shed? There's no harder work or greater fun. Every woman in this valley has taken her turn in the shed. The work creates a special bond. This makes you one of us, Lucy."

"I can only go back if I keep up with the cooking."

"You can do it," she said with more confidence than I shared. "Next year, things won't be so complicated. The world will be back to normal, I just know it. Perhaps your Pete will find his way to Palisade for a visit. Wouldn't that be nice?"

Picturing Pete in the orchard, his hair disheveled by the breeze and his face rosy from the rising sun—I liked that idea very much.

Lotti squeezed my waist. "It is a lovely thought, and you must keep it close to your heart." She rose on tiptoe to kiss my cheek. "For now, you better get going. The chickens need plucking. Get them cut up and into the buttermilk as soon as possible. And don't be stingy with the paprika. The recipe says a teaspoon but add three or four. It flavors the chicken up real nice. If I get a spare minute, I'll pop in to help."

Corky stood with his nose to the screen. "Have you ladies decided where you want that table?"

Lotti answered him, "Under the apricot tree. Lots of nice things have happened there. Today won't be any different."

Ada and Lotti sat with the sergeant and the corporal at one end of the table. As it turned out, we need not have bothered rousting out all those plates. Corky and Kansas Johnny preferred the company of Bessie to the Germans.

With their hair slicked back from a quick wash at the pump, the Germans buttoned their shirts to their necks. From peach fuzz and dust, their dark blue work clothes looked like chalkboards at the end of a school day. The men milled around the table, talking in hushed voices, uncertain of where to sit, all the while standing as straight as fence posts. They were a proud lot.

The sergeant stood to reach for the platter of chicken and asked Ada for the bread and beans. From the look on her face, I expected her to slap his hand. "Suit yourself, fellas," he said to the reluctant Germans, "but I haven't had nothing to eat since breakfast. You got twenty minutes to eat your fill before you're back in the trees."

I didn't know how, but the Germans got his meaning and pulled out chairs to stand with hands clasped behind their backs. With only a nod, two prisoners exchanged seats before the whole group sat as one. Corky's table of planks and sawhorses looked elegant covered by Lotti's linen tablecloth and napkins. Washing and pressing the linens fell to me, of course.

The Germans lowered their heads. A man with soft eyes and the start of a bald spot on the top of his head said the prayer. Lotti nudged the sergeant and we joined the Germans in lowering our heads. It took me back some to think of the Germans as churchgoing men. I figured them for murderers and thieves—who else would follow Hitler into battle?

"Amen," the man said.

The Germans studied the food, smiled tightly while they opened their napkins onto their laps. Before any of them touched the food, the prisoner with the blue eyes and quick smile offered the platter of chicken to Lotti. "*Darf ich?*"

Lotti startled at his attention. "Thank you," she said, taking the platter. "You're very...kind. Thank you."

The sergeant looked up from his plate, his lips shiny with grease. "It's good. The chicken is real good." All eyes were on him. "What?"

"Here's your napkin, sergeant," Ada said, handing it to him. "Continue eating. There's a lot of work to do."

"You ain't kiddin'." He sopped butter from the potatoes with his roll and popped the whole thing into his mouth. Had he cared at all that we'd been hoarding flour and yeast for months? From the strain of the buttons over his belly, I doubted Sergeant

Salvatore gave much thought to anything but his stomach.

Now that everyone was eating, I returned to the kitchen to slice the peach pies. By the time I returned to the table with a pitcher of water, the only sounds were cutlery against plates. You could bring enemies to the table. Evidently, you couldn't make them talk.

I poured water, starting with the sergeant and corporal because I was still nervous being that close to the Germans. Ada waved me off, so I filled Lotti's glass. I reached for the first German's glass and filled it. I'd taken note of him the minute he'd stepped off the truck. What his face lacked in width, it more than made up for in length. If he'd attended Palisade High School, his nickname would have been Horse-Face. I hoped the children of Germany were much nicer than I.

I set the glass of water down as close to the table's edge as I dared without drawing Ada's ire. My plan was to be invisible to the Germans. The stories I'd heard, whispered because we prayed they weren't true, were horrific. If they were true, monsters sat around the table, eating our chicken, heaping butter onto potatoes.

"*Die Dankebarkeit,*" the horse-faced man said.

Bitte, I thought but said, "You're welcome."

I chided myself to be more careful. I didn't want anyone knowing I understood German.

The sergeant spoke with a mouthful of chicken. "You made this chicken, sister? How old are you? My sister only knows how to open a can, and then she burns the hash. Have you ever been to Brooklyn? There's lots of guys in Brooklyn who would love this chicken, if you know what I mean."

Ada leaned over her plate. She bored a hole into the sergeant with her gaze. "She is going to college, not Brooklyn—definitely not Brooklyn." I vowed to thank Ada for deflecting the sergeant's attention. He'd been watching me since he'd arrived as he now looked at the platter of fried chicken. The hunger in his gaze made me queasy. If possible, I would avoid that man.

I scanned the yard for Goody and Mercy. It was reflex. An alarm sounded in my head at intervals throughout any given day, warning me to locate them. I'd set aside two chicken legs and substituted sliced peaches for green beans on their plates. Still, they were nowhere in sight.

I asked Ada if she'd seen the twins. Several of the prisoners looked up. Did they hear the panic in my voice without understanding the words?

"I haven't seen them," she said.

I hadn't seen them since breakfast either. Goody's stomach told better time than any watch. He should have been home with Mercy twenty minutes ago.

Lotti swallowed down a mouthful of roll. "Oh dear, I don't know where my head is. I sent them on an errand to the migrant camp. They've run out of soap at the community center. The twins are delivering a fresh supply." She frowned. "They should be back. Goody wasn't too happy when I called him away from the hoopie."

Sending Goody on an errand was like sending Odysseus on an excursion. The twins could have been halfway to China by then. I was untying my apron to start a search when the handsome German—I'd started calling him *Hans* in my mind—spoke to the man who had prayed. He tilted his head toward me. "She looks like the first girl I took for a walk in the forest, my first girlfriend but only until her father found out." He said this, of course, in German. His eyes turned on me. His smile was broad and hungry. Heat flared between my shoulder blades and swarmed my face.

"*Na, du hast mich verstanden?*" he said, eyebrows raised. I understood what he'd said, all right. I worked at retying my apron strings, willing my hands to stop trembling.

There was a clatter of service and plates. All conversation stopped. Every eye turned to me. Ada stood, shaking a finger at the sergeant. "I won't have the prisoners speaking to Lucy. Tell them! Tell them there are rules to follow. This is not a party. Tell them."

The sergeant made a sandwich of butter and two rolls. "I would love to, but I don't know a word of German, except them which can't be said in front of ladies."

Hans spoke to me. "You can tell that pig for me—"

The praying prisoner bolted to standing. He spoke to me in German. "We want to do a good job for your family. You are good people, this is clear. You are doing your best to make our lives in your country more bearable. The meal is simply wonderful—and the shade of this tree—your kindness overwhelms us. If we understood what they expected from us…we are only too happy to do it. Would you consider translating for us?"

These men missed nothing. Of course they wouldn't. Their very survival relied on reading the intent of people—enemies and friends—and they'd seen how I'd reacted to Hans' flirting. They knew I understood every word he'd said. *Now what?* I stared at him dumbly.

The sergeant pointed with a drumstick and asked me, "Hey, do you know what that guy's saying?"

I'd hidden my German language skills from my own mother. Hiding them from Ada and the United States Army wasn't a problem. I ignored the sergeant and the praying man, and returned to filling water glasses. Sweat loosened my grip on the handle. I steadied my hands by holding the pitcher to my belly. Its coolness settled my stomach.

"Gerland is right. We're tired of that pig shouting at us." The horse-faced prisoner nodded toward the sergeant.

"Lucy!" Ada called my name like an indictment.

The praying man sat down. "I'm sorry. I've made your mother angry."

I didn't think. I didn't consider the consequences. I simply shouted, *"Sie ist nicht meine Mutter!"* and dropped the pitcher to the ground.

Glasses thudded to the table. Someone cleared his throat. The heat settled on my shoulders. I dared not lift my eyes. The praying man—Gerland?—said, "I only thought...You look so much alike... Please pardon my assumption."

I looked to Ada whose face was a map of consternation. Why didn't she say something? Why didn't she send the Germans back to the orchard? Instead, Lotti rose. "Did your parents teach you to speak German, Lucy?"

There was no sense hiding the truth any longer. "Papa taught me."

"Do you speak with some fluency?"

"There are words I don't know, but yes, I understood everything the man said."

I could not read Ada's expression. She was either extremely angry or very disappointed. And most surprising to me, I preferred her anger to her disappointment. "This is unexpected," she said, simply, tightly.

"It's wonderful!" Lotti rushed around the table to me. I never got used to how quickly she moved or how her skinny arms squeezed the breath out of me. She picked up the pitcher. I was relieved to see it hadn't broken. "You must forget about your cooking duties."

"Wha—?" Ada started.

Lotti raised her hand like a crossing guard to stop Ada. "I prayed for someone to help us talk to the pickers, and here she is, our very own Lucy." She cradled my face in her hands, and still I felt Ada's eyes on me. "You aren't to be concerned about the twins either. I'll round up those two scallywags. Work with Ada and the sergeant. Talk to the pickers for us, and we'll get through this harvest just fine." Lotti walked toward the house, motioning me to follow. "Don't just stand there. Get these men their pie. They've surely earned it."

Ada pulled me away from the table, ushering me toward the house by the elbow, speaking into my ear. "This complicates as much as it helps. Call the packing shed supervisor. You won't be available for the rest of the season." I started to protest, but Ada shot me a look that would have curdled cream. "We have sheltered you. Fed you. Clothed you. And you chose to keep this knowledge to yourself."

"If you want us to leave, I must work at the packing shed."

"This isn't about leaving or staying. I want you to be truthful."

"I never lied to you."

"There are sins of omission, Lucy."

"And there are sins of pride."

Within steps of the house, she released my elbow, and I moved to put some distance between us, but she managed to catch up to me and grasp both of my hands. Her breath warmed my face. "Sin is always with us, but the peaches must be harvested now. We will talk of sin when the last peach has been hauled to the packing shed. Right now, nothing matters but the peaches. You will do what you must do, and I will do what I must do. Is this agreeable?"

Thunderous laughter came from the table. I followed the gaze of the men to Goody and Silver. Goody led the mule inch by inch up the lane. The mule stopped to nibble grass with every step. "You stupid ol' mule!" he said, pulling on the reins. "You're keeping me from the hoopie. You sure ain't no Silver!"

The Germans laughed freer, nudging one another as if anyone could possibly miss Goody's performance. They didn't need a translator for the scene before them. Were they thinking of their brothers? Their sons? Cousins?

"Where's Mercy?" I asked Goody when he came close enough to hear me.

He looked at me through his lashes, a sure sign he knew he was in trouble.

"You left her at the camp?" I said, fighting down a bubble of panic.

"It was her idea. She wanted to deliver the soap herself. You know how she can be. She don't listen to me."

Ada was at my side. "Lotti will get her. She's all right. You mustn't worry."

We had lived at the ranch with Lotti and Ada for most of a year, and still I struggled to share the responsibility of the twins with those two capable women. "Send Mercy to find me when she gets home," I said.

I pulled at my apron string but stopped when I saw the now-empty table that needed clearing, and the dishes to be washed, and remembered the next day's bread to be baked. I retied my apron and met Ada's gaze. "We can't lose them. The twins. We can't lose the twins."

"We won't, I promise."

And I believed her.

Sergeant Salvatore assembled the Germans in two rows on the lawn between the house and the barn. Not one tree grew there. Why Ada had chosen a place devoid of shade, I never knew. There were times when I believed Ada thought of ways to punish me, like when she played the piano at night. This was only conjecture but one that I believed wholeheartedly, especially with sweat running down my face.

Even though the men had been picking peaches for a day and a half, I translated Ada's instructions on how to determine a peach's readiness to be picked and how to use the picking sack as she strapped the canvas sack onto me. "Tell them to be careful how they dump the peaches into the baskets. They mustn't waste time, but bruised peaches have no place in the market. And make sure the sack is cinched up before they start picking peaches again. I won't tolerate dillydallying in the orchard. Work fast. Time is our enemy." She waited for me to translate. When I turned to her for more instruction, I noticed she was biting her lip. This meant Ada was about to say something difficult. I hoped she wouldn't undo all the goodwill that our lunch had created. "We have lost time to make up. I hope you will help us. This war has been hard. Perhaps we can, together, make the most of a difficult situation. You are being paid eighty cents a day."

I translated Ada's words.

"Play money, only good in the canteen," one of the men called out.

Ada looked to me for a translation before she answered, "Exactly my point. If you pick more than seventy bushels a day, I will pay you five cents—in U.S. currency—for each and every bushel you pick that day."

The horse-faced man smiled. "So, if we pick, say seventy-one bushels, you would pay us $3.55 beyond our eighty cents?"

"Yes. *Ja.*"

The men came to attention like Tonto when he heard a train's whistle in the distance. These men were still providers for their families, no matter that their families lived an ocean and half a continent away in Germany. The prisoners wiped the sweat from their hands, unbuttoned their shirts, and reached for the picking bags.

I walked from tree to tree with Ada and the sergeant, watching the men lift and twist the peaches from the tree, just as I'd told them. The men picked faster than they had before lunch. Ada offered words of encouragement to the horse-faced man.

"You have improved the most," she said. "You'll end up being my best picker after all."

The man struggled to stifle a grin. "You are a good teacher."

"You could pick faster."

"You just told him he improved the most," I said to Ada.

"He's still as slow as a sloth. Tell him."

"Ada," I pleaded.

"Tell him, now."

I spoke to the man in German. First, I couldn't be calling him Horse-Face anymore. "What is your name?"

"Steinhaus."

"My aunt says as you gain confidence, you will pick even faster."

He smiled. Nodded. "*Danke.*"

Ada returned to her tallying, especially important now that she was paying according to bushels picked. While she agreed I should continue instructing the pickers with only Sergeant Salvatore to watch over me, she insisted that he prove his rifle and revolver were loaded.

Meanwhile, Goody fulfilled his duties with only the corporal as an occasional rider. He took his responsibility of driving the peaches to the packing shed more seriously than I could have imagined. He never stalled the truck once. He eased the hoopie over every bump to prevent bruising the peaches. Not one complaint found its way back to the ranch. I wished Papa could have seen him.

But then, the war forced all of us to grow up faster. Until now, Goody had managed to maintain his childhood in the midst of deprivations and the constant reminders of loss around us. Just that week, a boy from a neighboring town had been written up in the paper as the latest casualty of the war. I hid the paper from the twins, but Goody brought the news home from his friend, Auggie. He retold the story casually, like a farmer talking about the weather. That night, however, he'd cried in his sleep.

The peach trees shimmied with the activity of the pickers, their slender leaves reflecting the glint of sun. The Germans worked in pairs, one on each side of a tree, plucking the peaches easily.

They spoke of their families with voices so clogged with longing that I could barely stand listening. One man, Markus, told his picking partner that his daughter's birthday was in just one week. She would be nine. He wanted to send her a letter, to assure her that he was coming home to her, but he hadn't heard from his wife or children in months. Letters from his relatives didn't tell him anything about his family's well-being.

"You mustn't give up hope, friend. They will be waiting for you just where you left them. It's the Brits and the Yanks. They're stopping the mail. They want to drive us crazy. They want us to give up. They want to break us."

"That's easy for you to say," Markus replied. "You hear from your wife."

"They can't stop all of the letters. If they did, they would be in violation of the Geneva Convention. No, just some of the letters are stopped. You mustn't give up hope."

I looked at Sergeant Salvatore. His face shone with grease. His table manners had made Goody look like a prince. Would he withhold letters from someone's family to win an advantage? The sergeant picked something from his teeth with his pinkie, sucked, and swallowed. I looked toward the trees and the prisoners, mostly hidden within the leaves, not wanting to believe my country would wrench families apart, even though Germany had drawn plenty of families apart with their ambitions.

Sergeant Salvatore held out his canteen. "You better take a drink. You look hot."

Who knew what floated inside that canteen? "We're almost done. I'll get a drink from the house. You better keep your water."

We came across the last pair of workers just as Gerland backed down the ladder with a bulging sack of peaches. "*Hallo*," he said to me, clicking his heels and bowing curtly over his picking sack.

"*Hallo*," I said, surprised by the journey I'd taken from the beginning of the row to the end. In that short walk, the Germans changed from monsters into men with families, struggling against the hopelessness of their situation, yet helping us in return for kindness. And they were terribly far from home, if home existed for them at all. Gerland deposited his peaches into a basket, overfilling it. I helped him move some of the peaches into another basket. The peaches were the size of softballs and deeply blushed from the sun. He had a good eye. Ada would be pleased. He hurried back to the tree, repositioned the ladder, and climbed into the green fringe of leaves.

Sergeant Salvatore called out to the corporal. They sauntered off toward the shade of the apricot tree, sipping on their canteens and laughing. Ada loaded full bushel baskets onto the hoopie as Goody eased the truck through the trees. I should have been nervous about being left with the Germans, but I wasn't. In fact, I enjoyed listening to their talk. The cadence of their words reminded me of Papa.

Gerland bantered with the man who had flirted with me. They picked from the same tree. "That's sixty-three bushels to your fifty-nine, Reinhardt. Perhaps you can keep your insults to yourself for one day."

"You'll still be an old man at the end of the day."

"Watch your language. The *fraulein* is listening in. In fact, you should apologize for getting her in trouble."

Reinhardt climbed down the ladder, smiled that smile of his.

I stepped back. "An apology isn't necessary. I get in trouble with Ada even in my sleep."

He said, "I regret that I caused you discomfort, but you should be proud to speak the language of the homeland. It is a language of strength and history. Your father taught you correctly. It is a foolish thing to be ashamed of who you are."

"I'm not German. My father was born there—"

His mouth curved into a smirk. "On a farm somewhere?"

"His father was a school principal in Meisenheim."

"And he left? To come where life is so easy? It is better for us all that the weaklings left the fatherland."

Gerland descended his ladder, his picking sack again full of peaches. "That will be enough, Reinhardt. How many times do you think this girl will forgive you in one day?"

Reinhardt's smile told me he had been forgiven many, many times by just as many girls. "You do look like one of the girls—"

"Enough!" Gerland shouted. "We have a lot of work to do, if we're to make up time."

"Can you be bought so easily, Gerland? Will a plump chicken and a few dollars buy loyalty from you?" Reinhardt flexed his hands, like I'd seen boys do before a fight.

I turned to the sergeant, hoping he'd noticed the growing tension. Not hardly. The sergeant sat on the bed of the hoopie, parked several rows over, eating a peach, and from the juice staining the front of his shirt, not the first of the day. Beside him, Goody struggled to hold the sergeant's rifle to his shoulder. If the sergeant hadn't put out his hand, a silent command for the rifle to be returned, I would have—what?—scolded the sergeant? I believe I would have.

Reinhardt nearly spat in Gerland's face. "The war is not over. The homeland stands in the balance. You better decide to whom you owe your allegiance."

"I have loved the homeland since I took my first breath. If you are looking for traitors, you'll have to look elsewhere." Gerland held Reinhardt with his glare.

"Do they shoot traitors in your country?" I asked, hoping to distract the men.

"On the spot," Reinhardt said, pressing his chest closer to Gerland.

"You will wish you had been shot when my aunt sees you dawdling."

Reinhardt turned to me and his gaze was a waterfall cascading down the length of me. He smiled. "And what incentive can you offer me, fraulein? It has been a long time since—"

Gerland dropped his picking sack.

I smiled back at Reinhardt, willing my eyes to catch the glint of sunlight through the trees. "I can see that you are served the fattest slice of pie tomorrow."

His jaw relaxed. "That will do for now." He moved his ladder to another tree where his friends greeted him warmly.

Gerland and I watched him leave. "Just because we fought side by side does not make us brothers in all things," he said in a low voice. "Reinhardt is a proud boy. He's young. It's killing him to be away from the action. Old men like me, we don't mind so much working in the fields. Battlefields have lost their allure. Reinhardt is from Berlin. He's been in the middle of the movement since he was very young. You understand what it means to want change to happen right now?"

I understood all right. I nodded.

"Not all Germans are the same," he said, "just as all Americans are not the same. There is good and evil on both sides."

"Terrible things are said about what's going on over there. It's hard to believe. The Jews…"

Gerland snapped the picking sack in place. "We are hearing these things, too."

"Just now? You didn't know?"

"We chose not to know many things for the sake of our families and our own necks. Now that these things are coming out in the open… I suppose it is the light that makes the difference. The darkness hates the light."

I didn't memorize Scripture verses like Mercy, but I'd heard this phrase many times. "You read the Bible?"

"That surprises you? We are fathers, sons, brothers, uncles, as well as believers, skeptics, agnostics, and atheists."

"Lucy!" Ada called.

Not until that moment did I question why the Germans had tumbled us into war. I pictured them as the posters portrayed them—muscled, brusque men with a perpetual scowl. I'd given no thought to families, occupations, or faith. These things belonged to America. They were our heritage. He'd caught me flat-footed. I wanted very much to understand, and Gerland was the man to tell me.

"Lucy, didn't you hear me? I need you." Ada looked to

Gerland. "Tell him to get back to work."

Gerland climbed the ladder quickly.

Ada led me to stand in front of two Germans. They had shed the dark blue shirts to work in white undershirts stained with circles of peach juice. Scattered on the ground, peaches lay flattened from the impact on their bodies. The men shuffled from foot to foot as if they'd been caught in a schoolyard prank. I struggled not to smile at the irony. Only weeks earlier they had been shooting to kill.

Ada said, "Tell them I won't have peaches ruined in play."

In German, I said, "The work is boring. You need to break the monotony."

"Tell them they are wasting precious time and each peach thrown takes food out of our mouths."

I said, "To stay out of trouble with my aunt, throw the peaches that have already fallen to the ground and only when she isn't looking. And keep your voices down."

One of the soldiers winked at me.

"What did you say to them?" Ada asked.

"They seem too young to be soldiers, don't you think?"

"These men are killers. In an orchard, on a sunny day, they may look like boys, but they are battle-hardened men. They are certainly not boys."

I told the Germans, "You better forget about throwing peaches."

Ada

April 19, 1994

Dear Lucy,

I've wandered away from a dull-as-dirt bingo game. If they come looking for me, I'll tell them exactly what I think of their foolish games and their trinket prizes. Just because we're old, doesn't mean we've developed a passion for inane games. Do send me a new crossword puzzle book, a really hard one like the New York Times, won't you? Go ahead and send the Sunday puzzles. Perhaps, what I really need is a good bit of humbling.

You're right as rain about the Germans. I absolutely hated that Lotti had registered for them to pick our peaches. I felt like a traitor. I do feel badly about not admitting later to Lotti how wise her decision had been. The migrants that did come that year came to work, no doubt about it, but they were as frayed as work shirts, older than usual, quite desperate looking. The Germans, for all their warmongering, had remained strong.

Up to that summer, the same migrant workers came to the ranch year after year. They picked and they left. A few became friends, the kind who exchanged Christmas cards. I hadn't known, or taken the time to know, who they really were or what they needed.

All that changed with Mercy in residence.

I remember my feet burning from all the walking back and forth through the trees, and up to the house, and out to the barn for more baskets. We had just finished cleaning the supper dishes, as I recall. There weren't many. Goody had suggested tomato sandwiches on toast, which I served on napkins. And that suited me fine.

197

I'd just sat in front of the fan in the kitchen to remove my shoes. I believe you and Mercy had already taken your baths and gone to bed. Before I allowed myself those luxuries, I called the broker to see if the price for peaches had remained strong. Goody, who should have been in bed as well, ran into the house as if a bear was chasing him. I told him to go back out and to come in like a gentleman, and I would not let him say a word until he did just as I'd asked. That rankled him good. He didn't do much better on the second try.

Finally, he tugged at my sleeve until I gave him my full attention. His words rained like pebbles. He insisted that a hundred people stood out by the fence, wanting to see Mercy. I expected to arrive at the door, only to hear him explain we were about to be bushwhacked by a hoard of Indians instead. His imagination didn't have an off switch, as I remember. (Is there any wonder why he is such a gifted storyteller? I'm on a waiting list at the library for his new book, although I think he should send me a signed copy. Tell him for me, won't you? I know he's very busy these days.)

It was just as Goody had said, nearly a hundred people stood at the road. They were absolutely silent. How they stood there after working all day in the orchards, I will never know. There were men, women, and children, infants as well as lanky teenagers.

I looked to the west, saw that the sun had slid behind the plateaus, and a sliver of moon dipped close to the horizon in a chambray sky. Soon the moon would be gone. I pushed open the screen and walked to the edge of the porch. Goody meant to pass by me and go to those people. I stopped him, of course.

I called out to the people to ask what they wanted. It was a wonder I wasn't afraid, or if I was, I've forgotten that part of the story. It's the faces, as unblinking as corpses, that I remember. Even the smallest children studied the house with solemn, hopeful eyes.

One man, hat in hands, stepped forward a few paces. In the fading light, I saw only that he stooped under some ominous weight. I pulled Goody to my side. At first, I couldn't follow what the man was saying. A woman had been healed? Mercy? Rheumatism? None of what he said made sense. Finally, I sorted out that he was the healed woman's son. At last, I understood that he believed Mercy had healed the woman's hands and feet.

That snapped me out of my stupor and made me steaming mad. I wish I could say it was all he'd said about Mercy, but my feet were killing me. I had it in my mind to get the Epsom salts out the minute I shooed those folks away, but they had brought a woman with a goiter and a baby with a weak heart for Mercy to touch. To tell you the truth, every last one of them had the look of forlornness about them. As the spokesman, he insisted they only wanted to see the goodness of the Lord.

It became clear to me they meant to milk their blessings out of Mercy. I stalled the best I could with all sorts of questions I don't now recall. I only remember a growing apprehension. The spokesman pulled a woman to stand at his side. If Methuselah had a wife, there she was. She held up her hands, turned them around for me to inspect. Then the man stooped to untie the old woman's shoes. I most certainly did not want to look at her feet. I'm not the squeamish type, but I didn't see any good coming from his actions. He persisted despite my protests, and the crowd eased closer to the house. This panicked me some. You know I don't like being painted into a corner, and I will play the fool to get out. Goody, on the other hand, offered the woman a chair on the porch. You would have been proud of his manners. That boy, I never knew what to expect next.

I found myself pleading with the man, something I did not appreciate, but he left me no recourse. I explained that Mercy was only a little girl, not a sideshow miracle maker. There had to be some misunderstanding. Mercy did not heal people. All the while, I recalled what had happened with Melba and the blistered handprint on Thelma's little girl, Veronica. Questions. I had many, many questions.

The old woman leaned on her son as he slipped the shoe off her foot and tugged on her stocking. I threatened to call the sheriff. Goody pleaded to see the woman's feet. I clamped my hand over his mouth. He promptly pulled it away and turned on the porch light. By then, we were both looking down at the old woman's feet. She wiggled her toes, her toenails glistened an exuberant red. She said her daughter-in-law had painted them. I'll never forget what that old woman said. "I guess the Lord won't mind if I show off His handiwork."

I backed with Goody toward the house. I fully expected the crowd to follow us, but only the son stepped forward. That man was poor, but this I remember: He possessed the dignity of a prince. He understood my anxiety completely, said he would do anything to protect his own daughters just like I was trying to protect mine.

Lord help me, I didn't correct the man. And I'll admit to you now that a spark of joy danced in my chest over the thought of someone, anyone, believing I was a mother, even if he was a total stranger and of questionable sanity (as I thought then). The crowd started to disperse when they saw I had no intention of calling Mercy out of the house.

Just when I thought the strangeness of the evening was behind me, a woman rushed forward, a baby wrapped in a pink blanket in her arms. She peeled back the blanket to show the child's face. I'm sure I gasped. In the coming dark, the baby's eyes were wells of blackness. This was the baby with the damaged heart. The doctors claimed powerlessness. (I don't know how you worked on the pediatric ward for all those years. That one child still haunts me and you nursed thousands!)

I almost capitulated. Did you know that? I wish I'd asked the baby's name. You see, don't you, why I didn't come for Mercy? I had no way of knowing what would happen. Those people could have trampled her.

I told that mother she had to leave or I would call the sheriff immediately. I sent Goody into the house to ring him up. Goody was pleased by the responsibility I'd bestowed on him.

The crowd melted away into the deeper hues of the night. I interrupted Goody's call to Sheriff Berg, told him myself what had happened, that the people were desperate but well-intentioned. I wished him and Elizabeth a good night. And then, I swore Goody to secrecy. No one in the house, especially not Mercy, was to know what had happened. That boy talked me into a pair of new cowboy boots in exchange for his silence. He didn't know I'd already bought a pair as payment for driving the hoopie. They're the ones he got bronzed, the ones he uses for bookends in his office.

I found you, Mercy, and Mother Heller fast asleep. I wept on my pillow that night out of confusion, guilt, exhaustion, and relief. Had I known how very wrong I'd been about Mercy and God's work, that would have been a very different night. I do hope I've learned something of His goodness since then.

Love,
Ada

Lucy

What was worse, a dream that played with reality in a maddening way or a dream that mirrored a horrible reality too closely? This was the question I kept asking myself.

I wadded my pillow into a tight ball as I stared into the blackness, waiting for the soft edges of the dresser, the bed post, and the window to emerge from the murkiness of night. I wanted to push away the dreams' images, but like the river's current, they pulled at me.

In the dream, I'd held Mercy's face just above the water. The current pressed my back into the log that held us in place. Mercy's legs drooped from my waist. I screamed in her ear to hold on, but her body softened and grew heavier.

Men on the shore, their sleeves rolled above their elbows, worked at tying a rope to a stout oak. Once the rope's ends were tugged tight, the men slapped each other's backs. I willed them to look in our direction and to take the rescue seriously. I even looked for Pete, but he wasn't there. In fact, I didn't recognize any of the men. Had they forgotten us?

Slewing toward us, a tangle of tree roots like a great hand pushed through the water. The men on the shore tipped back glasses of iced tea. They were so close I could see beads of sweat on their foreheads, but we were invisible to them. The tree pressed closer. My only chance to save Mercy was to let her go. The moment I opened my hands, the river snatched her. As she swept by, her hair brushed my legs and the great mass of roots drew ever closer. I woke thrashing against sheets.

This was the closest my dreams had ever come to what really happened in the Wisconsin River.

The Germans had eaten heartily their first day at our table, but not as much as we'd expected. It was a first date of sorts, and no one wanted to look like a pig on a first date. The second day, they scraped the bowls clean and looked at me expectantly.

"*Es gibt keine mehr?*"

No, there wasn't any more. So Mercy walked into town with me to help carry the groceries I would need for the next day. In truth, after the dream, I wanted her as close as possible.

Usually, Palisade was as quiet as a tomb. Now, the migrant pickers clogged every inch of the place. There weren't enough bathtubs or watering troughs in Palisade to accommodate the population surge. Mercy held her nose as we do-si-doed our way through the crowds and around vehicles that parked along Main Street like hungry piglets at a sow's teats.

The sun burned my scalp. By the time we stepped into Bancroft Grocery, my skin was slick with sweat under my blouse. Mercy's hand was as slippery as a freshly caught walleye. I shook her hand free and told her to hang onto my skirt instead. That was when I spotted Hank bent over the Coca-Cola cooler.

I wasn't one of those prissy girls who required every hair in place or I didn't go into public. That was plain silliness. But I'd been cooking and picking all day, so I looked a fright. I grabbed Mercy's arm and hurried down the bakery aisle, hoping to dodge Hank before he saw us. We edged around a woman with battleship hips.

"Lucy!" he called.

And there he was as crisp as celery. I wiped my forehead with my sleeve. "Hello, Hank. I'm in a bit of a hurry. I have a cake to bake."

He stepped closer. I leaned back into a shelf of pork 'n beans. "What's it like having those Krauts around? Are you afraid?" He smelled of Ivory soap and dust, just like a bank. He'd missed a few whiskers near his jaw. Someone bumped Hank from behind and he moved closer.

"I was. A little. At first," I said, inching away, very mindful of my souring sweat.

"Nazis don't belong here, especially not around the women and children." He nodded toward Mercy.

Over Hank's shoulder a man flipped through a *Better Homes and Gardens*. He wasn't the sort to be looking at a woman's magazine. I took him for a *National Geographic* sort of man with his high corrugated forehead and heavy eyebrows. And he wore a suit during the hottest part of the day. He surely didn't belong in Palisade. He looked up from the magazine and winked at me.

"I have to go, Hank."

Mercy chose that very moment to say much too loudly, "Sissy talks to the Germans."

Hank's eyes widened. They were the nicest shade of jade. I don't think I'd noticed that before. "You speak German?"

"A little." I waved off the importance of such a skill. "The prisoners work harder if they know what to do."

Mercy said, "She understands every word they say."

Hank raised his voice to be heard over two women exchanging recipes. "Doesn't that seem a little dangerous, talking to Nazi prisoners?"

Conversations around us stopped. Expectant eyes flashed our way. The onlookers leaned in and murmured. I could hear bits and pieces: *strange girl, Nazis, old woman.*

What old woman? I swiped my palms on my skirt.

Mercy continued, "Our papa taught her, but he didn't teach me and Goody. Mama said we were born Americans and we should speak American."

The man replaced the *Better Homes and Gardens* in the stand and picked up another, this time a *Movieland,* but he wasn't reading. He sauntered closer. His attention made me nervous. I'd heard of men who liked little girls.

I pulled Mercy past the canned vegetables. Hank stayed with us. "I should go, too. I'm helping Dad with the deposits." His chin lifted when he said this. He held up the bottles of Coca-Cola. "It's hotter than the blazes in his office." He touched my arm. "Do you think, before school starts, we could—?"

"I'm very busy," I said, hoping to stop the Palisade gossip mill before it started.

Crestfallen, Hank backed away and turned toward the checkout. The man with the magazine watched Hank leave and turned back to me. He smiled. My scalp prickled. I pushed Mercy through a klatch of women who were whispering about a woman being healed in the camp and wasn't this the little girl who had done it? I considered running out of the store, but Ada would play dirges all night long if I came back empty-handed. On the other hand, what did that man want?

"Stay with me," I told Mercy, squeezing her hand. "We're almost done."

"That man waved at me," she said, pointing to the man with the magazines.

"Remember what Mother said about talking to strangers."

Mercy waved back at him. "He didn't say anything."

I moved through the store, dropping potatoes, onions, and packets of yeast into the basket. I handed Mercy a ten-pound sack of flour to carry. I didn't want her encouraging the man's attention. No more waving for her.

The Germans sure liked their coffee, so I asked Mr. Amato to grind a pound.

"All I've got's chicory."

"That will have to do."

A woman I didn't know leaned in to ask, "Is that the little girl who healed the old woman?"

I pleaded ignorance, but Mercy said, "Her hands looked so sore."

"I'm sorry. We're not allowed to talk to strangers." I turned to put myself between the woman and Mercy.

Undaunted, Mercy leaned around me. "I touched her feet, but nothing happened."

"That old woman's been dancing a jig. I think you healed her, all right. What a blessing!"

"I'll have to come back, Mr. Amato," I said. "I forgot the ration book." This was a bald-faced lie.

"Your groceries will be under the counter until tomorrow morning," he said and turned to his next customer.

We ran all the way back to the ranch. I kept looking over my shoulder for the man with the magazines, all the while wondering about an old woman who claimed Mercy had healed her. I needed to hear the story from Mercy but not until we were safely back to the ranch.

The woman had called this miracle a blessing. Whatever was going on with Mercy didn't seem like a blessing at all. In fact, all this attention from God, if it was from God, was a huge inconvenience, if you asked me.

I was sure to be struck by lightning for such a thought.

Ada

Darling Lucy,

A young girl came from the high school to sing during lunch today, accompanied by her out-of-tune guitar. Her voice possessed an airy quality that grated at me. The girl didn't look up once, but this I find typical of anyone under a certain age. Most who come to "bless" the residents find our spotted complexions and droopy skin disturbing, and well they should. We're a reminder to all who darken the halls of Trail's End Retirement Home (my name for this place) of their mortality. That's why I treasure your company so. You remember me as a young woman, back when I rivaled the men in strength and endurance. I'm still that woman, as long as I don't look in the mirror.

Back to the singer. The activity director announced her, saying she was fulfilling her community service or some such thing. They don't let students graduate from high school these days unless they can prove themselves selfless for thirty whole hours. It seems to me they should aim a little higher. If my prayers are answered, the man with the accordion will return on Friday. He's the only one who will listen to Martin's stories, and he looks us straight in the eye.

Things were different on the ranch, were they not? Indeed, the world was different. The people were different. We depended on one another and trusted one another. Hard work wasn't a curse. It was a blessing.

I've put off admitting something to you in my letters. Lucy, I am glad for all this remembering you've forced out of me. I can't tell you what I ate for lunch yesterday, but the summer of 1944 is becoming more and more clear to me. We were all like Alice down the rabbit hole in those days. Nothing made sense. Now, I look back fondly on the mystery Mercy brought to my life and the verve Goody added. And you, Lucy, you were my prize, a browsy rose on a summer's day—sweet, fragrant, and a bit prickly. I love you so.

I had to laugh when you asked about Melba Wood. After the fuss she made over Mercy on Blossom Sunday, she was the last person I expected to see at my kitchen door that night. We were all so agitated over the migrant workers' continued vigil. And here came Melba, asking to see Mercy, like she was calling on the president of the United States of America.

I demanded her intentions, for I lacked the patience to deal with that irascible old biddy. She stood outside the screen, fiddling with a hankie for some time. One more second, and I would have slammed the door in her face. To my surprise, Melba spoke with an uncommon timidity, saying that Mercy would be safer with her.

After Mercy's first encounter with Melba, I wasn't about to send her anywhere with that woman. Somehow Melba convinced me to let her in. She actually apologized for her behavior, saying Mercy took her by surprise at the potluck. Her concern then was only for Mercy's safety. She feared those who held vigil may turn desperate as the days of the harvest dwindled.

The thought crossed my mind to push Melba down the kitchen steps, but what she said rang true. Who among us had the time to watch Mercy every minute during the harvest? Why the good Lord sent Melba Wood as our angel, I will never know. As you remember, Mercy shrank from her like a scolded puppy, and Tonto came within a breath of biting into her bony shin. Everything would have turned out differently, I'm quite sure, if Goody had not caught Tonto by the collar. That boy was quick.

I had known Melba since my first day in Palisade. Have I ever told you that? I answered an advertisement looking for a boarder in her home. She turned me down flat, said I looked like poor white trash, and it was not in her to shelter anyone who lived in an unholy manner. You can imagine how her words bit me. When I saw her after that, I crossed the street rather than pass her on the sidewalk.

And there she was, after all those years, standing in my kitchen, cooing at Mercy with tears streaming down her cheeks. The scene was too incongruous. I looked at the clock, the dishes in the rack, the toaster that needed a shining, anywhere but at Melba's contorted face. And for once, I kept my mouth shut. What was there to say? I didn't think Melba capable of such emotion and certainly not of saying she was sorry. I was shocked that her knees were capable of bending to Mercy's level. Her legs were as straight as pickets.

In the years since then, I've learned not to be so harsh in my judgments. I know you probably disagree, but it's true. For instance, our newest resident is a boorish man who displays horrific manners. Nevertheless, I have stalled any judgment on his character. His name is Phil. I haven't said anything before now about him because I had a theory to test. I believe he's trying to prove he doesn't belong here. We've all done it, acted hateful toward the staff in hopes they would send us packing. He'll settle in soon enough.

Oh dear, it's time for supper. I must have napped much longer than I thought. I won't have much time for writing in the coming days. Tomorrow, I have my hair done, and I make a trip to the doctor on Friday. It's nothing to worry about. Dr. Malik can't seem to get enough of me. He's such a nincompoop. I'm as strong as a very old horse with no teeth. Ha!

I'll drop this in the mail so you'll have it. I hope I've answered your question. I'm sure you'll let me know, if I've twisted things up again.

Love,
Ada

Lucy

Mercy stood with her hands loosely clasped behind her back, twisting one foot, and holding Miss Wood's gaze weightlessly. If Miss Wood wasn't crying buckets, you would have thought from Mercy's expression that she was hearing about the cookies Miss Wood baked that afternoon.

Mercy asked Miss Wood, "Did you remember Henry?"

Miss Wood lowered her eyes. "I never forgot him, not really."

What were they talking about? Henry who? "What is this about?"

Miss Wood met my gaze. "Your sister is a wonder. She saw right through my bluster. And she knew all about Henry." Miss Wood dried her eyes with a hankie.

"Did you talk to him?" Mercy said.

"Indeed, we have been communicating. We've exchanged several lovely letters." And then Miss Wood giggled like the girls at school when they're reporting that a boy held their hand or asked them to a dance. Ada and Lotti stilled their lips with their fingers, clearly trying not to laugh.

I'd known something had happened between Mercy and Miss Wood at the Blossom Sunday potluck, but this wasn't the usual. Mercy hadn't played matchmaker before, although she had pulled names out of the air, causing all kinds of fussing and consternation. And here was Miss Wood, speaking of shared intimacies with Mercy. Perhaps she'd fooled Mercy, but I wasn't about to trust Miss Wood with Mercy's heart.

"I think it's time you told us why you came," I said. "Or you can leave, Miss Wood."

She looked up sharply. "Hmph!"

This was more like the Miss Wood I'd come to know.

She lowered her head and breathed in deeply, rising with the help of the table. When our gazes met again, she seemed different. "I'm so sorry. I've gone and gotten completely sidetracked. I didn't come to talk about Henry at all. I came to rescue Mercy."

"Rescue her? From what? All that's ahead of her tonight is a good scrubbing in the bathtub and a very short story before bed."

"You haven't seen them, then?" Miss Wood said. She looked toward the front door.

Ada wore the weariness of the day's work. She was no longer laughing. "Melba, in case you haven't noticed, there's a harvest going on. We're tired. You're going to have to expound for us, please."

"This is no place for the girl. She simply must stay at my house. No one will bother her there. Only until the harvest is completed, of course, and the migrant workers leave town."

I remembered the red marks that had darkened to bruises on Mercy's arm from the way Miss Wood had pulled her through the Blossom Day crowd. "She's not going anywhere with you."

"I surely understand your reticence—"

Ada took a step toward Miss Wood. "For the love of all that is holy, listen to the girl, Melba. She knows what's best for Mercy."

Miss Wood's shoulders sagged but only for a moment, and then she stood as straight as a lamp post again. She motioned us through the dining room into the living room. We followed her out of curiosity, mostly. There she whispered, "The migrant people. They're out there." She pointed toward the door. "There must be a couple hundred of them. They want to see Mercy."

We'd had the shades drawn against the setting sun for hours. All of General Sherman's army could have been out there, and we wouldn't have seen them. But two hundred?

I knelt before Mercy and drew her into a fierce embrace, wondering how I'd let it come to this. How had I let this happen? Finally, I rose and led her by the hand to Ada, suddenly too aware of my inability to protect her, and more than a little afraid that Mercy's gifts would draw the attention of many, many more people. That somehow, Mrs. Nadel would follow Mercy's trail of miracles to reclaim the twins. Mercy shrank into Ada's chest.

"Where's Goody?" I asked, hoping he wasn't moving among the migrants and telling stories of Mercy's exploits to raise their hopes.

Lotti blinked. "Oh dear, I sent him to the henhouse for eggs."

I opened my mouth to ask her to retrieve him, but she'd already receded through the house. I jumped when the screen door slammed. I lifted the shade from the window. Miss Wood was right. Only now the crowd had moved away from road's shoulder to the lawn, and their numbers had doubled. I dropped the shade.

Mercy covered her ears. "They're calling my name."

I heard nothing. I pulled the shade back again, and Ada pressed in to look. Like a game of red light, green light, the crowd had inched closer.

"Lucy?" In my name, Mercy was pleading for—what? I didn't know, but I wanted to get her away from those people, not that I believed they would hurt her intentionally, but she was only a little girl. There were so many people with so many demands.

Ada backed away. "I'm calling the sheriff, and this time he'll come out."

Miss Wood peeked at the crowd, too. "There's more of them than when I drove in." She tugged me away from the window. "I want to help. Anything. I'll do anything."

Just then, Goody's boots drummed across the floor. "Sissy," he said, the worry line between his eyes deeper than I'd ever seen it, "there's a million people out there! They wouldn't stop tugging at my shirt and asking about Mercy. We gotta get her out of here."

I checked to see that Ada had taken Mercy out of hearing. I whispered to Miss Wood, "Are you still willing to take Mercy?"

As I folded a second dress in Mercy's suitcase she asked, "How long am I staying at Miss Wood's house?"

"Until the harvest is over. Five days? The migrants will go home then."

"Will you visit me?"

"Mercy, do you remember playing hide and go seek with the kids in the neighborhood back home? If you were hiding, you looked for a place no one would think to look, and then you sat there, stock still, hardly breathing and not saying a word."

"I remember."

"That's what going to Miss Wood's will be like. No one will think to look for you there. They don't know the two of you are friends."

"We're not good friends."

"No, but she wants to help you, and she seems to have changed. At least, she's changed a little. For the good, I mean."

"So, once I'm there I have to be real quiet, so no one will find me?"

"Exactly."

Miss Wood had parked her car in the back of the house, so she and Mercy could leave without anyone seeing them. Later, we all marveled at Miss Wood's subterfuge. That night, we watched as Mercy walked toward Miss Wood's car, looking over her shoulder only once to see me biting my knuckle. She blew a kiss and climbed in. As we'd planned, Mercy lay down on the seat to avoid attention from those holding vigil.

Miss Wood's car roared to life. Gravel popped under the tires as they rounded the corner of the house and disappeared. I stood there for some time, watching the dust settle. I felt like an apple being peeled with a very dull knife, and Mercy wasn't even gone yet, not really.

Although I couldn't see the crowd, I heard a murmur heave and swell to reach us behind the house. Had the migrants discovered our sleight of hand with Mercy? Were they growing impatient? Would the sheriff get there in time?

Lotti startled me with her warm breath on my ear. "Come in for a cool drink. Sending Mercy off with Melba wasn't an easy thing to do, and I had my doubts, but after hearing the two of them making plans, I do believe you've done what's best for the girl. Maybe that sheriff will take care of this crowd and Mercy can come back tomorrow night."

I didn't get a cool drink. Someone was banging at the front door. My heart pounded in reply, but then I remembered the sheriff's promise. He'd arrived in good time, better than I thought possible. I followed Ada toward the door. Lotti grabbed me about the waist and held me fast. "Ada can handle this."

The man at the door wasn't the sheriff. His voice boomed into the darkened room. "I'm Mr. Gurley, reporter for *The Denver Post*. I have a few questions about the miracle girl."

My heart sank. I'd been such a fool to think we could hide in this tuck of mountain with no worries of being discovered. Surely, this was the end of our sanctuary at Honey Sweet Ranch, and I would be discovered as a kidnapper. I wanted to see the man who would upend my life, so I stepped away from Lotti, but that mite of a woman pulled me behind the opened door so we could observe the man between the door's hinges. It took me a while, since he wasn't wearing his hat and the night had all but absorbed the day's light, but it was soon clear this was the magazine man. I seriously doubted that he wrote for a newspaper.

"Ma'am," the man said, taking a slender notebook out of his pocket and licking the end of a pencil. "Do you know why these people are here?"

I pressed closer to the opening. Sure enough, the crowd had followed the man nearly to the porch's steps.

Ada's words came out hot and biting. "You're wasting your time on Honey Sweet Ranch, Mr. Gurley. There's no story worth writing about us. Besides, we're smack in the middle of harvest. I don't have time to talk to you."

Ada moved to close the door, but Mr. Gurley stopped it with his foot. I disliked him even more, and the way he spoke with a feigned homespun quality made me distrust him all the more.

He said, "Can you explain, then, why these fine people are standing in front of your home? I've lived in my house for near on twenty years, and I've yet to attract such a fetching crowd. They're asking for a little girl named Mercy. Does she live here?"

I couldn't stand behind the door another second. "Why have you been following us?"

"He's been following you?" Ada said.

Mr. Gurley ignored the question. "Your sister is a story the world needs to hear, miss. The war is dampening our spirits. We need to know miracles still happen."

"The sheriff is already on his way," Ada said.

"Mercy is a little girl," I said. "She sleeps with a doll named Ruthie and loves to hear stories about princesses who live in castles. I think the world might be disappointed with a boring story like that."

"You're underestimating how wounded the world is these days.

People don't take their pain out into the marketplace. They hang
their gold stars in their windows and hunker down, hoping and
praying for a ray of light in their lives."

"Still, Mercy…"

His pencil scratched at his notebook. "Please spell her full name
for me."

Ada shoved his shoulder hard enough that he faltered. "You're
a brazen one, coming to my home to exploit children for your own
gain. Go find another story. Get off my porch, or I'll get my
husband's hunting rifle." With that, Ada pulled me behind the door
and slammed it shut, locking it for good measure. And then she
pulled me into an embrace and kissed my cheek. When she spoke
into my ear, she could have been Mother. "Go take a bath. You'll
feel better. Lotti and I will meet the sheriff."

I lay in that bath water until a film of soap clung to the porcelain at
the waterline. The water sheltered me. Once my feet touched the
bathroom floor again, I would need a plan. Yes, Ada and Lotti
were willing to stand against a crowd and put a pushy
newspaperman in his place, but where would their willingness to
fight go if they knew the truth of how I'd stolen the twins? When
Mercy's name hit the newspapers, we would no longer be safe at
Honey Sweet Ranch. The thought of leaving tightened my throat.
Lotti was the aunt I'd longed for. And I no longer hated Ada.
Depending on the hour, our relationship alternated between
coarse-grit sandpaper and a healing ointment. Unfortunately, my
only plan was to leave. I didn't know exactly where we would go or
what I would do when I got there, but the three of us must be
together. That was the most important thing, being together, just as
I'd promised Papa.

The bath water had chilled, which made me think of
California's perpetual summers and ocean breezes. I chided myself,
"Stay calm. Think rationally." I hadn't saved nearly the money we
would need to get there, let alone rent a room. And nothing in
California could be nearly so comforting and protective as Honey
Sweet Ranch.

Downstairs, I heard the authoritative voice of the sheriff. I
stepped out of the bath and wrapped myself in a towel and leaned
against the door. The man from the *Post* didn't have his story. Not

yet, not really. Ada had said nothing. Only I had been stupid enough to give him Mercy's name. I vowed to be watchful, not to panic but to be ready. But to be ready for what?

The day of harvesting, cooking, and watching Mercy ride away in Miss Wood's car had sapped us all, and yet Ada insisted on plaiting my hair for bed. She'd never done so before, and I had to stiffen my neck to keep her strong fingers from pulling my head back. Usually, her vigor would have irked me, but that night I coveted her strength and found comfort in it at the same time. When she was done, she laid her hand on my shoulder.

"I'll play something soothing. Would you like—"

The telephone rang. Lotti looked into the bedroom on her way down to answer and joked that Melba had already grown tired of Mercy's prattle. Ada followed Lotti downstairs. Goody crawled into my lap and Tonto parked his chin on my knee. A more woeful duo I'd never seen. "Is it your tummy?" I asked Goody.

"Nah."

"Is there something you need to tell me?" He did possess a keen, yet tardy conscience.

"Honest, Lucy, I've been good."

"Then why do you look like the end of the world is at hand?"

His forehead rested on my neck. "I don't know."

"I'm feeling a little blue myself." I took a chance and embraced him.

"Honest?"

"It started when Mercy left with Miss Wood."

"Are you missing her?" he asked.

"I am."

"Not me."

"This situation is only temporary, Goody. We'll be back together as soon as the peaches are off the trees."

"It's time for *Captain Midnight*." He pushed against my arms and slipped off my lap to race toward the parlor.

In the hall, Lotti spoke on the telephone. "Yes. It's been a long day. We're all very tired. Of course. I understand. That will be fine. Yes, we'll see you in a few minutes." Once she hung up, she spoke in a voice weighted by fatigue. "Pastor Pennington is coming to call, and he's bringing a Miss someone-or-other."

Ada was pacing in the kitchen when I entered. "Does he not understand the harvest is on? It's a little late for a social call."

"I'll make coffee," Lotti said, ever the hostess. "There are two pieces of Lucy's cake left. I'll slice them into wafers. Pastor has a greedy sweet tooth." She stilled her hands to look at us. "This has something to do with Mercy. I think we better listen to him. The lady is from some sort of child protection service. What's the world coming to?"

Ada trudged up the stairs. "You'll have to answer the door, Lucy. I better be dressed when the pastor comes to call, or I'll hear about it for months."

Ada stirred her coffee, clanking the spoon against the cup, even though she drank her coffee black. "Let me get this straight, pastor. People are gossiping, and you think the person they're talking about is the problem?"

"I can see how this rankles you, Ada, but that's not what we're saying. Miss Peasley is concerned that Mercy may be traumatized by the attention she's receiving, and I'm here to gain answers for my parishioners. Some are quite agitated."

"You can tell Rose Evelyn Bibelhauser and her band of vipers to mind their own business," Lotti said and wiped spittle from her chin.

Miss Peasley flinched and opened her notebook to take feverish notes. What did this woman know? What did she hope to learn? How long did I have before she connected the dots back to Baraboo? If feelings had color, I was green like a scummy pond in late August. No one seemed to notice, least of all Pastor Pennington.

"Ada. Lotti," the pastor implored, "these are extraordinary events for our small congregation. We must be patient. We're only here to ask a few questions."

"Mercy isn't here," I said, more to Miss Peasley than to the pastor. "We saw right away she was too young to be the center of this much attention. We don't know what those people are capable of."

Pastor Pennington deflated. "The girl isn't here?"

"We can answer any questions you have," Ada said, her anger still a freshly struck match.

"Has she gone far? Perhaps I could travel to her," he offered.

Lotti said, "We've arranged for her to be gone until the harvest is complete. You understand, don't you?" Pastor Pennington looked like a boy eyeing jars of penny candy with empty pockets. Miss Peasley heaved a sigh.

"Once the harvest is done and the pickers have returned home, everything will settle back to normal." Lotti sounded more wishful than certain.

Pastor Pennington scooted to the edge of his chair. "As you must realize, this topic is of great importance to me. Every man and woman of God longs to be used to further His kingdom. We hear of spontaneous healings, but they are always in faraway places. And yet, He has chosen to do this amazing thing through Mercy, a little girl, the very least of these, right here in Palisade."

"Ask your questions," Ada said, each word fixed with a lead sinker.

That made me look at her more closely. She slumped back in the chair. I'd never seen Ada slump, not ever. The woman possessed a two-by-four for a spine. I stilled my bouncing knees with my hands.

Miss Peasley touched Pastor Pennington's arm. "Pastor, my questions are of a completely different nature. Perhaps I could ask my questions first. My report is due first thing in the morning."

That perked Ada up. "What kind of report?"

"I write a report after each home visit."

"What are you looking for, exactly?"

"It's the child welfare office's mandate to look into any probable exploitation of a child."

Lotti stood and planted her fists on her hips. "I will have you know, Miss Peasley, children are highly regarded in this home. What's happening here is a mistake, and we have taken steps to protect Mercy from a crowd of misguided people."

Pastor Pennington waggled a finger to catch Lotti's attention. "I am not as sure as you are, Lotti, that those people are misguided."

"What are you talking about? They want Mercy to heal them. She's only a little girl, Percy. "

Miss Peasley stood. "Perhaps I should come back another time. My supervisor would be interested in this conversation."

I stood up too quickly and my uneaten cake slid to the floor. I gathered the mess, speaking to Miss Peasley, "Your supervisor?

We've told you everything, and we're doing all we can to keep Mercy safe. I don't see any reason to involve your supervisor."

Each Sunday, Pastor Pennington invited the children to the front of the sanctuary for a story. The children sucked their thumbs and waved at their parents. Their lack of attention was no matter. The story was for the adults, a simplified telling of the sermon in story form. He affected a tone of voice that drew our childlike hearts to listen. This was the voice he used to speak to Miss Peasley. "Our purposes are perfectly aligned, Miss Peasley. The welfare of the girl is of upmost importance. The gathering of details is how we begin to understand a mystery. This is how you come to an understanding of a home situation, is it not?"

Miss Peasley made a hyphen of her mouth. "Yes. Continue."

Pastor Pennington rubbed his knees as he thought. Finally, he blurted, "Does Mercy hear voices?"

Ada looked to me.

"No," I said.

"Does she speak of seeing angels?"

"No. Never."

"Has she ever healed anyone?"

"Of course not."

I believed Pastor Pennington was about to cry. Instead, he ran his hand over his chin and cast a wary eye at Miss Peasley. He said to me, "You know, don't you, a woman at the migrant camp has said your sister healed her rheumatoid arthritis? Her feet and hands were all but useless before Mercy touched her."

Ada rolled her eyes. "Come now, Percy, what good comes from repeating stories? You surprise me."

"The woman's family and other people from the camp, people who saw her sitting in her rocker day after day, corroborate the story. The lady—her name is a Mrs. Brown, Mrs. Lenora Brown— but that's of little consequence," he said, casting a glance at Miss Peasley. "Mrs. Brown is now seen bustling around the camp, running after her grandchildren and canning peaches over an open fire. She has knitted a scarf and started matching mittens for Mercy, all after the girl touched her hands and feet." He swept his gaze over each of us. "I talked to Mrs. Brown myself."

Miss Peasley drummed her notebook with a pencil. I pretended to study Gil and Ada's wedding picture on the side table. The clock ticked off the seconds. Pastor Pennington's face reddened. Was he holding his breath? Fine. He could turn blue and fall out of his chair before I would say anything. Besides, what was I to say? Mercy had only whispered the story to me the night before as I scrubbed the red earth from her scalp. And she'd said nothing about healing the woman's feet. I'd pressed her for details until her eyes glistened. "You have no idea what you've done," I told her.

"I was only trying to warm her hands," she said.

"In this heat?"

And then I regretted my harsh words because her lips set to quivering. I'd wrapped her in a towel without rinsing her hair to rock her until she had stopped crying.

Ada stood abruptly. "I can't give any more time to this. I have a harvest to oversee. You can come back when the peaches are happily on their way to the market. Until then, good night."

Miss Peasley folded her hands on her knees. "I would feel much better seeing the child before I leave."

"I'm afraid you'll have to leave disappointed." Ada gestured toward the door. "Lucy, make sure Goody isn't sleeping in front of the radio before you go to bed. Pastor. Miss Peasley. May I walk you to the door?"

Goody wasn't asleep at all. He sat with his back to the parlor door where he had listened to everything. His eyes were as big as dinner plates. He turned toward the sound of the front door closing. "That woman isn't going to take Mercy away, is she?"

"Never."

That night in bed, I reached for Mercy's hand in my sleep, only to be wakened by the coolness of the sheets. I flopped onto my back and tried to enjoy the expanse of mattress her absence afforded. I'd asked Goody if he wanted to sleep in the bed, but he'd refused, saying Tonto would be lonely on the floor without him. I must have fallen asleep again, but I was roused by Ada playing Brahm's Lullaby. By then, a slice of gray showed around the shade. Who knew Ada possessed the tenderness to play a lullaby? I rose on an elbow, smoothing the cool sheet where Mercy should have been. Goody slept like a cat behind my calves. When had he crawled into the bed? I ruffled his hair to wake him. He asked through a veil of sleep, "Are the peaches still on the trees?"

"Yes, the peaches are still on the trees."

Mercy

I was stuck like a bug in a jar.

Miss Wood made me stay inside day and night. She feared the migrant pickers would see me and storm her house. The migrant workers I'd met at the camp seemed nice enough, so I wasn't afraid, but there was no telling her that. And no matter how much my tummy twisted over missing Goody and Lucy, no telephone calls for me. According to Miss Wood, making one telephone call in Palisade was as good as calling everyone in the county. That's because someone named Miss Davis ran the switchboard.

Miss Wood's house was built with stone blocks like the kind they used to build castles. Other than the stones, Miss Wood's house was nothing like a castle. Not one fancy ball or banquet for me. According to Miss Wood, the stones kept the house cool and very, very quiet. The house was a little too quiet, so I thought to open a window, but Miss Wood said I wasn't to look around the shade at all. Miss Wood, on the other hand, couldn't stay away from the window.

"What's out there?" I finally said, looking up from reading *Little House in the Big Woods*.

She startled, played with the broach at her neck. I don't think she was used to being asked why she did this or that. Not one visitor came in the three days I'd been at her house. She clasped her hands together over her heart. "For your information, I am expecting an important piece of correspondence."

"From Henry?"

"Well, uh, I don't know. I mean, I receive important correspondence on a regular basis from all sorts of people." Miss Wood looked over my head as she talked. "I'm expecting a letter…" She cleared her throat. "A letter from my lawyer in Denver. He's looking over some contracts for me." She turned back to peek around the shade and then smoothed it in place. "Charles Crumpton is the most inept postal worker in these United States of America." With that said, she walked noiselessly from the room.

This was fine with me. My book made me homesick for the ranch in the nicest way. But a girl can't read all day. Miss Wood didn't own a radio. According to her, the programming was too carnal for a good Christian woman like her. I learned there were a lot of things good Christian women didn't do, like play Solitaire or dominoes or dance, even though I loved doing all of those things.

While Miss Wood made yet another trip to the post office with a fat letter to mail, I found a note Goody had pushed under the door: *Deer Mercy, Are yu stell alife? The kitens were born last nigt. Thar eys are closd. Thay canot walk good. Com home soon. Goody.*

That was some kind of torture, getting a note from Goody and missing the birth of the kittens.

"Only two more days," I told myself. "Only two more very long days."

Later, when Charlie finally delivered the mail, Miss Wood made me stand behind the door while she walked to the mailbox. I'd never seen her move so fast. By then, I was sure she was waiting for a letter from Henry. After all, I'd seen Aunt Ada and Lucy walk to the mailbox lots of times like they expected something special.

I ran from the front door to the kitchen to stand on a chair at the sink to watch as she shuffled through the mail. When she found what she was looking for, she folded the letter in half and stuffed it into her pocket. I jumped off the chair and slid it back to the table when she turned back toward the house, but she wouldn't have noticed anything out of place, least of all me. She went straight to her bedroom and stayed there. I didn't see Miss Wood again until suppertime.

While Miss Wood gathered the bread and cheese for our sandwiches, she hummed a breezy song. This made knowing how to please Miss Wood just about impossible. Only that morning, she'd scolded me for humming as I'd brushed my hair.

She took forever to saw the crust off the bread. For all her fussing, the sandwich didn't taste any better than the one she'd made the night before. The cheese and bread still clumped together into a wad in my mouth. I chewed and chewed, and as I chewed, I worked on asking a question just right, seeing as I wanted her to say yes more than anything.

"There isn't one soul who lives behind you," I said, careful to swallow before I spoke. "Can I play out there with Ruthie tomorrow?"

"You have far too many freckles as it is."

Was that possible? My papa had kissed the freckles on my nose and knees every night when he'd tucked me in. "Papa liked my freckles. He said I'd been kissed by the angels."

"Fanciful ideas like that are doorways for the devil's lies. You won't be spouting such foolishness in this home. Angels do not kiss children."

I was about to set Miss Wood straight on some things about angels, but just as I opened my mouth, I pictured Lucy's face, the way it squeezed together whenever I talked about heaven. I hated seeing Lucy sad or confused, or whatever it was she was feeling that wasn't happy. So instead of setting Miss Wood straight, I told her I was bored, which was truer than true.

She grabbed my hand and pulled me to the attic, which was as hot as you know where. Miss Wood knelt on the wooden planks to dig through a box until she found the game she was looking for— *Sorry!*

I hated that game. "Isn't playing games a sin?"

"Only if they're frivolous. This game will teach you to be flexible. Something is bound to come along in life to upset your apple cart. There's no time like the present to prepare for that eventuality."

I didn't have an apple cart, but I'd been upset plenty of times.

Miss Wood beat me three games in a row. She smiled so much, I got tired of looking at her teeth, especially the one that was as yellow as a dandelion. And she giggled, only it sounded like she had something caught in her throat. Finally, the clock in the hall chimed nine. I pushed away from the table, ready to be done with that stupid game, even if it meant going to bed.

"Where did the time go?" she said. "There's nothing to be done for it. We'll read *two* chapters of Deuteronomy tomorrow night.

Don't think I'll forget."

The whole time I brushed my teeth and put my nightgown on, she sang "Great is Thy Faithfulness" in her bedroom. Her voice was airy and sweet. I sure didn't expect that. She sang the chorus as she walked down the hall toward my door and walked in. "Mercy, would you like to join me for a glass of warm milk? Nothing else helps me sleep so well."

"Do you have cocoa powder?"

"Of course not. Such extravagant waste is not tolerated in this house."

"Then, no ma'am, not tonight, but thank you very much."

Miss Woods didn't move for the longest time. I wasn't sure what to do. She finally said, "Suit yourself," and left.

That was why I felt like a bug in a jar at Miss Wood's home and why I missed Goody and Lucy so much. Only two more days until I was back to Honey Sweet Ranch. Only two more days of runny poached eggs and two nights of sleeping on a big bed all by myself.

I wasn't at all sure I would make it that long.

Lucy

The Germans picked peaches from trees close to the house
lunch. Before they'd come, I'd expected ominous silence
shifty-eyed prisoners, but their voices, resonant and eager, so
as if they were at a church social rather than climbing up an
ladders all day. No doubt about it, they were having fun. Th
played a game called soccer during their breaks, which near
Ada mad. All this going on and I was stuck in the kitchen
oven blazing. Ada said I'd translated enough for them
what they were doing, so she'd reassigned me, again. It d
that Goody roared by every few minutes in the hoo
barking to clear the way. Mercy would have kept me
she'd been there, reading from Sunday school handouts
million questions about our parents. I missed her like
at twilight.

The instant I turned the bread out to cool, I trad
for a picking sack. I chose a tree some distance from
pickers and Ada's watchful eyes. She thought I woul
afternoon, and it would go better for me if she belie
long as possible. She would get her chance to scold
the heat no longer needled my skin. And while
would peel the peaches for tomorrow's crisp. N
Ada's tirades like watching me work.

I picked far enough from the Germans to a
but close enough to enjoy their banter. My Ge
and I still translated when needed, but there we

vocabulary. Frustrated by missing a word here or not being able to pluck meaning from the context, I mumbled Ada's name like a curse word and moved my ladder next to Gerland.

"What is *Verrat?*" I asked him.

"Treason."

"Treason? I thought you were talking about clubs at the camp."

"Not clubs as you're thinking but divided loyalties, I'm afraid. Nightly, there are heated discussions. Threats. The Nazis hate the communists, who in turn hate the fascists."

"And you?"

"I am a German, but I am a citizen of God's kingdom first, just like you."

He didn't know I lived on the outskirts of that kingdom. "Sometimes you sound like a preacher."

"I was. Not anymore. Probably never again." The smile faded from his eyes. I'd said the wrong thing, as usual, so I went back to listening. Before long, I was curious about another word I didn't know. I pointed to one of the prisoners and asked Gerland, "Does that one breed dogs?"

He paused his picking to listen. He called out to the men, "Mind your language, gentlemen! We have a young lady present!"

The men laughed and one said, "If she sticks with us, she'll have hair on her chest by the end of the day."

"Then keep your voices down."

I understood all too well everything Reinhardt said. He never missed an opportunity to wink or turn an innocent remark into a flirtation. No doubt, Reinhardt had made plenty of conquests all through Europe and North Africa that had nothing to do with soldiering. Gerland managed to keep the conversation between the three of us mostly appropriate, and when Reinhardt couldn't contain his tongue, I learned to roll my eyes and keep picking, but I think this angered him. Men could be as vulnerable as third-grade girls when it came to any kind of sleight, some more than others.

Gerland peppered me with questions about growing up in America, mostly, I think, to distract me from the men's conversations. We were both surprised to discover we had a lot in common. We'd both grown up in small towns, equally enjoying and loathing the intimacy of rural life. Our fathers preferred fishing and hunting, and he took care of his younger siblings, too. While my father worked in a factory and was a bit of a dreamer, his father

was a veterinarian.

"I was forever hitching up his buggy, so Father could look after someone's sick cow," he said.

"Did you go with him on his calls?"

"*Ja*, if school was out for the term. When I was seven, he was called up to doctor the officers' horses during the first war. When he was killed, we moved to the city to live with my aunt."

"I'm so sorry."

He shook his head against a memory. "I hated the city. Too many people. I missed swimming in the pond and chasing after the piglets that wriggled out of their pens. Mostly, I missed the silence, or what goes for silence, in the country. I especially missed the cows calling to be milked."

"And you missed your father."

"Very much so. We sat for hours under an apple tree, him reading *The Last of the Mohicans*, me exploring the American frontier in my imagination."

The Last of the Mohicans? What an unexpected, intimate connection. I'd gotten lost in the very same story. "I was the only girl in my class to read Cooper's book. The girls preferred *Little Women*." And then it dawned on me. Cooper was an American. He wrote in English. "Gerland, did your father read a translation of Cooper's book."

"No. Well, certainly there were translations, but my father read the book to me in English."

I stopped, holding a peach in each hand. "And you understood?"

"Every word."

"Then why pretend you don't speak English?"

Gerland stopped picking to look at me. A smile lit his eyes. "No one asked if I spoke English. They made assumptions. Besides, we are powerless here. We earn eighty cents a day in play money to be spent in the camp store. We see the far mountains, and yet, we cannot seek their beauty. Our language is something we can hold close to the heart." He resumed picking. "Will you tell?"

I shook my head, though he couldn't see me through the leaves. "My father also died," I continued in German. "My mother, too. I was afraid the twins wouldn't remember them."

"Both gone? That is a hard thing. Was your father in the military?" He asked this question as if testing a frozen lake under

227

his weight.

Would I talk to Gerland like this if my father had been killed by the Germans? I doubted it. There were people in Palisade who didn't appreciate the presence of the Germans because of the cost they had personally paid for the war, the war the Germans had started. I understood that. I'd feel the same about the Japanese if Pete were killed. "He worked in an ammunition factory," I said. "There was an accident. I guess I shouldn't tell you anything about that."

"No, no you shouldn't." We picked in silence, prickled by the reality of who we were. After a time, he said, "And your mother?"

At just that moment, Ada brought empty bushel baskets to exchange for the full ones. She wasn't happy to see me. "What are you doing? Get down, now! The sergeant—where is that deplorable man?"

I climbed down the ladder, prepared for a fight. But I wasn't prepared for the Ada I found. She trembled with tear-filled eyes. "What's happened?" I asked, sure that Goody had collided with a truck or that Mercy had been discovered or, worse, eaten by Miss Wood.

She waved a dismissive hand. "Nothing's happened. Where's the sergeant?"

Sergeant Salvatore trotted through the rows of trees from where he'd been lounging with the corporal. He saluted Ada, shamefaced for his laziness but not repentant.

"I don't want Lucy picking so close to your prisoners," she demanded.

The sergeant's shoulders relaxed. "There ain't nothing going to happen to the girl. I won't take my eyes off her." He crossed his heart. "I give you my word. And I hope to die if any harm comes to her."

"You will hope to die, if any harm comes to her," Ada said, scowling until the sergeant teetered back.

"Ada, I'm keeping up with the pickers. Let me help to make the most of the harvest," I said.

Ada dropped the baskets at my feet. Gerland and I watched her return to the barn before we climbed the ladders again. We knew how much it cost someone like Ada to relinquish a fight. She deserved a show of respect.

The sergeant kept his word about watching me. He flirted

almost as much as Reinhardt. I didn't take either of their attentions too seriously. Just about anything wearing a skirt—or overalls—received plenty of attention in those days.

Pete

Sweetheart,

Dropping you a few lines to let you know I'm still OKAY. I'm being as careful as I can. I want to make it back to you more than anything. Some of the guys wouldn't give a penny for their lives, and there's no convincing them otherwise. Your letters make me feel like a million bucks.

You say the land around the peach ranch is barren and the air is dry. It's hard to imagine endless blue skies. Anything dry sounds like a little bit of heaven. The jungles here are thick and hot. The only clearings are places bombed to smithereens. The clearings are tempting with all that space and sunshine, but we don't go there. The snipers wait for us there.

I should have said something about Mercy sooner. I can be such a dope sometimes. Anyway, it must be hard to be separated from her again, but I agree with your aunt. Mercy isn't ready for that kind of attention. This is all a mystery to me. I've never heard of a kid doing the things Mercy does. I talked to the chaplain about her. He couldn't think of one reason to doubt God is using her to bless others. He read a passage to me where Jesus says whoever receives a child in his name, receives Him.

What does it mean to receive a little child in his name? Not to hurt or take advantage of them, I guess. The chaplain says Jesus is making fools of people who consider themselves hotshots, but He blesses folks who stay like children. And we're left to wonder at what God is doing through her.

I hope this letter makes sense. I've never been more hot and tired in my life. I'm looking forward to sitting with you at the kitchen table with the smell of fresh-mown hay swirling around us. Instead of talking about Nips in the jungle, I'll tell you about another boring day at work. Let me know what you think about that idea. I hope you like it.

Love always,
Pete

Lucy

I positioned the ladder opposite Gerland and climbed. I'd been picking peaches with the prisoners for three afternoons, and my thighs no longer burned from going up and down the ladder. Although Ada didn't approve, I worked late into the night baking and peeling potatoes to buy time in the orchard. As I reached for the first peach, the men working nearby shouted out their approval of that day's meatloaf, but they called it *falsher hase* or false rabbit. Would they have preferred rabbit to beef? I didn't want to disappoint them, so I let their comments pass with a wave and a *danke*!

Gerland greeted me but seemed lost in his own thoughts. He'd admitted to me that he hadn't heard from his family in a long time. Friends and relatives had dispersed, looking for the one corner of Germany not damaged by the war's heavy hand, a lean-to against a wall or an abandoned apartment, not a motor lodge or a family's guest room. They were completely lost to one another. In a very small way, I knew how it felt to have your family out of arm's reach and subject to injustices and deprivation. As frail as our togetherness was, my gratefulness at having Goody and Mercy nearby had grown by befriending Gerland.

Gerland's pensiveness gave me time to think, mostly about Pete. Every letter that arrived revealed a different side of him, aspects that contradicted everything I thought I'd known about him. I'd never heard Pete say anything about Jesus, except when he was swearing. And now he seemed so sure God was involved in the things that happened around Mercy. Ada believed there was a reasonable explanation for why people acted the way they did, but then, she hadn't seen how people—Miss Wood had been the one exception—reacted to Mercy. As for me, I believed God considered Mercy special. She spoke his messages to people, and now, an old lady got herself healed without Mercy even trying. I hoped this was something Mercy would outgrow, like playing with dolls and chewing on her braids. Until then, I would do my best to keep God's affection for Mercy our little secret. That was getting harder and harder.

Gerland said, "You're quiet today. Is your boyfriend all right?"

Reinhardt climbed down his ladder, his sack of peaches filled to the brim. He stopped at the base of my ladder and leaned against the rails to look up. His eyes flashed with mischief. "Why are you mooning over a boy thousands of miles away when I'm right here?"

"Leave the girl alone, Reinhardt." Gerland sounded more tired than annoyed. Reinhardt waved him off and poured out the contents of his picking sack.

But Reinhardt had gotten it right. I was definitely mooning over Pete. And yes, I was worried. And the worry only grew as our letters became more intimate with the promises we'd exchanged. The thought of sitting across from Pete at our kitchen table, with our fingers laced, well, thinking about that set the butterflies loose in my stomach. Such thoughts also raised a sour bite of fear into the back of my throat. I was forever figuring out what time it was in Guam, if indeed Pete was still in Guam. I hadn't a clue. While I filled a picking sack with peaches, Pete was already living in tomorrow during its most dangerous hours. Was he sleeping? On guard duty? Alive?

Reinhardt climbed back up his ladder, two rungs at a time. "If he is lucky enough to come back, this boy of yours, he won't be the same. None of us are. No matter what he tells you in his letters, what he's seeing is worse. We don't tell the ladies everything."

"Your hands get lazy when your mouth starts flapping," Gerland scolded.

"I'm picking faster than you."

"With you, everything is a contest."

Reinhardt smiled broadly. "And I win."

Gerland climbed down his ladder and walked with me to dump our peaches. "How is your little sister? Mercy is her name? I haven't seen her. She isn't sick, is she?"

"She's staying with a friend." Friend? Did that stretch the truth to the moon and back? It was hard to say. Ada and I had driven to Miss Wood's house the night before to deliver clean clothes, a few books from the library, a drawing from Goody, and some of Lotti's cookies. I studied Mercy for a sign she wanted to return to the ranch with us, but she'd said, "Miss Wood and me are having fun, playing games and eating cheese sandwiches. You better go, so we can get to our Bible reading." In that moment, I'd been glad for Miss Wood. Even though the sheriff had scared off most who held vigil outside the house, a few returned each night. Lotti took to offering them water and something to eat. Ada hated that.

"The men at the camp talk about your sister." Gerland looked over his shoulder before he continued. "An *Obergefreiter*—Do you know what that means? He is a squad leader, no one too important, but he speaks English. We aren't exactly telling everyone. He heard about Mercy from the workers where he's picking. They know the woman in the migrant camp."

"What did he hear?" I asked, curious how far from the truth the story had wandered.

"That your sister has a special gift. That a woman who was once too crippled to walk is now dancing with her grandchildren."

I held two Elberta peaches, one in each hand. How did I find myself in this place, talking to Germans and worrying about Mercy? We poured out our peaches and returned to the tree.

"This perplexes you?" Gerland asked.

"Fairy tales are perplexing," Reinhardt said, rattling the tree's leaves with the ferocity of his picking.

Gerland rested his hand on my shoulder. "Verily I say unto you, whosoever shall not receive the kingdom of God as a little child—"

"Ach!" Reinhardt interrupted. "German children are dying from starvation as we feast at our enemy's table and harvest their bounty. God is not helping them. It is strong men who must do the helping. Your God is worthless." Reinhardt no longer picked with discrimination. His sack filled once more. He emptied it and carried his ladder to another tree, where the men were singing drinking songs.

Gerland said, "I'm sorry for him. He hasn't heard from his

family in months. The Russians are pressing hard on the borders. His father has been mustered, and his brothers are fighting in France. There's no one left to look after his mother and sisters. Their only hope of survival is to outrun the Russians."

Outrun an army? "But his mother and sisters are civilians."

Gerland held the bushel basket as I emptied my picking sack. "In war, it's not so easy to separate the combatants from the civilians. Besides, the Russians won't take such things into consideration, given all that's happened."

"Because of the Jews? Is what they say true?"

"I don't know how much the Russians care about Jews." He climbed into the tree. Gerland turned a peach in his hand before dropping it into his sack. "No, the Russians have their own reasons for forgetting mercy. They will be remembering Stalingrad when they cross our border. And they will cross soon."

I knew nothing of Stalingrad, but I was beginning to understand how hate gave us very long memories. Every citizen of the planet owed vengeance to someone. Would the war ever end?

I watched Reinhardt ripping the peaches from the tree. Like the other men, he'd taken off his shirt. Each day the prisoners grew darker from the sun. Was this who Pete would be when he returned from the Pacific? Would he be bitter? Distant? Muscled beyond reason?

"I finally received a letter from Eva, my wife." Gerland said, interrupting my thoughts. "I can't see how things could be much worse for my family. They are living in a cellar in Hamburg. The house once belonged to a distant cousin. The upper floors are nothing but rubble, and the cousin is not to be found. Twelve people live in that cellar. Eva is afraid to sleep. Someone must always be on guard. Others break in and take what little she manages to stash. There's no running water. No plumbing. No heat. Had I seen them safely to the country before I left...the country would have been better. Not so many bombs fall there. Eva could have kept chickens, perhaps some rabbits. As it is, she works as a helper in a bakery. For that, she earns whatever is left at the end of the day. Some days there is nothing."

I heard the pain in his voice but felt a searing pain that caused my stomach to churn. It wasn't difficult to recognize the source, not for me. Shame. I'd never even thought to ask Gerland the price this war had cost his family.

"She tells me she is grateful for her job, although she must leave the children unattended. They scatter to scavenge for food. Lenz, my boy, was caught stealing eggs from a farmer five kilometers away. He is ten years old and a thief, but I am proud of him for working so hard for his family. Everything is turned upside down. I pray it will all right itself when the war is over. But I can't be certain."

I studied Gerland as he picked. I had thought it was the picking sack that weighted him. How many prayers would it take to provide his wife and children with warm beds and food to fill their stomachs? How did a father reconcile such helplessness? Those questions seemed too cruel, so I asked, "Is it like Reinhardt said? Are you changed forever?"

"The decisions I made and didn't make have certainly changed me. I try not to think too far ahead. I pray I will one day be able to sleep without the parade of faces."

"The decisions you made?"

"*Ja?*"

"Is it possible to live with them?"

"You ask like someone who has made hard decisions. Is it true?"

I felt Mother's cold hand slip from mine and Mercy's hair slide over my thigh. "Yes."

"I'm sorry for that, Lucy. You are so young and tender, so much like what I hope my daughter will grow to be." Gerland moved his ladder. We worked in a companionable silence for some time. "As for your question, I may not be the best one to ask, but I do spend most of my waking hours haunted as you must be. As for me, for the sin I committed and the expediency of my actions, I don't expect peace. I don't deserve it. But I would like a sense of assurance, a feeling within my soul that I am agreeable to God. If that doesn't come in this lifetime, I will continue to stake my soul against the blood of Christ. I have no other hope. This is a new kind of faith for me, like new shoes that rub the heel raw. It is faith, but very, very different."

Nobody talked or sang about peace more than the people of Palisade Community Church. I'd always assumed they longed for war to end. But Gerland talked about peace like a man fighting for breath. Faith erased doubts, didn't it? Yet he seemed full of them. I supposed all that Gerland had seen churned his thoughts up. With all the thinking he did about faith and peace and such, he was the very one to ask a question I'd wondered about since Mercy was born.

"Does God like some people more than others?"

"Are you thinking of your sister?" Gerland whispered.

Who else?

He leaned closer. "Men I never expected to give God a glance, men embittered by all they've seen and done, are asking questions, hard questions." Gerland descended the ladder. I followed him even though my sack wasn't full. He asked, "Do you believe your sister healed the woman? Has she healed people before?"

Did I believe?

"I should believe, I guess. She's my sister, and I've seen her do things and say things that left our pastor completely flummoxed. But in every other way she's an ordinary girl. She loves her doll, and I have to remind her to brush her teeth every single night. She gets into terrible arguments with Goody but would defend him to the death."

"My children argue as well. I have a boy and a girl, only eleven months apart. They are either screaming at each other or conspiring against their mother and me." He winced, and I had to look away for the pain on his face. The snap of his picking sack clicked shut. "Do you mind satisfying my curiosity about Mercy? Has she always been special?"

"Since the day she was born," I said, although I hadn't meant to say this out loud. "She sees people I don't even notice. I walk by and she stops to talk. And she knows things. About the people. She's a real good listener, which is odd, I think, for a little girl. Sometimes, the people end up crying, and I feel bad about that, but they seem relieved, like some terrible weight has been lifted from their shoulders. But she's never healed anyone before. I would rather the story about the old woman wasn't true, but it probably is."

Gerland worked the straps of the sack between his fingers. "We live in a damaged hour, Lucy. Someone like Mercy, someone who is untouched by the war who still believes without hesitation, this is just what people need."

I was so very sorry I'd said anything to Gerland about Mercy. Clearly, he hungered for what Mercy could give him, and I wanted that for him, too. Were we friends? Shouldn't I exploit my influence over Mercy for his benefit? Was that what he expected? To explain away why I hoarded Mercy's gifts would mean telling him that I had stolen my very own brother and sister from the orphanage. What else could justify my stinginess with Mercy? By morning, my crime would be known by everyone in the camp. And if the camp knew, the town would know. Mr. Gurley would write a sensational story in the *Post*, and Miss Peasley would come back to the ranch with her supervisor. In the end, Mrs. Nadel would see the story and send for us. I couldn't let that happen.

"You're like the others," I said, climbing down the ladder. "You only want Mercy's help for yourself."

He nodded, taking in my accusation. "Am I so transparent?"

Mercy

Miss Wood snorted—I think she meant to laugh—as she carried a letter as fat as a pillow up the stairs to her bedroom. Whatever Henry had to say must have been a big secret.

Just the night before, she came to the kitchen where I was making a butter and honey sandwich. Her fingers were stained with ink and wisps of hair had fallen from her bun. It wasn't like Miss Wood to be untidy. Plus, she seemed surprised to see me. "Are you sick?" I asked. "Should I go get the doctor?"

She propped her chin in her hand and stared out the window, her pointy old elbows right on the table. Miss Wood believed elbows on the table were a sign of weak character, and her character was anything but weak. She blinked, straightened. "I don't know what I am. I think I might be happy." She chewed on the end of her finger. "Yes, I believe I am very happy."

She *believed* she was happy? Even Tonto knew when he was happy. He wagged his tail. I wasn't sure what to do about Miss Wood. *Should I call a doctor? Lucy? The post office?* When Lucy wasn't sure what to do with me and Goody, she asked if we were hungry. "I could make you a sandwich. It wouldn't be any trouble."

She frowned and I braced for a scolding, although I couldn't tell you what for. I was the one making my own supper.

"I have some peach jam. I've been saving it for—" She stared out the window again while I counted to twenty-nine. "I don't know what I was saving it for."

So we ate butter and peach jam sandwiches for supper and

239

breakfast the next morning. The jam was sweet and tart at the same time. The minute she finished eating, Miss Wood headed back to her writing desk. She expected me to be stone quiet.

I finished reading the books from the library and dressed and undressed Ruthie in her dresses many times. I made doll furniture out of boxes from the trash. I was proud of the way they turned out, but it wasn't any fun not having anyone to show, especially Goody, who had a way of saying when something pleased him without saying a word.

I sure was homesick for Honey Sweet Ranch, for Goody and Lucy and Aunt Ada and Lotti. I also missed Tonto and Silver, plus all of the kittens in the barn and the chickens, and even Corky who barely said a word, ever. And once the lonesome started on me, I missed Mama and Papa, Mrs. Devendorf and her oatmeal cookies and Pete's piggyback rides. I even missed my first-grade teacher, and she made Goody go back to Kindergarten after only one week in school. That was why we weren't in the same grade.

Finally, I'd had enough of missing people. So I left Miss Wood a note and set out for the ranch.

I'd just crossed the railroad tracks when a woman pulled her black car, as shiny as a beetle, beside me and leaned toward the open window. "Little girl, can you tell me how to get to Honey Sweet Ranch? It seems I've gotten myself all tangled up on these back roads."

When I told the lady I lived at the ranch, her eyes opened wide. With a grunt, she pushed open the car door. "Come on. I'll give you a ride, then."

I wasn't supposed to talk to strangers, although I did it all the time. What would Lucy say if I jumped into a stranger's car? Sometimes when I didn't mean to, I hurt Lucy, and when I did, she flinched like I'd stuck her with a pin. But the day was hot, and my feet burned inside my shoes, and the suitcase was rubbing blisters into my palms.

"You're right to hesitate," the lady said. "I don't know what I was thinking. Let me introduce myself. I'm Miss Peasley. I know your aunt and your sister."

Miss Peasley wore a dress covered with lilacs and a matching purple hat. She wasn't the kind of lady we usually saw on the ranch or in the whole town of Palisade, but I liked her right away. She didn't talk to me like I was a baby, and she didn't smile too much, like some people do when they're trying to get their way.

"You know Lucy?" I said.

"I met her at your aunt's house. I came with Pastor Pennington to talk to you, but you weren't home. They said you were staying with a friend. I was on my way in hopes you'd returned, so I could visit with you today."

The last time an adult came to talk to us, Goody and me ended up at the orphanage. I stepped back. "What's there to talk about?"

"People are awfully excited about you. Some migrant workers come to stand in front of your house every night. I've never seen anything like it."

Lucy had told me all about the people when she'd visited with Aunt Ada. "Lucy wishes they would go away."

"Maybe I can help. That's my job. I help children who...well, I help children who find themselves in uncomfortable situations."

I was all kinds of uncomfortable.

"We could go into town to the Palisade Drug Company. I hear they make the best sodas," she said, patting the seat. "Would you like that?"

I looked down the road toward the ranch. I could see the barn with its doors wide open. The new kittens were inside. And there were the cottonwoods, so fat with leaves I could only see the corner of the house. A breeze twisted the leaves to show their silvery bellies. I'd never seen a prettier picture in my whole life.

"You look awfully hot," Miss Peasley said. "They have big fans at the Drug Company."

Now that I thought about it, all I could expect at home was a good sassing for leaving Miss Wood's house. "Let's go, then."

Miss Peasley led me to a booth by the window. She said a booth was perfect for talking. I preferred sitting at the counter to watch Mrs. Richmond make the sodas, the closer to the chocolate the better. Each sundae started with three pumps of a silvery plunger that filled the bottom of a glass with a puddle of chocolate.

Of all things, Miss Peasley ordered a glass of milk. *Milk?* When there were raspberry, orange, grape, strawberry, cherry, chocolate, butterscotch, caramel, and lemon syrups? Milk was okay to wash down Lucy's gravy or for dunking cookies, but all by itself, milk was boring.

"They have other flavors," I said.

"I like milk. You have whatever you want."

"Anything?"

"Anything."

This proved she wasn't anything like Mrs. Nadel from the orphanage. Mrs. Nadel would have ordered a banana split for herself and a warm glass of water for me. I decided on a glass of chocolate milk, just to show Miss Peasley she didn't have to settle for plain milk.

"I meant it, Mercy," she said. "Order anything. I picked up my first paycheck this morning. I'm rolling in dough."

"You're rich?"

"For today I am." That's when I noticed Miss Peasley's broken tooth. I wanted to ask her about it, but Mrs. Richmond tapped her pad with a pencil. I took Miss Peasley up on her offer and ordered a chocolate soda with whipped cream.

While we waited, Miss Peasley asked me the kinds of questions adults think kids care about. I didn't want to hurt her feelings, so I answered them. I told her my doll's name and what kinds of games I liked to play on rainy days. Also, I explained why a twin brother wasn't as fun as a twin sister.

"What's your favorite subject in school?" she asked.

I'd just finished reading *Blue Willow*, about a girl who longed for a home. "I like reading the best."

"Why?"

This struck me as an odd question. "Are there a lot of things to like about reading?"

She leaned back against the booth. "When I was your age, I liked to read because the stories took me far away from the things that bothered me, namely Herbert, Clyde, and Richard—my brothers."

I would have liked to find a book like that.

"I talked to your teacher. You're a good student and a good citizen. Mrs. Zadrozny says she would like a whole classroom of students like you."

"I've heard Mrs. Z say that about lots of her students."

"I also talked to Mrs. Hanson, the school secretary, and Mr. Ramsey, the principal."

Then she would know all about Veronica and me leaving school without permission. "Am I in trouble?"

"Heaven's no. Besides, that's not my job. I'm not here to get you into trouble. Think of me as a friend."

I tried to think about Miss Peasley being a friend while I sipped my soda. As pretty and nice as she was, I didn't think she would like to dress kittens in doll clothes or set up a lemonade stand. "Don't you have any friends your own age?" I asked.

She laughed and scratched at a rash inside her elbow. "Mercy, tell me; why are you living with your aunt and Lotti? Where are your mother and father?"

"Aunt Ada invited us to live with her because Mama and Papa are in heaven."

"Oh, I'm sorry," she said and winced as if someone had hit her. "I should have known that. You must miss them very much."

Missing them felt like a deep splinter. Talking about them only pushed the splinter deeper into my chest. Since Papa and Mama died, I'd learned that most people had a sliver in their hearts. They whispered things like, "My daddy died when I was about your age," or "I lost my sister. She was only a babe, but I loved her so." Miss Peasley looked like she'd been left behind, too.

"Do you miss your Mama and Papa, Miss Peasley?"

She scratched the rash again. "That's a funny thing to say. They aren't dead. They do live far away. Have you ever heard of a place called North Dakota?"

I'd written a report about North Dakota. "The territory making up North Dakota was part of the Louisiana Purchase of 1803. North Dakota became a state on November 2, 1889. The state motto is: Liberty and union, now and forever: one and inseparable. I know just about all there is to know about North Dakota. The capitol is Bismarck."

"That is about all there is to know about North Dakota," she said and tipped her glass for the last of the milk.

I sucked on the straw and a glob of chocolate filled my mouth. I swallowed before I said, "But you miss someone you love very much."

Miss Peasley wiped at the corners of her mouth, even though she hadn't left one bit of milk there. Miss Peasley was the tidiest person I'd ever met, except for Miss Wood, who would be much happier with Miss Peasley as a house guest than me. Miss Peasley leaned forward and lowered her voice. "You can miss some people more than others and some not at all. Do you know what I mean by that?"

"I don't miss Dr. Warner. He gave us shots. Three nurses had to help Lucy hold Goody down. He gave us a lollipop afterward, but I don't think he was sorry for what he did."

"No one likes to go to the doctor, I suppose. But I'm talking about people in your family or people you live with. Even though these people love us very much, they can also hurt us, maybe more than anyone else." She wiped at a wet spot on the table with her napkin. "Mercy, is anyone hurting you?"

The bed at Miss Wood's house was like sleeping on a board, but that was not what Miss Peasley meant. Even I knew that. There were plenty of kids at the orphanage who arrived with scars and bruises, or looked like they'd been hollowed out from hunger. The only scratches on me came from climbing the apricot tree while Lucy wrote her letters.

"Sometimes Goody will tease me, but he feels real bad when he makes me cry."

"Well, yes, brothers will do that. I'm thinking more about the adults around you. You mustn't worry. You can tell me anything, even if they've asked you not to tell anyone. They didn't mean me. I'm the kind of person who can help you." Miss Peasley dug at her rash. The welts were red hot hills.

"Adults don't know how to say they're sorry. Have you noticed that?" I asked.

She pushed her glass back and took a notebook and a pen from her purse. "I have. Go on."

"It's best to forgive them anyways. Otherwise, you're likely to have a rash all the time."

Miss Peasley looked down at her arm and back at me.

"My mama used to get rashes," I told her. "When the itching got real bad, Lucy filled a bag with ice, and that seemed to help her rest. Lucy brought the bag with us. You can use it, if you want."

"That's very kind of you...How did—?" She wiped her eyes with a purple-laced hankie. "We're here to talk about you. Now, tell me about the people from the migrant camp who come to see you. How do you feel about them coming night after night? Do they scare you?"

"They come for help."

"But do they scare you?" she pressed.

This was a strange question. They didn't come to hurt me, but people sometimes got confused about what to be scared about.

"Do the migrant workers scare you?" I asked Miss Peasley.

Welts rose on Miss Peasley's neck. "Me? No. Scare me? I don't think so. No, they don't." She leaned back again. Crossed her arms over her belly. "Why would you ask such a thing?"

She sure looked scared, like she was afraid I was going to hit her. Maybe she'd talked to Veronica's mother. "I won't hurt you."

"Of course you won't. What made you say such a thing?" She twisted a strand of hair around her finger and looked to the ceiling. Kids did that when they didn't know the answer in school. "Has anyone—?" She scratched at her neck hard enough to leave red trails. "Those people, the ones who stand outside your house, do they pay your aunt money to see you?"

I hadn't seen anyone. "Aunt Ada won't let me go out to the people. Lucy, neither, or Lotti."

"Well, I'm glad they're watching over you. You should be careful. There are people, some of them children like you, with your presumed talents, who travel from church to church, and they collect a lot of money at those events. It's despicable, really, a complete sham." She spoke like a radio preacher. "Give us your money, they say. Seed your faith with an offering to the Lord. Give and it shall be given unto thee." She wrung her hands, but I bet she wanted to scratch her neck some more. Welts rose as I watched. "You know, Mercy, there's no such verse in the Bible, but the people who come for a miracle don't know that. They're hurting. Desperate. They're fooled like children at the carnival."

I'd gone and made Miss Peasley angry, and I didn't know how I'd done it. I'd never asked anyone for money, and I sure didn't quote made-up Bible verses. The odd thing about adults is that they can be angry about one thing and say they're angry over something very different. One morning, Mama burned the oatmeal, and when Goody said something about it tasting funny, she yelled real mean-like at him. I knew for a fact she did not want to yell at Goody because she was real sorry afterward. We learned later that Papa was looking for work again. Miss Peasley hardly knew me. If she was angry about something, I was pretty sure it wasn't me, but I wanted to slink away, like Goody had done when Mama got so mad. I pushed my glass to the middle of the table.

"Mercy? What are you thinking? Has something I said upset you?" Miss Peasley reached across the table to wrap her long fingers around my hand. "Mercy?"

I was angry now. "I don't have any money. If I did, I would buy Goody a new Lone Ranger badge."

"What about your aunt or your sister?"

"Lucy keeps dollars in a sock under the mattress, but she won't buy a badge for Goody. I already asked her. "

"Where does she get her money?"

"You're hurting my hand."

She released me. "I'm sorry. I'm very, very sorry. Would you like another soda? I didn't mean to hurt you."

"Miss Peasley, I'm sorry somebody hurt you."

"What?" She dug at her neck. "That's not why we're here. We're here to help you. That's my job. I help children who can't help themselves. I'm not very good at it, am I? Maybe I should have gone to business college like my father wanted. I would be typing in some office and married to Danny. There's no chance of that, not since he found out... It's better this way."

I waited for something to pop into my head, some words to soothe her, maybe to cool her rash. Not one word came to me for Miss Peasley, so I quoted a mercy verse. "'For as the heaven is high above the earth, so great is his mercy toward them that fear him.' Psalms 103, verse eleven."

Miss Peasley looked around the drugstore, like she expected someone to throw a rock at her. She pulled her white gloves on and buttoned them at the wrist. "I know all about fear. I know all about praying for mercy. It's time for us to go."

Ada

May 2, 1994

Dear Lucy,

You asked for my honest opinion of Melba Wood. She was a nitwit! My impulse was to reach through the telephone to wring her scrawny neck for losing Mercy. But I blame myself for entrusting our little darling to her. I should have known better. This is yet another regret I don't enjoy revisiting. Let's get it over with, shall we?

Like you, I thought first of the river, but I prayed Mercy had crawled into a cozy spot to read and had fallen asleep. You do remember her doing that, don't you?

In the moments after Melba called, I could barely breathe. I thought I was having some sort of attack. Now that I've actually had a heart attack, I know it wasn't anything of the sort. Whatever it was, I didn't let on. We had a job to do. Energy entered my muscles like fire, when only moments prior I'd announced supper would be toast and jam.

I saw fear in your eyes, but you kept your head about you. I desperately wanted to hold you in my arms and tell you how very proud your courage made me. I'm glad we can whisper endearments to each other now. Have we filled the chasm? Is it even possible? Are there enough words in the world? People who say they've lived free of regrets are either lying or delusional. I swim in regrets daily.

I've gotten sidetracked again, and it's time for supper. Pamela, the CNA who is pregnant with her third child, each from a different man, just called me to supper. She talks to me like I'm a child. Tonight, she said, "Oh, Ada, it's your very most favorite meal tonight." Corn dogs? My favorite? Not hardly! If I'm lucky, Joey has already eaten the corn dog off my plate. I'll finish this tomorrow, darling.

I'm not feeling so well today, my dear, but I promised I would finish this promptly. I don't want you cross with me when your visit is so very close. Seeing you will snap me out of the doldrums. Only six more weeks until you're here.

Back to the day Melba lost Mercy. After Melba called, you rounded up Corky and Kansas Johnny and some other people I don't remember. You gave each person an area to search. You saw I was too upset to go on my own, so you led me to the truck and we drove toward Melba's house. Did you drive? I don't remember that either, but we hadn't turned out of the lane when that Miss Peasley pulled in front of the house. Mercy sat on the seat beside her. She looked a little sheepish, didn't she? That imp knew she had worried decades off our lives. (If only she had!)

I'm sorry. I'll finish this tomorrow. I'm not well.

It's been three days, but I'm feeling much better. I should not have eaten that corn dog. I wasn't the only one who suffered. It's a good thing I only ate half of that dreadful thing. Another resident ended up in the emergency room.

I must take a step back. I've forgotten to write about Goody. His true self shone the day Mercy went missing. When I told him we needed to find her, he ran up the stairs. I assumed he had something better to do than look for his sister. The next time we saw him, he was all decked out in his Lone Ranger outfit atop that old mule. Had we ever seen Goody sit straighter? He harangued that mule into a trot! I nearly cried at the sight of him bouncing down the lane. I vowed right then to order him that badge.

As it turned out, Miss Peasley had found Mercy walking along the road and had taken her for something sweet at the drugstore. You and I both know that woman was looking for a reason to whisk Mercy away from us. Miss Peasley wasn't a bad girl, only a bit too eager. She went on and on about how she would be watching us. Your face went as white as death. I promised myself to have a little heart-to-heart with you once the peaches were on their way.

But we weren't afforded that luxury, were we?

Love,
Ada

Lucy

I'd long since kicked off the sheet. Between the heat, my aching muscles, and worrying about Miss Peasley coming after Mercy, sleep only came in fits and spurts. I ran my hand toward Mercy, looking for an inch or two of cooler sheet to claim. My hand reached until my fingers found the edge of the mattress.

"Mercy?" I whispered, groping the bed for her. I clicked on the bedside lamp. Tonto raised his head. Goody sucked in a sticky breath and whistled through his nose without waking. I looked under the bed. In the bathroom. In the kitchen. There was only one place she could be.

I found her out by the road, sitting among a handful of migrants. Someone had brought a lantern. Their faces shone amber and red with deep pockets of shadow for eyes. They leaned toward her, as if her words were the elixir of life. I recognized the young mother and her baby. An old woman with a goiter. Two women— I think one was the mother and the other the daughter—sat with arms entwined. The mother passed the daughter a limp hankie. The lantern's light glistened off their tears.

Well, this certainly sealed our future. We couldn't stay. If we left Palisade, our best hope was to stay one step ahead of the throng of people seeking Mercy's favor. Fatigue gripped my bones. I stepped into the lamplight and sat behind Mercy. I put my hand on her shoulder.

She turned to me. "They have questions; that's all."

"It's awfully late." I looked at the faces in the circle. They pleaded without words for more of Mercy's time. "You understand, don't you?" I asked them. "She's only a little girl."

"We was just about to send her in," the mother said. "But I admit her words are ointment to an old woman's fears."

"They're going home tomorrow," Mercy said.

I sighed. The damage had been done. There wasn't any sense in pulling her away now. I lifted her onto my lap. "Okay, but not too long."

The woman's goiter was the size of a melon. When she spoke, her voice was raw from crying. "Tell us again, child. You weren't on no cloud? You walked on ground as firm as this?" She patted the grass.

"It was a garden, the kind you see in picture books, not the kind you have to weed."

"And your mother was there?" This from the young mother.

"It was like a dream. Things happen in your dream, and you think to yourself, that can't happen. But Mother was there, and she'd been there for a long time. She knew everything, and I didn't know anything. She had friends who knew her, too. I watched her sew beads onto a fancy coat."

"She was working?" the younger woman said.

"It wasn't like beating the rugs or changing the sheets."

"But you said your mother fell in the river right before you. How'd she have time to make a coat? That don't make sense."

Mercy pressed into me before answering, "I didn't ask. There was so much to see. And I knew I couldn't stay. Mama smelled like the woods in spring."

"That's how my father smelled," a woman said and stilled her trembling lips with a touch.

Mercy's head lolled onto my shoulder. "I'm sleepy."

The woman with the goiter patted Mercy's knee. "You should get on to bed now. Coming out here like you done, well, you blessed us." They rose, the younger helping the older, and walked silently toward the camp. I carried Mercy to bed.

That was the most I'd heard of Mercy's trip to heaven. She'd asked me every so often if I was ready to hear, and I told her to keep her story to herself. I saw how it hurt her that I refused to listen. I had no reason to doubt what she said. No one was closer to God than Mercy. And I would be lying if I didn't admit a niggling curiosity. After all, I watched as the doctor pressed on

Mercy's chest and pounded her back after they pulled her from the river. It took an eternity for that first breath to come. I supposed her soul had to go somewhere. A person can't always say why they find something objectionable, like I disdained Mercy's stories of heaven, but, for a long time, I did.

Back in bed, watching the breeze lift the curtains away from the window, it came to me that I coveted the secret of my shame. I'd let go of Mother to save Mercy and released Mercy to save myself. I preferred to believe this secret was mine to keep.

I supposed only heaven knew everything.

Lucy

Kansas Johnny rocked back on his heels. "There won't be peaches worth picking when we're done today." He chugged down the last of his coffee. Grounds collected between his teeth. "Guess I'll be gittin' myself back home here right quick." With that said he ambled from the kitchen steps toward the orchard.

For the last day of the harvest, I was preparing my favorite—chicken and dumplings. Goody stood lookout for the prisoners' truck. Inside the kitchen, the pot of chicken bubbled on the stove. Lotti insisted a robust flame ensured the best flavor. Ada turned the flame down every time she walked through, and she questioned why I'd added onions, carrots, and celery. "You aren't cooking for the Queen of England."

"That's the way I was taught," I said through my teeth. We were all frayed by the work of the harvest and worry over Mercy.

Ada peered into the cooking pot. "This isn't Magda's recipe."

"How do you know?"

"Because I ate Magda's chicken and dumplings every Sunday in my parents' house. Magda didn't embellish. She covered the chickens with well water and simmered the pots slow. She always forgot the salt."

Ada spoke more and more frequently about her childhood with Mother. Sometimes her words were as tender as crumb cake. Other times, a twinge of contempt colored her words, like she'd tasted spoiled sauerkraut. As for me, I promised to find things to love about Goody and Mercy no matter how they managed to hurt me

252

through the years. Siblings know our vulnerabilities best and aren't afraid to exploit them. I didn't understand this at all. And yet, I wanted the three of us to be different.

"People change, Ada. They learn new things. Mother did teach me how to make chicken and dumplings." It was yet another lie. But I couldn't back down now. I'd watched Mother cook, but she avoided the kitchen by the time I was ready to learn. It was Mrs. Devendorf who had taught me to add the flavoring vegetables. She'd also taught me how to make dumplings as tender as baby kisses. I could have told Ada this, but it seemed to me she needed to try thinking the best of her sister, just that once. "Maybe you're remembering someone else."

Ada clumped down the porch stairs in her heavy boots. Walking toward the barn against the rising sun gave her a halo like the picture of her as a girl with Mother. I sure wished that girl would reappear.

I gathered the ingredients for Swans Down Devil's Food Cake, a recipe I'd found in *Better Homes & Gardens*. I'd raided every sugar bowl and canister in the house to gather the half cup needed for the cake, plus I crushed a few sugar cubes I'd pocketed from church.

Once I sifted the dry ingredients together, Ada's boots stomped the porch steps again. She spoke through the screen. "I loved your mother. I loved her very, very much." Ada was gone when I'd finally composed myself enough to turn toward the door.

Ada drove me crazy. Just when I thought I understood her, that I'd come to some sort of peace about her, she said something that crumbled that peace. There were days I wished I'd never learned of her existence. But we were all better off at Honey Sweet Ranch, even though Ada tested my patience daily, all while drawing me imperceptibly closer. She had panicked over Mercy's disappearance and cheered Goody's loyalty. And she loved my mother. I would try harder to see the good in her. She deserved that much.

With the cake in the oven, I sat by the open window with a cup of coffee. The pickers worked on the eastern edge of the orchard, so all was quiet except for the growl of the hoopie as Goody drove it up and down, up and down.

I counted on my fingers the months that had passed since I'd

discovered Ada's existence. Sixteen. Longer than I'd thought. It
had been the day of Mother's funeral. Mrs. Devendorf felt the
twins needed another night of respite at her house before returning
to the apartment, now devoid of our mother, so I'd returned to our
apartment to pack the twins' clothes.

I sat on Mother's bed, fingering the peaks and valleys of her
chenille spread. From that spot, I could reach everything in her
world. A globe. A jelly glass full of sharpened pencils. Bottles of
pills with names I couldn't pronounce. Stacks and stacks of
crossword puzzles and a dictionary with a broken spine. A tub of
Ponds Beauty Cream. Three library books, one with a bookmark
only pages from the end. A picture of Papa, me, and the twins
from Christmas. And a Bible swollen with use.

I touched all of these things—balanced a pencil, smeared cream
over my face, spun the globe to run my finger along the worn line
at the equator. The Bible crinkled when I picked it up. I fanned the
pages to release the smell of gardenia and sweat and old leather
when a photograph fell into my lap.

And there she was, my mother, a teenager standing self-
consciously in front of an old car. One hand covered her mouth to
hide the gap in her teeth, but her eyes were smiling. She wasn't
alone in the picture. A small girl, much younger and as fair as
butter, hugged Mother's waist. The little girl's head tilted back as
she laughed at what had to have been the best joke in the world.
They were salt and pepper, light and dark.

The girls' full names were written on the back with their ages,
and beside the little girl's name I recognized my mother's
handwriting. "My sister," she wrote. I slid that photograph behind
my library card in my wallet, but I never showed it to the twins.
Goody would rather eat worms than look at photographs of girls.
And I hadn't wanted to build an expectation in Mercy that couldn't
be realized.

That didn't stop the photograph from seeding a dream in my
heart that sprouted and grew, especially when the twins left for the
orphanage. I frequently imagined our aunt, Ada Christiane Stauffer,
baking in a sunlit kitchen with children flitting in and out from the
garden for a kiss and a cookie, for I'd counted the years ahead and
figured she was a full-grown woman by then. I often sat in the pale
light of Mother's bedside lamp and swallowed down the urge to
call out Ada's name. In my imaginings, I did call and she smiled as

if she had been waiting for me.

But how was I to find a little girl who was now a woman? She didn't live in Prairie du Sac. So I visited nearby towns to scan telephone directories, but the listings were mostly of men's names, and I didn't know Ada's married name. For all the longing the laughing girl in the photograph evoked, I held little hope of ever knowing her.

It was a hole in Goody's shoe that led me to discover Ada's address. At first, I tried gluing cardboard into the soles, but the cardboard worked loose before the end of the school day. My tip money wouldn't cover the cost of new shoes, not with a rent payment due. Left with no options, I looked around the apartment for something to sell. Most of our belongings came from tag sales, except for Mother's jewelry box, an anniversary gift from Papa from their early days, the only object of value in our apartment. Perhaps the pawn shop would give me the two dollars I needed for Goody's new shoes. When I dumped the contents onto Mother's bed, I found Ada's address taped to the bottom.

I didn't write her immediately. I knew Mother hadn't spoken of her sister for a reason. Maybe Ada wasn't a mother in a sunlit kitchen. Maybe she was in prison for murdering her husband. Or maybe Mother and Ada were like the Heesch brothers, old men who farmed on neighboring land but crossed the street rather than greet one other.

What had torn my mother and her sister apart? I couldn't imagine anything but death coming between me and the twins.

The director of the Sauk County Orphanage didn't give me a chance to discover what had happened between Mother and Ada, much less to find her and ask if she'd take us in. Mrs. Nadel visited unexpectedly, wearing a wool suit and a velvet hat on the hottest day of summer. If she'd called ahead, I would have emptied the drain board and dusted Mother's figurines. Mrs. Nadel took out a clipboard and pen. She asked all kinds of questions: "How old are you? Do you have a job? What do you feed the children? Who watches the twins after school when you're working? Are you taking them to church?"

After she left, I studied the photograph of Mother and Ada. Sure enough, I'd remembered correctly. Ada's eyes were wide and friendly. And so, it was the light in her eyes that emboldened me to write. In that letter I told her as much as I knew about Mother's life because a sister would want to know. It wasn't a long letter. I didn't know as much about Mother as I'd thought, and that embarrassed me but saddened me even more. I'd never thought to ask her about her childhood or anything, really. I ripped that letter out of the tablet and started again. In the second draft, I simply told Ada about the accident at the arsenal that took Papa's life and how Mother had drowned in the river. By the time Ada wrote back, the Child Assistance Society had already come for Goody and Mercy.

Ada's letter read simply, "Stay in Wisconsin."

It seemed a simple question given all that Gerland had been through. "After all that's happened to you and your family," I said, "do you ever doubt the existence of God?"

If the question bothered Gerland, he didn't show it. He plucked peach after peach off the tree and dropped them gently into his picking sack before answering. Finally he said, "I went weeks and months wondering if I'd wasted my life serving God. I was angry. Disappointed. Even now, I'm tired. I forget about Him. But then, something happens. A kindness is extended, like your wonderful dumplings. The sun's descent creates a cathedral of the clouds. I hear your brother calling for his dog. And I am pulled back from the blackness. God is real to me again, and I sense a faint echo of His love."

His answer revealed that Gerland still warred, even though he was far from a battlefield, not for the high ground but for his faith and freedom from his shame. And there I was, by then a seventeen-year-old girl fighting the same battles, needing the same answers. Because he was older, much more thoughtful, and because he had studied the Bible as a pastor, he seemed like the perfect person to help me find those answers. And since he would be gone soon, my questions were weighted with urgency. "The Bible says the righteous will never know hunger. How can that be true? Your wife and children, they are struggling for every meal."

His hands went limp on the picking sack as he looked toward the horizon.

Hope is a robin's egg in our palms. I knew this to be true, and yet I crushed the egg in Gerland's hand with my probing words. I regretted them immediately. "Gerland? I'm so sorry."

He closed his eyes. And then, Gerland reached for one peach

and then another, resuming his usual rhythm. Injuring Gerland like that sucked my marrow clean. I glanced at him as I picked, looking for his brow to relax. He finally said, "I worry about the children of Europe, and not only the German children but the children of Poland, France, and Italy, and certainly of Britain." He shook his head. "There were so many children. They played their games, but their sad faces belied their chatter and laughter. Their eyes no longer reflected the light. Children were asked to do things adults wouldn't do. How will they recover? Will they ever feel safe again? Certainly, shame will haunt them forever. My own children..." He sighed and his words trailed off.

I attacked the tree, snapping the peaches from the branches and dropping them into the sack.

"Easy, girl." Corky looked up, grinning. "What did that tree ever do to you?"

The weight of the sack pulled against my shoulders. "I got carried away. I'm sorry."

"If that tree doesn't survive another year, I'll have to report you to the high command." That meant Ada—Corky would never do that—but I took his warning. If the peaches arrived at the packing shed bruised, they'd be rejected. That was unacceptable. I was learning this peach business.

"I'll be more careful," I said.

Corky gave me a two-fingered salute and carried empty baskets to pickers at the end of the row.

"Lucy," Gerland said, "there are times when the light fades in your eyes, just like the children of Europe."

"It's the harvest, the heat. I can't sleep. It's nothing."

He laughed kindly. "I'll be gone tomorrow. You can tell me your secrets, Lucy. If the war has taught me anything, it is the power of confessing our sins."

I knew exactly what he meant, but I'd gone this long without saying the truth out loud. "Who listens to your sins?" I said.

"You're right, of course, to ask. Back in Germany, before this mess erupted, I met with a pastor friend every week for prayer. He lived in the next town. Pastors have their unique temptations, silly preoccupations, petty disagreements. We're human, very human. As the pressure increased to pledge loyalty to the state church, our meetings grew in importance. We met for five years. He heard all of my sins without judging me. When this is over, he will listen again, if he is able. He was mustered when the Russians entered the war. I don't know what I'll do if he is lost. I won't burden my wife."

I came very close to telling him everything, sheltered there among the leaves like a confessional, but forgiveness was for people like Gerland. He was a pastor, a godly man pulled from his life by no fault of his own. "I don't know what you think you see in me, Gerland, but I'm fine. I'm only a silly girl. I'm doing the best I can."

"I'm sorry—"

His sympathy would surely melt my resistance. I climbed down the ladder, dropped the peaches in the basket like stones. "I have work to do in the house."

Inside, every pot had been washed and every dish stacked in the cupboard. I tried reading, but my brain assigned no meaning to the words. When I'd read the same paragraph for the third time, I slammed the book shut. It didn't help that the house held the day's heat with unreasonable tenacity or that my skin itched from the peach fuzz. I'd expected to find Mercy inside, but she spent most of her time with the new kittens. I was much too alone with my thoughts.

I hadn't written Pete yet that day. The longer it took for his letter to arrive, the harder it became to write cheerful letters. I wanted to know where he was, and I didn't want to know. I'd seen a newsreel on the invasion of Guam. The announcer made it sound like recapturing the island had been child's play for the Marines. The tone of Pete's letters told a different story. Did anyone tell the truth anymore?

And Gerland wanted to be my confessor? I didn't shoot anyone. I didn't invade the countries of Europe. And I certainly didn't hate the Jews. I didn't know any Jews.

I went upstairs and lay back on the bed. The heat blossomed between my shoulders and prickled my hairline, just as it had that day in May. We'd had steady rain for several weeks, and then the temperatures flirted with the nineties. Much too hot for May. The humidity was a heavy hand. I'd worn a dress to church with lace around the collar. It itched like crazy. Mother came out of her room just as I'd decided to change. For the first time in weeks, she'd pin-curled her hair and applied makeup. That stopped me where I stood.

"Let's go to the river," she said. "The water is carrying all sorts of debris. People are gathering to watch. I heard about it on the radio."

Goody lay with his mouth near the fan, making his voice warble. "I'm game."

Mercy looked from Mother to me and back to Mother. "It will be cooler by the water, won't it?"

Only the butcher's locker would have been cool that day. Mother said, "Let's go, then. We don't want to miss the biggest thing to happen since forever."

I shook my head, trying to resist the pull of my memories, to direct my thoughts to things more mundane in the present, like the start of my senior year of high school or how I would talk Ada into having pancakes for supper. I raised the window higher, hoping for a breeze. Gerland picked close to the house. His steps were leaden as he emptied the picking sack, all thanks to me.

Despite myself, I played with how I would tell Gerland about that day at the river. The weight of those words squeezed my chest.

I pushed the screen door open until it slammed against the wall. Goody honked the hoopie's horn as he drove down the lane toward the packing shed. Sergeant Salvatore put a finger to his cap that I ignored, along with a wolf whistle from Reinhardt. I tugged on Gerland's pant leg. "I do have something to tell you."

"They are pressing us to finish," he said, looking down at me. "I can't stop. You better get a ladder."

I snapped on a picking sack and climbed into the shelter of the leaves. I couldn't look at Gerland as I talked, not into the softness of his eyes. I would cry and I needed to get my words out quickly. "I'm pretty sure my mother jumped into the river. People think she fell, but I saw her eyes. They said she was sorry, but she looked relieved, too. She tried to push Mercy toward me, but Mercy grabbed her dress and fell into the river with her.

"I couldn't think. There wasn't time. So I jumped in. The current, it was so much stronger than I expected. If it hadn't been for the tree snagged against the bridge, well, Mercy and I wouldn't be here.

"I worked my way to where Mother held Mercy against the tree's trunk. Mother wanted me to take Mercy from her.

"But I couldn't take her, you see, because Mother would let go."

Gerland touched my arm. "Lucy, climb down."

Once we were on the ground, he unclipped my picking sack. Now that I'd started talking, I couldn't stop. "Mother pushed Mercy into my arms. I grabbed at her."

"Your sister? You grabbed for your sister?" Gerland asked, his hands holding my shoulders.

"No. Yes. I pulled Mercy to my chest, but I caught the collar of Mother's dress, too. Her head went under the water. She looked up at me, pleading. Her hair wrapped around my arm. I feared her collar would tear off."

"How in the world were you holding on?"

"A branch under my arm. I held onto Mother's collar, but the current pulled at Mercy. I tried to lift her with my legs, but the river pried my legs away from her. I was losing them both." I was crying now.

Gerland pushed my hair away from my face. "Go on, Lucy."

"Mercy's head slipped under the water. I couldn't raise her. I had to let go."

Our eyes met. "You let go of Mercy?"

"No, Mother."

"You let go of your mother to save your sister."

When had he switched to English? "The branch cracked."

"What happened to Mercy? She's here. She's fine."

My words flowed now as insistently as the river's current. "To save myself, I grabbed for another branch. Mercy was swept away."

"Oh, my God. And you blame yourself?"

"I couldn't hold her."

"Your mother, Lucy, she could not have known you would jump in, that Mercy would follow her. You did the right thing in letting go. Mercy was saved."

"It took them three days to find Mother. The water was very cold. I had made a promise to my father. And still, I lost her."

"Lucy, listen to me. We don't have much time." He touched my cheek with the back of his fingers. "I'm sorry, *Schatz*. I never dreamed you carried such a burden. I can see why you asked your questions."

He drew a peach out of his picking sack and held it out to me. "This may not be the best example. We are all a little tired of peaches by now, *ja?*"

I agreed with a nod.

"Sometimes what we see of God is like this peach's horrible fuzz. It's irritating and seemingly incongruous with what we know is inside the skin. They remove the fuzz before they pack the peaches, *ja*? Who would buy them otherwise? Not me. Not you."

He twisted the peach to tear the fruit open, revealing the golden flesh veined with red. "Once you have tasted a peach, the fuzz is inconvenient. It's a mystery we may never solve, and we wish we didn't have to deal with it, but we love the peach too much not to work past the fuzz. It's not a perfect picture of God's nature, but this is what I mean by staking my soul on the blood of Christ. That He came is a historical fact. He died for our sins out of the purest love. That is the flesh of the peach—it is the flesh of Christ, the source of our hope. You and I, we must keep our focus on His love, not on what we don't understand, what is inconvenient or confounding about His nature. Someone as wonderful as Christ will always confound."

Gerland drew my other hand to encircle the peach. Its juice ran between my fingers. Its aroma sweetened the air. "You are a brave and strong young woman. Guilt, even when it is not deserved, erodes what is best of us. Look to the cross, Lucy. You will see the goodness of God and find the comfort you need. *Ja*, you will do this?"

"Are you done with your sermon, Gerland?" This from Reinhardt who stood with his hands on his hips.

Gerland wiped my tears with a hankie. "We are done here, I think." He smiled tenderly at me. Like a father.

Reinhardt turned sharply to walk through the trees to the truck.

Gerland held my hand with his sticky fingers. "We will be on the same journey although many miles apart. We won't give up, will we?"

I shook my head and he gave my hand a squeeze.

Ada called from several rows away, "Pickers to the trucks! The harvest is done! Good work, everyone!"

Gerland unsnapped his picking sack. I hated the war for many reasons, especially, just then, for how it brought people together and ripped them apart. I laid a hand to Gerland's arm. I wanted to say something, but what? He'd set aside his pain to contend with mine. "I'll pray for your family. And for your friend, the pastor, that he'll be waiting for you."

A light sparked in his eyes. "And I will pray for you." He dug

261

the pit out of the peach I held and worked the pulpy flesh clean with his fingers. He handed it back to me. "Keep this in your pocket, a reminder of where we put our trust, *ja?*

Lucy

Practically the whole town of Palisade came out to watch as the last boxes of peaches were loaded into ice-cooled train cars for destinations to the east. And with the peaches gone, the migrant workers prepared to leave with them.

Tents lay along the roads and in fields like popped balloons as the workers stowed blankets and pots and children into their vehicles. The hoods of cars rose snootily, weighted as they were by the many jars of peaches wrapped inside blankets in the trunks, some to sell to neighbors and some to save for a sunless January in Iowa.

Just because the pickers left, didn't mean rest came for those of us staying in Palisade. We swept and scrubbed the migrant cabins until Lotti declared each one clean. And there was our own canning to do—peach jam, peach halves, and spiced peaches. But the work seemed downright lackadaisical after the frenzy of harvest. Best of all, with the town emptying of pickers, shoppers no longer jostled for a place at the checkout counter, giving me plenty of time to browse movie magazines.

With the pantry shelves glowing gold with jars of peaches and the bushel baskets stacked in the barn, hardened muscles and tanned faces were all that remained of the harvest. Even as a newcomer, I was proud of what this small town had accomplished. The peach harvest of 1944 was the largest in the history of Palisade. Over a million bushels of peaches dripped down the chins of children in Kansas City and Chicago and points beyond. That made me smile.

The war news subdued our celebration, however. Instead of the usual band concert in the park, we filed into church to give thanks and to pray. Right after the service, we gathered around the radio. Ada reached for my hand as the reporter spoke with an urgent and solemn voice about troop movements in Europe. Gil had been mentioning Geronimo, his code word for yet another jump behind enemy lines in every letter he wrote. He could very well be in France or on Germany's doorstep.

Every night Ada played the piano long into the night while I lay on the sofa with a pillow and blanket to keep her company. The darkness tormented my thoughts about Pete. It had been over three months since his last letter. What did that mean? Had he been injured? Worse? I tried not to think about what his silence could mean. The days were endless, stuffed as they were with all of my questions.

And yet, the heat of summer did, at last, yield to the softer days of September. Ada and I developed a routine. After homework for me and milking for her, we sat under the apricot tree to write letters to Pete and Gil. Part of me wasn't sure Pete wanted to hear from me. Maybe his silence signaled a cooled heart. That was just too bad. Pete would hear from me whether he wanted to or not. He wouldn't come home wondering how I felt about anything, especially not him.

One day, Ada opened a V-mail from Gil. She'd held it in her pocket since Charlie had delivered it around noon. Her self-control astounded and annoyed me. I hoped she didn't expect me to wait that long when word from Pete's finally arrived.

After reading the letter, she pressed it to her heart. "Thank God, he's back in England. At least he was as of two weeks ago. Let me read this to you. He says, 'Do you remember the Wrights? They're the family with eight children in a tiny cottage near the base. Our platoon keeps them supplied with whatever we can scrounge food-wise. Well, we hit the jackpot last night. Lots of guys were off the base, and the mess crew managed to cook up a halfway decent Salisbury steak. We packaged up as much as we dared without drawing too much attention to ourselves and delivered the meat to the Wrights' cottage. You should have seen the children eat, Ada. Their mother told us they hadn't eaten meat in months. We have to finish this damnable war and do it quick.

These children need the world to get back in order. We won't be lolling about here long. Geronimo is being groomed again.'"

Ada squeezed her eyes shut. I looked away, embarrassed at her show of emotion. I pretended to consider what to write Pete. She sniffed and our eyes met. "I thought you would enjoy the story about the children. That's Gil for you. You're going to like him."

I liked him fine already. "He sounds nice."

"He is." She folded the letter and put it back in her apron pocket. She focused on the horizon. "It's been difficult for you to concentrate on your studies." She turned her eyes on me. Gold flecks orbited her pupils like moons. "You're distracted. That's to be expected. I might be able to help in that regard. I was going to save this bit of news for a surprise, but I can't."

The only surprise I hoped for was seeing Pete walk up the lane.

"Gil has agreed to help with your college expenses. Of course, I've told him many times how brilliant you are. He wants you to have this opportunity."

Typical of Ada to make plans without talking to me. I swallowed hard. There was no time like the present to pop Ada's bubble. "Pete and I are getting married the moment he gets back."

Ada closed her writing pad, sat up straight. "How long have you known this?"

He'd asked me in June. I'd answered him the next day. "I'm not sure he's received my answer."

I hooked my pen on the writing pad, preparing for the debate on whether women should attend college. She'd convinced me long ago that I should go, but didn't Pete deserve to have his dreams realized, too? We couldn't both afford to go.

Ada shifted. "Still no letters from Pete?"

She already knew the answer, so I kept quiet. A rogue breeze rustled the leaves and played with my skirt. I held the writing pad to my chest. Ada scooted closer, hooked my hair over my ear and rested her hand on my shoulder. I was glad for the weight of it, for surely I would dissolve and scatter with the next gust of wind.

"It can't be easy getting the mail through," she said.

"He sounded different in his last letter." I leaned ever so slightly toward Ada. Her arms encircled me. I spoke into her shoulder. "I shouldn't make any plans until..." Until what? Until Pete came home? Until he wrote to break up with me? Until, somehow, I learned he'd been killed? And how would that happen? It wasn't as if the Marines would send their telegrams to me.

Ada wiped my tears with her apron. "Lucy, married ladies go to college. It's harder, but you aren't one to shirk away from a challenge. Or you could wait to get married. Knowing someone through letters isn't the same as living with them day after day. I hope you'll consider your options."

I'd known Pete most of my life. He was the only future I'd allowed myself to think about. All other possibilities seemed painfully singular. "I'll think about it."

Ada drew me closer. Her breath warmed my scalp. "We should visit a college or two. We have time. A train trip to Denver is in order. There's Denver University and The University of Colorado in Boulder."

That far from the twins? "Why a university? What about the community college in Grand Junction? Lots of girls are going there."

Ada thought on my question too long. "Yes, I suppose Mesa is a possibility, but you don't want to limit yourself. Is Pete an academic? Does he have plans for college?"

Pete and I had exchanged letters about cars, houses, even babies, but nothing about school. And no, Pete wasn't an academic. He'd barely made it through geometry. But then, he'd changed in almost every other way. Why wouldn't he want to go to college? "I'll ask him."

Ada kissed my hair. I would definitely write Pete about Ada's tenderness. That qualified as cheerful news.

Hank stood when I entered the drugstore. An empty malt mixer and glass sat on the table, along with a dozen napkins folded into airplanes. "I didn't think you were coming."

I slid into the booth. "I couldn't find Goody. I'm sorry. Of all things, he was painting the mule white with shoe polish. He wanted the mule to look more like Silver." I showed him the polish that clung to my cuticles.

Hank leaned back into the booth and had a good laugh.

"My aunt would have a fit. Fortunately, he'd only painted one leg. That boy. You weren't like that, were you?" I said.

Hank crushed the napkins into a ball. He wasn't laughing anymore. In fact, I'd never seen Hank so serious. Did he know why

I'd agreed to meet him? "Maybe we should save that conversation for another time. I'm trying to make a good impression here."

He'd already made quite an impression on me. He was much smarter than he let on. I saw that in how he quietly helped struggling students during lunch in the library. Ada said his prospects were better than average. Even so, she didn't know I'd come to meet him at the fountain. She was awfully funny about boys. She all but worshipped Gil, never hinting at one snag in their marital happiness, but she considered every other man a threat to my future. Was she selfish? Prudish? I'd heard enough to know her parents had been strict. She'd surpassed them on that front, of that I was sure. But if they were that strict, how did she end up in Palisade as a single young woman? I'd never thought to ask. Another mystery about Ada. I shook my thoughts of her away.

I was sitting with Hank. Heads turned when I was with him, and I would be lying if I said I didn't swell a bit at the attention. He was good looking in a fresh, confident way that sent a thrill through me. Too bad I was there to put an end to his attention, even though his attention had only amounted to a walk home from school now and again. I was an engaged woman, and it was time to start acting like one.

Mrs. Richmond buzzed from table to table before she pulled out her pad at our booth. "Can I get the lady something?"

Hank ordered another malt for himself. "My brother warned me to eat as much as I could before basic." I ordered a cherry cola, which I intended to pay for myself.

Hank folded and unfolded a napkin as we waited. "I'll be leaving soon. My folks signed me off, so I don't have to wait until I'm seventeen. They aren't too happy about me quitting school."

Mrs. Richmond brought our drinks. She wiped her hands on her apron. "I hear you've gone and enlisted, Hank. I sure wish this thing was over. I'm tired of seeing the kids I've watched grow up going to war."

"I can't let my brother get all the glory," Hank said, looking at the tabletop.

Mrs. Richmond heaved a sigh. "Me and Mr. Richmond, we'll be praying for you, son." She laid her hand on Hank's head, and I half expected her to call down the power of God right there and then, but she only ruffled Hank's hair. It was clear Mrs. Richmond didn't think much of the pursuit of glory and neither did I, but saying

267

anything now would only be mean-spirited, even though I felt sick inside. Hank was on his way to war, plain and simple. Mrs. Richmond patted Hank's shoulder and walked off.

"I'd heard the rumors," I said. "It's a good thing you called me."

"Honest? I didn't know. You're a hard girl to figure. I would have called sooner. The harvest tied me up pretty bad. I helped Dad at the bank most of the morning and picked peaches in the afternoon."

Like an old farmer, I asked, "So, you had a good harvest?"

"Best ever. Dad put a big hunk of cash into my college account. He says I'll need a nest egg when I get back." Hank got all earnest, like a boy did when he was trying to act older. "There will be school, of course, but a man has to prepare for every eventuality."

"Every eventuality?"

"I'll be awful lonesome over there. It sure would be nice to come home to someone."

Hank was the exact kind of boy a girl would wait a lifetime for, but I'd made my promise to Pete, and I'd meant it. I pushed the cola aside. "This isn't a time to be coy, Hank."

Hank looked as happy as a robin staring down a fat worm. "I like that about you."

"You're the only one who does," I said, but from the grin on his face he'd missed the irony of my statement.

"You'll write me, won't you? You're the only person I want to hear from, excepting my folks, of course. You're special, Lucy. I was hoping—and I might be making a giant leap here—but I thought you might feel the same about me."

"You aren't going to make this easy, are you?" I sighed.

He leaned back. "Oh boy. I don't like the sound of that."

Right then, my stomach roiled, thinking about how Hank would change after he'd gone overseas and saw the kind of things Pete was seeing. "You should have waited to enlist, Hank. Did you ask your brother about what the war is like? Did he tell you it's all glory? If he did he's as crazy as you are."

"Whoa, wait a minute." He leaned toward me and spoke in a soothing voice that only made me feel worse for breaking his heart. "I know what it's like over there. As for my brother's letters, I can read between the lines, and I watch the same news reels you do."

So maybe I'd underestimated Hank. And yet. "The news reels

don't tell half of what's going on over there. There are guys in the Pacific wishing they were dead. They're seeing their buddies shot and worse. They never sleep. They can't. The Japanese just keep coming."

"Who's telling you this stuff?"

This conversation wasn't going at all how I'd planned. I sipped at my Coke, but it tasted bitter. "I write a boy from my hometown. He's in the Marianas."

"Then he's got it pretty bad."

"I haven't heard from him in months."

"Is this guy special to you?"

I lowered my gaze to the tabletop, not wanting to see his disappointment or his relief. "I agreed to marry Pete when he gets home. It wouldn't be right..."

"No. No, it wouldn't."

We sat there for the longest time, heads down, hands in our laps. "I'm sorry, Hank. I should have said something sooner."

"Don't worry about it. Ma will write." Our eyes met then. He smiled weakly. "I hope Pete makes it home okay."

"Me too."

Mercy

Miss Wood and Mr. Henry Adler were as old as dirt. That didn't stop them from acting like two lovebirds. And somehow, and I didn't get this at all, they thanked me for their happiness. Miss Wood smiled all the time now. Some people just shouldn't smile that much.

Lotti cut thin slices of zucchini bread and put the teapot to boiling. Thin slices meant Lotti hoped they ate quickly and left. She still watched Miss Wood with a wary eye. Aunt Ada drank her tea straight down and set her plate on a marble-topped table. She hadn't taken one bite. Tonto left Goody where he lay on the floor to sniff at her plate. I took another look at Miss Wood and Mr. Adler. They'd stopped cooing at each other and were looking at me.

Henry leaned forward. "I have to know. How did you know my name? We've never met, have we?"

He wasn't going to be happy with my answer. "I don't know."

Goody talked around the zucchini bread in his mouth. "I don't see why I have to be here."

"Children are meant to be seen, not heard, young man." Miss Wood didn't say this mean-like, but that didn't stop Goody from crossing his eyes at her, which she didn't see on account she was looking at Mr. Adler.

Mr. Adler cleared his throat. "Back to you knowing my name, Mercy. Did you see my name in your mind, like it was written on a piece of paper? Did someone or something whisper it in your ear?

270

I'm completely befuddled by all this."

Adults sure liked details, but I didn't have any for Mr. Adler. "I just knew, sir. Miss Wood got all flustered when I asked who you were, so I figured I was right."

His cheeks pinked up real bright.

Miss Wood played with the latch on her purse. "I nearly forgot." She unfolded a newspaper clipping with this headline: "Miracles Come with Mercy."

Lucy groaned.

Miss Wood was too proud of her show-and-tell to notice how unhappy she'd made Lucy. "Henry clipped this out of *The Denver Post* Sunday last. It's a lovely piece."

"What's this?" Lotti said, setting her plate down with a clank.

"Can I see that?" Lucy reached for the clipping long before Miss Wood had a chance to answer.

Ada and Lotti stood behind Lucy to read over her shoulders.

"Hey, read it out loud," Goody demanded.

Lucy handed the article to Ada. "You read it."

Palisade peaches are finally filling produce shelves. The long wait is over, and our war-weary hearts are glad for a sweet and juicy diversion.

Another bud of hope grows in Palisade in the form of a little girl named Mercy Richter, 9. The girl with the unusual name, a relative newcomer to this notch of a valley, is a miracle worker.

Just ask Lenora Brown, 72, of Ulysses, Iowa. Mrs. Brown has been traveling with her family to Colorado every year since she was a newlywed, but Mrs. Brown hasn't walked in decades due to rheumatoid arthritis.

According to Dr. Albert J. Welch, Sr., physician to Mrs. Brown, she has suffered with arthritis from her late teens to the present.

"Her joints were horribly misshaped by the disease," he said, "leaving her hands and feet all but useless. She was in constant pain. Besides pain drugs, which she refused, there wasn't anything more medicine could do for her."

As this reporter watched, Mrs. Brown tightened

canning lids without any show of discomfort. When asked what transpired the day she was healed, she said, "I was sitting right there in my rocking chair, waiting for my family to return after a day of picking [peaches], when this little girl offered to fetch me some water. What happened next will surprise the pants right off you."

Lucy stood flagpole straight, her forehead filled with worry. "We can't stay here. We have to go. This place will be swimming with people looking for Mercy."

I didn't like the sound of Lucy's voice, all tight and squeaky. I crawled onto Lotti's lap. Nothing made me more nervous than seeing Lucy all worked up. I tried to think of a mercy verse, but my mind buzzed and wheezed. Nothing made sense.

"Don't stop reading now," Goody said. "Maybe he wrote something about me."

Lucy started to pace, and Aunt Ada looked around like the house was on fire. She grabbed Lucy by the waist. I expected Lucy to push her away, but she didn't. Aunt Ada said, "You aren't going anywhere. This is your home."

Miss Wood and Mr. Adler stood at the same time. She said, "This is a disproportionate amount of drama for a simple story in the newspaper. I thought you would enjoy the article."

"You were right in bringing it." Lotti tightened her arms around me. "Now, you'll have to excuse us. We need to plan for this unexpected attention."

Lucy closed her eyes and pressed her fingers against trembling lips. She made to go upstairs, probably to pack, but Aunt Ada held her tight. I was awfully glad someone as strong as Aunt Ada was there to look after Lucy.

Mr. Adler bent over me. "You'll be famous, little miss. The reporter filed with the AP. Why, folks all over this world will be reading about you. You shouldn't be troubled." He dabbed the sweat from his head.

Miss Wood pulled on her gloves and sniffed. "Most people would enjoy the attention. I should have known you would see things differently, Lotti."

Mr. Adler put his arm out for Miss Wood. "Shall we?"

Miss Wood squeezed his arm. She talked to us, but she looked at Mr. Adler the whole time. "Wish us luck. We're off to get our marriage license. We hope Mercy will agree to be our flower girl. The wedding won't be much, but a flower girl seems like an appropriate extravagance given her special role in our finding each other. Henry, we better take our leave." She picked lint off his lapel. "We'll stop by Hargood's to buy a suit to your liking."

They finally headed for the door. Henry said, "I've never met a suit I liked, but I sense my freewheeling days are behind me. Brown or black, Miss Wood?"

"Brown," Miss Wood said, leaning into him. "We're too happy for black, Mr. Adler."

Once they left, tension squeezed the house. Ada watched as Miss Wood drove her car down the lane. "I should have talked to that reporter, tried to explain to him the can of worms he would be opening."

"You tried, Ada. Don't go beating yourself up." Lotti pulled my head to her shoulder, and I was glad for its softness.

"They'll come," Lucy said. She wasn't a scaredy cat, but she sure sounded like one. "Everyone will come. We can't stay. I don't want to go, honest, but I don't see another way."

"Your care for your sister is admirable, but you're not alone, Lucy, not anymore. We'll think of something. There hasn't been an onslaught yet." Aunt Ada studied the clipping. "This story is only a few days old. We have some time. We'll talk to the sheriff and Pastor Pennington. In fact, we'll build a ten-foot fence if we have to."

"They'll be here soon enough. People are desperate. They're on their way. I should be packing." Lucy made to leave the room, but Aunt Ada caught her by the hand this time. I was surprised to see relief in Lucy's face when she turned back to face Aunt Ada.

"Can I go now?" Goody said, filling his pockets with the remaining bread.

Lotti handed him a napkin and thought better of it. "Yes, you can go. You don't need to hear all this. And take your sister. The kittens made a terrible ruckus this morning. You better look after them."

Goody had grown tired of the kittens. I followed him until he ran through the orchard toward the river to meet up with his friends. I returned to the house to sit under the parlor window, where I could listen in on the plans Lucy made with Ada and Lotti.

"Leaving will only add to your problems," Lotti said.

No doubt about it, I was the problem. None of this would have happened if I'd minded my own business, like Lucy had made me promise.

"We don't know there is a problem," Aunt Ada said. "It would be foolish to jump to conclusions."

Lucy wouldn't like being called a fool. She spoke real soft. I stood on tiptoe to listen. "It's up to me to protect Goody and Mercy. That's the way it's been. I won't stop now."

Thinking of all Lucy had given up to be more of a mama than a sister to us set my stomach rolling, a feeling I'd almost forgotten. Ada pleaded with Lucy, and you know, I wasn't sure if she was begging Lucy to be sensible for Goody and me or for herself. "Lucy, I'm asking you from the bottom of my heart to stay. Here. With us. We have come to love you all so very much. Losing the three of you would be more than we could bear. Let us protect you and the twins. We promise no one will hurt any of you."

The parlor got real quiet. I wondered if I might be missing something. Maybe Lotti was whispering like she did when she was spilling over with love. I stood on the downspout. Lucy spoke through tears, "I don't want to go. Can you help us?"

I sat on the ground and leaned against the house. Lucy had asked for help. Glory be, we really were in trouble.

Pete

My dearest Lucy,

I picture you sitting under the apricot tree when things go crazy over here. You're wearing that blue dress, the one you wore the night I taught you how to drive. You look beautiful in that dress. Wear it every chance you get.

I worry about not telling you plainly enough how very much I love you, how much I've always loved you. That might be hard to believe with all the pranks I played on you, and I'm awfully sorry about that, but please believe beyond any doubt that I love you with all of my heart. You're the most beautiful girl I've ever known, and the smartest. No one loves like you, Lucy. I've been watching you take care of your family for years. You're the best person I know.

Sweetie, death is very real here. In fact, I'm surprised I've made it this long. Please know that I'm fighting like hell to come back to you, Lucy, but if you've received this letter, my time on this earth is over. Oh God, I so want to come back to you. I'm praying this letter stays in my buddy's pocket until we sail home. Lots of fellas are writing letters like this. I'm carrying three in my pocket for my friends. This is a grim business, but I worry you won't find out, that you'll think I stopped loving you when my letters stop. I'll never stop loving you, Lucy.

Honey, it's been my plan for some time to drive you back to Wisconsin and make things right when I got home. The director of the orphanage needs to know that I deserve the blame. I'm sorry you have to do this without me, but I really think you should. Don't go alone. Take your aunt with you. When they see you've been living with your aunt, I'm sure they'll let you keep the twins. And you can forget about being arrested. You made the best possible decision for Goody and Mercy. I don't want you to be afraid anymore. Living in fear is the closest thing to hell we can live—I know this for a fact. When you're in Sauk County, be sure to go by and see my mom. She'll be happy to see you all.

There are days when I see that Paul was right. Death will be a relief. You see, I'm not afraid at all. Grandpap will be there to introduce me around to all the other Devendorfs. If they play cribbage in heaven, that's what I'll be doing.

I want you to be happy, Lucy. Fall in love. Have lots of babies. Cling to God in the tough times and thank Him for all that's good. There will be good for you. I'm so, so sorry you are reading this letter.

With all of my love forever,
Pete

Ada

May 23, 1994

Darling Lucy,

And so we come to the day you received the letter from Pete. I've made you wait too long, I suppose, but I couldn't think of writing these thoughts with my fellow residents constantly parading by my open door, and if I close the door, they're forever knocking to see if I'm okay. These days, my only privacy is the bathroom.

Fortunately, this place empties on the days the bus takes residents to Wal-Mart. I meant to write last week, but I couldn't trust Doris to buy the correct kind of toothpaste, and so I was forced to go myself. Do we need so many different kinds of toothpaste? Why not make the best possible toothpaste and leave it at that? Who has time to read one hundred labels?

I'm back to stalling. The longer I think on that day, the clearer (is that a word?) it becomes. In that way my stalling has served your purpose. I see it all. I see your face twisted by pain, how you fell to the dirt and curled yourself into a ball, but I'm getting ahead of myself. I tend to do that these days.

As I remember it, this all happened on a Saturday. There was something amicable about the sun's reach into the parlor window that afternoon. And yet, my fingers were absolutely wooden as I practiced "Fairest Lord Jesus." Gil's letters came too infrequently. My mind buzzed with worry. It didn't take much to draw me away from the piano that day.

Like you, I watched for Charlie. As I came to the screen door, you ran by—with unfathomable optimism—toward the mailbox. I watched the whole thing, how Charlie teased you with Pete's letter and you jumped to grab it from his hand. I would have pulled him off his horse if he'd tried to tease me like that.

You held the letter to your heart as you walked back to the apricot tree. The change in your composure addled me. There you were, savoring the moment, or were you afraid? I couldn't guess. I said a prayer and stood in the shadows to watch. Who knew what Pete had to say for himself? I never imagined, not for a second, my dearest, that you would be torn in two by his words.

You fumbled with the flap and finally ripped the letter open. The envelope skittered away. You could not have read more than a paragraph when you doubled over. The letter fell to the ground, scattering in the breeze. I ran to you and pulled you into my arms. You resisted at first, but I would not be dissuaded. Your keening tore at wounds I had long thought healed. I nearly sprung off the bench to escape the pain, but I'd let go of you once. I would not do it again. You finally stopped fighting and clutched the back of my dress.

I heard steps on the porch. Goody called out. "What's wrong with Sissy?" He sounded annoyed, how he still sounds when he's worried. I waved him off, told him to get busy and stay busy. I don't remember where Mercy had gone. Do you? It's probably not important.

I asked to read the letter. You didn't protest, but it took some time for you to release me. We took our time. There was no hurry. I gathered the envelope and the V-Mail. Eventually, I understood why he wrote that letter, but at that moment, after reading it through, I hated Pete for his self-indulgence, the pure drama of what he'd said.

You lay against my chest as I stroked your hair. I willed the mountain to topple over us. But it stood as it always had—a thing of immensity, so barren yet strong. With some thought, I realized Pete's words were a gift, the very thing I would have wanted from Gil.

I asked if you'd read the whole letter. When you tried to say no, your sobbing began afresh. Mother Heller drove up the lane. By then my back ached like fire. She saw us there and started to come. I begged with my eyes for some time with you. She took my meaning, pressed her palms together to say she would pray. Before she reached the kitchen door, her cries rivaled yours. I sat there completely dry-eyed. To this day, I don't understand how I pulled off that piece of magic.

Bessie lowed in the barn. Cows don't hold their milk happily. Moments later, Mother Heller walked toward the barn with the pail, blowing her nose and blotting her tears.

I read Pete's letter out loud as you cried softly. Goody came out of the house again, asking after supper. Between cows and little boys, it's a wonder women broker any time for their heartaches.

After reading the letter and learning that you'd taken the twins from the *orphanage, I finally understood why you seemed always to be looking over your shoulder, always looking for a reason to leave. My poor rash darling. It was all clear how Mercy's gifts were more than a magnet for the desperate. They were the very thing that could grind you to powder.*

I know this letter will reopen old wounds for you, dearest. I wish it weren't so, but this is the price we pay for loving well. And you love well, Lucy.

Love,
Ada

Lucy

I wanted to go back to Wisconsin immediately, as Pete had suggested. He was so right about fear. I counted out my dollars and change, but the three of us would only make it as far as Denver, not Wisconsin. I asked Ada for the remaining fare. When had she become approachable, the one I sought out to share my morning coffee and my deepest heartache? That was like asking which pull of the oar had drawn me closer to shore.

Despite Pete's promises that returning to Wisconsin would only release me from fear, Ada insisted that we should be prepared for the worst. If the authorities took me into custody, she would take care of the twins, so she insisted on coming along. Also, Ada promised to hire a lawyer, if the need arose, and I was more and more certain I would need one.

Ada convinced me to delay our return to Wisconsin. The waiting part didn't settle well with me. Ada wanted Gil to come home from the war before we left. First, she insisted it was because she didn't want to leave the ranch untended. That was nothing but an excuse. Corky and Lotti were more than willing and able to take care of the ranch, especially now that it was fall. The real reason was the mailbox. It was Ada's only connection to Gil. I surely understood that.

I agreed to wait, but I doubted we would have until the end of the war to settle things in Wisconsin. In the moments that prequeled sleep, I pictured Mrs. Nadel laughing with glee as she read the article Mr. Gurley had written before she rang up the sheriff. But there was no hurrying Ada once she'd made up her mind.

I spent all of my unclaimed moments under the apricot tree. I rubbed the pit from Gerland's peach like a worry stone or like those beads the Catholics use to pray. I ached for comfort, questioned seriously whether I would see God's goodness in the cross or anywhere as Gerland had encouraged me to do. And yet, I kept the pit hidden in my pocket, reached for it when the darkness pressed me.

The desperate still found their way to Honey Sweet Ranch, looking for Mercy. Although I resented the people who came, they reminded me that suffering wasn't something to be weighed. It came to everyone, no matter their station. Some drove up the lane in long, shiny cars. Others came in wagons or pulled carts on foot. Most came while we were in school and met the business end of Corky's rifle, if they persisted. They all looked tired. Lotti gave them water and prayed with them. For those who waited for Mercy, Ada stayed right with her as she met each pilgrim. I didn't know what Mercy said to those folks. Grief pressed me so hard I couldn't take a breath to ask. But when the people made their way back to their cars and wagons, they walked with lighter steps, buoyed by hope, I reckoned.

Pastor Pennington tapped the microphone. Ceiling fans stirred the heavy air, the humidity of breaths and bodies and heat all squeezed together. "Thank you, one and all, for coming out this evening. Your willingness to help a family with a unique situation demonstrates the true nature of this community, and I, for one, am proud to be counted among you."

The crowd filled the seats and stood along the walls of the community center. All stood a bit taller with Pastor Pennington's words. They applauded and nodded approvingly at their neighbors.

"Mercy's family has been inundated with people wanting the little girl's help. Most people have been gracious, but as you might imagine, some have allowed their desperation to make them act in an unseemly manner."

I nudged Ada, whispered, "What? When?"

She put a finger to her lips. "Later."

A man called from the back. "Is the little girl here? Can we see her?"

I didn't like how he sounded, all hopeful and demanding at the same time. I kept my eyes forward. Mercy wasn't the best of show, for goodness' sake.

"For obvious reasons, Mercy and her brother are not here tonight." The speakers squealed. Pastor Pennington stepped back.

A woman stood. "If God has given her a gift, won't He also protect her?"

"The disciples were given gifts, and all but one were martyred." This said by a man standing along the wall. His words squeezed my heart.

Pastor Pennington raised his hands. "That will be enough, people! Let's have some order. The family is asking for your cooperation. Folks are coming into town and asking for directions to the ranch. Lotti and Ada only ask that you encourage these folks to go back home and seek out the help of their own pastors and neighbors. Please, remind them that Mercy is a little girl, nothing more."

Murmurs filled the room.

Pastor Pennington dabbed sweat off his forehead with a hankie. "They don't want you to lie. You must understand that the flood of people is very disruptive. I believe, and so does the family, that the flow will subside if we can dissuade folks a bit."

A woman in the front row stood, holding a sleeping child. She turned to where I sat with Ada and Lotti. "I surely understand your desire to protect Mercy but I'm wondering, is there a way to consider the needs right here in Palisade? We suffer from rheumatism and heart failure—" She kissed the forehead of the sleeping child. "And diseases no one can name. The children of our community need her." The woman sucked in her lip until she regained composure. I slipped a hanky out of my purse to dab my eyes. "Maybe Mercy was sent to us for a reason." And she sat down.

"That's right!"

"It only seems fair!"

"You can't hide your light under a bushel!"

Pastor Pennington approached the microphone again, his arms rose as a plea. "People! People! Listen up. I'm as intrigued as you are. The Bible says signs and wonders will follow us. I've loved God all my life. I've prayed for hundreds of people in the years of my ministry. Not one of them has been healed. Perhaps my faith isn't strong enough. Perhaps my theology isn't what it should be. Perhaps my God is smaller than Mercy's. But that's not the topic for discussion here tonight."

"It's the topic if you're the one who's sick!"

"Amen!"

"Tell him, brother!"

"The little lady has it right!"

"God has answered our—!"

"A little girl is not the source of your hope." Pastor Pennington's word's bit the air. "The source is the heart of God, people. It's there for everyone who calls on His name. Maybe we're standing back, hidden by the shadows because we don't come as children.

"I've thought long and hard on how to respond to God's work through Mercy. I was like you. I harbored the hope she would whisper a word from God's own lips to me, just as the prophets of old had done." He hung his head. Nothing but the whoosh of the fans disturbed the quiet. "I'm not going to wait for that word to come. I intend to become a child again—a balding, pudgy child, but a child nonetheless. I want to see my Father as He really is, the way the Scripture say He is. He is not an intellectual exercise. He is God or he is a huge waste of time. I intend to find out.

"It's quite possible we will never understand why God chose to work through a girl. None of that matters. I hope you will join me in protecting Mercy from a grabbing world. Will you?"

By a show of hands, a majority of the people declared their support. As the auditorium emptied, the woman with the sleeping child drew a crowd. I couldn't hear what she said, but she looked over her shoulder toward the three of us, and she wasn't happy.

On the way home, Ada said, "They're good people, Lucy, but they may all change their minds tomorrow. That woman may start selling maps to the ranch on the corner of Third and Main. We can't put off that trip to Wisconsin."

The very next day, we boarded the 2:25 train. I didn't have a minute to consider what might happen once I showed my face at the orphanage. Preparation for the trip left little time for sleep. Lotti filled a picnic basket with fried chicken, bread, egg salad, apples, canned peaches, and an apple pie. I wasn't sure how to pack for the twins. Would they be staying at the orphanage? I must have stared into the suitcase for an hour. Ada finally led me downstairs for a cup of tea. "Rest. These hours have drained you. I'll pack for the twins. Have you packed for yourself?"

"Not yet."

"Drink your tea. You'll feel better. We aren't journeying to Troy and back, only Wisconsin. You shouldn't need more than a couple dresses."

On the train, soldiers shifted and bullied their buddies to switch seats, so the four of us could sit facing each other. Goody used his schoolbooks as a footstool, but only until the train gathered speed. Then Ada grabbed his math book. "I intend to catch you up a grade before we reach Wisconsin. We'll start with computation."

Ada made sure the twins had plenty to do and kept them from bothering the other passengers. That first night, the windows reflected my fear back to me. Goody slept with his head in Ada's lap and Mercy leaned against me. Ada slipped her foot out of her shoe and rested it on mine. I woke in the night, startled, wondering where I was. I sought her foot in the dark and found comfort in its warmth.

Lucy

We stepped out of the taxi into the affable light of a Wisconsin fall. But I'd lived in the area too long. I knew this kindness of warmth and color wouldn't last. Harsh arctic winds would blow. Snow would accumulate. Ice would harden the ground, so I shrugged off the sunshine.

Ada paid the driver and started up the steps of the orphanage. She stopped, turned. "Come on," she coaxed.

Goody and Mercy pressed into me.

Ada smiled weakly. "They can't hurt you anymore."

Mercy tugged on my skirt. I bent to listen. "'The Lord will perfect that which concernth me: thy mercy, O Lord, endureth for ever: forsake not the works of thine own hands.'"

"Amen." I squeezed the twins to my belly, felt the warmth of their breaths, questioned the wisdom of being in this place. And prayed for mercy.

Ada returned to us and extended her hands to Goody and Mercy. They grasped at her like a life line. They were almost to the door when I followed them up the steps.

Miss Floss wore a polka dot dress straight out of the Montgomery Ward catalog and the wide-eyed gentleness of a Jersey cow. "What you're saying is new to me," she said, looking from Ada to me. "I eventually replaced all the staff when I took over the directorship of the orphanage. While I'm not at liberty to tell you anymore about the previous director, I suppose that's why I hadn't heard anything about the twins. But still, I read through the files. I don't remember anyone with those names. Goodness and Mercy would certainly stand out. But I may have missed something. You've caught me completely flat-footed. If you'll excuse me, I have one more place to look for the twins' files."

She stepped into an adjoining room. Drawers opened and closed. There was a shuffling of papers. Miss Floss returned to her office holding a fat file. She walked to the window overlooking the playground. "Are those the twins there, sitting on the bench?"

I followed her to the window. Mercy left the bench to tie a little boy's shoe. Goody sat rod straight in his white cowboy hat and mask. The shirt Ada had made for him rose high above his wrists. When had he grown so tall?

"They're almost ten, are they? Well then, I should talk to them." She searched my face. "Do you mind?"

"No, I don't mind." But inside I did mind. I minded very much.

Mercy

Lucy didn't think me and Goody knew, but we did. We knew she took us from the orphanage when she wasn't supposed to. The kids who had lived at the orphanage for a long time liked to talk on the playground, usually near the woods, where the grownups wouldn't hear us.

The only way out of that place was to be adopted or to get too old. They all agreed that me and Goody would be living at the orphanage for a long time because we were already eight years old when we came, and not at all pink-cheeked or toothy like the ones who got picked right away. One boy, older than both of us, thought a farmer might like Goody. Farmers liked boys because they helped with the chores and grew up strong enough to lift the heavy bales. Girls like me cost too much to marry off.

Sitting on the playground with Goody again, I tried to picture myself living at the orphanage. They'd painted the building yellow since we'd left. Someone was trying to make the place cheerful. There wasn't much to be cheerful about when your family was long gone. But still, I appreciated the effort.

Miss Floss wasn't anything like Mrs. Nadel. For one thing, she smelled better, more like flowers than medicine. When she smiled, her eyes lit like two stars. She asked if she could join us on the bench. She didn't ask Goody to take off his hat, but I made motions at him like I'd seen Lucy do in church, so he finally pulled it off.

"Lucy has agreed to let me talk to you," Miss Floss said.

That didn't sound like Lucy. But then, Lucy hadn't been herself since she got the letter from Pete. If she would have listened to me about heaven, she would feel a lot better. I hoped she wanted to hear soon. I was beginning to forget things.

Miss Floss frowned into the setting sun. "Is it okay with you? To ask a few questions, I mean."

Goody slapped his hat against his leg. "You'll ask your questions anyway."

"Goody!" I said.

"It's true." Miss Floss looked Goody straight in the eye. "You've found me out. I really want to hear your answers. No one else knows what happened to you here. Will you answer the questions, if I'm more honest with you?"

Goody squinted down on Miss Floss. "I reckon we can."

"Some of the questions may make you uncomfortable, although that's not what I want, and that is the honest truth."

Goody shifted his weight. "Will answering your questions help Lucy?"

"Quite possibly."

"All right, I'll do it."

"Since you're willing, my first question is for you, Goody. You had your difficulties during your stay—"

"Is Lucy in big trouble?" he asked.

I glanced over my shoulder to see that Lucy and Aunt Ada were watching from inside the orphanage. Lucy wouldn't be happy that Goody had interrupted the lady, but Miss Floss didn't seem to mind. She leaned back and cocked her head. "Do you think she should be?"

"Heck no, she took us all the way to Colorado, so we could be together. I wasn't so sure at first. I wanted to go back to our apartment. I gave Lucy a pretty hard time. I even kicked her real hard, but she never let go. Once Lucy gets a hold, she doesn't ever let go."

"She's a good sister, all right," Miss Floss said. "I can understand your concerns. Did you change your mind once you got to Colorado?"

"It's about the most perfect place on earth, except they don't have lightning bugs and it ain't Texas. You see, they don't have no Texas Rangers in Colorado."

She smiled kindly. "Maybe you can take a trip to Texas when

you're older."

"Do I have to take my sisters?"

"You probably should, or they'll feel left out." Miss Floss flipped through papers from her folders. "Do you get plenty to eat at your aunt's house?"

"Heck no!"

"You don't?" I could tell Miss Floss hated the idea of hungry children, but I didn't know what Goody was talking about.

He said, "Aunt Ada won't let us have no candy. Lotti gives us lozenges on the sly, but they ain't the same."

Sometimes I wondered if Goody's hat squeezed his brains too tight. "Miss Floss isn't asking about candy. We get three meals a day, the best we've had in a long time and a lot better than we had here." I'd gone and said too much. I clamped my hand over my mouth.

"That's okay, Mercy. It's hard to beat home cooking." Miss Floss turned back to Goody. "You seem to have strong opinions. Let me ask you this: Do you feel loved in your aunt's home?"

"She makes me take a bath every dang day."

"Goody!"

He pulled at his shirt front. "She made me this shirt. It looks exactly like the Lone Ranger, don't it?"

"It's very nice. I have a nephew who would love a shirt like that." She turned to me. My heart beat like a war drum. "Mercy, is there anything you want to say? Are things better or worse for you in Colorado?"

A breeze scattered leaves that had collected where the sidewalk met the lawn. One broke from the pack to cartwheel past our toes. It was a marvel to see, only from the looks on Goody's and Miss Floss's faces, they had completely missed it. I couldn't help smiling.

Miss Floss touched my knee. "Mercy? You're smiling. Are you thinking of your new home in Colorado?"

I wasn't. I watched where that leaf fell. I was thinking of pressing it between the pages of our dictionary. Before I could stop myself, I leaned in close to Miss Floss, "He hasn't forgotten you."

"Who hasn't?"

"That's what you told your daddy, that God had forgotten you, but He hasn't."

Goody spoke through his teeth. "Mercy, remember what Lucy said."

"I remember." And I did. I'd tried to ignore the movement of the air, the way it made the leaves scrape the sidewalk, but I couldn't. Jesus was near, and He was crazy about Miss Floss.

Miss Floss looked toward the woods. Her chin dimpled and shook. Goody left the bench to play dodge ball with some boys, which was just as well. But Lucy wouldn't like that either. There was no turning back now. I scooted closer to Miss Floss. "You won't need those little pills you cut in half anymore."

"What little...? How...? Wait a minute." She flipped through one of the files, scanned a page with a red fingernail until she found what she was looking for. "I think Goody has the right idea. It's too pretty a day to answer questions. Why don't you play on the swings while I talk with your family?"

I got a sick feeling in my stomach then.

Lucy

Ada and I returned to our seats when we saw Miss Floss turn toward the building. My thoughts raced. I envisioned the worst thing happening—the twins plodding down the hall of the orphanage toward the dormitory and me toward the county jail. Would my jailers put me on a road crew? Lock me away and forget to feed me? Shave my head? As I was considering the possibility of sharing a cell with a murderer, Ada started rubbing the tight place between my shoulder blades. I forced myself to consider the very best outcome—the twins and I going home with Ada.

Miss Floss sat behind her desk and laced her fingers over the folders. "You've done the right thing coming back, Lucy. I can only imagine how difficult this is for you. I wish I could say your ordeal is over, but the decision to release the children to you or your aunt isn't mine, although our preference, always, is to place children with capable and loving family members. It's quite possible you broke the law in taking the children, but I'm not a judge. I'll talk with the board members, let them know what you've told me and give them the report of my interview with the twins. This might take a few days. Do you have someplace to stay?"

I scooted to the edge of the chair. "Will the twins stay here?"

"I don't have enough."

"There's someone in Prairie du Sac I need to see."

"I don't know. Prairie du Sac is a bit of a drive. I'm not sure if the board—"

Ada stood to rummage through her purse. She laid her driver's

291

license on Miss Floss's desk. "If I leave this?" she asked.

"If the board—"

Ada tugged her wedding ring off with some effort. "We will not leave without my wedding ring."

"I'm not sure about the legality of—"

Ada pulled a chain over her head and added it to the pile on the desk. "My mother gave this necklace to me when I left home. It's very precious, from my grandmother's side of the family."

"Mrs. Heller, you're asking me to make decisions I'm not prepared or authorized to make."

I tugged on Ada's skirt and she sat down, but she kept talking. "There's a woman in Prairie du Sac. She helped deliver the twins. Mrs. Devendorf. She's very close to the children, and her son was Lucy's fiancé." She glanced at me before continuing, "He won't be coming home from the Pacific."

Miss Floss swallowed. "Leave me the telephone number and the address. I'll call when the board is ready to meet you." She stood, wringing her hands. She looked straight into my eyes. "You must realize the risk I'm taking, letting you leave Baraboo. I would give anything to see my fiancé's family, so I understand. I hope your time together is healing for you." She scooped up Ada's belongings. "If you don't mind, I will keep these until I see you again."

My knees buckled once we stepped into the sunshine. Ada supported me with an arm around my waist. "I'm very proud of you, Lucy. You managed yourself like a grown-up woman in there. I know for certain I could not have done better, especially at your age."

"Do you mind going to Prairie du Sac?"

"It's the thing to do."

The Devendorf family home was nothing but a box with windows and a door and a pitched roof, but the sight of it sent shots of gladness and dread and outright anguish through me. Nothing had changed about the home when everything else in the world had tipped and split. The lawn alternated in diagonal rows between silver-green and the color of moss on a rock, this by the careful hand of Mr. Devendorf with his lawn mower. I breathed in the bouquet of the river, separated from us by a stand of trees, the mud as old as life, yet fresh and careless. As we drew closer to the house, Ada set down the suitcase. A service flag hung in the Devendorfs' window. The blue star that had stood for Pete was now gold, the color for a vanquished hero.

Mrs. Devendorf threw open the screen door. She moved faster than I'd ever believed she could, and she drew me into a tenacious embrace, where we emptied our sorrow onto each other's shoulders. This was home, what I'd been longing for all along.

Goody said, "Are you going to cry all day?" We probably would have, but Goody's question served as a reminder that life kept moving forward no matter how relentlessly the ache pulled us back.

Although I'd hoped to stay in the apartment, new tenants had just moved in. Mrs. Devendorf sent Mr. Devendorf upstairs with our suitcases and took command of the kitchen. She lay out a supper of ham, chicken, macaroni salad, bread and butter pickles, deviled eggs, coleslaw, and raisin pie. After we ate, I sat with the adults at the cleared table to drink coffee. Mrs. Devendorf excused herself and returned with a shoebox of Pete's letters. She poured them across the table, walking through the envelopes with her fingers until she found the letter she sought.

She smiled. "I knew something was up. You don't birth a son and not notice he's hiding a piece of his heart. He told me in this letter that you were going to be my daughter-in-law. I was a little perplexed seeing how the two of you fought like cats and dogs, but I was happy, Lucy, real happy."

It hit me then that I hadn't only lost a love, I'd lost a family, and the weight of the loss nearly flattened me.

Over the next couple of days, I saw every photograph ever taken of Pete, plus his baby book and a display case of his Boy Scout badges. I saw him with fresh eyes. The strength of his grip on a bat. The way he smiled shyly at the camera. How he held his baby sister in her first hours. In all of my dreaming of our lives together, I'd severed the past, but Pete would have brought all of this with him. It was odd to think about, but it made me feel crowded and lonely at the same time.

I never, in all of that discovery and longing, forgot Miss Floss was presenting our case to the orphanage board. When she finally called, saying the board wanted to see us the next day, Ada asked me to take a walk. We buttoned our sweaters to our necks and walked arm and arm toward the river.

"I suppose this place brings back many fine memories," she said.

"I keep thinking Pete will show up."

"Yes, of course, you would. Do you think of your mother and your father?"

"Always."

Her face shifted from grimace to smile before she covered her face to cry. I tried to comfort her, thinking she grieved her sister. Words didn't help much, so I wrapped my arms around her. Cheek to cheek. Shoulders level.

Finally, she loosened her grip. "We have to talk."

We sat on the very same log where Pete and I had discussed my taking the twins. We stared at the river a long time. My words hadn't done much good before, so I waited for Ada to compose herself. What was the hurry? Time unwound in all my uncertainty. Even the river seemed ambivalent, shifting from blue to green to brown. Close to shore, the water rippled over river stones. The current turned glasslike in the middle. A pair of swans tipped below the surface, tails like white party hats. All that was missing was Papa's fishing boat.

Finally Ada lifted her head. "Pete was a very special young man. I'm sorry I didn't get a chance to know him."

"And?"

She stood to pace. "I'm very happy you want to come back to Colorado. No matter what happens tomorrow, we will get you back there. But there are hurdles you don't know about, things I need to tell you."

"What hurdles? Unless I'm in jail, I'll be on the train tomorrow night."

She stopped, hugged herself. "Yes, we will do that, but there are questions, more for you than for me. I want you with me, Lucy. Always."

"What sort of questions?"

She lowered her head. "I should speak plainly. I promised myself I would."

"What's up, Ada? You're scaring me. Is Gil all right?"

Her eyes shot up. "I don't know. I hope so." She opened her purse and took out a piece of yellowed paper. "I had hoped to wait until Gil got home. He should know first, but this isn't the kind of thing you put in a letter, not if you can help it."

"Ada? Are you sick?"

"No, I'm fine. Lucy, darling girl, I'm desperate to make things right with you and the twins. Perhaps, if the board of directors knew…perhaps, they would feel more, I don't know, comfortable with our arrangement."

"They have Miss Floss to answer their questions. Besides, our arrangement isn't that strange. You *are* my aunt."

"True. But this isn't a time to withhold information, especially with what's at stake."

Her evasiveness was getting on my nerves. "What do you know, Ada?"

She unfolded the paper and handed it to me. It was a birth certificate from Sauk County. The baby's birth date matched mine. I looked to Ada for an explanation.

"Keep reading," she said.

I held it out to her. "Whose is this?"

"Yours. It's yours."

"You have it?"

"I felt a bit possessive, mostly of what the birth certificate said of me. Who has held the birth certificate and why they held it isn't the point, not now. I'm hoping that showing the birth certificate to the board of directors will work to our advantage."

I read the baby's name. "This can't be mine. They have me down as Baby Girl Stauffer and left the father's name blank." And then I read the mother's name: Ada Christiane Stauffer.

I stood abruptly and paced back and forth as Ada sat, waiting, searching the far shore, looking like she expected to be slapped.

This made no sense. My mother was Magda Stauffer Richter. She was always there, the one who came when the terrors visited in the night, the one who came early to schoolroom pageants, and hers was the first voice I heard each morning, whistling a hymn or a child's tune. Papa had bragged that she couldn't put me in the church nursery until I was three. To have me out of her sight panicked her. And yet, she had left the three of us completely alone. Had she considered the consequences, what it would take for me to keep our shrinking family together?

I sure didn't look like Mother, although the twins did. My face was round compared to her angular cheekbones and chin. Had she simply lost too much weight? She was a sapling, graceful in her movements, yet fragile. I possessed the grace of a baby moose. I was all legs, big-boned, strong.

I studied Ada.

We shared honeyed hair with cheeks appled by the cold. We were tall, too muscled, and too tanned. We both chewed at the calluses on our fingers and valued duty above all else. Her eyes, though, were blue. Mine were brown. And she'd asked me not to come when I needed her most. How could she do that? And yet, her name filled the space for *mother* on my birth certificate.

I thrust the paper under her nose. "Explain this."

"This must be so unsettling. I'm very, very sorry."

"Ada," I pleaded with opened hands.

"Okay. Yes. I'll tell you." She took a big breath. "Magda tried and tried to have children. The years passed. She was told nothing could be done. It broke her heart, and then, and I'm not proud of this, I found myself with child and not married. So we decided it was best that you live with Magda and Thomas."

Ada stood, reached for me. I stepped back. "You're telling me this now?"

"This is hard to explain, harder now that I know you and love you."

I couldn't stand to look at her. I turned to walk back to the Devendorf's house.

Ada grabbed my arm, but I shook her loose. "When we came to you at midnight, you told us to leave. The twins and I were in danger of freezing to death, and you told us to leave."

"I deeply regret that night, Lucy. Please, let's sit down and talk."

The sorrow in her gaze cut me, but I wasn't prepared to face her remorse when I choked on my own.

"I made a promise, Lucy, to your mother and Thomas. They asked me to never contact you. And then you wrote, many years after the promise, of course. But I was still frightened. Gil was gone, and I didn't know how Mother Heller would react to the news I was a mother."

I stopped. Dropped the birth certificate to the ground. "I already have a mother. No matter how sick she was, she never would have refused to help me. You are not my mother." I turned then and left Ada at the riverbank. I avoided looking at her or speaking to her the rest of the day. I lay on Pete's bed, cursing the day I pointed his car toward Colorado and Ada.

That night as Ada and I lay side by side in Mrs. Devendorf's guest bedroom, the very room I'd envied when Joanne had painted the walls lavender, I waited for Ada's breaths to deepen, but they never did. There we were, two women with tumbling thoughts. I had come to understand why she'd told me, understood the possible leverage our new relationship afforded us with the orphanage board, although it seemed Miss Floss was content with her being our aunt. More than anything, I hated her for fogging my view of the past when the future was still so uncertain.

Rain pummeled the roof all night long, splashing over the gutters and slapping the ground. I'd become accustomed to Ada's sleep noises on the trip, the great press of air and the bubbling of her lips. Ada now lay silently beside me. But if I dared to look, surely she fingered a fierce tirade of notes on the mattress, like I'd seen her do on tabletops when her piano was nowhere in sight. I almost nudged her, invited her to drink coffee in Mrs. Devendorf's kitchen to wait for the morning.

I couldn't.

Ada was my mother. My *mother*.

This explained a growing list of traits we shared. Not the color but the shape of our eyes. A tendency to stiffen under pressure. Competitiveness. A holding back. A love for music. Preference for leading rather than following. She was smart, capable, creative. But my mother? No wonder she felt justified in bossing me around and appointing herself my protector. This instinct had arrived rather tardily for my tastes.

Not everything could be explained by my parentage. I kept remembering the night when the twins and I had arrived at Honey Sweet Ranch, the hateful words Ada lobbed at me, demanding that we leave immediately. In my most vulnerable moment, she turned her back on me. Mothers didn't do that. They didn't shrink away. They ran toward trouble to help their children, not away.

But Ada was here now. She stood where Pete would have stood, ready to barter her future away to protect me and the twins.

And yet.

And yet.

Did I want this mother?

I dozed off with that question buzzing in my head and woke to its droning. I shook it away to focus on the day ahead. My destiny teetered on a knife's edge. Fall one way and the world would turn gray and cold. Metal. Stone. Porcelain. Fall the other way? Oddly, that would be less certain. Perhaps Mrs. Devendorf would let us live in the garage apartment again.

The room was as gray as a mottled moon. Color hadn't managed to bloom yet. I set the time just before dawn. The sheets where Ada lay had gone cool. I tiptoed to where Mercy slept on sofa cushions on the floor. I lay my hand on her chest to feel its rise and fall. I drew close to breathe deeply of her, now with the scents of river and the woods and Mrs. Devendorf's donuts clinging to her hair. My throat stung.

There would be time for tears later.

I bent over Goody, pushed his hair from his forehead. The crust of sleep had collected in his eyes. Such a boy. I moved to sit on the floor with the twins until the alarm sounded at seven.

We took our turns in the bathroom and dressed as if the whole world slept but us. Even Goody whispered, "Is it gonna rain all day?"

Ada stood at the bedroom door in her Sunday suit. "I have a new Lone Ranger comic in my suitcase."

Goody frowned. "I don't feel much like reading."

"I'll bring it. You may change your mind." Her words were as soft as butter left on the counter. She tried to smile, but the effort was too much. She slipped silently away.

After breakfast, Goody excused himself to return to our room. I called to him for the third time. "We have to go, *now!*"

Down he came, his new shoes tapping the stairs. He wore the button-down shirt Ada had bought him for the Christmas pageant and a bowtie with flannel trousers still creased from the store. His part was a pale road of flesh right down the middle of his head. Rivulets of water ran down his neck from the water in his comb.

"You look nice," I said, squeezing Mercy's hand, hoping she would know better than to say something.

Goody plunged his fists into his pockets and studied his shoes.

"Sometimes a man has to do the hard thing."

I sure didn't need Goody acting strange. "What do you mean?"

"Nothin'."

"Goody—?"

Ada came through the front door, water running from her coat. "Mr. Devendorf is waiting."

Mercy shot me a questioning glance.

"Let's go," I said.

The drive to Baraboo was interminable. No one talked, except for Mr. Devendorf, directing Ada's attention to points of interests. There was the first house in Sauk County with indoor plumbing and the farm where a two-headed calf had been born. Ada looked out the window, nodded.

At the orphanage, Miss Floss rushed down the orphanage steps, carrying a briefcase and an umbrella. Ada rolled down the passenger window. Miss Floss bent to talk to us. "The board wants to meet at the bank. It's more convenient. Follow me."

The bank accused me with its arched windows and stone eyebrows. A woman took our wet coats and umbrellas and marched us past brass teller windows and curious eyes, trying very hard not to be obvious.

The woman ushered us into a conference room with a long table. Along one side sat a man in a gray suit, another man writing on a pad of paper—already?—and a woman in a purple suit. Her brooch, in the shape of a clown, winked from the lamp's light. We sat across from the threesome, the board of directors of the Sauk County Children's Home. A policeman entered to sit next to me at the end of the table. I smiled weakly, trying but failing to keep my gaze from the handcuffs on his belt. Miss Floss acted as the hostess, making sure everyone had a glass of water and paper to take notes. My throat was too swollen to drink a drop.

The president of the bank also served as the president of the board of directors, a Mr. Adams from his nameplate. He cleared his throat. "From the looks on your faces, you're expecting to be brought before a firing squad. You can put your minds at ease. This is simply an inquiry. Quite frankly, this is a brand-new situation for us, so we're going to walk through this in the serious manner the situation warrants, but we don't want to drag this out forever either.

"Miss Floss has already summarized her meeting with you, Lucy Richter and Ada Heller. And we've read her notes on her interview with the children. I don't intend to rehash all of that here. Our greatest concern this morning—" He looked at the paper in front of him. "Our greatest concern is for the well-being of Goodness Richter and Mercy Richter." He nodded at the twins.

He turned his attention to me. "Our first order of business is to determine if a crime has been committed, Miss Richter. As I'm sure you will appreciate, your future greatly affects the children. Let's start there, shall we? Officer Larsen, can you update us on the status of this case?"

Ada rose from her chair, smoothing the creases from her skirt. "If I may speak, I can offer information that may make any questions of illegal activity moot."

Ada was the last person I wanted speaking on my behalf. She'd had her chance to be my champion. Besides, I wasn't ready for the whole world, or, at least, Goody and Mercy to know Ada was so much more than my aunt. Hadn't they experienced enough loss and confusion? And who was to say Ada wouldn't change her mind when she had to choose between her own security and protecting ours? She'd already done that once, twice. Too many questions had been left unanswered to trust this moment to Ada.

I turned to the bank president, looked square into the eyes of the other board members. They looked like good people, the kind you trusted to act on their consciences and not to cut in line at the movies. They sure weren't the kind to contradict the law. I had no choice. "I prefer to trust the judgment of the board. I'll tell you everything you need to know. I don't need Mrs. Heller to speak on my behalf. In fact, I don't want her to."

"Lucy, please let me help you. This isn't the time to stand alone."

The bank president set down his pen, sighed. "Mrs. Heller, I think the young lady has a point. We don't want to muddy the waters here. I'm determined to stick to our agenda. That means we'll be hearing from Officer Larsen. Do sit down, madam."

Ada closed her eyes, steadying herself against the table before sitting down.

Officer Larsen scratched his chin. "Well then, interestingly enough, no report of missing children was ever filed by the previous director of the orphanage, Mrs. Nadel, and so, no charges are presently pending. Now, that being said, there is no statute of limitations on kidnapping. Charges can be filed at any time. Miss Richter, the fact that you came back to Baraboo tells me you don't take the law lightly, although you have demonstrated a lapse in judgment. We are willing to—"

Goody stood and planted himself toe to toe with Officer Larsen, slapping his Lone Ranger badge onto the table. "Sir, I surrender my badge to you and offer myself in exchange for my sisters. It's all my fault for what happened. Lucy wouldn't be in this mess, if she wasn't trying to save me from Mrs. Nadel breaking her promise. And Mercy, the orphanage was a hard place for her, too. I heard her crying lots of times. I sure don't want her to go back there." Goody held his wrists out for Officer Larsen to cuff.

Ada was back on her feet. The bank president looked at her as if she were a recalcitrant child, and she sat back down.

Officer Larsen lowered Goody's hands to his sides. "No one's getting cuffed today, son. You can relax yourself." Officer Larsen leaned forward in his chair to give Goody all his attention. "Where do you expect me to take you?"

"To the farmer's house. That's what started this whole mess. He's the one who wanted to adopt me. That's what upset Lucy. But I can see now that going with him is the right thing to do."

I opened my mouth to protest, only to meet Officer Larsen's cool gaze. My thoughts froze.

Officer Larsen returned his attention to Goody, nodding slowly, considering all that Goody had said. Clearly, he'd never met a boy like Goody. He said, "Living on a farm is a boy's dream. There's hard work, but there's lot of fun to be had and plenty of good food. Why do you think your sister was so upset?"

"The farmer said if I gave him a hard time, if I complained to my sister like a little baby, then I wouldn't never see Mercy again. And I guessed I wouldn't see Lucy neither."

"Is that so? And yet, you're willing to be that man's son."

Goody looked over his shoulder at me and back to Officer Larsen. "Yes, sir."

Officer Larsen dropped his head and swallowed hard before he met Goody's gaze again. "I have two sisters. They gave me nothing but grief my whole growing-up years, constantly telling me I needed a bath and yelling at me over the silliest things. They screamed over a frog in the bathtub. Can you imagine?"

"Yep, I believe it."

"And they tattletaled on me with some regularity."

"That's how sisters are," Goody said.

"And you're willing to do this thing for your sisters?"

"Yes, sir. They sure like living in Colorado, although Wisconsin's a fine place, too."

"Since we're talking straight with each other, tell me something. Did your sister force you to go to Colorado?"

Goody peeked over his shoulder again. "She wouldn't go back for my Lone Ranger badge, but she done what she said, she kept us together, and Aunt Ada got me a new badge."

"And at no time did she tie you up?"

"Heck no, I tie her up when we're playing Cowboys and Indians. I need to keep my knot-tying skills sharp to be a Ranger."

"Well, young man, my concerns are satisfied." Officer Larsen addressed the board. "What happens next is up to you. I don't see any reason to extend this ordeal for these fine folks." He shook Goody's hand. "It's been a pleasure to meet you, son, an honest-to-goodness pleasure, yes indeed. You'll be a fine Ranger." He stood. "Unless you have other business for me, I'll be heading on over to the diner. It's rhubarb pie day. I never miss it."

Ada

June 2, 1994

Dear Lucy,

I'm taking two sleeping pills each night, and still I toss and turn. I don't understand these movie stars who expose their dirty laundry to the world. Have they no shame? And people gobble up that trash. I'm too old to understand this fascination with baring one's soul. In my time, we gossiped for weeks if a woman's slip showed. Now, girls wear their underwear to church!

All of this is to say, I'm not thrilled to relive one of my more foolish moments and write it down in my own hand. I made my grand announcement about being your mother at the worst possible time, and my clumsy technique nearly ruined everything between us. We had become closer over the months, hadn't we? We no longer stiffened in each other's presence. I believed you tolerated me more than well. I should have been content to let it be, and I should have trusted God to orchestrate a moment for us to talk. But no, I panicked. I acted rashly.

Here is how I remember it all: After our meeting with the board of directors, I worried you would stay in Prairie du Sac with the Devendorfs. I had listened as you volleyed remembrances with Mrs. Devendorf. You stepped so easily into her arms to comfort and be comforted. And, of course, you shared a deep love for Pete. In truth, I was terribly jealous. (Yes, I was a wretch!)

I don't know why you returned to Palisade with me. I was afraid to ask. I'd learned my lesson. I decided to enjoy you at whatever cost, even if that meant more mystery than I endured well.

We certainly didn't pick up where we had left off. You withheld yourself, and I couldn't blame you. You were cordial and attentive to a point, but it took some years for us to settle into our new relationship. I'd believed presenting your birth certificate would draw you into my arms. On that account, I was more than wrong.

It's two in the morning. I haven't slept a wink. We've never been the pair to spill our affections, but I realize this was a mistake on my part. And so, I want you to have these words to mull over before you arrive. I'm choosing them carefully. I don't want to botch this up again.

I believed I'd made my love for you clear over the years. And here you are, no longer a child but very much asking as any abandoned child would for a mother's reassurance. This is why you've asked me to write my memories down, isn't it? Am I that difficult to approach? In light of your reticence, I must be. It's quite possible you're fed up with me, that any attempt to explain away my choices would only distance you further. And yet, I can't resist the temptation to tell the story, our story. You've never asked, and I never felt compelled to give voice to my deepest shame. My hope in telling you now is to benefit you and you alone. I pray to God I'm correct in doing so.

My Lucy, my beautiful and precious daughter, please forgive me for abandoning you. You will contradict me on this. You're a smart woman. You understand what sorts of pressures I faced, but my darling, that is head knowledge, not a heart's reconciliation. It's true; I didn't have a crystal ball. I didn't know God would bring a man like Gil into my life to love both of us—and Goody and Mercy as it turns out. I wish I'd had some inkling to the goodness coming my way, the beautiful provision of love waiting for me and you. This was a shortcoming of my faith and startling evidence of my pride.

When I learned I was with child, I was scared, awash with shame, and feeling very stupid. I knew to wait until marriage, although, truthfully, I wasn't entirely sure what I was waiting for. (You can only learn so much from the barnyard.) Hans, your biological father, was older, a gifted pianist. He'd lived in Milwaukee. He knew things. Must I say anything more?

In offering to take you, Magda was only trying to be kind, and, as it turned out, to procure happiness and fulfillment for herself. She welcomed me into her home when Father threw me out. In doing so she lost Father's approval as well. He returned all of her letters unread and sent a telegram saying that his daughters had been killed in a tragic accident.

It was Thomas who convinced me to leave you in their care. He spoke of stability and the love of two parents. Even though they lived in a tiny apartment, it was more than I could offer you on a piano teacher's earnings.

As I prepared to leave their home without you, Magda insisted I wasn't to *contact you, that all of our correspondence would be reserved for emergencies only. She made me swear on her Bible. She said I would confuse you, and perhaps I would have. They're awfully loosey goosey about these sorts of things anymore. Anyway, for what I believed was an act of love, I left you in Magda's arms and traveled by bus to a couple in Iowa. The woman was Thomas's cousin. I always meant to go back there to thank them. I fear they're no longer with us. In any case, I have long since forgotten their names.*

What more do you need to hear, my darling? I will tell you what I longed to tell you every day from the moment I first saw your face:

You are the measure of beauty in my life. Love for you seared my heart. I thought of you every waking hour. I dreamed about you every night. When I heard a baby cry or children laughing in play, I turned in hopes of seeing you. I studied the calendar like Holy Scripture, supposing when your first tooth arrived and sharing the expectation you must have felt as another birthday approached.

Now we must address the night I refused you shelter after our Magda died. My words won't satisfy this lingering question, for what is there to say in my defense? I've mentioned my promise to Magda. I took that promise seriously. But I also lived under a false understanding of our good Father.

When you arrived at the farm, you must have wondered why Gil and I had no children. We both wanted them desperately, especially Gil who was part child himself. Each anniversary that passed underscored our disappointment. Secretly—because how could I tell Gil I'd born a child from another man?—I believed my sin had left me cursed, like the women of the Old Testament whose wombs God had closed. Despite Gil's disappointment, he never stopped loving me. Wasn't he a wonder?

And here you came. I'd been living a lie and wallowing in shame for sixteen years. Yes, I'd made my promise to Magda, but more than that, I could not, would not, expose myself or Gil openly to my shame. Your arrival, I believed, would have done that. Instead, you brought goodness and mercy that even I could understand. I wish you'd come much sooner.

I love you so,
Mother?

Lucy

I graduated from Palisade High School a few days before V-E Day. Out of habit I kept an ear out for news about the Pacific. The Japanese looked done for, but they weren't ready to cry uncle quite yet. How I ached for the families still waiting for their boys who were over there.

I came to the apricot tree often, whether it offered shade or not, whether snow covered the ground or those fat weeds the chickens loved to peck cushioned my feet. I'd come to believe the fist that squeezed my heart would never loosen its grip. Maybe I'd reached my limit of pain, and I would never recover. Ada sometimes called me lazy when I slept in or read until my eyes watered, but she didn't mean it. She wanted to soothe me. She just didn't know how.

Mercy came out of the house with a plate of cookies and a pitcher of lemonade. She was a filly of a girl, all legs and arms with soft mounds hinting at changes to come. I took the heavy pitcher from her.

"The cups are in my pockets," she said, turning one way and then the other for me to retrieve them. After she ate her cookies and drank her lemonade, she lay with her head in my lap.

I stroked her hair. "I think I'm ready," I said. "To hear about heaven."

"I'm starting to forget things."

"You saw Mother?"

"Yes. I saw her first thing, the moment I stepped through the gate. She looked wonderful. Beautiful. I almost didn't recognize her."

"And she was happy?"

"It's not the kind of happy you're thinking about. Happiness there is different. Something big fills you up. I should have written it all down, the things I saw and the people."

We sat quietly, listening to the drone of the bees and the gurgle of water slewing through the irrigation ditches. This was the question I'd avoided asking all this time, "Did you want to stay?"

She sat up, searched my eyes. "Yes."

I remembered her ragdoll body on the riverbank. "I'm very glad you didn't."

"I should tell you about the river, not the Wisconsin River but the river beyond Mother's garden wall." Mercy's bittersweet eyes reflected the blue of the sky. "The river flows from a high mountain. I've never seen a mountain like it, not even in Colorado. I felt the sound of the river in my chest. I couldn't think of anything else. But I wasn't afraid, Lucy. Not ever. Mother called it the River of Mercy. At first, I thought she was teasing me, and I asked her if there was a River of Goody, too. She smiled like I'd never seen her smile and said the river was for the people on earth, not heaven. There's more than enough mercy for everyone, if only they will cup their hands and drink."

She could not mean there was enough for me.

"There *is* enough for you, Lucy, even if you drink and drink and drink."

I played with the peach pit in my pocket, the one Gerland had given me, now smooth for all my rubbing. "Did you see Papa?" I asked, but I was thinking about that river, a whole wide river of mercy, running clear and calm over stones rounded by the current. Picturing the river evoked a powerful thirst.

"Not as much," she said. "He spent most of his time fishing." She shielded her eyes from the sun. "Hadn't I told you that?"

Had she?

"Are you thinking about Pete?" she said.

Sitting on the bench under the apricot tree, I felt the river's current, gentle yet persistent, not at all like the day I'd followed Mother and Mercy into the Wisconsin River. That river had demanded my surrender. This river wooed me with its glint and the song of its ride over the stones. I wanted to plunge my hands into the water and drink, but I didn't know how.

"Mercy?" I asked, not even knowing how to voice the question.

She drew her knees under her skirt and rested her chin on her crossed arms. "I'm having a hard time remembering Mama and Papa back in Prairie du Sac. I can't see their faces anymore, but I do remember little things, like eating raw corn from the field with Papa. We traded bites in the shade of the tree, the one beside the garage. The corn was so sweet."

"We did that, too, when I was younger." I'd thought the memory was mine alone but sharing it with Mercy made me feel less lonely, more a part of something that flowed along, deep and cool, and satisfying.

"And I remember a time at the lake. Papa held me up, his hands barely touching me, and I floated like a leaf on the water. Papa turned until his shadow fell across my face and I could see him smiling. He said, 'I'm so very proud of you.' I knew better. He was holding me up. I couldn't float by myself, but I didn't want to make him feel bad for seeing through his trick. Lucy, the odd thing is I think he knew I saw straight through him, and he was still proud of me for lying across his hands, not worried one little bit about sinking to the bottom. Papa was like that."

I'd worried that we didn't have enough photographs to remember Mother and Papa, so the twins might forget our parents. Remembering, I now saw, was much more about how a person made you feel than how they'd looked or the very words they'd said.

I smiled my first smile in a long time. "Papa was very much like that."

Just then, a car turned onto the lane. The dust of a thousand miles subdued the car's green paint, and a hand pressed the horn to nearly cover the shouts of the men inside. A man in the backseat stretched out of the window, his eyes closed, breathing the scents of the ranch. The moment the car stopped, he jumped out and ran toward the house. Mercy and I stood. Nothing like this had ever happened at Honey Sweet Ranch before.

Ada intercepted the man on the lawn and dove into his kiss. Gil was finally home. All of the letters and the longing were done for Ada. His buddies cheered as the kiss went on and on.

Mercy tugged on my hand, urging me to move closer. "Shouldn't we go meet him?"

I pulled her back. "Let's wait. They haven't seen each other in a long time."

The screen door banged, and Lotti quick-stepped off the porch with a rolling pin in her hand. I grabbed Goody as he ran by, hoping to give Ada and Lotti time to welcome the man they both loved. But there was no stopping Tonto from barking and sniffing at the men who stood behind Gil and Ada, elbowing one another. Corky approached from the barn, wiping his hands on an oily cloth. He stopped short to study his fingernails once he saw what was happening.

Goody wriggled free of my grip. "Ah, shucks," he said. "If I wanted to see this kind of mush, I could sit in the back of the movie theater." He whistled and Tonto followed him toward the river, where his friends had built forts to play, of all things, war.

I should have taken Mercy into the house or, at the very least, looked away, but the power of Ada and Gil's embrace held me in place. We'd all been anticipating Gil's return, but I hadn't imagined anything like this. Truthfully, I'd expected Ada to slap him on the back like one of the guys.

This was very different. It was raw, emotional, intimate.

Lotti stood some steps back, the rolling pin at her feet, her hands over her heart, her head bent. Corky worked at the dirt under his fingernails. Yes, we all believed we should turn away, go to the kitchen, offer Gil's traveling companions something to eat, but none of us moved a muscle, but none of us looked either.

The ache seeded in my chest blossomed into a searing pain, thinking of Pete, knowing we would never have a homecoming, a moment of intimacy to share with our whole world. I let my tears fall silently, not wanting to taint what Ada and Gil shared.

With Gil's arrival, a light switched on in Ada. In all of us. Up until then, we'd all been sitting in the dark. Lotti canceled her numerous committee meetings to prepare meals as if none of us had eaten for weeks. Bags of hoarded sugar and coffee were hauled up from the basement. When Ada sat with Gil on the bench after supper, she laughed freely and tipped her chin to blush at the things he whispered in her ear. They took long walks, starting in the orchard and spilling out toward the river or town. Once, she came back with her coiled braid completely unraveled. Around Gil she was more girl than woman. In fact, she looked like her young self in the photograph with Mother. This transformation confounded and pleased me. Did I know the real Ada?

There were times when Ada and Lotti loosened their holds on Gil to attend to their lives beyond the ranch. While they were gone, Gil performed magic tricks for the twins and built a tent out of old painters' tarps on the lawn. He invited me to join them under the canvas to hear stories of growing up on the ranch, but I begged off to read a book, although I stayed on the porch to listen in. I was much too grown up for such things, I said, though in my heart I thrilled at the sound of the twins laughing, having someone both strong and fun around the ranch for Goody, especially.

Industrious Corky couldn't leave Gil to his games too long. He interrupted play with news of a broken fence or to remind Gil that thousands of packing boxes waited to be assembled for the harvest. Gil knew the running of the ranch inside and out, but he'd just gotten back from a war, for heaven's sake. Corky, clear and simple, was a stick in the mud. Gil knew how to work and have fun. No wonder Ada had fallen in love with him. The twins didn't seem to mind the interruptions. They simply trotted off with Gil wherever Corky led him.

After supper each night, Ada played love songs that we all knew from the radio. No more icy marches for her. Gil sang along, his voice was clear and careless. He sure wasn't the man I'd pictured for Ada, even though photographs of him populated every tabletop around the house. He smiled easily, which Ada had not. Now, she smiled like those women in the newsreels selling war bonds. She was nothing but teeth. No, despite the photographs, I'd imagined Ada with a dour man with pale skin and bad teeth who said, "Yes, dear" and "You're absolutely right, my sweet" and nothing else. Who would have dared? But that was before Gil had returned to the ranch.

Now I knew better.

Gil was as tan as a saddle with white teeth that lined up like proper soldiers. His forearms rippled with muscles. And the sky spilled from his eyes. When he turned his gaze on me, my words stumbled out, not that I was nervous or that he was good looking enough to rattle me. No, it wasn't how he looked. It took me some time to understand his effect on me, and then I stopped stuttering like a schoolgirl. Gil liked me for no other reason than that I was present and accounted for. Such acceptance gave him tremendous power over me. We never mixed words. I simply bent and did whatever he asked. I was completely cowed.

I supposed that was another way I was like Ada. I was definitely her daughter, which made our relationship easier to understand. She feared I would follow in her footsteps, and she feared I wouldn't.

Once word got around that Gil was home, visitors walked up the lane with hands outstretched in greeting. Gil ushered the men to the apricot tree to smoke cigarettes and share stories. Ada carried pitcher after pitcher of iced tea out to the group, sometimes sitting on the arm of the bench alongside Gil as she combed his hair with her fingers. She eventually returned to the ladies, who waited for her on the porch. I listened to the men as I leaned against the wall below my bedroom window. They never spoke of the war. They speculated on the start of the harvest, whether the Mexicans would come to pick the peaches that year, and the weather. Always the weather.

And why not? July baked the valley. We counted the days of consecutive one-hundred-degree temperatures or higher. By the third week of the month, we'd been pressed for nine days of crushing heat. The twins and I had finished our chores and sat stupefied, waiting for a breeze. None came.

Gil strode through the orchard toward the house with a muddied irrigation shovel in his hand and an energy that nearly sucked the breath out of me. When he got within shouting distance, he called out, "Get your bathing suits! We're going swimming!"

Ada came out on the porch. "Are you finished already?"

Gil threw the shovel into the dirt and took the steps two at a time. He hooked Ada by the waist to pull her back into the house. "Come on, kids. My brain's on fire."

I followed along, not dragging my feet but not making any attempt to keep up with the rest. Gil and Ada leaned in to whisper and laugh softly, all of the hurry drained out of them now that they walked hand in hand. Even in love Ada was contrary. She foiled my plan to dillydallying my way out of the procession and back to the ranch.

Lotti wasn't any help either. She carried a stack of towels that needed adjusting every few steps. Mercy walked beside her, looking over her shoulder to check if I was making good on my promise to come to the river. I would go to the river. I'd dressed in the swimsuit Lotti had bought me the summer before, wore the old shoes she'd recommended for walking over stones, but I had no intention of actually going into the water. None.

Only Goody seemed eager to get where we were going. He rolled an inner tube Gil had found, patched, and pumped full of air while we'd all changed into our swimsuits. Goody doubled back several times to hurry us on.

Brothers.

I watched from the bank as Ada played motor boat with Mercy, my heart pounding in my chest the whole time. Of all of us, Mercy should have been the most afraid of water, deep or not, but she giggled and shouted for Ada to spin faster and faster. I prayed Ada wouldn't let Mercy slip out of her hands, that my sister wouldn't have to depend on me to save her and find me lacking again.

In deeper water, red with silt, Gil taught Goody how to swim like a frog on his back. It seemed to me Gil allowed more distance than was wise between him and Goody. When Goody tired, he flipped to his stomach to dog paddle, sputtering and sinking under the surface before Gil reached out to lift him above the water. When he was safely in Gil's arms, I was able to breathe again, but my breaths came shallow. I sat on a rock to avoid falling face-first into the rocky shallows.

Mercy caught my eye and smiled knowingly. That girl thought she knew everything. The others had already tried cajoling me into the water. I told them I wanted to work on my tan. But something in Mercy's smile drew me closer to the water's edge, made me drop my towel into the fine red silt, and walk over the stones into the eddy. When the cold water covered my knees, I stopped. This was craziness. I took a step back and waited for my pulse to slow. Within moments, the water went from cold to refreshing. I scooped water onto my shoulders, where the sun had already reddened my skin. Tan indeed.

"Aren't you going in?" Lotti asked from where she sat on a rock. She munched cookies she'd plucked from the picnic basket.

"I'm not much of a swimmer," I lied.

Papa had made sure I'd learned to swim by the time I could walk, living as close to the river as we had in Prairie du Sac. Remembering Papa, swimming into the murky cool with him— pulling, pulling with tireless arms, never fearing I'd lose my way back to him—made me look at the Colorado River again with the smallest deposit of longing, only until I remembered the passion of Papa's words to me, *Don't lose them.* But I did lose Mother and Mercy. I'd released them both into the flood waters to save myself. I couldn't be trusted, not when it mattered.

I took the wink of light off the water as a challenge, a gauntlet of sorts: Can you hold onto Mercy today? I wasn't at all sure I could, especially with my heart beating so fast. I shook off the river's challenge, bending, scooping more water over my hot face, and watching through my fingers as Mercy held onto Ada's shoulders, kicking wildly at the water as Ada backed toward me. "I'm getting tired," she said over her shoulder. "Can you take over?"

Mercy's wet eyelashes made stars of her eyes. "I want to go to the bottom with you, just like you did with Papa at the lake."

There had been a time when I'd bragged about swimming with Papa. Mercy was little more than a toddler and desperate to follow Papa everywhere he went. But he'd walked through the trees toward the river by himself. I saw my bragging as cruel now. Mercy could not have known that mothers and papas changed, that it wasn't her he'd walked away from so much as his powerlessness to make Mother happy.

"I don't want to get my hair wet," I said.

Ada raised an eyebrow. "Are you going somewhere?"

She knew I wasn't, *wouldn't* go anywhere.

"Maybe."

"Please, Sissy, please," Mercy begged. "Just like you did with Papa. Maybe we'll find a turtle."

"Or an alligator," I said with a hint of menace in my voice. Would nothing dissuade that girl?

Mercy rose from the river with shimmering water droplets on her skin. This should have been a happy scene, but my heart pounded. "There are no alligators in the Colorado River," she said with some smugness.

"Piranha?"

"Not one."

I closed my eyes against the image of her lifeless eyes under the water. "Beavers can be really mean."

"Sissy!" She waded closer. She motioned me to bend toward her whisper, "The water is soft like the lake."

In her ten-year-old way, she was telling me that the water wasn't angry and demanding. It wasn't like the flooded Wisconsin River. Gil had brought us to a place off the main channel, a ribbon of water as smooth as glass that twisted back on itself to create an eddy. Someone had added a wall of boulders to deepen the swimming hole and to calm the water. Probably many someones. Maybe Goody and his friends. Most definitely Gil.

Goody paddled the inner tube toward us. "Hey, if you're scared, you can use this."

I stood straighter, tried to smile. "I am most definitely not scared, young man. You'd better keep the inner tube," I said, avoiding his gaze. "You aren't an Olympic swimmer yet."

"I'm cold." Sure enough, Goody's lips were tinged blue from his time in the water. That boy hadn't an ounce of fat on him. He climbed out of the water up the slippery grass, to sit by Lotti, where he shivered in a towel. He accepted a fistful of cookies. "I'm coming back so hurry up!" he said.

Mercy lounged in the inner tube as I pushed her into the deeper water where Gil and Ada floated holding hands. When I couldn't touch the bottom, my breaths came as pants, and I looked back to the shore, not really so far away, but we hadn't been far from shore in the Wisconsin River either. Mercy took advantage of my distraction and slipped into the water.

"What are you doing?" I sounded angry, but I was afraid, and that did make me angry. "Do not let go of me, ever. Do you understand?"

Mercy moved to my back and grabbed onto my neck. "I'm ready."

Something touched my leg. I kicked wildly at whatever it was, but it must have been a fish, not clawing grass or Mercy's silky hair.

"Sissy? Are you all right?"

"Something rubbed against my leg," I said as matter-of-factly as I could manage.

"You'll have to let go of the inner tube to dive."

A newcomer to the eddy cannonballed into the water, sending waves that lifted and beat the inner tube like a drum. I felt the rip of Mother's dress, the slide of Mercy's hair over my thigh, watched the ruthless press of the tree's roots through the current. "It's too choppy, Mercy. We'll have to dive another day. Let's get out."

Mercy moved to face me. Our noses nearly touched. Before she quoted a mercy verse or tried to change my mind, I told her the truth. "I'm afraid." And my lips trembled to prove my words genuine.

No flash of panic or surprise showed on Mercy's face, only implacable certainty. "You're a good swimmer, Sissy, the best ever."

"I might let go," I said, not as a warning as much as a reminder to myself of what I was capable of.

"You won't."

I needed more assurance than Mercy could offer. "Did Jesus tell you that?"

"I don't think so."

"Mercy…"

She inched closer and whispered, "You won't let go. You *won't.*"

I never spoke with that much certainty, not at ten and not at eighteen, maybe I never would. But her words shifted something in me. A pop. A settling. Something rearranged. My chest didn't hurt. My breaths came easy. "You must hold your breath the whole way down and back up again," I said. "Can you do that?"

Mercy nodded emphatically.

"If it gets too hard, squeeze me tight. I'll turn right around. Do not take a breath underwater."

"I know that." I was exasperating the closest person to an angel I knew.

"Maybe I should go by myself first, see how deep it is. There might be a hole."

"Sissy!"

"All right," I said with all the command I could summon and turned for Mercy to wrap her arms around my neck again. "When I count to three—"

"I'll hold my breath."

I counted and dove into the depths, pulling and kicking with everything in me. Mercy held tight. I touched the bottom before I'd expected. My fingers wrapped around a rock, not a turtle but a token to mark the day. I pushed off the bottom. The sun burned a spot on the water's surface. I reached for it and broke into the stunning brightness of the day.

"Are you okay?" I asked Mercy over my shoulder.

"Let's do it again."

She'd been right. The river was soft. It made no demands, only offered escape from the blistering heat. I threw the rock to shore and counted for the next dive.

No one would mistake an eddy on the Colorado River as the River of Mercy, but I collected twelve smooth stones from the river bottom that day. That was mercy enough for me.

The river didn't wash away the hard memories or the aching loss that had lodged in my chest, but as I dredged up rocks from the bottom, the hard places I'd built against the pain began to tumble, just a little.

Gil asked if I planned on building a wall to rival the Great Wall of China.

"Not today but maybe tomorrow," I said.

The twins and I wore a path through the trees to the swimming hole that summer. Goody met up with his friends and swam as far away from me and Mercy as possible. Many times, friends from school or church came to swim, so I started bringing a bag of Lotti's cookies.

Sitting on a rock in the sun, waiting for my body to stop shivering—snowmelt water never reached what you would call warm—I remembered how Hank had invited me to join him at the river, and how I'd lied about not being able to swim. Now, I found myself looking for him every time we came to the swimming hole, even though I knew he was somewhere in the Pacific. Thinking of Hank there filled me with a churning dread.

I reminded myself that Hank's story could end like Pete's, and I found my heart hoping for the impossible, that Hank would return to Palisade and ask me to go for a swim. How I dared to dream such a thing could happen, I never knew.

Lucy

On his eleventh birthday, Goody announced that he was finished with the Lone Ranger. We'd seen the evidence of his retirement in the months prior, but making the Little League team sealed the deal with his new identity as a member of the team. He was now number seventeen, a number, according to Goody, of great mathematical importance because it was a prime.

Losing the Lone Ranger created its own mix of loss and hope in me, but mostly I was relieved that Goody had gleaned something from the classroom, despite consistent reports from teachers that he was a daydreamer and a doodler. How would that boy ever make a living?

Mercy, absolutely and positively, did not outgrow her name. People still found their way to Honey Sweet Ranch, mostly with ailments or injuries, coveting Mercy's prayers and wisdom. The wonder of seeing a person walk away from her upright and whole filled me with a dazzling joy. God was definitely near at those times.

Some people, however, went away disappointed, not healed, not released but bent from the burden of their pain, physical or otherwise, leaving Mercy and me clutching each other—me silently giving God an earful and Mercy whispering indecipherable prayers. Other times, and this was just as difficult to understand, the healings only came with hours and hours of intense prayer. When God bided His sweet time like that, I imagined Mercy wrestling with Him, just like Jacob, and I do believe she limped for a few days afterward.

To the people of Palisade, Mercy was that strange girl on the Heller's ranch who appeared to know what God was thinking. Reporters stopped coming, but churches from around the country invited her to touch their sick. All of us agreed—and by all, I meant our Palisade family—that Mercy would decide where to travel with her gifts once she turned eighteen, if she wanted to travel at all.

The war had been over in the Pacific for months, and Hank hadn't made a public appearance, especially not to Honey Sweet Ranch. Could I blame him? I only knew he'd come home because his mother sought me out at church to encourage patience. But just as school started, he'd left for college in Boulder without ever saying hello or goodbye. I doubted patience would ever be enough to draw Hank closer.

Other young men did come to the ranch, not to see me but Mercy. By the time they arrived at the farm, they had tried everything to relieve their pain or to steady their gaits or soothe their nightmares. Mercy was their last hope. Usually, they arrived late in the afternoon to insure Mercy would be home from school. I supposed it paid to be accommodating, if a person was hoping for a miracle.

The peach trees were all puff and circumstance, wearing their flowery bonnets of pink. Keeping my mind on studying took every ounce of concentration I possessed, all to memorize the parts of the digestive system. I loved nursing school more than I would ever tell Ada.

I'd just sat under the apricot tree to quiz myself with a stack of index cards when I looked up to see a young man at the end of the lane. I hadn't heard a car. Had he simply materialized? Some of the boys—I still called them boys since I'd gone to school with many of them, and, like Pete, they would forever be boys. And like this boy, some struggled to find the faith to walk the last part of their journey.

The boy leaned heavily on a cane, and Mercy wasn't even home. She'd asked to play at a friend's house. She wouldn't be home for another hour. There was nothing to do but walk up the lane and meet the pilgrim to urge him closer. I hoped he didn't expect company until Mercy returned. Although it was Easter break, I needed every minute to prepare for the anatomy mid-term once break ended. I would get the boy seated on the porch and bring him a glass of cool water, the extent of my usual ministerial duties.

I wrapped a rubber band around the stack of index cards and started down the lane. The soldier dipped his head, probably embarrassed that his hesitancy had forced me to walk to him. He looked up just as I came close and studied me with cool jade eyes.

I stopped. My breath caught. "Hank?"

"So, I'm still recognizable?"

He was definitely still recognizable. Still handsome. Still tall despite leaning on a cane. "Did you come to see Mercy?" I managed to squeak out.

"That might not be such a bad idea, but I came to see you." Hank shifted his weight on the cane. "Is this a bad time? I could come back."

His earnestness nearly broke my heart. "This is a great time, really, but I'd almost given up hope of seeing you. The last time I saw you...I wasn't very...I've changed, Hank."

He dipped his head, nodding. "We all have."

I took his free arm, not as one offering help but because I was genuinely glad to see him. Hank walked cautiously, concentrating on every step, slightly dragging the foot of his wounded leg. I slowed my steps.

"You're home for Easter?" I said.

"Mom's been putting food in front of me since I got off the train. I'll have to go back before I explode."

"But not before Sunday?" I said, not hiding my panic.

"I'll be here a week." He stopped, turned toward me. "Lucy, I'm real sorry about Pete. I'm sure he was a great guy."

I swallowed down the loss that still harassed me. "Thanks, he was."

Rather than ask Hank to climb the porch steps, I said, "Let's go to the apricot tree. The sun is warm enough. I've been studying there, and truthfully, I was getting a little drowsy." *A little drowsy?* I sounded like an English dowager. I'd waited and waited for Hank to visit, and now the words I'd imagined myself saying had turned to vapor.

Hank lowered himself onto the bench with some effort. Beads of sweat dotted his lip.

"How about something to drink?" I said. "Something cold?"

"A glass of water would be great," he said, wincing as he

straightened his leg.

Inside the house, I leaned against the door and prayed that Lotti would linger at her committee meeting, that Gil and Corky would clear one more row of irrigation ditch, that Goody would loiter at the ball field with his friends, and Mercy, just this once, would return home late. And Ada, I prayed the exhaustion of growing a baby would extend her nap for another half hour. If I got that long with Hank, it would be a miracle, but I was more inclined to believe in that sort of favor lately.

Water glasses in hand, Hank and I stared toward the far horizon, where the San Juan Mountains stood startlingly white against the sky. The gentility of the sun wrapped us in a kind of embrace that hinted of promises, at least that tomorrow would show up bright-eyed, and that seemed like enough.

Hank ran his finger around the rim of his water glass. I turned my back toward the sun. Time ticked relentlessly on. I thought of something to say and discarded my ideas quickly. All of the things we used to talk about—football, peach farming, the future—involved physical ability and endurance. Could he talk about such things without resentment?

"Did you decide on a major?" I asked, the first line of inquiry among college students everywhere. That seemed safe enough.

"Accounting, I think. A desk job." He looked toward his outstretched leg when he said that last part.

A bubble of anger rose in me. Hank would hate a desk job. "Is that your idea?"

He took a good long drink of his water. "It's pretty much the only idea."

Moving gingerly, I knelt on the ground before him and met his gaze, asking silent permission. I put my hand on the knee of his injured leg. "I want to see what they did to you. Can I?"

"Lucy," he said, pleading. "No. Please. It's not pretty."

"I'm sure it's not." To lighten the mood, I touched his other knee. "So, this leg *is* pretty?"

He smiled tightly. "Lucy…"

At the sound of my name on his lips I started blabbering. "You've been home from the Pacific for months. You rushed off to college. We're friends, aren't we? But you didn't come to see me. That's a long time for a woman—"

He raised his eyebrows, smiled that cocky smile of his. I

couldn't help myself. My heart fluttered and I smiled back at him. This was the glimpse of the old Hank I'd hoped for. He was still there, lurking. Wanting to flirt with me. "So, you're a woman now?" he said.

"That's what my patients at the hospital think."

That wiped the grin off his face. "Aren't you still in school?"

"They believe in learning by doing around here."

Guys like Hank, the kind who had experienced the glory of running faster or throwing farther than anyone else in their schools, were awfully funny about the wounds they'd brought home. They'd left for war fresh-faced and eager to prove themselves, and in a matter of a moment their warrior bodies, the ones that had only months earlier carried them over goal lines to cheering crowds, now slowed them to a snail's pace. Back in their hometowns, they stood out in a whole new way, and they didn't like it.

I'd seen the returning soldiers' struggles over and over in the wounded-soldier clinic at the hospital. Some of the wives had never even seen their husbands' injuries. Their husbands dressed in the dark and slid under the bed covers rather than show their wives how the war had altered them. That was what the women had told me, desperate for someone to know the loneliness they faced.

I wasn't afraid, not of seeing what the war had done to Hank. I never wanted him to think he had to hide from me. I did worry that I was pushing Hank too hard, but it was too late. I'd already started toward something I couldn't back away from.

I sucked in a breath and waited for Hank to look at me. "Whatever they did to you, I want to see it. How else can I show you it doesn't matter, not to me?" I started to roll up the hem of his pant leg.

He stopped me with a touch. "Maybe not coming here had nothing to do with my leg. Maybe you broke my heart so bad I feared for my soul."

His eyes glinted some, so I smiled as sweetly as I knew how. "It's a small town..."

He grinned wryly. "Meaning you've been talking to Mom."

"Like I said, it's a small town. Word gets out. She suggested that I wait, be patient. You can imagine how well that went over, but I stayed put. And now you're only here for a week."

Our eyes met. We studied each other for what seemed like

forever until Hank removed his hand, so I could continue rolling up his pant leg.

At the clinic I would have laid Hank face down on an exam table to inspect his wound. Instead, I leaned in, dunking my head low and behind his leg to see his calf. Whatever had hit him took a big bite out of his gastrocnemius muscle. The scar tissue was still fire red, but there were no signs of infection. The redness would fade in time. All in all, the surgeon had done a decent job of knitting Hank back together. For that, I was thankful. A wound like that would make walking difficult, not impossible and certainly didn't limit him to a desk job. I rolled his pant leg down and sat next to him, closer.

"So," he said, "do I pass muster?"

Looking at the wound had shifted me to nurse mode. "You usually wear a brace, don't you?"

Hank squirmed. "I was trying to impress you."

"I am impressed. I've never seen anyone with that much muscle loss walk so well."

Hank's shoulders slumped. "My foot flops around like a landed trout."

"You should wear the brace. You'll be more stable. No one who cares about you will give a lick."

He shot me a dubious glance.

I leaned closer. "I'm so very sorry they got you, Hank." I squeezed his hand and didn't let go.

"They got some other guys a lot worse." Hank's eyes emptied of light. More than likely, he was seeing those other guys, his buddies, who had been torn apart. I would never be able to share any of his horror with him or even understand what the seeing could do to a man. But I remembered what Reinhardt had said, that war changed soldiers forever, that they would never tell their loved ones everything they'd seen. He'd been right. The war would always be with us. Times would come when Hank would dive into his hell like this, and I wanted to be there when he came up for air.

I reached into my pocket for the peach pit Gerland had given me, now varnished for all the rubbing it had gotten whenever I needed reminding to look to the cross for the goodness of God. "I have something for you."

He turned the pit over in his hand. "A peach pit?"

I snatched it back from him, a little embarrassed by the

lowliness of my gift. We spat a thousand peach pits to the ground in the course of a season. But this one was special. "This isn't just any peach pit."

"I'm sorry, Luce." He put his hand out for the pit. Our gazes met again, held. "What should I do with it?"

Tardily, I realized I was no Gerland. I completely lacked his ability to speak simply yet eloquently of hope. "Put it in your pocket."

The line between Hank's eyebrows deepened. "And?"

"And," I echoed. True, I wasn't Gerland and certainly not Mercy, but I owed Hank my best effort. "And I'm going to tell you a story."

"Does this story of yours have a happy ending?"

"The happiest."

"Tell me everything."

Since he'd found the courage to show me his wound, it only seemed fair to show him mine. I told him all about the day Mercy first spoke for God, how Papa had died and Mother fell in the river with Mercy, and how I jumped in after, only to lose them both. That Ada was my real mother. By the time I got to the part about Gerland ripping open the peach to show me the heart of God, everyone had returned to the ranch, tipping caps and waving shyly but not coming one step closer to the apricot tree than necessary. Very odd. Definitely a miracle.

And just like that, I wished Lotti would come out of the house with a plate of cookies, and for Gil and Ada to spread a blanket in front of us, Gil patting Ada's fat belly to introduce the baby to Hank. Even in my imagination, Goody followed the plate of cookies and Tonto barked until Lotti finally threw him one. And Mercy. I pictured her coming home early from her friend's to sit right next to Hank. She would listen as the rest of us talked, and soon her hand would light on his wounded leg. He wouldn't think anything of it, so natural was the gesture.

Hank slipped the peach pit in his pocket. "I should warn you. I'm likely to rub clear through this thing."

If he did, I knew where to find more. "I'll send you a replacement whenever you need one."

"Then you're finally going to write me?"

Had I been too presumptuous? "Is that all right with you?"

"Only if you agree to meet me at the swimming hole."

Acknowledgements

Special appreciation for the guidance and friendship of my editor, Traci DePree.

The constant support of my blog partners at www.Novel Matters.com eased the journey—Bonnie Grove, Kathleen Popa, Latayne C. Scott, Sharon Kay Souza, Debbie Fuller Thomas. You are women of outrageous talent. I love you so.

My long-suffering and doggedly determined critique group— Sharon Bridgewater, Muriel Morley, and Darlia Sawyer—you may whip me into shape yet.

Priscilla Walker, founding chairman of the Palisade Historical Society. No question was too small or too allusive.

The many wonderful people of Palisade, Colorado who endured my interviews with grace and generosity—Harry Talbott, Richard Skaer, Carol Zadrozny, Ron Jaynes, Phyllis Barker, Marilyn Christensen, Bonna Moody, Joy and Randy Capp, Margaret Coe, Forrest Tilton, Audre McDonough Jaynes, John Lindstrom, and Bill and Lucille Floryancic. If I've forgotten anyone, my deepest regrets. You were all fabulous.

The helpful staff of the Museum of Western Colorado, Loyd Files Research Library, Michael Menard, director.

The character of Pete was inspired by the service and faith of PFC Harold Albert "Al" Tesch USMC. He served his country well with the Third War Dog Platoon.

Exuberant thanks to my husband, Dennis, for his unwavering faith and unreasonable support. I adore you.

CPSIA information can be obtained at www.ICGtesting.com
Printed in the USA
LVOW08s1746230713

344258LV00017B/785/P